His Mystery Lady

M.A. Nichols

Books by M.A. Nichols

Generations of Love Series

The Kingsleys

Flame and Ember
Hearts Entwined
A Stolen Kiss

The Ashbrooks

A True Gentleman
The Shameless Flirt
A Twist of Fate
The Honorable Choice

The Finches

The Jack of All Trades
Tempest and Sunshine
The Christmas Wish

The Leighs

An Accidental Courtship
Love in Disguise
His Mystery Lady
A Debt of Honor

Table of Contents

Chapter 1

"**S**tand and deliver." Three small words, yet that clarion call of the highwayman struck fear in the heart of every traveler—especially when followed by a pistol jabbed into one's back.

Katherine Leigh merely sighed.

"Give me all your valuables, and no one need get hurt." The brigand's voice rumbled, dark and menacing, as he prodded her once more.

Nudging her spectacles back into place, Katherine crossed her arms and glanced over her shoulder to give the blackguard an arched brow. "Will you shoot me or run me through?"

All swathed in black, the figure stared at her through the mask obscuring the top half of his face. His tricorn hat sat at a jaunty angle, belying the sneer that formed on his lips.

"Don't play around, lass. You don't want trouble."

"Tonight is liable to be nothing but trouble, Mr. Archer." Katherine scoffed and shook her head, turning her gaze back to the ballroom and the figures skipping about with all the abandon one expected of a masquerade.

The pistol dropped, and the gentleman straightened, his mouth pulling into a genuine frown. Or as much of one as he was wont to give.

"You are spoiling the fun, Miss Leigh."

"As I am often accused of doing so, why not embrace my role as resident spoilsport?" she replied with a dry tone.

But Mr. Archer merely shook his head and came around to stand before her. "Don't be ridiculous."

"I thought the point of a masquerade was to be ridiculous, though you are quite capable of doing that wherever you are, whenever you wish." For the briefest moment, Katherine's heart constricted, and she wondered if she'd pushed the jest just a hair too hard, but Mr. Archer smiled and shook his head.

"You are correct, Miss Leigh," he said, taking off his hat and sweeping into a low bow. "About me, that is. Though entirely incorrect about yourself."

Katherine merely turned her attention back to the dancers moving about the floor to the choreography with varying degrees of success. "Well, I cannot be correct all the time or it would inflate my pride to untenable levels."

But Mr. Archer didn't laugh. When she finally looked at him, she found his gaze fixed on her. Though the shadows of his mask didn't allow her to see his brows, Katherine felt the furrowed brow beneath the strip of black fabric.

"You needn't scowl like that, sir. You are at a masquerade—the land of merriment and ridiculousness."

His eyes swept down her, giving her drab gown a pointed look. "I will scowl as often as I like when you refuse to participate in said merriment and ridiculousness. I am not Mr. David Archer, but the infamous Dick Turpin, terror of the roads and stealer of purses..." Then, with a low dip in his voice, he added with a rascally smile, "and hearts."

Katherine laughed. For the first time in days, she felt it bubbling inside, and she let it out—she couldn't help it. Mr. Archer's gaze brightened at the sound, though he adopted a mock scowl.

"Do you doubt my prowess, good lady?"

"I do not doubt how highly you esteem your prowess, Mr. Archer. However, your roguish claims would be more believable if you weren't wielding sham pistols and spending your evening with a spinster."

With a sigh, he straightened and gave his first genuine frown. "I know you do not wish to dress for the masquerade, but much of the fun comes from the pretense. Let go of your inhibitions, Miss Leigh, and embrace the evening's ridiculousness. Feign ignorance of the person beneath the costume, and play along."

His words were hardly a scolding, but Katherine fought to keep her cheeks from burning. "I apologize, but today has been especially beastly."

Mr. Archer tucked his pistol into the edge of his sash, which was tied about his waist in a fashion better suited for a pirate, yet still seemed fitting for his roguish costume. Mr. Archer's brows peeked up above the edge of his cloth mask, and he didn't need to speak the words for her to know the question nor did she need to answer: both were always the same. Yet she spoke anyway.

"Mama was pestering me all day," she murmured with a sigh. "Forever demanding that I leave my spectacles behind—as though they are the sole impediment to my marrying. Rosanna decided to add to the cacophony, forever needling me about wearing a costume to her all-important masquerade. Apparently, the evening would be ruined if I didn't dress for the occasion—never mind that I never have."

Katherine drew in a deep breath and didn't bother to elaborate upon all the many other reasons for her sour mood. It wasn't as though her life had suddenly grown more dark and morose. Her siblings ignored her. Mama harped at her. Papa derided her. Society dismissed her. However, some days that load weighed heavier on her heart than others. And realizing that Mr. Archer was the first person pleased to see her today only added to the sentiment.

The gentleman's mouth pulled into a frown, and Katherine held up a hand.

"Do not fret, dear sir. You know I am made of sterner stuff. I am merely in a mood, and it shall pass soon enough. Do not let me spoil your fun, Mr. Turpin."

But the gentleman's expression remained fixed on his face as he watched her. Holding his gaze, Katherine pleaded with him to let it go. There was no good to be had in bemoaning her life, and she had wallowed in self-pity for long enough.

Thankfully, he seemed to accept that silent petition and threw himself back into his role, flourishing his pistols.

"That is a mighty fine dress, lass. Clearly, you are a woman of taste and refinement, so give up your jewels before I'm forced to take more drastic measures."

Running her hands down her skirts, Katherine tried not to let his words affect her. This was Dick Turpin speaking, after all, and not Mr. David Archer. Nudging her spectacles up her nose, she glanced about the gathering, though no one paid her any mind.

"It is hardly a fine dress, and I have no jewels." No truer words had been spoken, for though Katherine liked this gown, it was hardly one to draw the eye. A simple white muslin hardly stood out amongst the rainbow around her, but with the columnar styles of the past decades waning, the fuller skirt and natural waist gave her figure far more definition, and the wide neckline that was gaining more prominence in fashion allowed Katherine's only good feature to be shown to advantage.

Not that shoulders were much of an attraction, but when one had nothing else, one embraced what one could.

"Nonsense." Some of the dreaded Mr. Turpin's tone faded, and Mr. Archer waved his pistol about as though motioning at her dress. "You look nice tonight. That is a fetching gown, and it suits you perfectly."

When one did not anticipate dancing, one didn't often require a fan, but Katherine wished she'd borrowed one of

Mama's, for her cheeks were determined to set her ablaze. For all that she tried to remind herself to be calm in such a moment, her heart gave a happy thump—but thankfully, that was not noticeable to anyone but herself. And thankfully (or unfortunately, depending on one's perspective), she had practice enough at keeping a calm facade when Mr. Archer inspired such ridiculous, swoony behavior.

With a flash of a cocky smile that belonged wholly to the rascal beneath the costume (and not the character he played), Mr. Archer added, "Being a spoilsport is such a unique costume, after all. And to be so devoted to the role that you play it year after year—that is commendable."

Despite the small pang in her chest, Katherine smiled. "If nothing else, I am committed to my part."

"There you are, David."

With those four words, Katherine's ribs constricted, though she managed to school her expression. In and of himself, her brother was no cause for alarm, but where there was one Leigh, more would soon follow.

Coming up beside Mr. Archer, the Roman soldier threw an arm around the highwayman's shoulder, and Katherine struggled not to look at his bare arms and legs. Masquerade or not, it was unnerving to see her baby brother in such an indecent state, though he was hardly the only one in deshabille.

"I was beginning to think you'd decided not to come tonight," said Benjamin.

"When in doubt, look for a pretty maiden. You're likely to find me at her side," replied the roguish Dick Turpin.

Benjamin's eyes darted to Katherine and back to his friend, the movement as clear as any words. The last unmarried Leigh daughter was hardly one to attract the attention of any man, whether he be real or imagined.

"That's kind of you to keep my sister company," said Benjamin.

Katherine's heart twisted. A bit of charity? Was that all her brother believed motivated Mr. Archer's friendship? But she supposed that was what everyone believed. Heaven forfend that Mr. Archer might actually enjoy Miss Katherine Leigh's company. No one else seemed to.

"On the contrary," said Mr. Archer. "She has been kind enough to keep me company."

Benjamin's brow furrowed, and he smirked at his friend with a shake of his head. Then, ignoring that statement, he said, "I wanted to speak with you concerning this business in the newspaper—"

"Am I going to have to give you the same lecture I gave your sister?" asked Mr. Archer with a playful sigh. "We are at the Tates' annual masquerade, but it is their family who are determined to keep us grounded in reality. Can we not embrace a bit of merriment for one evening?"

"Well said, Mr. Archer," added Rosanna as she drew up beside the others. Katherine forced herself not to grimace. Not that she disliked her sister's intrusion, but as she had feared, the family was gathering. Wherever Rosanna went, Mama was soon to follow, and Katherine couldn't bear having the Leigh matriarch intrude on her time with Mr. Archer. It was bound to happen, but Rosanna needn't rush it along.

"Do not tell me we have more prudes in the company," said Rosanna whilst frowning at her siblings. "It is bad enough that public opinion is turning against masquerades, but I cannot bear the thought that my own family is betraying me. It is naught but a bit of fun. I adore our annual ball, and I am not ready for the tradition to end."

The goddess glanced at the others, and though she didn't linger on her sister's costume (or lack thereof), Katherine felt Rosanna's disappointment. But then, if Katherine looked even half as lovely as her elder sister did whilst swathed in little more than a fancy bed sheet with her hair cascading down her back, perhaps she might wish to embrace costumes as well. Granted, Rosanna looked gorgeous in everything she wore, so dressing as the Goddess of Love and Beauty was redundant; despite being nearly forty years of age and the mother of six, Mrs. Rosanna Tate looked more like Katherine's younger sister.

Rosanna tugged at the shoulder of her toga as her blonde brows pinched together, fairly begging them to assure her that the evening was, in fact, delightful. Had no one intruded on her conversation with Mr. Archer, Katherine might even have agreed.

But then Rosanna gave her sister's dress another frown. "If you wish for a mask, dearest, I have plenty at the ready by the door."

Katherine's jaw clenched. She refused to think about that wretched endearment, so casually tossed about. Crossing her arms, she turned her gaze away from her family and looked out at the dancers. It wasn't as though she was the only one to eschew fancy dress, and her reason was far more understandable than the others'. Yet it was she who earned the disappointed looks and constant verbal nudges.

There was no point in defending herself, for this was a conversation they'd had every year since Mr. Malcolm Tate had appeared in Greater Edgerton twelve years ago, stolen away the heart of Rosanna, and settled into local society every autumn with their annual masquerade ball. Katherine Leigh could see, or she could wear a mask; until they created spectacles that fit beneath the mask or a face covering that worked around the spectacles, she would be forced to choose. And she wouldn't be swayed.

Unfortunately, even after years of attempting to persuade her, neither would her family.

A brief nudge of an elbow drew Katherine's attention to the gentleman at her side, and from beneath the shadowed edge of his mask, Mr. Archer winked at her. Such a small thing. So simple and unnoticed by anyone but her, yet Katherine's heart stuttered, her breath catching as she stared into his light brown eyes.

Did he have any idea how that gaze affected her?

The question was silly. Katherine went to great lengths to

ensure he never saw just how much she loved gazing into his eyes. And much more. But at two and thirty, she knew better than to flirt openly with any gentleman—let alone such an eligible one. Nothing scared a man more than to have a plain spinster throw herself at him. Especially one who was five years his senior.

Be his friend. Be patient. Surely he would see the truth for himself with time. It wasn't as though only beautiful people ever found love. Plenty of plain-faced people secured adoring spouses, and such an attraction didn't happen in an instant. He already counted her a good friend, and with time, something more might grow from that platonic affection.

The others continued to gab, but Katherine stood there, watching Mr. Archer smile. At her. All while she attempted to keep her heart from beating out of her chest.

Be his friend. Be patient. But like all good advice, it was easier said than done.

Chapter 2

A n arm slid through Katherine's, giving her a start—but not half as strong as she felt when her mother said, "Here you all are, my dear children."

The lady's hold on her arm was like a vise, and Katherine struggled to keep her expression impassive as her jaw clenched. Yet another prayer for patience flitted through her heart.

"And Mr. Archer," said Mama, batting her lashes. "So lovely to see you."

"I fear I do not know any Mr. Archer, madam. But I am quite pleased to meet you this fine evening," said Mr. Archer, sweeping into another gallant bow before brandishing his pistols once more. "However, I am very sorry to announce that I am here to rob you..."

Though he hid it well, Mr. Archer's voice faltered as he tried to discern the lady's costume. Feathers in her hair bobbed around her, looking all the more ridiculous for the pink confection of a dress she'd chosen for tonight. The mask was gilded and painted until it looked like a golden garden, but that gave no hint as to what the lady's intention had been for her costume.

Mr. Archer's gaze darted to Katherine, and she mouthed, "Love."

For all that Rosanna had chosen to be the Grecian embodiment of the sentiment, Mama had decided upon a far more direct route, yet her execution made it far more obscure.

"You look fetching tonight, Mrs. Leigh," he said, his gaze darting between her and her mother. All the while, Katherine continued to mouth the word to him.

"Would you say you *love* her costume?" asked Katherine.

Mr. Archer straightened and nodded. "Ah, yes. Of course, I would. Brilliant interpretation of love."

Mama beamed, reaching out with a fan to jab Mr. Archer. "I knew you would understand. Can you believe no one else has been able to guess it?"

"I cannot, madam. The rest of the party's wits are lacking," he answered with utter gravity, though when he hazarded a glance at Katherine, Mr. Archer's eyes shone with a silent laugh, and she fought to keep it from showing in her expression as well.

Giving him another jab (which was hard enough to make Katherine wince at the sight, though Mr. Archer made no show of displeasure), Mama gave him a narrowed look. "A gentleman of your age and situation ought not to be standing about like a lout, sir. Tell me you intend to stand up with our dear Katherine."

Years of practice ensured that her heart didn't show in her face, but it sank to her toes like a lead weight, sending her stomach into a fit of indigestion. Thankfully, Katherine's blushes hardly showed or her cheeks would be as pink as Mama's ridiculous gown, but her eyes shot away from Mr. Archer, unable to look at his reaction.

Of course, she longed to see pleasure there, but Katherine knew too well that shock or horror was more likely to be present—as it was on her siblings' faces. She only hoped theirs was due to Mama's social faux pas and not the idea of their sister standing up with Mr. Archer.

Benjamin let out a halting chuckle. "Really, Mother. You are being far too direct."

"Rubbish," said Mama, flicking her fan at her boy as though to brush away his words. "Mr. Archer is a dear friend of the family, and there is nothing untoward about him standing up with our dear Katherine or my entreating him to do so."

As Mr. Archer was the only gentleman who ever asked to stand up with Katherine, she had supposed he would do so tonight as well—if Mama didn't make him so uncomfortable that he avoided the whole lot of Leighs tonight.

"Mama, leave him be," whispered Katherine.

But rather than answering in kind, Mama scoffed and replied with enough volume that everyone in their circle could hear. "Don't be missish, Katherine. You do nothing to encourage the gentlemen to approach, so I must do something on your behalf."

Curse Francis for marrying and leaving Mama with nothing to do but fret over her sole unmarried daughter. At least when the youngest Leigh had been about, the lady's attention was divided. Really, it had been focused entirely on Francis, for Mama had long despaired over Katherine. However, in the six years since that felicitous occasion, Katherine had become the sole recipient of Mama's matrimonial endeavors.

One might believe that being well past thirty would've deterred the lady's efforts, but one would be wrong.

Turning her attention back to the gentleman in their little circle, Mama jabbed him once more with her fan and said, "As a gentleman, you must agree, Mr. Archer. What man wants a bespectacled bride who dresses dowdily and refuses anything more than a cursory attempt to style her hair? You've seen Katherine at enough of these functions to know that it has done nothing for her but label her a wallflower and spinster. If I demur in my duty, she will never marry, and what sort of mother would do such a thing?"

"You do your daughter a disservice, Mrs. Leigh." Mr. Archer's words forced Katherine's gaze to his, but his attention was fixed on Mama. Though much of his face was obscured by his mask and costume, Katherine saw the signs of his displeasure in the corners of his lips, and she could well imagine the furrow in his brow. "A gentleman of sense wants a wife of substance and not merely an ornament to hang on his arm—"

"Here, here," echoed Rosanna.

"—and there is far more to attraction than outward beauty."

Though Mr. Archer's words were meant to comfort, Katherine's heart sank further, seeping into the ground at her feet until there was nothing left.

Despite the inference that Katherine possessed attractions, Mr. Archer's words were clear enough: he didn't believe her to be beautiful. Such a sentiment was not new to Katherine; even if she were able to forget the many gentlemen who'd rejected her, her mother and father were keen to remind her daily.

With or without spectacles marring the image, her features were too sharp to be arresting, which was the best description she could hope for. Her coloring was unremarkable. Her height was just a touch too tall, but that would've been forgivable had she a figure worth looking at. Katherine Leigh was the epitome of plain. Not ugly, but ordinary, unremarkable, and easily overlooked.

Having heard as much from her family for the majority of her life, Katherine had learned to ignore it. She possessed no outward beauty, but that did not mean she was without value or merit. One could not help one's appearance, after all, and it did no good to fixate on what one could not change. But hearing Mr. Archer agree with her mother's assessment pained Katherine, opening old wounds.

Ridiculous. What did she expect? Her hope for the future was that Mr. Archer would come to his senses and realize they were well-suited for one another—despite her lack of outward enticements. So, how could she then be hurt when he stated a simple fact?

Glancing at the others, Katherine inched backward. They continued discussing the subject, and though she had been the catalyst, no one paid her any heed. So, she saw no reason to remain.

"Excuse me," said Miss Leigh, not looking at anyone as she stepped apart from their ground. Despite that small sign of pain, she held herself erect, and if one were to overlook her gaze, one might believe her to be entirely unaffected by her mother's criticisms.

David Archer longed to curse at Mrs. Leigh, which was an entirely new sensation to him, as it went against everything he'd been taught. Foul language on its own was a wretched thing, but directing it at a lady was unthinkable. Yet David couldn't help but feel that anger burn in his chest as he watched Miss Leigh walk away with little haste but solid determination.

If not for the fact that Mrs. Leigh immediately latched onto his arm, David would've followed after, but the lady's grip was firm, and unless he wished to drag her along, he was stuck.

"I do not understand that girl," murmured Mrs. Leigh with a heavy sigh. "I try my best to guide her, but she is never happy. Such a dour, unhappy creature."

"On the contrary, she's exceptionally amusing," replied David.

Benjamin gave a wry chuckle. "That is kind of you to say, Archer."

"It isn't kindness. It is truth."

Yet the raise of her brother's brows said he was unconvinced.

"I have all but given up helping her," added Miss Leigh's sister with a shake of her head. "All my efforts are for naught as they are met with a harsh retort before she scurries away."

And was it any wonder if her family's idea of assistance was harping at her? But David knew better than to say anything of that nature. The Leighs were an odd puzzle, and for all that he spent much time in their ranks, David was no closer to deciphering them.

"Do you know a gentleman who might suit her?" asked Mrs. Leigh, turning her gaze up to David. "Someone who can overlook her pittance of a dowry, plain features, and blunt-speaking?"

Thank the heavens for his fancy dress, for they couldn't see the way his brows climbed upwards at that question. He might be a close friend to two of her children and a regular fixture amongst the family, but that did not make him privy to such a private discussion.

"My husband cannot be bothered to bestir himself," said Mrs. Leigh with a frown. "And despite Rosanna's many invitations, Katherine refuses to join them when they are in London." Patting her daughter on the hand, she added, "I do not blame you, of course. You have tried your best with the girl, and she refuses to listen."

Then the sharpness in Mrs. Leigh's tone and gaze softened as she turned to her son. "And our dear Benjamin is too young to be of much assistance. Most of his acquaintances are closer to his age—none of whom would be interested in a lady twelve years their senior. But with all the time you spend assisting your father at the mill, you must be acquainted with men of varying ages. Surely you know older gentlemen who are in want of a wife."

David's smile didn't falter even the slightest: he had too much practice to let even a casual remark discompose him. Rawlston Mill was owned and overseen by Mr. Thaddeous Archer. His son and heir merely aided him. That was all.

Instead, David focused on the second half of her statement. "I am well-acquainted with many gentlemen and mill owners, but I fear Mr. Ambrose Ashbrook is the youngest amongst that set, and he—like most of the others—is married. The rest are closer to my father's age."

But Mrs. Leigh simply watched him as though not comprehending a single word he'd spoken. "I am certain there must be a widower amongst their ranks. Or some confirmed bachelor finally ready to settle down."

David couldn't imagine wishing to marry off one of his sisters to a gentleman who was in his sixth or seventh decade of life and had only just decided to marry. Such a fellow would be either a bounder looking to secure an heir or a tyrant who didn't wish for the annoyance of a wife. Neither of which was likely to ensure matrimonial bliss.

Yet Mrs. Leigh stood there with her gaze fixed on him, waiting for him to answer.

Thankfully, Benjamin saved David by announcing, "Miss Rothschild is expecting me."

"That girl?" Letting out a sharp tsk, Mrs. Leigh frowned. "Her parents own a mill."

"Mama," said Mrs. Rosanna Tate in a gentle reproof, though the lady seemed not to hear it.

Benjamin slanted a raised brow at David, and he held back a snicker. As usual, Mrs. Leigh did not seem to know or care about the implications of her words and what they might mean to the mill owner's son standing before her. Or the hypocrisy rife in the fact that she had just been trolling those lowly mill owners on her daughter's behalf.

"I must dance, Mother," said Benjamin.

Patting her boy on his cheek, she smiled. "Yes, you must, and you cannot help it if all the ladies are desperate to secure you for their partner. Go, enjoy yourself, my darling boy."

Benjamin attempted to do just that, but Mrs. Leigh released David's arm and latched herself to her son, fairly squeezing his cheeks as though he were a lad of three.

"You are such a handsome young man. It is little wonder they are all fighting for a chance to stand up with you."

With a strained smile, Benjamin met David's gaze as though begging him to intercede, but David knew better than to engage in losing battles. Instead, he gave his friend all the sympathy he deserved at such a moment.

"I heard they were casting lots to see who would have the honor of approaching him first," said David, a smirk tugging at his lips, and Benjamin's gaze narrowed.

"Oh, my dear, wonderful, perfect little boy," said Mrs. Leigh. "It is precisely as it ought to be. You are a catch, and far better than most of those ladies could ever hope to secure. It is little wonder Miss Rothschild is chasing after you."

David cast a glance round about, but the noise of conversation and the music in the air covered her words enough that only the busiest of bodies might've overheard. And they were all occupied elsewhere.

"I could speak with Malcolm about Katherine," said Mrs. Tate with a considering look into the crowd for her husband. "As we do not spend most of our time in Greater Edgerton, he does not have as many acquaintances as we do in Town or at our family seat in Kent, but he might know of candidates we haven't explored before."

With care, Benjamin extricated himself from his mother's grasp, and David knew better than to linger. Whilst Mrs. Leigh was occupied turning back to her daughter, he slipped away. Though not fast enough that he didn't catch the beginning (or continuation, rather) of their assessment of Miss Leigh's matrimonial prospects, weighing the many options available tonight.

David held back a shudder. Thank the heavens his parents were too distracted to give any thought to his matrimonial state. Father didn't care one jot, and Mother was still reveling after Agatha's marriage last winter and too occupied with her three other daughters to give her son much thought. David had enough to manage at present without being bothered by their machinations or adding a wife to his list of duties.

Turning his gaze to the gathering, he searched the sea of faces for Miss Leigh. The lady had scurried away before he'd secured a dance with her. Not that he needed to rush matters, for he knew well enough that her dance card never filled, but in the past two years since he'd come to know Benjamin and the Leigh family, David had discovered her night always fared better if someone—even her scraggly friend—stood up with her early.

And perhaps he could warn her of her mother and sister's

plans. Not that they were anything new, but there was a determined edge to their conversation that was troubling.

Skirting the gathering, he scoured her usual haunts, though it was slow going, as people insisted on interrupting his hunt to lob social niceties at him. Each pause ate up the time until he extricated himself once more, and matters weren't helped by the fact that he must've missed her during his first turn about the room and had to make another before he spied her hiding in the back corner of the room, slightly obscured by the musicians.

Ensuring that his hat was once more resting at a jaunty angle, David lifted his pistols and invaded Miss Leigh's sanctuary.

Chapter 3

"Stand and deliver," said David with a low growl.

The lady raised her hands in placation, though her gaze held more than a hint of impatience. With a wooden tone, she said, "Do not hurt me, I beg you."

David straightened and tucked his pistols away, and with more than a hint of teasing he said, "Spoilsport."

"It is my costume, after all."

Tucking his hands behind him, he paused and wondered what to say. Which was an odd sensation, as from almost the very beginning, conversation had never been a struggle with Miss Leigh. David didn't understand it any more than he understood why so many found her company irksome and her humor incomprehensible.

But with her mother's words burning in his brain, David didn't know what to say. He never did in such moments. After witnessing all the vitriol Mrs. Leigh was able to cast upon her daughter, he ought to know how to tend Miss Leigh's wounds, but all the placating words he employed with his sisters or mother didn't seem right.

Miss Leigh wasn't some wilting miss who needed a healthy dose of encouragement to thrive. Again and again, she stood firm against her mother's railings and never shrank. But even the strongest of spirits suffered injuries at times.

"You left before I was able to speak to you properly," he said.

"Extricating myself is the easiest way to hold my tongue," she replied in a wry tone.

"With how often you must do so, it is a wonder you haven't relocated to another county."

Miss Leigh's lips quirked into a smile that shone with her dry humor. "I shall, one day. But what did you wish to speak to me about, Mr. Archer?"

David's brows rose in challenge. "What do you think I would wish to speak to you about *at a ball*?"

"The rising price of cotton." The answer came quickly and was delivered with such a serious demeanor that if David didn't know better, he might've thought her retort genuine. But behind those spectacles, her eyes sparked with a laugh, if anyone bothered to look.

Chuckling, he shook his head. "You are ridiculous."

"The point of a masquerade is to be ridiculous. I am simply embracing the *joie de vivre*."

"There you are!"

Miss Leigh's smile vanished at her mother's call. Her eyes widened, begging him to rescue her, but before a plan formed in his mind, Mrs. Leigh swept in and took her daughter by the arm, dragging her from her sanctuary.

"Your sister and I have found the perfect gentleman for you," said Mrs. Leigh, leaning close.

As their backs were to him, David felt free to grimace, for he could only imagine whom she might've chosen, but his curiosity was quickly answered as her sister led the promised partner to Miss Leigh.

"Mr. Mowbry is quite keen to secure an introduction, Katherine," said Mrs. Tate, glancing between the pair with a bright smile as though this were the finest match anyone could hope for.

Even in his prime (which must've been some decades before), Mr. Mowbry didn't seem like much of a catch. Though not acquainted with the gentleman, the way his gaze swept along Miss Leigh gave David a pretty clear understanding of who he was. Mr. Mowbry's attention lingered where it ought not to, which was poor enough, except the bounder's frown made his disappointment clear.

David's fingers curled into a fist.

"Miss Leigh, your mother and sister have been singing your praises," said Mr. Mowbry as he bowed his head.

"I can well imagine what they've said," replied Miss Leigh, and David couldn't help but smile at the meaning rife in those little words.

Meanwhile, her mother and sister watched the exchange with varying degrees of delight. At least Mrs. Tate had the good sense to look a touch troubled, though Mrs. Leigh held no such compunctions and beamed as though this were the greatest conversation she'd ever witnessed.

"Our dear Katherine is such a fine reader," said her mother.

"I have managed to master all my letters, A to Z," added Miss Leigh. "I will admit I had some troubles with V and G, but with practice, I prevailed."

David snorted a laugh, and the others turned furrowed brows at him. When Miss Leigh met his eyes, the only hint of humor in her expression was the laughter hidden in her gaze.

Mrs. Leigh blinked at him but then shook herself free from her puzzlement and continued to speak to Mr. Mowbry with all the enthusiasm and skill of a horse breeder at auction, pointing out her daughter's various enticements and interests, though they were sadly lacking truth. Not that Miss Leigh wasn't a fine reader or skilled with a needle, but the descriptions were vague and utterly lacking any of Miss Leigh's heart.

How did they understand her so poorly? The whole thing was a mystery to David—as was their clear delusion in thinking Mr. Mowbry suitable for Miss Katherine Leigh. Anyone with sense would know in an instant that such a fractious man was unlikely to enjoy her biting wit.

Thankfully, there was something David could do about it. Even if it was small. But just as he opened his mouth to ask Miss Leigh to dance, Mr. Mowbry took her by the hand and led her away without bothering to ascertain if she wished to stand up with him. The pompous fool.

Miss Leigh cast David a glance from over her shoulder, her eyes narrowed. He could practically hear her chastising him for not rescuing her, but there was little to be done at this juncture that wouldn't cause a scene. And nothing would deter Mrs. Leigh from securing Mr. Mowbry as her daughter's dance partner once she set her mind to it.

David gave her a sympathetic cringe, and though she gave no other outward sign, Miss Leigh's gaze held a sigh, resigning her to her fate. He sent her a look in return, silently promising to stand up with her afterward, and despite being too complicated a message to convey with a single expression, Miss Leigh's gaze brightened as though she understood him clearly.

"Ah, Mr. Archer—" began Mrs. Leigh, but David gave her a quick bow.

"Please excuse me, but I fear my partner is waiting for me," he said before hurrying away in search of someone with whom to dance.

Curse her wretched mama and sister, curse this dreadful bore Mr. Mowbry, and a double curse on that sneak Mr. Archer for not rescuing her. Katherine didn't bother hiding her sigh. With the dance and music covering any subtle sounds of the ballroom, she was free to show her displeasure in that little way.

Not that Mr. Mowbry would've noticed had the room been empty and silent, for he expounded at length about his tannery, which she might've found interesting if he knew the slightest bit about his business, but like many of the high-minded middle class, he wouldn't dirty himself with such low work. Never mind that an intelligent owner ought to know about every facet of his business.

No, the gentleman rambled on about ledgers (which was more of a none-too-subtle hint at his income) and his disputes with other tradesmen Katherine didn't know, concerning things she didn't understand. He filled the air with the puffed-up ramblings of someone who either believed there was nothing more interesting than himself or inflated his pride to hide his fractured sense of self-worth.

Either way, Katherine couldn't wait for the dance to end. Thankfully, the quadrille didn't allow for him to be at her elbow the entire time. Unfortunately, this particular dance was simple enough that her thoughts drifted, pulling her in directions she didn't wish to go.

It wasn't as though this was the first time her family had foisted a bachelor on her; Katherine couldn't even say that Mr. Mowbry was among the worst of the offerings. However, the comparison between the prospective beaus chosen for her and those chosen for her sisters still pricked her heart.

Of course, no one was good enough for Rosanna, and it was a miracle that someone of Malcolm Tate's quality (namely, income) had stumbled into Greater Edgerton. Prudence was no beauty, but she was capable and intelligent, and Papa was convinced that in marrying a mere physician, his eldest had stepped down in the world. Francis had been paraded before every bachelor of passable looks and fortune until one was finally prevailed upon to carry her off.

Katherine, on the other hand, was fobbed off on geriatrics whose only discernible trait of worth was a middling income. A Mr. Mowbry was the best Mama hoped for, and even in that possibility, the lady despaired.

A mother's duty was to secure good husbands for her daughters, after all, and an unmarried daughter was a mark against a mother and a blight on her family. Until that all-important wedding was performed, Katherine was a bane, leaving Gertrude Leigh forever tainted by association.

Mama would never love her. Not truly. But then, such a

selfless emotion was impossible when one's focus was on one-self. With her sense of self so wrapped up in the outward success of her children, Mama could never love them as they were—unless they were perfect.

This was not the first, second, hundredth, or even thousandth time Katherine's thoughts had dwelled on that undeniable fact, yet her heart still squeezed tight. That old pain echoed through her, and gazing out at the swirling people around her, she couldn't help that her mind drifted down familiar paths. A sea of faces, all laughing and smiling, and not one of them spared a single thought for the solitary Katherine Leigh.

Surrounded by people, yet she was alone.

As this was hardly the first time she'd felt thusly, it ought to be familiar by now. But with two and thirty years to her name, Katherine was old enough to know some wounds never healed completely. Like an old soldier with a limp that acted up when the weather turned, Katherine's gave her little trouble, only twinging at times. But at times like these, she couldn't help but feel that pang and wish for things to be different.

Thank the heavens, the music came to a close, freeing her. Katherine bobbed a curtsy to her partner and turned to leave, but Mr. Mowbry took her by the elbow and hooked her arm through his, not even pausing in his speech about his difficulties with another tannery in town, droning on about the nuances of their petty squabbles.

Perhaps when she'd been in her twenties, any man's attention would've soothed her wounded pride, but despite what others believed about the pitiable state of spinsters, there were far worse fates than being unattractive and unmarried, and being Mrs. Mowbry was one of them.

Drawing in a deep breath, Katherine cast her gaze about for some escape; she may have a reputation for abruptness, but that didn't make her rude. Then her salvation appeared.

"Do excuse me, Mr. Mowbry, but I really must speak to Mrs. Kitts." Not allowing him time to respond, Katherine yanked her arm from his and slipped between the other guests, weaving through the crowd as though the hounds of hell were nipping at her heels.

Although Pamela was dressed in costume, like most of the gathering, Katherine recognized her friend beneath the slight half-mask covering her eyes. When Pamela spied her, she raised a hand in greeting, but her smile died away at the sight of Katherine's widened eyes. Snatching the lady by the hand, Katherine dragged her from the ballroom.

"Help me," she said, leading her friend from the fray.

As Pamela was the best of women, she didn't argue or slow as they wove their way to the door.

Chapter 4

As Boxwood Manor was her sister's home, Katherine knew where to escape. Ducking down a corridor, they scurried into the library, which was closed to the public. With only a low fire burning in the fireplace, there was little light by which to see, but it was clearly empty. Katherine shut the door behind them and sagged against the wood.

"Is your mother matchmaking again?" asked Pamela with a wry smile as she straightened the turban sitting atop her head.

"I had a few months of blessed peace. I had thought she'd accepted the inevitable, but she and my *dear* sister are at it again," mumbled Katherine as she nudged her spectacles up her nose. Straightening, she studied her friend, in the flowing pants and robes of a sultana. "You look lovely, Pamela."

Her friend preened and turned about, the gauzy robes and sash flowing behind her. "Isn't it magnificent? I do love fancy dress parties."

"You must save me," said Katherine, dragging them back to the subject at hand. "If I am forced to spend the evening with Mr. Mowbry, I shan't be responsible for my actions."

"You are at a masquerade, so the solution is fairly obvious," said Pamela with raised brows that inferred her meaning as much as her tone.

Katherine sighed and crossed her arms. "You know I cannot wear a mask and my spectacles at the same time."

"Would you rather see or be pestered by Mr. Mowbry all night?" Though it was phrased as a question, Pamela's tone made it clear there was only one answer she expected.

And heaven help her, Katherine knew she was correct. If stumbling around blind provided an escape, it was well worth the price. Her friend took her by the hand and led her back into the corridor. Tip-toeing back into the entryway, Pamela searched about and found the stack of masks Rosanna had provided for those who hadn't brought their own. With a quick word to the footman, Pamela summoned her shawl before dragging Katherine back down the corridor and out of the sight of prying eyes.

Plucking Katherine's spectacles from her nose, Pamela tucked them beneath the edge of Katherine's elbow gloves and tied a black mask in place. It was larger than the masks so many favored, which covered only the eyes and nose, and stretched up to her forehead and down her cheeks, leaving only her mouth and jaw uncovered.

With a flick, Pamela opened the shawl and draped it over Katherine. The cream fabric was large enough to cover her head and shoulders while still cascading down far enough to obscure her bodice. Twisting the edges, Pamela arranged it like a mantle, concealing her friend's face in shadow. Without hesitation, she reached into the folds of her outfit and pulled free a few pins, using them to secure the shroud in place.

"You need those—" But before Katherine could mount any proper objection, Pamela gave her a narrowed look that brooked no refusal, though the sultana's costume now drooped a touch in a few places. But when Pamela inspected her creation, she frowned. Reaching to her lapel, she freed a butterfly brooch and affixed it to Katherine's shoulder, holding the drape of the shawl firm.

Stepping back, Pamela smiled. "No one will be able to identify you, though I would avoid vigorous dancing, as it wouldn't hold up to much jostling."

"Are you certain?"

"Absolutely," she said with a nod. "I cannot see your face or hair at all. Unless Mr. Mowbry recalls your dress—and I doubt he was that observant—he won't recognize you. And even much of that is obscured. Besides, he won't be looking for a lady in fancy dress. Not even your family would recognize you."

Katherine longed to see for herself, but there was no looking glass to be found (not that her eyesight would allow her to make out her appearance even if there was); so, she had to have faith in her friend's assurances, and besides Mr. Archer, there was no other soul she trusted so much as Pamela Kitts.

Ensuring that her spectacles were secured in her glove, Katherine took Pamela by the arm. The world was naught but a blur, though the differences in color and sizes of the shapes allowed Katherine to navigate around obstacles—but having Pamela's guidance gave her the emotional fortitude to face the ballroom once more.

The pair snuck in through a side door and eased along the edge. Thankfully, she'd seen the room beforehand, so it was easy enough to identify the green fuzz along the walls as the floral arrangements Rosanna had slaved over. And the writhing mass in the center was the dance floor, though she couldn't tell what they were dancing precisely. The music sounded like a country dance.

Pamela tightened her hold, and Katherine turned her gaze to her friend's hazy form.

"Mr. Mowbry just walked by and didn't even pause when he glanced past you," she whispered. "Success!"

And Katherine couldn't even tell that one moving shape had been him, but as long as her disguise worked, she wasn't going to complain about a little blindness. This wasn't about vanity, and Katherine would do much more to protect her sanity.

"You have my undying and lifelong adoration, Pamela Kitts."

"Mine, as well."

The new voice gave Katherine a start, though it was clear enough from the vague shape of the person who joined them that it wasn't Mr. Mowbry; the new gentleman was taller and quite thinner than that stocky fellow. Katherine squinted as much as she could and thought he might be wearing a matching sultan costume, though it was difficult to tell, for it was just a smear of colors.

"Good evening, sir," said Pamela in a coy tone that told Katherine the blur's identity.

"You are by far the loveliest lady in attendance," said Mr. Ralph Kitts with a sweeping bow.

"You are too kind," replied his wife like a prim young maiden.

Katherine gave the pair a smirk, but she cursed her blindness at present, for it was impossible to see if a jest hit its mark if one could not see the target's expression. And the flirtatious pair certainly deserved a good tease.

"You both are nauseating," she murmured.

Fully ignoring her, Mr. Kitts swept into another bow. "My dear lady, might I be so bold as to beg a dance from the most fetching woman in attendance?"

Pamela turned her face to her, and though she couldn't discern the expression there, Katherine knew her friend well enough to suspect that it was troubled. Which was ridiculous. As much as Katherine would love to keep Pamela by her side the entire evening, this was one of the few moments in which husband and wife could behave like a courting couple once more.

Why society had declared it uncouth to dance with one's spouse was a mystery. Yes, it was better not to monopolize any individual's time for an entire evening, but really, why should a courting couple be allowed to stand up together and a married one not? To say nothing of the fact that the pair rarely had time together, away from their children. But swept up in the masquerade, no one would think anything of it. Such rules did not apply when one was in fancy dress.

Katherine tried not to feel a pang of disappointment for that fact.

With their strictures, typical parties allowed her unfettered access to her dear friend. Before she'd become Mrs. Kitts, Pamela had spent many an afternoon with Katherine, but as her friend's world expanded, her focus shifted—as it ought. She did not begrudge Pamela for it, but it left her heart aching the slightest bit; these evenings together were few and far between, and Katherine couldn't help but be a miser about their time together.

Relationships changed, and Katherine knew better than to bemoan that fact. And she had plenty of practice spending an evening alone.

"Go, you silly woman," said Katherine, nudging Pamela toward her husband. "Enjoy yourself."

For all that she spoke those words with utter sincerity, her friend required a few more prods before finally relenting. Turning, Pamela embraced her, and as her face was mostly obscured by her disguise, Katherine felt free to smile.

Even if her parents were the sort to dole out affection in such an open manner, Katherine would never have been the recipient of such displays. Their favorites certainly earned embraces from time to time, and her siblings bestowed tendernesses freely between each other, but they had little place in Katherine's world. So, she reveled in the feel of her friend's arms around her.

A little thing that so many took for granted, but it helped to close those troublesome wounds once more.

"I shall be back, soon," whispered Pamela, before leaning back and straightening Katherine's covering once more. Then, taking her husband's arm, she disappeared into the writhing mass of colors and shapes.

...

With a wild swing, David brandished his weapons once more and gave Miss Peck a wicked grin, his brows bobbing up. "Stand and deliver, my lovely lass."

The massive plumage erupting from her coiffure bobbed as she giggled. "You are a tease, Mr. Archer."

Holding up a staying hand, David frowned. "Alas, I fear you are mistaken. I am the rogue Dick Turpin, not this Mr. Archer. Though he does sound like a handsome and engaging fellow. The best of men, no doubt."

"No doubt," echoed the gentleman to his left, his tone matching his sardonic smile peeking from beneath the bottom of his mask. David thought he recognized the voice, but he couldn't be certain whether it was Mr. Mandrell or Mr. Garrison disguised as the dashing naval captain.

If Miss Peck was so certain of his identity, perhaps he required a better mask, or to employ a different voice for the rest of the evening. Much of the fun came from trying to uncover the identity beneath the costume. But David supposed there was little to be done about it at this juncture.

Miss Peck lifted her fan, which matched the plumage in her hair, and attempted a coy look from over the edge. It was not her best effort, but David supposed it was difficult to flirt when one was dressed as an overstuffed pigeon.

"And does the rascal Dick Turpin plan on stealing the hearts of any ladies tonight?" asked Miss Peck.

David laughed at that. "Is a certain swallow hoping to entrance me with her plumage?"

Miss Peck gaped, her eyes sparking with humor as she snapped her fan closed and reached over to whack his arm with it. However, as feathers added so much to the length, the young lady missed her aim, only hitting David with the downy tips and not the hard skeleton beneath.

"You wretched man," she said with mock affront. "You know I am a peacock and not a swallow."

"But you are dressed in bright plumage, and as it is male peacocks and female swallows who are thusly adorned, I stand by my comment," replied David with a grin.

Miss Peck glanced at the naval captain, and the fellow gave her a chagrined smile.

"It is true," he said. "Though I will add, Mr. Turpin, that female swallows are often brown as well. In the animal kingdom, males are often more brightly colored than females."

Her teasing expression fell, and Miss Peck glanced down at the swaths of blue and green fabric draped about her person. Dropping her head, she held her fan up to her face to hide her laughter.

"I suppose I did not think my costume through, gentlemen."

"Yes, but—" began David, but a hand at his elbow had him stopping as he turned to see his mother standing there. She was easily identifiable, as she eschewed a costume and gave only a passing nod to the masquerade with a mask stick, which seemed entirely useless, as it only covered the face when one wished to cover it.

Mother said not a word, but then, she didn't need to do so when she looked at him in that manner. All raised brows and questioning eyes—it was an expression David knew all too well. Giving the others his excuses, he allowed himself to be dragged away.

"Do you know Mr. Gould?" she whispered, glancing at David for the barest of moments before turning her eyes back to where she'd come from, and he followed the movement to see two of his sisters standing together with a gentleman. Although Clarissa was the most talkative of the trio, the gentleman's attention was fixed on Irene, who was smiling brightly back at him.

"I do not." However, that would not remain for long. "Who introduced him?"

"The Leggatts."

The tension in his shoulders eased. "That speaks well of the fellow then. They wouldn't encourage an introduction if Mr. Gould was a bounder. However, I will ask around."

David's gaze drifted to the dancers, and he spied Flora with Mr. Kellen, which was far more disconcerting than the mysterious Mr. Gould. Though he was not well-acquainted with the Kellens, the rumors surrounding their heir were enough to give any brother indigestion.

"He was quite determined to secure an introduction," said Mother, nodding at Mr. Kellen as her fingers worried the stick of her mask. "Your father wasn't concerned, but I do not feel easy around him."

And rightly so, though David wasn't about to speak those thoughts out loud. The tightness to her eyes and lips said enough that any troubling news might shatter the last of her nerves. What had Father been thinking? But that answer was easy enough: he hadn't.

"Do not worry, Mother." David forced a warm smile and nodded towards his sisters. "Look after them, and I will find out more about this Mr. Gould."

Brows pulling tighter together, Mother nodded but didn't move. Shifting in place, she drew in a breath and shook her head. "I hate to be a bother, but your father has been at the card tables for some time now…"

A genuine grin grew at that. "The Tates are not allowing high stakes, so if he loses, he cannot lose much."

But for all that his words ought to have comforted the lady, Mother's muscles were strung taut, and if her mask had been made of fabric, it would've likely been shredded with the way her hands worried the wood.

"I will keep a weather eye on him," said David. "Go, enjoy the evening with the girls. Leave Father to me."

Granted, he had no intention of speaking to Mr. Thaddeous Archer. With penny stakes, the man could do far less damage than if he were left to wander the ballroom and chat up the gentlemen who were occupied with speculating. No doubt, they'd have him purchasing farmland in South America or investing in canals to nowhere. Again.

"Of course." She nodded and some of the strain eased from her features, though that ever-present concern remained in her gaze. "You always know what's best."

"Trust me, Mother. I will manage it all," he said, nudging her towards her daughters.

With great reluctance, and a few more prods, she drifted off back to her previous position, and David shifted his shoulders to ease the tension, though it did no good. Drawing in a breath, he tried to clear his mind, but with the magic of the evening broken, and thoughts of upcoming meetings with mill owners, the workers' wages, and the vacillating economy swarmed him. With the addition of Mr. Gould and Mr. Kellen.

David had already done as much as he could to secure healthy dowries for his sisters, but perhaps it was time to be more assertive in marrying them off. Mother was doing her best, but he could nudge good gentlemen into their paths. Not that Agatha's nuptials had done anything to alleviate David's burden. Now, he had to keep an eye on her husband and his business ventures as well. But surely, securing the girls good husbands like Ezra Endicott would limit the megrim he was taking on with each addition to the family.

Pain pulsed at the back of his skull, and David tucked his pistol away in his sash and rubbed at the throbbing point, though it did nothing to alleviate the pressure building there. Adding Mr. Gould and Mr. Kellen to his ever-growing list of things to manage later, David drew in a deep breath and focused on the room around him.

The circle of people he'd just left remained, but standing about wasn't going to do much to lift his spirits at present, and he wasn't about to waste this evening pondering over his many duties and tasks. The Tates' masquerade was too special an evening. Now was the time to dance.

Chapter 5

Adjusting his hat and mask so that they were properly situated, and righting his coat, David glanced around for a partner. He still hadn't secured his dance with Miss Leigh, and she was bound to lift his spirits. Her humor and teasing were bound to set his mood to rights.

Yet as he searched her usual haunts, she was nowhere to be seen.

His fingers drummed an unhappy rhythm against the hem of his trousers, his brows furrowing as he scoured the scene once more. The only thing that kept that slight unease from turning into a proper fret was discovering Mr. Mowbry buzzing about some other poor lady; if Miss Leigh was free of him, then she couldn't be in dire straits, which was a comfort.

As this was her sister's house, she'd likely escaped into one of the family's private rooms, leaving him unable to follow. Perhaps she would resurface again, allowing him the chance to stand up with her, but there was nothing else he could do but hope and pray. The realization settled heavily upon his heart, dimming the candlelight burning above.

But despite it all, David's feet still itched to dance, and so he turned his attention to the ladies scattered among the edges, overlooked and forgotten. Why gentlemen ignored the wall-flowers was a mystery to him. Nothing livened the spirits quite like standing up with one of their ranks; their expectations for the evening were low, so any partner was like manna from heaven, and it was thrilling to see their joy blossom at the un-expected invitation.

Tucking his hands behind him, David allowed his gaze to drift along the edges of the room and nearly overlooked one lady standing with her back against the wall. Whilst many in the company employed enough of a mask to meet the requirements of a costume, others embraced the mystery and had their faces entirely covered. David certainly thought the latter much more enjoyable, and surely this lady did as well, for her identity was entirely obscured.

Her frock was on the plain side, but that made the shawl draped about her head and shoulders all the more interesting. It was of fine quality, and though the base matched the cream-colored muslin gown, there was an explosion of deep blue em-broidery across the edges that took the piece from ordinary to extraordinary. Even from his distant location, it was easy to see the fine craftsmanship that had gone into the piece.

More than that, it shrouded her in shadow, giving her an air of mystery that was quite at home at a masquerade. And when the lady turned, the edge pulled back just enough to show a flash of a mask affixed to her face. It was a simple covering, blending into the black of the shadows so that only her lips and chin showed in the darkness.

A simple costume, to be certain, but far more interesting than Miss Peck's explosion of feathers and silks. Smiling, David stalked forward and drew out his pistols.

"Stand and deliver," he said, affecting his most thrilling highwayman timbre. "The daring Dick Turpin is here to relieve you of your valuables."

"Oh, dear me. Whatever am I to do?" she asked with a stilted tone that held more than a hint of humor.

"No need to worry, lass. Hand over your money and jewels,

and no harm shall come to you."

"Am I to take the word of a brigand?"

"Ah, but I am an honorable brigand," he said, freeing his hand by tucking one pistol in his sash before placing it over his heart.

"Quite the contradiction." Her voice was low, and one corner of her lips quirked upward. "No doubt, other ladies would swoon at the thought. After all, so many of the Gothic heroes are sinful and broken, giving females everywhere the hope that they might inspire a fallen angel back into his heavenly realm as only their love and beauty can lure him away from his immoral life and heal his fractured soul."

David fought back a grin and tried to affect a serious demeanor, though it was difficult. How many times had he heard his mother and sisters sigh over just such a character?

"And you do not?" he asked.

"Call me a fool, but I think it better to win the heart of a tedious banker or unremarkable tradesman than to believe someone so prone to wickedness will be content with a quiet life. Inevitably, they will return to their ways, and then the lady is forever bound to a bounder. Dull is better than having a husband with a wandering eye or a careless purse."

Somehow they'd ventured into quite the serious subject, and David found himself blinking at the lady, wondering how that had happened, though her tone was as light as ever.

"So, a brigand doesn't impress, but what if I said I was like Robin Hood of old, stealing from the rich to aid others?" Even though she couldn't see it, David found himself arching his brow in a teasing challenge.

And despite her face being hidden from view, it was easy to hear her own arched brow in her tone. "As I haven't any jewels or money to offer you, I am hardly rich. That makes you a highwayman, plain and simple, you brigand."

"Stuff and nonsense. That is a mighty fine dress, lass. Clearly, you are a lady of means, so give up your jewels before I'm forced to take more drastic measures." David nodded at the broach anchoring her shawl. "Like that bit of sparkly. And the shawl—that is worth a pretty penny."

The Mystery Lady laughed. "You are a poor thief if you cannot discern paste from real gems. But I fear neither it nor the shawl are mine. A friend lent them to me for the evening, and I shan't surrender them to a halfhearted robber."

"Then keep your baubles, but as recompense, you must dance with me."

She paused, and David longed to pull back the mask and see the emotions playing out across her face. Though her lips were visible, they showed so little, but there was something so animated about her conversation that he couldn't imagine her outward expression being stoic or unreadable. Yet there was a wryness to her teasing that had him questioning that assertion.

Who was she? David stared at her mask, searching for some sign. The lady stood alone like a wallflower, but there was a fire to her that belied the usually quiet demeanor found amongst those ladies.

"A bit of gallantry from the roguish Dick Turpin? Are you certain your reputation will survive?" she asked in a low tone that quickened David's pulse.

Clearing his throat, he tried to waggle his brows, though it was difficult to do the movement justice with the mask across his eyes.

"Ah, but I will brandish my pistols and shoot anyone who dares look at my lovely partner. That is certain to keep my character as blackened as ever."

The Mystery Lady let out a humming chuckle, and David couldn't help but smile at the sound.

"So, what say you?" he asked, nodding at the dancers. "If you cannot fatten my purse, you might as well entertain me for a few minutes."

"I fear I am not dancing tonight. My costume doesn't allow it."

David glanced between the dancers, skipping about to the bright reel, and the lady's delicate shawl draped in a manner that was unlikely to hold given the rigorousness of the steps. And considering his heavy coat, mask, and hat, David knew just how uncomfortable a rousing dance was in the rig. He'd barely kept his pistols in place when he'd stood up with Miss Jennings; they were forever attempting to slide down his trouser leg.

Clearly, both he and the Mystery Lady ought to have planned better for their fancy dress. But heaven smiled upon ridiculous gentlemen at times, for at that very moment, the last strains of the song ended, and the next dance was called.

"Come now, a waltz is unlikely to unsettle either of us." Then, sweeping off his hat in a courtly bow, he added, "Please, my dear lady, do me the great honor of standing up with me."

"I thought this was to be recompense for some imagined debt I owe you."

David straightened and plunked his hat back on his head with a laugh.

"You are right, of course. Do forgive me if my highwayman manners are lacking." Wrenching a pistol free of his sash so he had both in his hands once more, David leveled them at the Mystery Lady. "Now see here, woman. You're going to stand up with me, and you're going to enjoy it."

"When threatening my person with toys is the only way in which you can secure a dance? Highly unlikely. It doesn't speak well of your lightness of foot."

David stifled a laugh and nudged her towards the dancers. "Come now, accept your fate."

While he expected another witty retort, the Mystery Lady remained fixed in place, her face turned to the dancers. David straightened and tucked away his pistols, his mask hiding the furrow of his brow as he studied her. Had he pushed their jesting too far? Made her feel obligated or uncomfortable?

Before David could think what to say to this strange turn of events, she spoke in a whisper that barely carried above the noise of the ballroom.

"I fear I am not a very good dancer at the best of times."

Despite wishing to frown at the fear in her tone, David used the only part of his face she could see, giving her a warm smile.

"It is a slow waltz. The steps aren't intricate, and you need only hold fast to me, and I will keep you from toppling over." He paused, his grin lifting to one side. "And if anything happens, tell everyone I'm the clodhopper who tripped you."

He couldn't be certain that it was a laugh he heard, for it was low and halting, but he offered up his arm and added, "If at any point you do not wish to continue, simply tell me, and we will stop."

It was silly, but David's heart lightened when she threaded her arm through his. Guiding her in amongst the other couples, he turned to her and took her in a simple hold, eschewing some of the more elaborate dance positions and placing his hands at her waist so as not to upset the shawl draped around her head and shoulders. The Mystery Lady hesitated only a moment before placing her hands on his shoulders.

Then the first strains of the music began, and the two stepped easily into the rhythm of the dance. For all her objections, the Mystery Lady moved with enough fluid grace that David felt like the clodhopper he'd jested about.

Generally, when any gentleman deigned to ask Katherine to dance, it left her feeling giddy and anxious (except Mr. Mowbry, of course). No matter how much she knew it was only kindness and friendship that prompted Mr. Archer's request, she couldn't help but think about the beautiful possibilities that might arise from that moment. Especially in a waltz, when one's attention was fixed exclusively on one's partner.

But Katherine's heart was thumping a rapid beat not from anticipation but nerves. It was a strange sensation to be so wholly at another's mercy. The room swirled about her, and she could see enough to spy the dark blotches moving near her—but not well enough to judge whether or not they were about to crash into another couple.

Trust, it seemed, was a terrifying thing. Even with Mr.

Archer.

But there she was, embracing the ridiculousness of the evening as he'd prodded her to do, and when Katherine allowed herself to relax into the dance, she couldn't help but see the enjoyment to be found. Even when blind.

"And what has brought you to our gathering tonight?" asked Mr. Archer—or Mr. Turpin, rather, for he continued to employ that roguish tone.

Katherine had a quick and ready answer that was likely to make him laugh, as her reason had more to do with obligation than desire, but the memory of their previous conversation surfaced, reminding her that unless she truly wished to be the spoilsport she'd labeled herself, a bit of frivolity was warranted. Not that she cared much about others' opinions, but Mr. Archer was one of the few people who saw her for what she was—and liked her.

It wouldn't do to trample on his fun.

Besides, it was quite amusing to play the part alongside him. A masquerade was all about playacting, after all. And if she was stuck hiding behind a mask, then she might as well embrace the moment as Mr. Archer had prodded her to.

Adopting a low tone more suited to the character she played, Katherine said with a dramatic turn, "I fear I am on the run from a blackguard who is determined to marry me."

Chapter 6

Positioned as they were, David was allowed unfettered access to stare at her face, but the shadows cast by her shroud made it difficult to tell much about her eyes, except that they were a dark color and were alight with laughter. The color itself was unremarkable, but they shone with a vitality of spirit; the feeling was contagious, seeping into David until he felt ready to dance the entire evening.

"Ah, so this is not fancy dress for you, but a shield and protection from his nefarious plans?" he asked.

"Most definitely." Her tone was quite dry, but there was the perfect hint of humor to it.

"I am honored that such a desirable lady would choose me as her dance partner."

"You threatened me with your pistols."

Again, such a serious delivery made the words seem cold and unfeeling, yet there was a warmth to them that set David laughing. Subtle humor was the best sort, for it was like a secret jest between the pair of them, and he couldn't help but stare at her face, hoping to discern some hint of who was beneath it.

As they turned about the floor, the two pieced together the poor Mystery Lady's lurid past, in which she had to flee from her home and safety to keep herself from being trapped in a most wretched marriage to the vile creature who hunted her.

Though much of their conversation was fraught with silliness, bits of the person beneath the mask shone through. The lady had a clear view of the world, seeing through the short-sightedness and illogical nature of society, and she teased and twitted David, meeting his wit without flinching. A confident and outspoken wallflower seemed like a contradiction, but she stood before him.

Who was she?

The music wound to a close, and the pair surrendered their place on the floor. David offered up his arm once more, and his heart gave a distinctly happy flutter as she took it, but as he guided her back to where he'd found her, the thought of releasing her had him frowning.

"Is something amiss?" asked the Mystery Lady.

David forced himself to smile again and shook his head. "What could possibly be amiss when I am keeping company with such a captivating partner?"

"Again, I will remind you that I am here by force, so I am more captive than captivating," she retorted, drawing another laugh from him.

But a pause followed that, and when she spoke again, there was nothing humorous in her tone (dry or wry). "Is it your sisters? I noticed Mr. Kellen was pestering Miss Flora earlier."

David straightened at that clue, small though it may be. She knew his sisters? And logically, that meant she recognized him as well. "I will admit that has me a tad concerned, but truth be told, I was having an epiphany."

"Concerning?"

"I have decided to keep you captive for the entire evening," he said.

"You have decided that for me?" she asked.

David tapped his pistols. "I did say 'captive,' and I have already established the lengths I will go to."

She paused a moment before asking, "Even if it raises eyebrows? Surely you have something more important to do with your time."

David paused and turned to look at her. "I assure you, I do not. And as it is a masquerade, where unseemly behavior isn't out of the ordinary, I see nothing wrong in commandeering you for the rest of the night, Mystery Lady."

Katherine forced herself not to fidget, her mind whirling with questions as she struggled to fill her lungs. What was happening? Having known Mr. Archer for some time, she'd watched him flirt with ladies, but never had he turned such sultry tones on her. It was impossible to see his expression clearly, but the vague lines of his face seemed to form a smile of some sort, though everything she knew about the gentleman made her believe it wasn't a jest.

Mr. Archer cleared his throat. "If you do not wish it, I will leave you be, but—"

"Not at all," she said, feeling rather pleased that her tone was so even. "I was simply considering whether it was better to spend the evening alone or in the company of the horrid and terrifying Dick Turpin. Should I attempt an escape?"

With a laugh, he shook his head. "I am certain that is a difficult decision to make, but surely such a specimen of manhood ought to ensure you are protected tonight from your blackguard with nefarious plans. I wouldn't wish to see you come to harm."

There! Katherine blinked, grateful that her mask hid her furrowed brow and that she had sense enough to keep from gaping at the tone that was so dissimilar to the one he usually employed with her. For all that she thought herself a sensible lady, Katherine's heart picked up its beat and her thoughts spun with the possibilities.

Was Mr. Archer finally seeing her as more than a chum? Too many hopes were wrapped in that little question, and she hardly dared to give them free rein.

Nodding in the direction they'd been walking, he guided her along, and Katherine had no choice but to follow. No amount of doubt or common sense would allow her to do anything else. Whatever the reason behind this shift in behavior, she wouldn't surrender the opportunity. Clinging to his arm, she followed his lead as she avoided colliding with the blurry shapes around them.

Mr. Archer opened his mouth to speak, but before he could say something silly, Katherine said, "I wouldn't concern yourself over Mr. Kellen. He is a cad, but he grows bored very quickly. Even if he is serious in his attempts to woo Miss Flora, he'll move along when someone else catches his fancy. However, if you cause a fuss, he is more likely to remain interested—to twit you, if nothing else."

"Are you speaking from personal experience?"

"Heavens, no," replied Katherine, not bothering to smother her laugh. The question was just so ridiculous, as was the tone with which it had been spoken. She couldn't pinpoint precisely what emotions drove it, but if she were any other lady, she might've thought Mr. Archer was jealous. Which was ludicrous.

"I was speaking as one who has witnessed the comings and goings of many a ballroom and parlor," she added. "When one is a wallflower, watching people is the only entertainment to be found in such gatherings."

"No doubt you are more skilled at gathering intelligence than the Home Office, with all their spies," said Mr. Archer.

"Didn't you know that we are all employed by that venerable agency?" That earned her another laugh, which made Katherine's steps all the lighter, but before he could divert the conversation towards more jesting, she said, "You really needn't be concerned about Mr. Kellen. Your sister is a sensible young lady."

"Isn't it an elder brother's duty to fret and fuss over his sisters?"

Katherine considered that. "All older siblings fret and fuss over their younger siblings. It's in our nature. However, there is no need to work yourself into a dither."

Standing side by side as they were, Katherine was close enough to discern his expressions, and she spied a grin he was all too quick to use when sloughing off others' concern. His own troubles always remained tucked close to his heart.

"Do I look as though I'm working myself into a dither?" he asked.

"Yes. For all that you hide it well behind jests, smiles, and flirtation, you are almost always in a dither about something."

It was such a strange sensation to have another profess such a personal observation without knowing the identity of the person who'd spoken it. David feigned a laugh, but the lady turned to face him, her lips pulled into a smirk, condemning his deflection more fully than with words.

"Perhaps you are correct," he said with a wince. No answer followed that, but it was no introspective silence.

David couldn't put his finger on the feeling wriggling through him at that moment, for he'd never felt such a thing upon meeting another for the first time. Granted, it seemed likely that he knew this lady in some fashion (however distantly), but as he didn't know for certain, this counted as their introduction.

With his mother in a panic over his sisters, his father forever on the brink of economic failure, and his concerns over the health of the business, quiet and calm were in short supply. Yet as they walked the ballroom, muscles he didn't know were tight loosened, and the pressure in his chest eased. No words needed to be spoken, for that peace seemed to simply seep from her into him. The Mystery Lady demanded nothing of him, content to simply be at his side as they circled the gathering.

And whether it was the connection he felt with her or the anonymity surrounding her identity, David felt himself saying something he hadn't intended to say.

"I think I've been working myself into a dither since I was a young lad," he admitted.

"I imagine it's difficult not to when you feel such responsibility for them," she replied.

He slanted her a look. "I am not sure whether I should be flattered or terrified that you seem to know me so well."

"Flattered, of course," she said with a haughty lift of her chin. But she lowered it once more and answered in serious tones, "Everyone ought to have someone who knows his true self. I know all too well how easy it is to hide behind a persona, much as I have this mask, and I am grateful for the few who go to the effort to peek behind it."

The words made his chest burn, though David couldn't say whether it was his own longing making itself known or sympathetic pains for the loneliness rife in her tone. For all that the Mystery Lady seemed to know him, there was no way for her to know how true that statement was. Or how much he longed to peer behind her mask.

Saints above, what was happening to him?

He fought to keep his hand at his side, though it longed to reach up and lift the bit of *papier-mâché* and solve this mystery once and for all—but they had an entire night together, and he wasn't about to break the spell.

As David led her along the edge of the gathering, their conversation moved about like a honeybee, zipping haphazardly between the silly and the serious, quickly touching on something personal and real before flitting off into the ridiculous, though it felt far less like the avoidance his Mystery Lady had mentioned than it was simply a byproduct of a personality that preferred amusement to tears. Not hiding from the reality of life but embracing the ludicrousness of it all.

Despite his better judgment, he found himself confessing far more than he ought to a relative stranger, but something within the lady begged him to trust her. He couldn't explain it any more than he could find the words to describe this connection he felt with her.

David paid only the slightest attention to the others—only enough to ensure that they did not cross paths with anyone who might interrupt him. And with each passing hour, the urge to snatch off her mask grew.

Chapter 7

Good gracious, Katherine couldn't stop smiling! It took every ounce of self-restraint not to beam like a fool as the evening wore on. Yet still, Mr. Archer remained at her side.

In the two years since their first introduction, they'd spent countless hours in each other's company, speaking about personal subjects. However, there was something more to their conversation this evening. Deep in her bones, she felt it. Mr. Archer was finally seeing her. Truly recognizing that Katherine, *his chum*, was so much more than that. Try as she might, she couldn't understand what had altered, but she wasn't about to question her change in fortune.

Heat filled her, though it had as much to do with their location as it did the gentleman at her side. Between the warmth radiating from the dancers, the candles filling the chandelier and sconces, and being covered in this shawl and mask, sweat gathered at Katherine's temples.

Glancing towards the far wall, she spied the dark blur that indicated a doorway, which led to the outside courtyard. She longed to step through them; despite the doors being propped wide open to let in the air, the room was stifling. Yet as much as she yearned for a few minutes outside, she didn't know if she was bold enough to suggest such a thing.

But with each passing minute, the heat grew, and there was nothing to be done. It was either escape into the autumn night or risk fainting dead away. Katherine tugged on Mr. Archer's arm, nodding towards the doors.

"I must insist we get some air," she said. "I fear I am liable to melt."

The gentleman didn't fight her, but his smirk was clear for everyone to see. "My dear lady, if you wish to steal away to the garden to tarnish my virtue, you need only ask. There is no need for the pretense."

Katherine scoffed, though she was loath to admit it sounded more like a snort. "Do not pretend to have any sensibilities now, sir. I know full well that you have no compunctions about stealing embraces in gardens. From what I hear, you are quite the skilled kisser."

David gaped, and he was grateful they slipped through the door and out into the cool autumn air, for he was certain he was blushing enough that his mask couldn't hide it.

"Do the ladies of town gossip about me?"

"As if that is any surprise," she murmured. "Miss Woodhouse has told every young lady in town that you are far more skilled than Mr. Breadmore. 'Titillating' is the word she uses most often."

The pair strolled into the dark. Despite the moon hanging high in the sky, the light from the ballroom made it difficult to see much of the garden, but they followed the paved pathway past the shadowy shrubs and flowers.

"With so much responsibility resting on my shoulders, you cannot fault a man for seeking diversions," he replied, guiding her further into the greenery as the autumn breeze helped to cool his flaming cheeks.

"Ah, so rather than taking up riding or hunting, you prefer

kissing?" she replied with a laugh. "Certainly a different sort of sport. They say practice makes perfect, and surely you've mastered it by now."

Reaching up to straighten his hat, David wished he could defend himself from the accusation, but there was no defense to make—though he also couldn't help but smile at the Mystery Lady's pluck. A gentleman ought to have a lady strong enough to humble him when it was needed.

"Would you care to see what a bit of practice can do?" For all that he'd intended the question to be another of their many jests, when he turned to face her, his hand rested at the small of her back, holding her to him in a manner that erased the laughter from his tone.

The moon hung high above him, casting light upon her face and allowing him to see her eyes widen at his question. She stood stiff in his arms, but she didn't back away, either. David's gaze fell to her lips, and though sanity demanded he release her, he couldn't.

Tonight was so fully unexpected, but then, love was not on a timetable, set to arrive at certain intervals. And perhaps it was silly to say "love," for he hardly knew the Mystery Lady. However, something deep in his bones recognized the kindred spirit hiding behind that mask.

David refused to believe in soulmates. Despite how popular it was to speak of love in such terms, it ignored so many important truths. Love wasn't an accident into which people "fell." Love was a choice. It required effort and compromise. One could not love properly if one was not willing to give of himself.

"Soulmates" made it sound as though magic were involved, erasing all hurdles to irrevocably bind two hearts together. It implied that all other love was a poor imitation and that only the truest of affection was based on fate dropping another into one's life on a whim. The idea of soulmates was the antithesis of pure love, and David couldn't accept that such things existed.

Yet he couldn't deny the deep connection he felt with this woman he hardly knew.

Despite her placid exterior, every nerve snapped and sizzled at the feel of Mr. Archer's hand on her back. Katherine stood fixed in place as he stared at her. Had she truly heard him correctly? For all that she had almost convinced herself that he was, in fact, wooing her, hearing Mr. Archer ask such a bold question set her mind and heart into a frenzy.

Mr. Archer wanted to kiss her?

Was that what he was asking?

And not in jest but an earnest desire to kiss her?

For the briefest moment, Katherine wondered if she were sleeping. Perhaps the carriage had crashed on the way to the masquerade, and she was in heaven, living out her greatest fantasies. Of course, any version of heaven she could imagine wouldn't include Mr. Mowbry leering at her.

But Katherine knew all that was silliness anyway, for this was real. Mr. Archer was standing with her, under the moonlight, asking to kiss her. And she was standing there like a gaping fool, unable to speak.

"I do not treat such things lightly, sir."

Where had that come from? She longed to throw herself into his arms, but for all that she dreamed of embracing the fantasy of this moment, Katherine knew her heart wouldn't survive if Mr. Archer were merely amusing himself. Not that he was the sort to toy with a lady's affections, but clearly, it did not mean as much to him as it did to her.

"There is nothing light about my feelings at present," he murmured, drawing closer.

Katherine's breath caught, her eyes widening as he stopped just a hair's breadth from her lips. His eyes held hers, and for one glorious moment, she forgot anything else existed in the world but her and him. Even with her spectacles gone, she saw his face clearly; neither the stripe of black cloth across his face nor the nighttime enveloping them could hide the warmth in his eyes, holding her gaze with such intensity.

Then his lips touched hers, and tingles ran down her spine

as she stepped into his embrace. His arms came around her, and Katherine rested her hands on his chest, allowing only one final jolt of surprise to pass through her mind before she lost herself in the feel of his kiss.

Her mask, still in place, poked at her cheeks, but Katherine didn't notice it as the embrace deepened, sweeping her into sensations she'd all but given up hope of feeling. Her heart felt so light that she might blow away, and tears pricked in her eyes. If not for the energy thrumming through her at his touch, her legs might just very well give out on her at the thought that Mr. Archer cared for her.

This was all she'd ever wanted. All she'd ever hoped. All hesitancy was gone. Though some quiet concern in the back of her mind wondered if she was doing it properly, Katherine reveled in the feel of him surrounding her, and the ardor leaching from his touch that couldn't be feigned. And he felt it for her!

Her arms rose and drew around his neck, and she tried to convey all the things she'd never dared to say. How much he meant to her. How his friendship sustained her. How she valued the time they spent together.

Her Mr. Archer.

Footsteps against the pavers forced Katherine's eyes open, and she drew back. Mr. Archer leaned in once more, but she pressed against his chest and listened.

"David?" called someone from the far side of the courtyard.

Katherine stiffened at the sound of his sister's voice (though she couldn't say which one it was), and though she tried to step away, Mr. Archer's gaze was fixed upon her as he leaned in. She opened her mouth to say something, but he captured her in another kiss, and Katherine's muscles slackened once more as she threw her arms around his neck, pulling him closer.

It was a dangerous thing to do. She knew it. However, logic couldn't penetrate her fogged mind—not when Mr. Archer was so enamored that he hadn't noticed the interruption. Intoxicated with her! The thought that Katherine Leigh could catch any man's eye seemed impossible, but for someone like David

Archer to be so enchanted that he was deaf and blind to the world around him was too thrilling to allow something as silly as logic to ruin the moment.

David Archer was a fool. For all that they'd teased each other about his flirtatious past (harmless though it may have been), he couldn't help the guilt twisting his heart as he reveled in his Mystery Lady's kiss. Her comments and tentative movements made it clear she was unpracticed, and for all that the others had been diverting in their way, at this moment, he rather wished to erase that entire history.

But then he wouldn't know just how special this embrace was.

The others had been merely touches of skin, but this felt as though she reached into his chest and plucked out his heart. The sensation was strange, and David didn't know what to do with it, for just as he didn't believe in soulmates, he detested the idea of love at first sight. It was lust masquerading as something more meaningful; one could not feel true affection without knowing a person.

Yet how else could he describe what bound them together? Did he love this Mystery Lady? A few hours of conversation and a couple of fevered kisses surely wasn't enough to build a strong foundation for that sentiment, but neither could David dismiss this as mere affection.

Did she feel the same way? With no comparison, how could she recognize the remarkable connection they shared? Had David ever felt this electricity coursing along his nerves, he would never have made it to seven and twenty without marrying, and his heart pounded against his ribs, begging him to hold fast to her.

But then she was pushing him away again as she whispered, "Someone is coming."

"Let them come," he replied, leaning in once more.

The Mystery Lady pressed a hand to his chest and glanced

over her shoulder at the intruder. David cursed the person to perdition, but that anger allowed his thoughts to clear enough to recognize the prudence of her action. Blast it all!

Yet still, he longed to cast it all aside and sweep her into his arms again. What did it matter if they were caught together? He didn't plan on cutting ties with her any time soon. Or ever.

"Are you here?" called Irene from somewhere behind the shrubs. "Mama is not feeling well, and we need to leave."

David rested his hands on the Mystery Lady's hips, but she kept looking over her shoulder, and he was vaguely aware of his sister calling for him, drawing ever closer.

"Until tomorrow," whispered the Mystery Lady, pressing a quick buss to his lips.

His foggy thoughts had him nodding, and David let her go as she slipped away and ducked behind the shrub at his back. Reality sent a jolt of realization that cleared his muddled mind, and David scoured the shadows.

"What do you mean?" he whispered into the night, turning on his heel to search the darkened garden for any sign of her. "Tomorrow? I—"

"There you are," said Irene, swooping in and taking his arm. Pulling him back to the ball, she echoed her previous words. "Mama needs to leave."

David wanted to call out to the garden and demand the lady's name, but when he shook off his sister's hold and looked behind the shrub he'd thought the lady was hiding behind, he found nothing.

His Mystery Lady was gone.

Chapter 8

On bad days, people called Katherine Leigh dour. On good ones, they said sensible, which sounded like an improvement, but not when that word was only tossed out like a crumb of kindness when one could think of nothing better. It was not the pinnacle to which people aspired. No, they preferred "attractive," "intelligent," "creative," or any number of enviable traits.

But this morning, Katherine was neither dour nor sensible. She felt like a hummingbird, needing to be in constant motion as she flitted about the halls of her family home, attempting to complete her tasks for the day. Energy—electric and crackling—pulsed through her, making it impossible to sit.

With Grandmama Cora gone, no one at Whitley Court desired Katherine's company, leaving her alone most of the day. Which was for the best, for they would think her bound for Bedlam. A great smile stretched across her face, and no matter how she tried, she couldn't contain it. Even when she could, there was nothing to be done with the joy shining in her gaze, if anyone bothered to notice.

And no one ever did. Except David.

Now she was grinning again. For the briefest moment it

dimmed, but the thing resurfaced the moment her control slipped, which was often as her thoughts remained fixed on the previous night.

Katherine felt as insubstantial as a cloud, floating about on a summer's breeze. Had she known kissing David Archer would elicit such euphoria, she would've taken matters into her own hands long ago. That thought made her chuckle to herself, for it was entirely insensible. Despite having longed to do just that for some time, she never would've had the courage to act on that impulse.

David had kissed her! Despite having been party to that interlude, Katherine still couldn't believe it. Though she'd imagined such a moment occurring and hoped that it might come to fruition someday, a part of her had never fully expected it to happen. It had been impossible. Improbable at best.

Lifting a hand to her lips, she flew down the stairs with little hopping steps as she beamed at everything and nothing. Arriving at the parlor, she schooled her expression: it wouldn't do to draw Mama's attention. However, it required a herculean effort when she spied David standing in the parlor. Alone.

"I thought that might be you," she said with a casual tone, as though she hadn't been listening keenly for the doorbell since the break of dawn.

"As you see, though I hope my far less dashing attire today doesn't disappoint," he said, giving a sweeping gesture towards his person. Katherine's gaze followed the movement, and she couldn't see anything wrong with the plain jacket and trousers. But then, David looked appealing in everything he wore.

The pair stood facing each other; his eyes smiled as they were wont to do, and Katherine felt like sighing in a manner as she was never wont to do. What did one say in such a moment? She was beyond the age of needing her father's consent, and David knew her well enough to realize she wouldn't welcome him speaking to Papa. But she had to admit that having some set course of action might be a blessing, for then she would know how to proceed.

And wasn't that a laugh? Whether she knew the next step or not, she hadn't the foggiest notion what to do with a beau. Her theoretical knowledge provided vague guidance but no true ability—like a lad in school studying the great battles of old and believing himself as skilled as Wellington.

What did one say to the man she had kissed?

"It is good to see you." Oh, that was brilliant, Katherine. Revolutionary.

"It is good to be seen," he replied with a cheeky grin.

She stepped closer, her hands itching to hold him close once more as her lips felt the phantom touches they'd shared last night. Would it be appropriate to simply launch herself at him? The impulse was certainly there. Katherine's heart pounded at that audacious thought. Could she be so bold? But then, was it truly that shocking when they had shared such tendernesses last night? Several, in fact.

Lifting her arms, she reached for him.

"What in the world are you doing here at such an hour?" called Benjamin, striding through the doorway. "You pulled me from bed."

David scoffed. "It is well past noon, you lazy fellow."

"After last night's festivities, it is a wonder I rose from my bed at all." He punctuated that with a broad yawn that he didn't bother to stifle. Glancing at Katherine, he raised his brows. "Have you been pestering David again?"

Katherine's heart constricted, but before she could think of what to say, David leveled a narrow look at Benjamin.

"She has never pestered me. Not now, not ever."

Benjamin's brows pinched together, his gaze darting between the pair.

"Despite what my family believes, there are some who value my company," said Katherine in a monotone.

Holding up his hand in surrender, her brother replied, "No offense meant, Katherine—"

"Is she being missish again?" called Mama, striding into the room to give her son a buss whilst entirely ignoring the subject of her question. Patting Benjamin on the cheek, the lady frowned. "What are you doing up at this hour? You were up so late, and you must get your rest, my dear, dear boy."

Benjamin stiffened, his gaze swinging to David with an inaudible sigh, as though being the apple of his mother's eye was the greatest of burdens. The poor, poor boy. Katherine forced herself not to scoff, though it was a near thing.

"I'm awake because my friend called at a wretched hour on the day after our sister's grand masquerade," replied Benjamin, slumping into an armchair.

"It is a matter of great importance," said David. "Though I wouldn't say it is life or death, it certainly feels like it."

Katherine's breath stilled, and she stared at the gentleman. His tone was far too significant to be ignored, and the rest of the Leighs clearly believed so, for they all watched David with varying levels of curiosity.

"I believe I am in love," he announced with a laugh.

Everything within her stilled at that declaration. Those beautiful words threaded their way through her, and as they wove deep into her heart, energy pulsed once more. Katherine was trapped in this delicious agony, caught between freezing in place and flying apart at the seams. Certainly, her heart could not handle such strain, and it felt ready to leap free of her chest.

He loved her. Yes, that declaration had been qualified with "believe," but even that was far more than she had ever hoped to hear. David loved her.

"And as much as I hate to be a bother, I'm here because Mrs. Tate mentioned last night that she was going to visit today, and I desperately require her assistance," added David.

Katherine frowned at that. What did Rosanna have to do with any of this?

"You are correct, but I fear she is late," said Mama, sitting once more whilst motioning for him to do the same. "Tell us about this direly important assistance you require."

However, he remained where he was, casting a glance at Katherine. Of course, he was waiting for her to sit first; her brother may have the manners of a dockworker when it came to his sister, but David was a gentleman through and through. Unfortunately, Katherine couldn't move.

What did Rosanna have to do with this? Her mind pieced together possibilities, but each was ludicrous and nonsensical.

Standing there, she stared at David, and a chill started at the tips of her fingers, spreading through her to settle deep in her heart and causing it to sink beneath the weight of that unnamed dread. This was David. Her David. Katherine batted at that awful foreboding, which had no place inside her during such a pleasant moment, but its hold was too firm for her to break.

Something was amiss.

"I met the most magnificent lady last night, and I was certain Mrs. Tate might know who she is," said David, glancing at Katherine. Just moments ago, she would've taken that as some secret laugh or communication, but there was only mild curiosity in his gaze. No doubt wondering why she kept both of them on their feet.

The strength seeped from her legs, and Katherine sank into a seat as he went on to give an abbreviated version of his evening with his "Mystery Lady." But her ears refused to work. His words were muffled, and Katherine sat there, staring at him as he spoke with all the animation of a man truly ensorcelled and convinced his lady was the finest in creation.

Her thoughts stuttered. Last night had seemed improbable, but this mistake felt impossible. How did he not know her? Her mind stuck on those questions, unable to follow the conversation. Having replayed the evening countless times since she'd snuck out of Rosanna's garden, the memories came quickly to her call, and she scoured them for any sign.

Surely this was a jest. David had known it was her. It wasn't as though she had hidden her identity beyond blocking her face. Yes, she had masked her voice at times and played the part of the Mystery Lady, but he knew her far too well to be taken in by that weak ruse. The way they'd spoken. The things she'd shared.

How could he not recognize the soul beneath the mask?

But a realization struck her with such force that Katherine couldn't breathe. Couldn't move.

Expectations colored perspectives, twisting reality until it was unrecognizable. If one did not expect to see something, it was easy to overlook. And Katherine was so far from being a viable romantic option in David Archer's mind that he couldn't recognize the truth staring him in the face.

Her stomach turned, and her muscles cramped, holding her in place like a statue as she stared at the far wall. Her breaths came in pants, and though her heart began to crumble, she forced herself to remain calm. Immoveable. Impassive. Fighting against the pain vibrating through her, Katherine forced herself to show no sign of distress. The others laughed and teased, speaking of the evening in grand terms whilst her world toppled to the ground.

And no one noticed.

Mr. Archer's gaze turned to her, and Katherine's eyes prickled, though she refused to let them compound her pain by revealing her shame. Had she truly thought he loved her? That one evening of dancing and talking would suddenly alter everything about their relationship? His brows furrowed, but Katherine drew in a deep breath and kept her chin lifted.

"Might it be Miss Pelham?" asked Mama, tapping her chin with a finger. "Or Miss Chorley?"

"Impossible," said Benjamin with a laugh. "Miss Pelham is quite enamored with Mr. Tomlinson. And I doubt Miss Chorley would tolerate such a poor excuse for a beau as David Archer."

"You wound me," replied the gentleman with a laugh.

Ticking off her fingers, Mama rattled off several other names in quick succession, but Katherine's attention waned once more. Until Benjamin responded.

"You are forgetting one eligible lady," he added with a teasing smile.

Mama frowned. "Am I?"

Brows raised, Benjamin nodded at Katherine. Her mother

didn't even hesitate before she chuckled.

"Don't be a ninny, Benjamin."

It was the same sort of dismissal Mama always gave. Katherine couldn't recall a time when the lady had ever paid the slightest bit of attention to her daughter—except to criticize. So, it ought not to hurt now. But Mama's words struck her heart like a dagger. The Mystery Lady had entranced Mr. Archer, drawing forth a declaration of love (however hesitant it was) in the short span of an evening, and the thought that Katherine could be that lady was so ridiculous her mother thought her brother's suggestion was a jest.

And perhaps it might've been. With Benjamin, she couldn't say for certain. But did it even matter?

Shooting to her feet, she strode from the parlor with her head held high. Let them talk. Let them laugh. But Katherine refused to sit there and listen to it.

Chapter 9

Speaking kindly to kind people wasn't the mark of a good person. Treating another as they have treated you was not difficult, and living tit for tat was no true test of character. Facing down cruelty and meeting venom with goodwill took far more strength. How could one claim to be good when that goodness was contingent on others' behavior?

David knew plenty of people who thought decency was reserved only for those who showed decency in return and that reciprocating poor treatment was the only way to help others see the error of their ways. But that was lunacy. Maintaining the higher ground wasn't easy and didn't always gain the victory in the argument, but sinking to a lower level never won the day. Thoughts and behavior couldn't be badgered or belittled into changing.

But heaven help him, David longed to rail against Mrs. Leigh. Heat swept through him as he stared at the lady, who didn't notice her daughter marching away. Her treatment of Katherine was inconceivable.

"Benjamin is correct, Mrs. Leigh. Your daughter was there and unmarried, so he is not a ninny," David managed to say, only when he was certain he wouldn't say something regrettable.

Mrs. Leigh laughed and waved a hand. "She refused to wear a costume, so she can't have been your Mystery Lady. And even if she had, surely you would know her."

That explanation was sound enough, but the lady's flippant dismissal of her daughter sat uneasily with David. Her laughter hadn't been born from such practical thoughts. But just as he was about to get to his feet and follow after Miss Leigh, Mrs. Tate swept into the room.

"There you are, my dear," said Mrs. Leigh, rising to greet her daughter as the menfolk did the same. "Mr. Archer is quite determined to speak with you."

But then, glancing behind Mrs. Tate, Mrs. Leigh frowned. "Didn't you bring the boys? I long to see them."

Stiffening, Mrs. Tate met that with a tight smile. "They *and* their sisters are at home at present. It's time for their lessons. Besides, I called on Prudence before coming here, and I didn't think it was wise to bring a herd of children to her home when she's feeling so poorly. She has her hands full enough with her brood."

Benjamin straightened. "What is the matter with her?"

Mrs. Tate waved his concern off as she set down her basket by the door and dropped her gloves into it. "The same thing that troubles most expectant mothers. I brought a tisane that helped me some with Gregor, so I hope it will alleviate some of her discomfort. But I fear she won't be able to enjoy any of the Michaelmas festivities. Parker insists she needs to remain in bed for some time."

"Such fuss. Her discomfort is nothing compared to what I suffered bringing you children into the world. Such vexation!" Pausing, Mrs. Leigh's gaze softened as she looked at Benjamin. "Except for you, my dear boy. You've never been anything but a pleasure."

Benjamin huffed and dropped back into his seat without meeting his mother's eyes. "David was hoping to speak with you, Rosanna."

Mrs. Tate's brows rose as she and her mother took their seats. David joined them and dove into the explanation of the previous night—only omitting how the evening ended between him and the Mystery Lady.

Just thinking of that moment heated his blood, and David had to force himself not to grin like a fool. It wasn't as though he'd been a wilting flower before; he was well acquainted with flirtations and little tokens of affection, but the kiss he'd shared with his Mystery Lady had outshone all other experiences, leaving all the others as naught but pale comparisons. Mere shadows.

"And you do not know her identity?" asked Mrs. Tate. "But what hints did she give? Is she from Greater Edgerton or a town roundabout?"

David shifted in his seat. "I do not believe she said either way."

Mrs. Tate nodded with a puzzled frown. "Was she familiar with my family? Our invitation list was long, and not everyone was a close friend of ours."

"She didn't say directly, but it was clear that she knew me by reputation if nothing else."

David scoured his memory for any other tidbit he had gleaned that might indicate her identity, but adoring music and reading were hardly noteworthy. But then, that was part of the appeal of their conversation. They had spoken together as though they were already dear friends, glossing over the inconsequential and diving straight at the heart of things.

However, David couldn't help but feel a pang of discomfort when he realized how much of that conversation had revolved around himself and his interests. But then, he hadn't expected her to disappear so suddenly.

"I recall seeing your Mystery Lady," said Mrs. Tate with a furrowed brow. "But I cannot remember greeting her when she arrived at the party. There were a few ladies with simpler costumes, like what you describe, but I cannot say for certain that any of them fit your description of her. And there are many of our guests whose fancy dress, or lack thereof, I cannot recall."

"I will take any guidance you can offer," said David.

"Miss Hooper meets the costuming criteria the best, though I do not think she matches in any other fashion. Sweet girl, but she's very young and incredibly timid. And I do not believe you are acquainted with her at all."

David shook his head, but that did not signify anything. He may not know her, but that did not mean she was ignorant of him. Wallflowers saw all, and many of them embraced that role because of a natural propensity towards timidity. So, a quiet stranger was a possibility.

Mrs. Tate tapped a finger on her lips. "But if I had to guess based on personality, I would say Miss Seward or Miss Lyons—"

"Miss Seward was dressed as a queen," interjected Mrs. Leigh. "Her gown was quite gaudy and not easily mistaken for anything else."

Nodding, Mrs. Tate amended, "Miss Lyons, Miss Heber—"

"She was otherwise occupied with Mr. Brookman much of the evening," said Benjamin.

Mrs. Tate gave her brother a narrowed look and sighed. "Am I going to finish my list or am I going to be interrupted every other word?"

Lifting his hands in surrender, Benjamin smirked.

Watching him for just a moment, Mrs. Tate turned back to David and said, "Miss Lyons and Mrs. Ellery are your likeliest bets, though I cannot recall their costumes." The lady paused, her brow furrowing. "I cannot say I am certain about the latter, though. I do not believe she is eager to remarry so soon after her husband's passing."

"Nonsense. She is so very young and too pretty to waste herself on widowhood," replied Mrs. Leigh with the smile of one who knows a great secret. "Besides, he left her quite destitute—"

"Mama," scolded Mrs. Tate with a frown. "That is unkind."

Mrs. Leigh waved it away. "I am merely speaking the truth."

That silenced the group, though the significant looks that Benjamin and Mrs. Tate sent each other and David spoke clearly enough. When people veiled criticisms in the cloak of "honesty," it was simply an excuse to make themselves appear virtuous, for truth-speaking didn't require one to spout every cruel thought that entered one's mind.

But correcting Mrs. Leigh was like attempting to bail a sinking boat with a teacup.

Clearing his throat, David turned back to the subject at hand.

"I had Miss Lyons and Mrs. Ellery on my list of possibilities as well. I didn't know if they had attended last night, but of the ladies I know, they are the most likely to...fit the bill." David managed not to stumble too much over the words, though he was certain a blush was stealing across his cheeks.

Those ladies were foremost on his list as they were the only ones he knew who were bold enough to kiss him in such a fashion, though he wasn't about to admit that to the Leighs. Yet David would wager a large sum that the lady he'd embraced was uncertain in their kiss. The timidity of someone unused to such affection.

And wasn't that a contradiction? Demure enough to be shy in those overtures, yet bold enough to steal a few kisses at midnight.

"Miss Sheridan!" exclaimed Mrs. Tate.

"Who?" asked her mother before David could do the same.

Straightening, Mrs. Tate raised her brows as a smile stretched across her face. "Little Miss Rebecca Sheridan. She was there, and I am certain her costume was akin to what Mr. Archer described."

"She's hardly more than a child," said Mrs. Leigh with a laugh.

But Mrs. Tate shook her head. "She had her coming out last year, Mama."

Casting his thoughts to the family, David tried to see her in that light. As the Sheridans resided in his parish, he was acquainted with them as much as occasional conversations after Sunday services afforded a person, but he couldn't say with any certainty that he knew Miss Sheridan well enough to judge whether it had been her beneath the Mystery Lady's mask. However, she was a pretty young lady, and the little he knew of Miss Sheridan spoke well of her.

"I would say of all the possibilities, Miss Sheridan is your best," said Mrs. Tate with a decisive nod. "The more I consider it, the more convinced I am that she was wearing the costume you described."

However, there was no reason to discount anyone at this juncture. Better to widen his search than to overlook one of the ladies. Miss Hooper, Miss Lyons, Mrs. Ellery, and Miss Sheridan. Four possibilities. Surely one of them had to be his Mystery Lady.

Turning his attention back to the matrons, David asked, "Do you know what mornings they entertain?"

"Why pay calls?" asked Benjamin. "They are all likely to be at the Hyatts' picnic next week. You can spend a little time with each and not waste your time traipsing about town."

"Paying a call on a possible sweetheart is hardly a waste of time," said David with a huffing laugh.

Benjamin shrugged. "You rarely have time to spare."

And there was a lot of truth to that. As he sat in Whitley Court, his work was multiplying, and David knew all too well how easily it became overwhelming without constant care. His schedule was filled to the brim already, and finding any time for social calls during his busiest hours was hardly going to help matters.

"Perhaps you are right," said David. "I doubt I'll have time to make all the visits before the Hyatts' party, and it shouldn't take long to identify which lady it is, so there's no reason not to be efficient."

"You speak of courtship like another task to be completed, Mr. Archer," said Mrs. Tate with a scoff. "Surely you should take some enjoyment from it."

"He will have enjoyment enough once he locates the lady," said Benjamin with a waggle of his brows.

Mrs. Tate's cheeks heated. "Benjamin!"

But his mother merely laughed and murmured her usual endearments for the man who would forever be her "dear boy." For his part, David fought to keep from tugging at his collar as it was strangling him at present. The innuendo rife in Benjamin's tone would make any young man blush—especially as it was accurate.

Turning away from her brother, Mrs. Tate drew in a steeling breath and continued, "While your plan certainly seems...economical with your time restraints, I fear that it is of no use when it comes to Miss Sheridan. If I recall correctly, her mother said they were leaving this very morning to visit her sister in Whittingford for a few weeks. I believe they are to return by Michaelmas, but they shan't be around for the Hyatts' picnic."

David frowned, his heart sinking at the prospect. Courtship and marriage hadn't been foremost on his thoughts before last night, but he couldn't deny the appeal of it now that the possibility landed in his lap, and the thought of having to exercise patience was like sitting on the church pews every Sunday—uncomfortable but necessary.

"I suppose there is nothing to be done about that," he mumbled.

"You'll be busy enough sorting through the other ladies," said Benjamin in a dry tone that sounded so very much like Miss Leigh that David couldn't help but smile, despite the daunting task before him. "The Hyatts' picnic is the best setting—"

"Enough of that nonsense," said Mrs. Leigh, waving her hands at the gentlemen to break up that conversation and draw their attention back to her. "What about Miss Heber? How do you know what she was up to last night?"

Holding his hands up once more, Benjamin shook his head. "I have no interest in the young lady."

Mrs. Leigh narrowed her eyes. "No, but she is good friends with Miss Rothschild—"

"Not this again, Mother," said Benjamin, straightening. "Miss Rothschild is a fine young lady and from a good family."

"But hardly worth noting," she replied with a scowl. "You can do so much better. If you insist on looking beneath you, Miss Heber is a better choice."

Benjamin sent David a pleading look, though there was nothing David could do to save his friend from that quagmire. Mrs. Leigh was a force unto herself, and none of them could rein her in. He'd seen the eldest daughter have some luck with it, but as Mrs. Tate had said, Mrs. Prudence Humphreys was settled in her own home and too indisposed to manage her mother at present.

Rising to his feet, David thanked Mrs. Tate for her assistance. When Benjamin moved to follow, Mrs. Leigh grasped her son's arm and dragged him back to his seat. David winced in sympathy but fled while he still could.

Chapter 10

Once out of sight, David listened to the house, certain of what he would hear. The murmur of the conversation was behind him, but the muted notes of a piano echoed in the distance, and climbing the stairs, he followed the sound to the drawing room. David eased the door open and found Miss Leigh seated at the piano. Her fingers flew across the keys, her head canted to the side and her eyes closed as she listened to the song streaming from the instrument.

David was no musician and couldn't begin to guess at the composer, but the tune rang in the air, running up and down with such speed that he wondered how her fingers didn't trip over themselves. He was well aware of the unkind opinions of Greater Edgerton, but he didn't understand what they found lacking. Her music sounded brilliant to his ear, and it was impressive to watch her lose herself in it.

Whatever her skill, it was clear Miss Leigh loved that piano. Despite the frustrations that had driven her from the parlor, the lady sat there with a level of peace David didn't often see resting upon her. But was it any wonder that tranquility was in short supply in Miss Leigh's world when her family and society as a whole judged her vexing?

And not for the first time, David found himself wondering why she garnered such ire.

Having the drawing room to herself was a double-edged sword. Katherine appreciated the solitude and freedom to do as she wished (as the room was often ignored during the daytime); however, it pricked her pride every time she shut herself away in this forlorn corner of the house, for it reminded her of the day Mama had made the change.

The lady hadn't bothered to soften the truth or tip-toed towards an explanation. The family couldn't stand to hear Katherine play, so it was better to exile the piano from the heart of the house. And every time Katherine crossed the drawing room threshold, she was reminded of those words—and that sentiment was made all the more bitter and sharp because of her current disappointment.

Mr. Archer hadn't known it was her.

Katherine's heart twisted in her chest, though she was able to keep a tighter rein on the resulting pangs and focus the sentiment into her fingers. She pounded on the keys, letting the pressure build through her and come out in the notes.

No tears. No more, at any rate. Those would be reserved for the dark of night whilst tucked away in her bed. There would be no stopping them then, but in the here and now, she refused to give them control. In the waking realm, she was mistress—not them.

The song came to an end, and applause forestalled Katherine from selecting another. There was no need to turn and look at the intruder. There was only one person it could be. Closing her eyes, she took a fortifying breath.

"Brava, Miss Leigh," said Mr. Archer. "That was quite impressive."

Katherine scoffed, her eyelids lowering as she stared at the black notes scattered across the page. "You will forgive me if I do not believe you, sir."

"Am I not a reliable source?"

"When you are my only supporter? I fear that makes your opinion suspect," Katherine didn't bother to soften the sardonic tone.

Footsteps sounded against the floor, but she studied the music, shifting through her sheets.

"I will admit I prefer the more modern sound to these old pieces, Miss Leigh, but I am still in awe of your skill," he replied.

"I play these 'old pieces' because I haven't the skill to do the modern composers justice, Mr. Archer. Trust me when I say there is little to admire in my playing. I do so because I adore it—not because of my skill."

Mr. Archer moved to stand beside the piano, but Katherine couldn't look at him. Wouldn't.

"The lady doth protest too much," he murmured, and though she wouldn't turn her gaze to see the expression, she heard the arched brow in his tone and knew the exact manner in which his lips turned up at the corners. "I find it impossible to believe you have such a poor opinion of yourself when you are so quick to put yourself forward. I hear you are not only playing a solo at the Garrisons' concert next week, but you are accompanying several young ladies. From what I understand, you are doing more than any other lady."

Katherine frowned, her eyes jerking to him of their own accord. "Firstly, I do not have a poor opinion of my skill. Knowing one's limitations is not self-denigrating. Whilst I am very capable with certain styles of music, I haven't the touch for emotive music, which is what dominates modern music tastes. I know it, accept it, but that doesn't tarnish my value or make me a lesser person. It simply is. Not everyone can be the best at something, and I am perfectly content to do what I can to improve and accept I haven't the talent to reach loftier climbs."

Yes, Mr. Archer was watching her with that amused and disbelieving look of his that he always employed when she was speaking of herself. But Katherine didn't know what else to say to convince him. Having played in public for so many years, she knew precisely how she compared to others, and acknowledging her mediocre standing was hardly slandering herself.

"Secondly, I am only accompanying several young ladies because they asked me to, hoping to keep me too busy to manage a solo. Which is ridiculous, as I have little else to do with my time but practice, and I enjoy performing—"

Forcing her mouth closed, Katherine turned her gaze back to her music.

"And thirdly?" prodded Mr. Archer. "And don't feign ignorance, Miss Leigh. I heard it in your tone."

Katherine sighed to herself, her shoulders dropping as her hands fell to her lap. Her gaze drifted to him, and she found him watching her as he always did. As no one else ever did. There was no censure or mockery there. Only curiosity and concern.

And her heart fractured anew.

Straightening, she forced herself to swallow past the lump and shook off that sentiment. It was of no use at present, and she refused to allow herself to be undone by it.

"And thirdly, I do not volunteer because I believe my talent deserves to be showcased." Turning her gaze back to the music, she studied the notes. Warmth suffused her chest at the flurry of black marks on the page. Talented or not, it took effort to master such a piece, and she had done so.

Katherine focused on Mr. Archer again, fully intending not to say another word, but he watched her so intently. Not demanding an answer, though she was certain he knew there was more. He always did.

Drawing in a breath, she forced herself to continue, "I know I am not as skilled as the other ladies, but performances push me to try new pieces. It gives me a reason to improve. A deadline of sorts. I enjoy attempting it, but if left to my own devices, I do not know if I would go to the effort. I would simply plod along, playing the same pieces over and over."

Mr. Archer watched her, his gaze holding hers, and Katherine's heart reached outward, pressing against her ribs as though begging him to see her. The gentleman may be the only one who saw her as anything more than a pest, so surely he could see past the plain facade and recognize the lady who had captured his attention last night. For a long moment, they watched each other, and Katherine's heart slowed, each beat releasing another pulsing hope.

As he was the only one who ever noticed her for any pleasant reasons, surely he would see her. Realize the truth sitting before him. The silence stretched out, and it felt as though her dreams pressed down on her, as though the very air had weight to it.

"I feel like I should apologize for your family," he said.

Like a soap bubble on the breeze, the moment burst and evaporated as though it was never there. Katherine rested a hand on the keys and studied her fingers.

Giving herself a moment to steady her voice, she said, "As their behavior is none of your doing, I do not see why you need to." She drew in a deep breath and hurried to add, "And you needn't fret. I am quite used to their ways, and though I cannot pretend I am wholly unaffected, it doesn't disturb me much anymore. Not like when I was younger."

Mr. Archer shifted, drawing himself to the edge of her line of sight. "And what changed?"

For the first time since she'd entered this room, a hint of a smile drew up her lips. "With age comes wisdom, and with that, a true sense of self that isn't rattled by others' opinions. Receiving little outward validation of my value, I was forced to find it within myself. I know my worth, and it is no longer dictated by them. Though it helps that I have an escape planned."

Katherine stiffened and wished she'd employed a bit of her self-control on her tongue, for she hadn't intended to tell anyone that detail.

"Ah, you are planning to sail away and join a pirate crew?" asked Mr. Archer with a teasing grin.

Eyes narrowing, she stood and gathered the sheet music with sharp movements. For all that his rascally ways often drew her from the doldrums, her present mood was not the sort that could be laughed away, and Katherine wanted nothing more than to see the back of him.

Mr. Archer held up his hands. "I meant no disrespect, Miss Leigh. I was only jesting. But I am very curious about it. What is your plan?"

"It is none of your business," she replied whilst nudging her spectacles back into place.

"Do tell," he said with a smile. "I am quite good with plans, after all. If I can navigate my family's mill through the economic turmoil of the past four years, I am certain I can be of use in helping you escape your parents."

"No." Her tone was tarter than intended, but Katherine couldn't help the bite. Exhaustion blended with the tumult of the past half hour, leaving her heart wrung out.

Silence followed that pronouncement, and she couldn't meet his gaze as she busied herself with the music. Even if she were in the mood to speak about such things, it truly wasn't a wise thing to do.

"I apologize, Miss Leigh. I didn't mean to pry." For all his jesting before, Mr. Archer's tone was quite earnest, and Katherine could well believe that he meant every syllable. But that didn't change her answer.

Grandmama Cora had been very clear in her instructions, and Katherine couldn't help but see the wisdom in the lady's plan. Whether or not she trusted Mr. Archer, it was best not to tell a soul about the money. If Mama and Papa were ever to discover—however inadvertently—they would not stop until they secured the funds for the "good" of the Leigh family, and there was a reason Grandmama Cora hadn't left it to them in the first place.

No, the money was quite safe where it was, awaiting the time when Katherine needed to leave.

"If you cannot speak of that escape, perhaps you could tell me of the one you made last night, Miss Leigh."

Though his tone was passably light, there was a distance to it that made Katherine's shoulders drop. More so when Mr.

Archer continued.

"I had planned on dancing with you, but I couldn't find you anywhere. No doubt you were hiding from that wretched Mr. Mowbry, and I am quite put out that I didn't get the chance to squire you about the floor, though I cannot blame you for hiding if it meant you could avoid that fellow."

How could one feel so giddy and disappointed in the same instant? Katherine's heart couldn't decide whether to rejoice that Mr. Archer sounded quite put out about it or weep because he was so entirely blind to the fact that they had danced. And so much more.

So, her heart decided to alternate between the two, leaving it beating erratically in her chest as her thoughts struggled for an answer.

What would he say if she told him that his Mystery Lady and his friend were the same? Mr. Archer would never mock her as her family was apt to do, but could a gentleman who was so determined not to view her in a romantic light welcome the revelation? Her family's jeering laughter rang in her memory, shredding her resolve.

The whole debate was ridiculous, for Katherine knew what her course of action would be. It was the same that she'd taken since the moment her heart first stirred for Mr. David Archer. Men never welcomed her overt attentions; subtlety and patience were all she could employ whilst hoping he came to the conclusion on his own.

But that didn't mean she couldn't help to nudge him in the proper direction. Scouring her memory, Katherine tried to recall precisely what they'd said the previous night. Despite her lack of a costume, she forced herself to don the guise of the Mystery Lady.

"I was hiding from Mr. Mowbry, as you said," she replied, lowering her voice a touch as she had the previous night. "I could've used a dashing highwayman to help run off the brigand."

Would he recognize the reference? They'd spoken at length

about her evading Mr. Mowbry, even if they hadn't said his name.

Mr. Archer's brows rose. "Is that so? It is a shame, for I proved myself quite adept at safeguarding ladies from brigands. I kept my companion from being spirited away, and I could've extended that protection to you as well. I am sorry I was unable to do so."

Katherine's shoulders fell, the guise dropping as she stared at him. Was it truly so impossible to connect her with his perfect Mystery Lady? Her heart cracked open, but thankfully, it was hidden away. She didn't allow the pain to show in her expression, for that would only bring more questions she couldn't answer.

If Mr. Archer was so determinedly blind, she knew she couldn't simply tell him. Patience and friendship were a potent combination, were they not? With time, he might see the truth of his own accord. Surely that was better than springing it on him without warning.

For all that she'd just claimed to be a confident and mature lady, even Katherine Leigh—who brushed aside her mother's savage comments and her siblings' indifferent treatment with ease—did not have the fortitude to lay her heart on the line when whether or not Mr. Archer would welcome her as his Mystery Lady was entirely unknown.

Vulnerability always led to pain.

Chapter 11

Despite the weather's changeable nature, people met every season with shocked expressions about the "unusual" temperature, precipitation, winds, and what have you. Too many wet days in a row garnered lamentations about the previous summer's beauty, and when a chill settled in the air, it was considered unseasonably early.

They compared the present with the past, their infallible memories of childhood supplying a never-ending parade of pristine snowy winters and clear summer days. Those same people who recognized that their childish understanding of the world was very narrow and unreliable spent far too much of their time mourning the changes nature wrought, leaving their present far bleaker than in their idyllic youth.

And how those complaints were out in full. Yes, the evenings were already growing brisk with the sharp smell of winter tinging the autumn air, despite not having passed Michaelmas. And yes, it was earlier than the previous year, but neither was it out of the ordinary. Averages were merely a generalization—a spectrum of possibilities—and not hard and fast facts. It certainly wasn't cause for alarm, especially as the days were plenty warm enough to enjoy without layers of cloaks and furs.

There were far more pressing concerns than whether or not the Hyatts' picnic would take place—like the mountain of correspondence staring back at David from the top of his desk.

Foul language was not appropriate. Despite how much he longed to let loose a few choice words in the confines of his mind, the lessons of his youth were too ingrained. But that did not mean he couldn't be creative as he cursed his father's meddling. Shakespeare had a keen brain for such things, and David contented himself by letting loose a string of the Bard's most interesting ones.

That starveling, eel-skin, dried neat's-tongue, bull's-pizzle, stock-fish! The words made little sense, but the meaning was clear enough to the lad who had memorized them so long ago.

Where were the letters he was meant to review? David had laid a stack of them just to the side of the desk, but they were nowhere to be seen. Father's usual flair for disorganization meant the surface was covered in old newspapers and rubbish, and David shifted the mess about to give some order to the area.

Not that it ever remained so for very long. Although the fellow rarely used the study for anything more than smoking cigars and escaping the rest of the family, Father always made his mark on the space. It was his, after all. Even if David was the only one who used it as such.

Glancing at the pocket watch he had propped against his inkwell, David frowned. The morning had disappeared in a trice; the hour was fast approaching for the Hyatts' picnic, and there were still too many tasks to be completed.

Where were the blasted letters?

David allowed himself that one curse, though it did nothing to lighten his mood. Pulling open the drawers, he found a pile dumped inside, and with a sigh, he retrieved them, shifting through so that they were in the proper sequence. At least they hadn't been thrown into the fire.

Rolling his neck, he stretched his back and set this morning's ledgers aside to dive into the correspondence, though his thoughts remained fixed upon the ticking minutes. He needed to go to the picnic. It was the best opportunity to uncover the Mystery Lady's identity, but there was so much to do. Bills to review, advice from the family's man of business to analyze, investments to investigate, and there were still too many questions regarding the household accounts. Mother was not a spendthrift, so there was no reason the expenses ought to be so high.

To say nothing of the concerning reports about the cotton trade in America; having witnessed enough wild speculation on Britain's shores, David was all too aware of how quickly an industry could spin out of control and destroy everything in its path like a tornado. Especially when one considered how many other fools in town were shortsighted and wouldn't survive yet another financial hurdle like the country had seen in these past few years. When one mill fell, more than that single business was affected.

Thankfully, the Archers' income was spread into more than just the mill to avoid just such a possibility, but it was troubling nonetheless.

Rubbing at his forehead, David worked through the first letter, making notes here and there for him to address. All the while, he glanced at the pocket watch.

The door swung open, and Mother flew through the entrance. "Mrs. Littleworth said you were here, but I could not believe it."

Lifting his eyes from the missive, David frowned. "As I spend far too much of my time here, I cannot see how it is shocking."

"Not this afternoon. You cannot go to the Hyatt's party in such a state," she said, wringing her hands. Mother gave his crooked cravat and ink-stained hands a narrowed look. "You are hardly fit to be seen, and we must leave if we are to arrive in time. You know I cannot bear to be tardy."

Setting down his pen, David gave his mother a crooked smile. "I fear that as much as I wish to attend, I cannot escape my work. There is far too much to be done."

"But your sisters will be so disappointed," she said, her shoulders falling.

"I thought Father could escort you."

Mother straightened once more, her brows pulling together. "You didn't hear? He left this morning."

Leaning back into his seat, David didn't wish to ask the next question, for he was well aware of what the answer would likely be, but he couldn't help it. "Where did he go?"

A handkerchief hung in Mother's hands as her fingers worried the lace. "He mentioned a race or match or some other bit of nonsense near Liverpool."

Without bothering to mention when he was expected to return, no doubt. David's hand rested on the desktop, his fingers drumming at the polished wood. Before he could think how to phrase his next question, Mother answered it.

"We cannot attend unescorted, David. Even if we were to go there and return without an incident befalling the carriage or horses, there is the matter of your sisters." Mother's frown deepened as she paced before him. "Mr. Kellen was so overt in his attentions at the masquerade, and though Mr. Gould does seem good and proper, I would feel more at ease if you were there to help me watch over them. For all that I ought to be at ease after seeing Agatha so happily settled, I fear I am growing more anxious by the day that I shan't do the same for her sisters."

David's shoulders felt close to buckling as she talked, his gaze falling to the physical manifestation of his other cares. So many letters. So much to do. So much to consider. And that did not take into account any worries concerning Father's likely mischief.

But one of the great skills a tradesman must learn was prioritization. Success relied on one's ability to examine the tasks, weigh their relative importance and merits, and plan accordingly. It was a talent that was sadly lacking in the world as a whole, and having been thrust into this role as unofficial head of the Archer family, David had done much to hone that ability.

As much as the work before him needed attending, a few hours' delay would not cause as much fuss as Mother's fretting. He would simply have to finish it all tonight.

Forcing a smile, David rose to his feet. "Ready the carriage, Mother. I will freshen up and be ready in a trice."

...

Like gardening, berry picking was an activity that yielded wonderful results yet exacted a massive toll on those who attempted it. Though hours at the piano had strengthened Katherine's back greatly, the constant bending and stretching was wearing on her, and she straightened, stretching those muscles. With a nudge, she set her spectacles back into their proper place, though the perspiration dewing on her skin made it impossible for them to remain there.

With a quick swipe, she wiped her forehead with the back of her hand. Pausing, she lowered it and frowned at the marks marring the skin. For all that work gloves would protect against the stings and scrapes during her battles with the brambles, she was more likely to crush the delicate berries. So, Katherine was left to brave occasional pain to protect her bounty.

Puffing out her cheeks, she let out a heavy sigh whilst rubbing at her neck. Little dots of black amongst leaves taunted her, promising so many delectable treats if she continued. The shrubbery was thick with winding paths throughout, allowing people to pick to their heart's content, though few people availed themselves of the berry picking.

The brambles stretched out, curving out around a swath of green large enough for several blankets. People gathered together and reclined on pillows, laughing and chattering as they picked at the food the Hyatts provided. The party was a merry one, but Katherine's gaze drifted over it quickly, hardly noting a bit of it.

No matter how she tried to stop herself, it was as though

her eyes couldn't help themselves. Whenever she appeared in public, they were always scouring for some sign of *him*.

As she'd spent the past two years being Mr. Archer's friend, surely it should be an easy thing to continue—though Katherine didn't know why she thought to lie to herself. How could she speak to him whilst knowing what it felt like to be held in his arms? The tenderness of his kisses? How could she think to keep her mind on their conversation when even now, the memory of their intimate embrace replayed in her thoughts?

Her cheeks heated, and Katherine forced her gaze back to the blackberries. Plucking the branches bare, she dropped the fruits into her basket, the dark and shiny mountain growing with each move.

"Good afternoon, dear sister of mine," called Benjamin.

Katherine's teeth clenched at the endearment and she straightened, pulling her hand free of the bush as she dropped more berries into her cache. But when she turned to greet him, she found her brother studying her gown with a furrowed brow. It was an expression she knew all too well, though her heart panged at the sight of it on his face.

Her apron was worn and smudged, but what fool picked blackberries without some protection? Granted, as Katherine glanced about her, she realized the pristine gloves and gowns surrounding her were a clear answer. Of course, most didn't bother with the activity, and those that did never dug deep into the bushes, focusing solely on the surface fruits.

It was clear from their small mounds that berry picking was not the priority for them, but Katherine's heart lightened at the sight of the quickly filling baskets at her feet. Mrs. Tomkins could do wonders with such a bounty; the cook had quite the talent for blackberry tarts, and Katherine fairly salivated at the thought of the buttery crust slathered with the filling. That perfect balance of sweet and bitter.

Benjamin's smile faltered as he studied her, and Katherine's chin jutted up. But he said nothing as another gentleman drew up beside him. Though she knew nothing of the fellow, he seemed a strange companion for her brother.

The gentleman appeared to have a good decade over herself (giving him two over her brother), and it was clear from a glance that he didn't possess Benjamin's or Mr. Archer's easy manners. In a word, he looked stern. His heavy brow was pulled low, and if the gentleman ever smiled, Katherine would eat her bonnet, for he sported not a single wrinkle at the edge of his lips to indicate such a thing—despite boasting a few small ones between his eyebrows.

"Ah, here we are, Katherine," said Benjamin, clearing his throat as he turned to the newcomer. "I wanted to introduce Mr. Clarence Moody."

Katherine and the gentleman exchanged pleasantries whilst Benjamin watched the pair of them with a level of interest that had the back of her neck prickling. Though she sent her brother questioning looks, Benjamin gave no indication of what he was about, and Katherine couldn't think what to do but let it unfold and see what was to come.

But once the introductions were formed, the trio stood there, staring at one another.

Chapter 12

"Do you need a trug?" asked Katherine, nodding towards the brambles. "The berries are quite thick here, and you're sure to fill a basket quickly. Mrs. Hyatt has quite a few—"

Mr. Moody raised a hand to forestall her, his smile straining. "My thanks, but I do not wish to pick berries this afternoon."

"You do not wish to pick berries at a berry picking party?" asked Katherine with a furrowed brow.

"I am here to enjoy the picnic and the company," said Mr. Moody, waving out to the people lazing about. "Lawn games and berry picking aren't my idea of entertainment."

Katherine's head canted to the side. "I cannot say I enjoy berry picking, but if I wish to have blackberries in my cakes and tarts, I must roll up my sleeves, so to speak."

"That is quite industrious of you." Despite the complimentary words, there was an edge to his tone that made it feel like a genteel insult.

Slanting a look at her brother, Katherine stared at him, and Benjamin merely looked back at her with his brows raised high as though urging her to say something more, but she couldn't think what to say to such a man.

As one who was often mistaken for unpleasant, she knew too well how fallible first impressions were, but there was an air to Mr. Moody that made her uneasy. When one boasted a dry sense of humor, one could easily identify those who shared similar sensibilities, and nothing about this gentleman begged a further acquaintance.

"I understand he is quite a reader," said Benjamin, his gaze darting between the two. Having spent years with Mama and Rosanna forcing such interactions, it took little reasoning to guess that Benjamin was presenting a possible suitor to Katherine. What she couldn't reason out was why he was doing so now.

"Most people read," replied Katherine. "It is a question of what they read."

Mr. Moody's brows rose. "Too true, Miss Leigh. I am a lover of poetry."

"Ah, yes. I cannot claim to be well versed in verse," she replied, though neither man gave any sign of amusement at her play on words. Mr. Archer would've given her at least a chuckle at that, poor though it had been. "However, there are a few poets I enjoy."

Mr. Moody's gaze lightened a touch, though his expression didn't soften at all. "I believe Byron and Shelley are amongst the finest to ever grace this world. I doubt we shall ever see any others match their poetic genius. The beauty of their prose and their view of the world is so unique, don't you think?"

For all that his words denoted a passionate heart, Mr. Moody's expression altered little, his words coming in a monotone. But it was his statement (not his delivery) that had Katherine's brows rising.

"I will agree that their imagery and use of words is quite impressive, sir, but I cannot say I like their view of the world or wish to be better acquainted with it."

Mr. Moody straightened, his furrowed brows pinching closer together, putting the wrinkles at the corners of his eyes on full display. "Do not say you are like too many who cannot separate the actions of the artist from his work."

"Actions are a manifestation of one's thoughts and true desires, which colors one's perception of the world. That, in turn, impacts one's work. Poets write of the world as they see it and what they wish it to be, so I cannot separate my distaste for their personal lives from what they publish. They are intrinsically linked."

The gentleman puffed up, looking as though her opinion was an affront to his dignity, rather than that of two men he'd likely never met. Mr. Moody launched into a diatribe, listing all the reasons the two ought to be celebrated, but Katherine was not swayed in the slightest. Both men had abandoned families to seek after their own pleasures, and she could never admire such self-centered behavior, especially as that jaded view of love and honor pervaded their works, seeking to justify their poor behavior and encourage others to do the same.

Turning back to the bushes, she continued to strip the branches of their berries. "I appreciate you are passionate about them, sir, and you are welcome to your opinion, but I assure you I am not swayed by your arguments. As I said, I do not care for them or their values. I am not insisting you believe as I do, so why are you so insistent that I come to your way of thinking?"

"Every man must educate when faced with ignorance. Your view of the world is narrow and ought to be widened, but I suppose I am a fool for expecting more of someone so poorly read as yourself," he replied with a frown. "No doubt, you fill your head with silly romances and Gothic tales that have as much intellectual stimulation as a card party."

"Such praise! I didn't realize you hold romances and Gothic novels in such high esteem," said Katherine, raising her brows and widening her eyes with feigned innocence. "As card games require an understanding of mathematics and strategy, it takes intellect to master them. I find card parties quite engaging, for they allow one to pit one's skill against another and provide excellent mental stimulation whilst entertaining."

Mr. Moody scoffed, his nose lifting and eyes narrowing as though he expected her to cower, but Katherine merely watched him with an impassive expression before he finally turned on his heel and marched away.

"Why did you run him off?" asked Benjamin with a frown. "You could've made yourself more agreeable instead of mocking him."

Ice swept through her, and Katherine straightened, meeting her brother's gaze. "Ah, I see. I ought to bow and scrape before any man who dares to give me the honor of his presence."

Benjamin sighed, his shoulders dropping. "That is not what I meant, and you know it—"

"Oh, I understand far better than you do, *dear* brother," she said, fairly gagging on the endearment. How she hated the sound of it. Like iron scraping together, it shuddered down her spine. "My entire life, our *dear* mother has tried her best to change me because I am so very unpalatable as I am. No one can ever desire my company unless I alter everything about myself."

"You are putting words in my mouth," he said, his hands resting on his hips. "You were cold and argued with him."

"And what should I have done?" she asked with narrowed eyes. "Fluttered my lashes and feigned ignorance? Or simply lied and claimed a change of heart to impress him? I expressed an opinion politely, and he chose to be offended. Why are you standing here, lecturing me, when it was he who was rude?"

"But you needn't be argumentative and cold—"

"What is going on here?"

The pair turned to see Mr. Archer striding up, and the tightness in Katherine's chest eased at the sight.

"My sister is being unreasonable," said Benjamin, flicking a hand at her. "She seems to listen to you, so perhaps you can talk some sense into her."

"In my experience, your sister is generally reasonable and sensible if treated with respect," replied Mr. Archer.

Katherine's throat tightened, and it felt as though someone

had dropped a burning ember in her chest. Doubly so at the certainty in his tone, as though it were an indisputable fact that only a fool would misunderstand. Not even Benjamin's huff of disbelief could penetrate the glow in her heart as the warmth wove through her.

"I simply wished to introduce her to a fine gentleman, and when he tried to speak to her of poetry, she insulted his preferences and refused to engage in an intelligent debate," said Benjamin.

Staring at him, Katherine wondered how he got all that out of that conversation—but then, everyone seemed to believe her opinions and words far harder than she intended them to be, so was it any wonder that her brother was quick to adopt the rest of the family's opinion?

Despite her history in the Leigh family, Katherine had hoped that one of the siblings might come to know her. Or at least form their own opinion rather than allow themselves to be colored by their parents' poor opinion of her.

Prudence and Rosanna had been too busy with their friendship to be bothered with knowing their younger sisters, and the latter had only attempted it after Prudence had married, leaving Rosanna alone. Katherine wasn't worth her notice when someone better was around, and when she refused to embrace the role as the second-best friend or to be made over in her sister's likeness, Rosanna grew offended, just as Mr. Moody had.

Francis was Mama's lapdog, so there'd been little hope of the two of them ever building the sort of relationship the elder Miss Leighs had. But Benjamin had left for school at a young age and spent most of it away from their parents' poison; since his return, his treatment was never particularly warm, but their shared friendship with Mr. Archer often threw them together, and Katherine had hoped Benjamin might come to appreciate her.

Apparently not.

Had he only tolerated her presence because Mr. Archer

welcomed her friendship? That was a question she couldn't answer at present, nor did she have the emotional fortitude to attempt it.

"Mr. Moody is a bore, Benjamin. Why in the world would your sister find anything he says interesting?" said Mr. Archer. "I cannot imagine your sister being openly rude to him, though I can well believe he was in return. The fellow cannot stand to be disagreed with, and she is no wilting flower."

Turning his gaze to Katherine, he added, "Good on you, Miss Leigh. There is nothing wrong with having an opinion and expressing it politely. If he took offense, that is his own doing."

In this light, a hint of green shone in his eyes, making them more hazel than brown today. Katherine refused to turn away. From deep within her heart, she pleaded with him to realize the truth. Gathering all her strength of will, she sent out a silent prayer that he would see past that silly mask.

His Mystery Lady was standing before him!

"Well, I am glad you are here," said Benjamin, drawing Mr. Archer's attention away. "I had almost given up hope that you would be."

Katherine sighed, her shoulders dropping.

"It was a near thing, as I have been busy all day, but Mother and the girls wanted an escort, and Father is unavailable," said Mr. Archer.

Benjamin's brows rose, and with a significant tone, he asked, "He's *unavailable*?"

Mr. Archer merely smiled broadly and waved it away, and her brother nodded, his expression relaxing once more, though Katherine's own tightened, her brow furrowing. Staring at him, she waited for some other reaction, but Benjamin began rambling about the picnic and the various people there.

Did he truly believe Mr. Archer's deflection? Katherine studied her friend's expression—one she knew all too well. It was easy enough to believe the grin and jaunty tilt of his hat, the carefree manner in which he laughed. But one needed only to look at his eyes to see how false it was.

That the elder Mr. Archer had left town was no surprise, for the gentleman never remained long in Greater Edgerton; there was too much sport and amusement to be had in other places, after all. However, that did not mean that his son was unbothered.

Katherine had never met the elder Mr. Archer, and she had only a passing acquaintance with the rest of his family, but she'd heard her friend speak of them enough to know Mr. David Archer was far more of the patriarch than his father had ever been. The work to be done that awaited him at home, the duty to his mother, and the concern for his sisters' futures all rested heavily on Mr. Archer, and Katherine longed to pull him aside and ask him all about it, though this was neither the time nor place to do so.

Schooling her features so as to not give away her thoughts to Benjamin, Katherine watched her friend, though she couldn't help the slight pinch of her brows. Mr. Archer's gaze turned to meet hers, and though he attempted to give her a dismissive grin, she didn't believe it.

There was so little she could do for him at this moment, beyond offer sympathy. Channeling all of those feelings into her gaze, she hoped her eyes would say all that she couldn't. And Mr. Archer's own softened. That corner of his lips turned up in something far more genuine. He didn't pause in his conversation with Benjamin, but Katherine felt his understanding and acceptance. His gratitude.

"There you are, Mr. Archer!"

Mama's voice shattered the spell, and Katherine fought not to flinch as the lady swept forward, dragging a poor young lady along.

Chapter 13

The girl was from the younger set, and her cheeks flushed red as she stared at the ground. Katherine longed to slap Mama's hand away from the girl and hurry the poor dear away. Who knew what precipitated this moment, but it was clear it had not been a pleasant interlude for the young lady.

"I had wanted to introduce you to Miss Hooper," said Mama, nudging the girl forward, leaving Katherine absolutely flummoxed.

The meaning was clear, for Mama had all but trussed the poor girl up as an offering to Mr. Archer, and though Katherine had not been privy to that portion of the conversation, it was obvious from the eager gleam in Mama's gaze that this Miss Hooper had been deemed one of the possible candidates for his Mystery Lady.

Dear heavens. Katherine's heart ached, though it had naught to do with Mr. Archer or his search. As much as she wished to dislike Miss Hooper on principle, the way the young lady shrank in on herself called to Katherine's sympathies. She knew all too well what it felt like to be the object of Mama's matrimonial machinations.

"It is a pleasure to meet you, Miss Hooper," said Mr.

Archer.

Mama glanced between the pair, but no one spoke beyond that. The young lady looked incapable of it, whilst the others simply shifted in place.

"It is such a fine afternoon," said Katherine. "Miss Hooper, would you care to pick blackberries with me?"

With a scoff, Mama swiped a dismissive hand. "Nobody wishes to pick blackberries with you! Leave the girl be."

Years of such moments had given Katherine a tolerance for public embarrassment, but even her nerves of steel couldn't keep her cheeks from heating. However, she kept her head erect and allowed no other sign of discomfort.

"I would love to pick blackberries," said Mr. Archer. "Won't you join us, Miss Hooper?"

Katherine's blush grew until she was certain it showed, but for an entirely different reason. Her ribs squeezed her heart, and she turned her gaze to the brambles; with her bonnet, they couldn't see any of her expression, which helped some, but the swing from pain to pleasure was too extreme for her to manage with an audience.

"Mrs. Hyatt has more baskets," he said. "Miss Hooper and I shall fetch some."

"None for me," said Benjamin, waving away Mr. Archer's offer. Though Katherine couldn't see his expression, his tone was rife with a grin when he said, "I have other business to attend to."

"It'd better not be that Rothschild girl," said Mama.

Miss Hooper attempted not to stare at the group, but the stiffness in her posture and the pinch of her lips made it clear she was all too aware of the conversation. Katherine slanted Mr. Archer a look, hoping the gentleman would take the hint, but rather than making his escape with the girl, he remained at Katherine's side.

Did Mama have no shame? Katherine had often wondered what it would be like to flit about the world without ever caring what others thought, but as it often produced people as selfish and self-absorbed as Gertrude Leigh, Katherine was grateful for the humiliation burning through her. It was an unpleasant sentiment, but it was far better than the opposite.

With a haughty little sniff, Mama narrowed her gaze at her son. "You know better than to waste your time on that girl. Your father and I have been quite clear about the quality of lady you ought to court."

Benjamin adopted that slanted grin that had often won his arguments for him. "You know I am far too young to be thinking of marriage. One ought to explore the world first before settling down."

"That is true. You are such a good boy and deserve to have your fun." Mama reached over and patted his cheek. Then she paused and added in a hard tone, "As long as you understand your duty when the time comes—"

"It is difficult to believe the Garrisons' concert is in a sennight," blurted Katherine. "Despite being so focused on my preparations, the evening has snuck up on me."

Mama's hand dropped, and she turned a scowl towards her daughter. Drawing her strength close, Katherine refused to flinch.

"Oh, really! Must you remind us? It is bad enough that you insist on embarrassing yourself at every turn. Must you do it in public? I swear, Katherine, our standing lowers a little every time you venture out into public."

"Steady on," said Mr. Archer, glancing between mother and daughter, but Katherine's attention was on her brother. Benjamin stood there, staring at the exchange; she wanted to glare and shout at him not to waste the opportunity to escape, but doing so would only draw Mama's attention.

"As it is my role in this family, I ought to do it well," said Katherine in a dry tone, ignoring Miss Hooper's gaze darting between them.

"What have I ever done to deserve such disrespect?" said Mama, clutching a hand to her chest.

The better question was what she had done to deserve any

respect, but Katherine knew prodding her in that manner was a step too far. The group stood there in silence as mother and daughter stared at each other.

And still, her brother remained where he was.

Katherine darted a glance at him, narrowing her eyes and nodding away when he met her gaze. But there was little point, as Mama's attention followed the exchange, turning away from her greatest disappointment to her son.

"Surely you won't be as cruel as your sister and disobey us at every turn," said Mama.

Katherine turned to the brambles and closed her eyes. She'd done what she could to distract Mama, and Benjamin had wasted the opportunity. A hand at her elbow testified that someone still paid her mind, though she didn't look to see who it was. Benjamin and Mama bickered back and forth before their voices grew distant as he finally tried to escape and she followed after.

"So, it looks as though we need baskets for two," said Mr. Archer with a strained tone while Miss Hooper said nothing. "We shall return once we've fetched them, Miss Leigh."

Katherine kept her face turned to the brambles and nodded, reaching for her own trugs.

Footsteps moved behind her, and she hazarded a glance over her shoulder to find the pair walking off together. Her heart sank to her toes, leaving an aching void behind. If anyone bothered to look at her, Katherine knew they would see the pain etched in her gaze and the tightness of her lips. But no one ever did—except Mr. Archer and his attention was currently fixed on the young lady at his side.

Glancing about the area, Katherine moved deeper into the brambles, weaving between the massive bushes until she was well and truly hidden from view. It was one thing to know Mr. Archer was pursuing better candidates for his Mystery Lady, but it was another thing altogether to witness his attempts, and Katherine's heart couldn't bear another beating today.

...

"Oh, dear!" said Miss Lyons as the shuttlecock fell to the ground once more. "I am such a dunce."

David forced himself to smile, despite wishing to agree with her (which was not a very kind thought at all). Shaking the stiffness in his shoulders, he waited while the young lady fetched it and hit it back at him. The shuttlecock flew at him with such accuracy that her innate skill was quite clear, no matter how she pretended otherwise.

They managed a few volleys before she swung in such a wide arc that she was more likely to strike herself than the shuttlecock, and when it fell to the ground once more, she stamped her foot.

"I am such a goose, Mr. Archer," she said with a pout. "I fear you have chosen a poor partner."

That was certainly true (though not in terms of this game); however, David wasn't about to say it aloud.

Spinning the battledore in her hand, Miss Lyons cocked her hip and tipped a smile up at him. "I do think I am holding this all wrong. Can you show me your technique?"

David drew in a deep breath and held onto his affable expression. As irritating as her feigned ineptitude was, he couldn't hold it against the poor girl. Plenty of ladies adopted a helpless facade to appeal to a gentleman's pride, and as plenty of beaus prized that sort of behavior, David couldn't blame women for attempting it—even if he found it irritating.

Surely, anyone who required such delicate handling was hardly a wife worth having. Miss Leigh would hardly stoop to such methods, as her handling of Mr. Moody had made quite clear. David had enough ladies in his life who truly required his assistance that he couldn't imagine choosing to marry another.

Lifting the racket, he showed his hold on the handle, and Miss Lyons fawned over the display as though he were Hercules of old, having just completed one of the infamous labors of legend.

"But I fear I cannot seem to mimic it," she said with another coy smile. "Perhaps you can position my hand for me?"

Drawing closer, he stood before her, but the young lady gave a little huff.

"I cannot see it properly," she said, shifting so that she was standing with her back pressed to his chest. Glancing over her shoulder up at him, she asked, "Now, how do I do it?"

Miss Lyons was a pretty girl, and having her stand so close was not an unpleasant experience. But as she stepped into him, David couldn't help but wish there was some space between them. The bluntness of her attentions wasn't disagreeable—for determination was to be applauded—but something about it had his insides squirming.

"There you go," he said, stepping away and hurrying to take his place.

Miss Lyons swung the racket, her gaze fixed on him with a smile that attempted to blend innocence with invitation, though it failed with the former. With a quick hit, he sent the shuttle-cock towards her, and she struck it with ease, sending it back to him.

"A hit, a very palpable hit!" called Miss Lyons.

Was the girl flirting using Shakespeare? And choosing a line from the tragic end of *Hamlet*, of all things? She beamed as though she'd won the game, but David suspected it was because Miss Lyons believed herself to be winning something other than their match. Unfortunately, her display only proved she was not entirely as senseless as she claimed to be.

Miss Lyons was far more intriguing than Miss Hooper, but only in that the latter had refused to speak more than two words the entire half-hour they'd spent together. His Mystery Lady was no shrinking violet, so it was clear that Miss Hooper did not fit the bill. Miss Lyons, on the other hand, displayed all the confidence but none of the wittiness or intelligence.

They continued for several more minutes, but thankfully, another pair were waiting nearby for their turn at the game, and David was able to use it as an excuse to finish.

"Isn't the weather magnificent?" asked Miss Lyons as she took his arm. "Though it is unseasonably chilly for September, don't you think?"

David smiled to himself at that second question, though he thoroughly agreed with the first.

The sky was the bright blue one saw only on the sunniest of days, and not a single cloud marred its perfection. The day looked as though it ought to be stifling, but the slight nip of autumn kept them from being overheated whilst the sun above kept them warm enough to enjoy the outing. And the grass at their feet gleamed with the last vestiges of summer, giving one final push before giving way to the coming winter.

"It is quite fine," he said before grasping at anything more interesting. "Do you read, Miss Lyons?"

"Oh, dear me, no," she said with a shake of her head, which set her blonde ringlets bouncing. "I prefer dancing and embroidery. Music, as well. I haven't any interest in spending my days lost in books like some bluestocking, though I am certain you read extensively. You are so intelligent, Mr. Archer."

Brows raised, he agreed with her first assumption concerning his interest in books but didn't know why she had said the second. Not that he considered himself a dunce, but she didn't know him enough to make such a claim. Of course, the Mystery Lady had spoken as though they'd known each other for some time—but her comments had been truly insightful and not empty flattery.

Before he could say anything on the subject, David caught sight of Flora standing on the far side of the gathering with Mr. Kellen leaning in. She stepped away, but the fellow closed the distance once more, forcing her backward again. With slow steps, Mr. Kellen herded her away from the rest of the party, and David's feet moved before he made a conscious decision to do so, dragging Miss Lyons along as they crossed the lawn.

Chapter 14

"**G**ood afternoon, Flora," said David as they stopped before the pair, though the warmth in his voice faded as he gave the gentleman a nod and a curt, "Mr. Kellen."

His sister gave him a tremulous smile, though she did an admirable job of hiding her relief at seeing him as he offered up introductions between Mr. Kellen and Miss Lyons.

"Mr. Archer," said Mr. Kellen. "I hear my father wishes to broker an alliance with your family's mill. In fact, I believe he was planning on discussing it with your father this afternoon. Some business about cotton investments in America."

"Is that so?" David's muscles clenched, and for once, he was grateful Father was occupied with races. Perhaps he'd stay away long enough to forget about whatever business it was, which was unlikely to benefit anyone but the Kellens.

"I was speaking to your sister about it," said Mr. Kellen, his gaze turning to Flora.

"As I said, Mr. Kellen, Father never speaks to me about business, so I have nothing to say on the matter," she replied, whilst stepping closer to her brother. In the same instance, Miss Lyons dragged David nearer and positioned herself in front of the other gentleman.

"Your reputation precedes you, Mr. Kellen." Her words might've been censorious (given the fellow's reputation), but the tone with which she spoke was anything but. Miss Lyons grinned at the gentleman, and though her hold on David's arm was quite firm, he felt her attention shift.

"Ought I to be afraid?" Mr. Kellen asked with a wicked grin.

If the blackguard didn't leave Flora be, David would make certain he was very afraid. However, Miss Lyons tittered. Glancing at the lady on his arm, he studied the expression she gave Mr. Kellen, which matched her flirtatious conduct during their game of battledore and shuttlecock.

Perhaps it was simply to make him jealous, but David's heart lightened as that uncomfortable itch in the back of his mind solidified into an epiphany. Miss Lyon's behavior was unsettling because it was indiscriminate. Each coy compliment and flirtatious comment hadn't been intended for David specifically. Any gentleman would do.

David didn't begrudge a bit of flirtation, for it was quite a diverting pastime, and he wasn't ignorant of the expectation placed on ladies to secure good husbands. However, there was an edge to Miss Lyons that left him feeling like a fox being run to ground. Hunters weren't particular about which fox they chased; they only wished for the sport or to catch themselves a prize. Even if Miss Lyons were his Mystery Lady, that evening meant little to her.

Clarity on the subject was welcome, for an answer—even a disheartening one—was better than having none. Neither Miss Hooper nor Miss Lyons was his Mystery Lady.

"I do believe Mother is looking for us," said David, gently pulling his arm from Miss Lyons, who continued to flirt with Mr. Kellen as though her previous partner hadn't even spoken, and his heart constricted for the young lady who was so undiscerning in her hunt for a husband.

Flora quickly took hold of him, and David led her away.

"Thank you for rescuing me," she whispered. "I do not

know why he is determined to annoy me, but I swear I gave him no encouragement. I still do not know how he managed to separate me from the others. One moment, I was surrounded by my friends, and the next, Mr. Kellen cornered me."

"Do not fret, Flora. Men like him amuse themselves by plaguing young ladies who have too much sense to play their games. If we make too much of it, he might redouble his efforts, but if we simply ignore him, he will grow bored."

David parroted the words Miss Leigh had given him, and again, they offered some solace; action was preferable, but the lady's advice was too wise to ignore. There was no need to tell Flora that elder brothers had ways of discouraging less savory gentlemen from paying court on their beloved sisters. Thankfully, David didn't think it would come to that.

"Are you certain?" she asked, and David gave her arm a squeeze.

"Unfortunately, that is the way of gentlemen with too much time and money on their hands."

Flora nodded and fell silent, allowing David's thoughts to wander as he led her over to where some of her friends stood. And in that moment of quiet, a new question popped into his mind, shattering his clarity like a hammer to a window.

What if Miss Lyons was his Mystery Lady, and the masquerade had simply been a game to her? David's limbs grew heavy as he considered that, and though certainty burned in his heart that Miss Lyon's conversation was nothing at all like the Mystery Lady's, he couldn't help but wonder if he was holding onto a false hope.

If that evening had meant anything to her, why hadn't the Mystery Lady made herself known? True, she couldn't call on a bachelor without causing a stir, but paying a visit to his mother and sisters was possible. But then, he hadn't been home when Mother had entertained visitors this past sennight. And there was no guarantee that their social circles overlapped enough for her to do so.

Despite the lawn stretching out before him, David was able

to get to the other side and deposit Flora amongst her friends once more before wandering off in search of something else to do. And that was when he spied Mother, watching him with furrowed brows and twisting hands.

No doubt she'd witnessed Mr. Kellen and Flora's interlude. Not that there was anything to be done about it at present, but telling her so wouldn't make the slightest difference, which was why David ended up ducking behind another group and slipping out of sight, all whilst praying for forgiveness. Honoring his mother may be a commandment, but managing her fretting required more stamina than he had at present.

For all that today's efforts hadn't been physically taxing, David felt as though he was plodding through mud as he edged around another group. Drawing in a deep breath, he tried to soothe his swirling thoughts, but they refused to calm. It was bad enough that he had a mountain of work awaiting him at home, and now his mind was awash with Flora and Mother.

And where was Miss Leigh? The lady had disappeared without a trace whilst he and Miss Hooper had fetched their baskets, and she was still missing.

With vague nods and smiles at those he passed, David trudged along. He couldn't leave. Not when his mother and sisters were still partaking in the merriment. No matter how much he needed to. David shifted his jacket, straightening it as he fought to keep his grin in place.

What he needed was a distraction—something that had nothing to do with ladies. And when he searched the gathering, he spied the perfect option. Benjamin raised a hand in greeting and called David over. Once within reaching range, his friend took him by the shoulders and drew him into the conversation.

"You are just the man I wanted to see," said Benjamin, giving David a friendly shake. "I was just telling Mr. Pine about our excellent Katherine."

David's brows rose. "You were?"

"Of course," he replied with a puzzled smirk, as though speaking of his sister in such laudable terms was an everyday occurrence, despite the fact that David had never heard a single one of her family ever do so. Her brother was rarely openly critical, but that was a far cry from the beaming fraternal pride he was showing at present.

Releasing his friend, Benjamin clapped him on the shoulder. "I do not know why gentlemen overlook her, for she has the makings of a good wife."

David's brows rose, though it was not in response to the statement as much as the man giving it and to whom he was speaking. Mr. Pine might only be a decade older than Miss Leigh, but his face was lined and cragged, making him look like her grandfather. Not that appearance was the only measure of a person, but David thought it said much of the fellow that he'd never seen Mr. Pine smile.

"She's quiet and keeps to herself most of the time," said Benjamin. "As long as you keep a piano on hand for her, she can entertain herself all day long."

With a scoff, David couldn't help the genuine smirk that emerged. "Your sister isn't a toy to trot out whenever you are bored and ignore the rest of the time."

"Of course not," said Benjamin with a wave of his hand. "I am merely saying that she isn't one of those ladies who inserts herself into every facet of a man's life. She's content to keep her own company, which is quite an asset to some men."

With a nudge, Benjamin nodded for David to say something, but what could he say to that?

"She's far too serious for my tastes," said Mr. Pine, and it took all of David's willpower not to snort at that declaration.

"Her wit is subtle, but I assure you, it is there," David said, though his remark had less to do with convincing Mr. Pine as it had to do with his own honor, which demanded that he defend Miss Leigh in the face of such bald-faced misunderstanding. "She is one of the most amusing people I know."

Mr. Pine wrinkled his nose and shook his head, turning away from the pair, and David was happy to see the back of him. With a chuckle, he turned to Benjamin, though his friend watched the departure with drooped shoulders.

"I had thought he might be a good match. Clearly, she is far too shy to find someone on her own and requires assistance," he mumbled.

David couldn't help himself. He laughed. Not some little chuckle but a true, full-bellied laugh—enough so that it drew others' attention. He couldn't decide which of his friend's statements was more ridiculous.

"That is brilliant," said David, clapping his friend on the shoulder, but when Benjamin merely stared at him in return, the laughter died, and David straightened. "You aren't teasing, are you?"

Benjamin gaped. "Why are you so shocked? Mr. Pine is a fine gentleman—"

"I do not know why you are attempting a bit of matchmaking, but I would leave it to your mother. She may be no better at it, but at least only one ridiculous family member would plague your sister instead of two. Three, if I count Mrs. Tate, who seems just as determined to fob her off on any man who will take her."

David paused and crossed his arms. "But why are you tossing gentlemen at her?"

Scratching at the back of his neck, Benjamin shifted in place. "I want to see her happily situated. Besides, it is only a matter of time before Katherine gives in to Mother's prodding, and that lady is indiscriminate in her choices for Katherine's husband. At least I can ensure that she doesn't end up with someone who would treat her poorly—like Mr. Mowbry."

David arched a brow. "She has withstood your mother for over a decade. Do you really think your sister will give in now?"

Benjamin tugged at his jacket cuffs and squirmed. "You never know. I just want to see her properly settled, but she is determined to remain a spinster."

"Is it any wonder when you present her with gentlemen like Mr. Pine or Mr. Moody? Surely spinsterhood is better than a cold marriage," replied David, though the words brought to mind his conversation with Miss Leigh.

Ever since she had mentioned it, he couldn't leave the thought be. What was the "escape" she had planned? The choices for unmarried women were few and far between, so there were few possibilities. Yet still, David couldn't imagine what it was. Nor could he help the twist his stomach gave at the thought of Miss Leigh venturing out into the world alone. She was a capable and intelligent lady, but that alone did not guarantee safety or security.

Benjamin huffed. "Rather than pointing out the flaws in my plan, perhaps you could make a suggestion of someone else who would suit her?"

"I would rather point out that your sister is unlikely to accept anyone chosen for her," replied David. "She is one of the most stalwart people I know and will not be swayed by others' opinions. She knows her own mind."

Leaning back, Benjamin studied him for a long moment. "You really do enjoy her company, don't you?"

With a furrowed brow, David huffed. "Is that so surprising? We are often together."

"No." Benjamin paused and changed course. "I mean, yes, you do, but I suppose I had always thought you were simply doing so out of pity, as she has no friends."

Ignoring that ridiculous statement (for she had at least him and Mrs. Kitts), David shook his head. "Why is your family so determined to think ill of her? Your sister does have a sharp wit, but she is far kinder than you give her credit for."

"Forgive me for disagreeing, but I have only ever seen her curt and dismissive of others. But if you enjoy her company, then I am glad for it."

"I do," said David. "I count her one of my closest friends, and I will not stand by as you try to marry her off to men like Mr. Pine and Mr. Moody."

Benjamin's brow furrowed, and his friend stood there, studying him in silence.

"What is it?" asked David.

With a shrug, Benjamin turned his gaze out to the crowd. "If you do not wish to help me 'toss' gentlemen at my sister, would you prefer to talk about the riots in the South?"

Pinching his nose, David groaned. "Are those my only options? I have told you my opinion on the matter. They will likely spread here, but as long as you prepare for that inevitability, there is no reason Whitley Court cannot weather it."

But no amount of assurances appeased Benjamin, and David succumbed to another long discussion on the matter. Thankfully, he'd given the speech many times over the past few weeks, and he could do so with little thought.

Chapter 15

Despite the main draw of the afternoon being berry picking, the majority of the party had chosen to avail themselves of the picnic spread on the grassy knoll. Blackberry bushes stretched out along the sides of the clearing, but few even pretended to pick. Katherine had four trugs settled beside her on the blanket, and despite wishing for more, her back demanded she stop.

"Oh, how delightful," said Miss Kipling, stopping by the dark treasures and reaching for a berry.

"They are not for eating," said Katherine, pulling the basket out of reach.

Miss Kipling straightened with a laugh. "I just wanted one."

"There are plenty over there," replied Katherine, nodding towards the bushes.

"It is only a single berry, Miss Leigh." The young lady stiffened, her brow furrowing as she straightened her skirts. "You needn't be so testy about it."

"As everyone who wishes to steal a bit of my hard-earned berries claims it is 'only one,' you will forgive me if I am not feeling particularly generous. Especially as you are quite capable of fetching some yourself. This is a berry picking party. If you wish for berries, pick some."

Miss Kipling huffed and turned, marching away.

Katherine let out a hissing sigh through her teeth and took several deep breaths before she was able to relax once more. Why was she always made to be the villain? Perhaps her answer had been a tad curt, but as she had spent the better part of a half hour defending her bounty, was it any wonder that her patience was worn a tad thin?

Not a single thief bothered engaging her in conversation before or after (except to scold her), yet it was she who was heartless and greedy because she wouldn't part with her hard won treasures. They acted as though they were the dearest of friends when attempting to nip a berry, but the minute they were thwarted, all pretenses dropped.

And of course, the fault was all Katherine's.

Even now, she spied Miss Kipling sauntering off towards a group of gabbing girls, all tittering like overeager songbirds (if such delightful creatures sounded like metal scraping together). It took no leap of logic to know precisely what she was saying when the gaggle glanced at Katherine with narrowed eyes before they began an agitated critique of all that was wrong in the world. Namely, Katherine Leigh.

Shoulders dropping, she sighed. There was no point in leaving. It was too far to walk, and Mama would not be prevailed upon to call the carriage until she was ready to depart, but Katherine longed to escape. Watching Mr. Archer pursue Miss Hooper and Miss Lyons was difficult enough without the added burden of such blatant displays of how disliked she was.

It was no mystery that Katherine was detested. With few exceptions (namely Pamela and Mr. Archer), people tolerated her at best and openly despised her at worst. As it was her natural state of being, it no longer surprised or wounded Katherine. She didn't understand it any more than she understood why some were so universally adored, and fretting about it had only brought her more misery.

But from time to time, Katherine wished for more.

Or at least to leave this party. That would be a start. Oh, how she longed for a bit of quiet. To hide away in her bedchamber. Or steal a few minutes with her music.

For all that everyone else adored parties and balls, Katherine couldn't help but feel exhausted by them. It was enjoyable when Pamela or Mr. Archer was on hand, but when left to her own devices, she had only her thoughts to entertain herself. In most circumstances, Katherine was quite content to do so, for she simply turned her mind to books, music, or puzzling out the rest of her day; it was impossible to be bored when one could simply slip off into her musings.

But not when Mr. Archer occupied the whole of her thoughts.

Ridiculous. Katherine Leigh was no young miss in the throes of infatuation. She ought to have more control, but it was impossible to scrub her mind of Mr. Archer when the gentleman in question appeared before her.

"Please hide me," he muttered as he tossed his hat to the ground and flopped onto the blanket beside her.

"Are you being hunted?"

"You have no idea." Mr. Archer groaned and scrubbed at his face. "I cannot bear to talk to anyone else today."

A voice called out for him, and Katherine spied a gentleman scouring the area. Her gaze dropped to Mr. Archer, and he groaned.

"I shan't be responsible for my actions if I am forced to have one more conversation about the riots," he mumbled.

But just before the gentleman drew up, Katherine tossed a shawl over Mr. Archer's face, covering him as best she could. The gentleman glanced at her but did what everyone did—identify and ignore. With no more than a passing glance, he walked right by without noticing the male legs stretched out beside her.

Peeling back the edge of the shawl, Katherine looked down at Mr. Archer. "It is safe. For now."

The gentleman tucked the covering under his head as he stretched out with a sigh. "Your shawl is magical."

Katherine's stomach flipped as she recognized the possibility set before her. Not allowing herself to rethink her actions, she adopted as much of a significant tone as she dared to employ and said, "Yes, I've found shawls are very good at hiding people. So well that it can be impossible to recognize even your closest friends."

But Mr. Archer merely hummed in agreement and settled in as though he was about to nap.

With a sigh, Katherine let the moment pass. "Has it been a difficult day?"

Mr. Archer peered out at her with one eye. "Your brother pesters me about the riots in the South, which he is certain are going to infect our county and destroy everything we hold dear. My father disappeared to lose appalling amounts on racing. My mother believes our family is going to be ruined at any moment. My sisters give me palpitations every time we go out into public. Scads of work await me at home, but I am stuck here at this wretched party. It has been a perfectly delightful day."

Katherine smiled and chuckled more from sympathy than amusement. "That is quite dire, indeed. What has happened?"

"Naught but a string of failures," he mumbled with a heavy sigh. And before she could ask for clarification, Mr. Archer began to speak of his hunt for the Mystery Lady.

For all that the gentleman was quite intelligent, Katherine couldn't understand why he was so blind. He expounded more about the lady he'd met, and the closeness he'd felt, yet never once did he seem to recognize just how much this conversation aligned with the ones he'd shared with his Mystery Lady.

Could he not see how much he talked with her? Shared with her? Trusted her?

The pressure in her chest built as she longed to shout the truth at him. A dozen scenarios played out in her head, imagining what such a conversation would look like, but despite all the hope buried deep in her heart, she couldn't picture a single one that ended happily.

Mr. David Archer was her friend, which was miracle

enough. Would she press her luck by attempting more?

Katherine easily imagined what would come to pass if she did. Mr. Archer would be kind. Polite. He'd hide his revulsion behind a mask of gentility. Then he would take his leave and never speak to her again. And once more, Katherine Leigh would be left to her own devices. Alone.

Worse than that, the ties that bound them could not be severed altogether. As he was her brother's close friend, Katherine would be forced to see Mr. Archer regularly. The gentleman would never be so cruel as to give her the cut direct, but her rejected feelings would be a wedge between them, impossible to forget or ignore.

Mr. Archer had fallen for the Mystery Lady, after all. Not Katherine. Would he have been so free with his affection had he known who was beneath the mask? The face beneath it didn't possess a fraction of Miss Lyon's beauty or Miss Hooper's youth.

Surely only a foolish person repeated the same action again and again, expecting new results, and Katherine was no fool. Or she tried not to be. The past was a stern teacher, and Katherine knew better than to expect even the great Mr. Archer to be wholly different from everyone else.

Vulnerable hearts were trampled, and forcing the issue only increased the chances of that happening.

So, Katherine nodded and listened. She was his friend, and this was what a friend did. And she loved him enough to simply be his friend if that was all he desired. Better that than to lose him altogether.

"I cannot help but worry that I won't find her again," he said with a frown. "I have already cut my list in half. What if she isn't among the remaining? What will I do then?"

"I have no doubt you will sort it out." It was easy to speak the words, for Katherine felt they were entirely true. Mr. Archer always had a knack for seeing her; surely he would eventually discover his mistake. And perhaps she could nudge him along.

Drawing in a deep breath, Katherine swallowed and forced

her voice to remain calm as she said, "Perhaps you underestimate just how much the costume hid your Mystery Lady. Simple though it may have been, clearly her mask obscured her face and voice, altering her in ways you do not recognize without the costume. She could be sitting right beside you, and you might not realize it."

Mr. Archer opened his eyes once more and turned to look at Katherine, and she met his gaze without flinching. Pouring her hopes into her eyes, her heart begged him to shake off this ignorance. To recognize. How could he not? Every time he described his Mystery Lady, he described her. Not merely because they were one and the same, but independent of that phantom, Katherine met all the desires he had expressed for his lady love.

"There you are," called Benjamin.

Katherine fought back a scowl as she cursed her wretched brother.

Chapter 16

When Benjamin Leigh had returned home from school, it hadn't taken long for David to build a friendship with the fellow. His company was easy and effortless, and Benjamin had a talent for making merry, so it was little surprise that he was a favorite amongst Greater Edgerton society.

Yet at that moment, David despised him.

For the first time today, he was simply enjoying himself, and Benjamin had to interrupt. And with the other gentlemen on his heels, David knew the subject they wished to discuss.

"I was trying to explain what you were saying about that business in the South, but I fear I am doing a poor job of it," said Benjamin with a smile, nodding at David to join a group of gentlemen, but with the sun shining down on him and Miss Leigh's conversation to entertain him, he was quite content to remain precisely where he was.

"There is little to say on the subject," said David, trying valiantly to keep the exhaustion from his voice. "Yes, the riots will likely spread farther and touch even our corner of the country, but it is unlikely to be any more disruptive than years with poor crops or heavy taxes."

"Having the worker rise up and destroy our land and machinery is hardly a small matter," refuted Mr. Pitt with a frown. "They are wrecking any improvements the gentry attempt to make to their lands."

David rubbed at his face and forced himself upright. "That is what happens any time new improvements alter the way things are done. The new threshing machines are replacing the laborers, and they are understandably unhappy. We saw the same with the Luddites and the mills, but progress cannot be stopped. With innovation there is always a period of unrest when everything and everyone are at odds, but the world will right itself again and move forward—altered, to be sure, but it will move forward."

"But I have just arrived from Kent, and the gentry are in fear for their lives," said Mr. Standish. "I have been trying to convince my father that we should remove to the Continent for a time, but he refuses to leave our home unprotected."

Why did people seem determined to fear the very worst from every upset? It was as though each generation expected theirs would be the last to walk the planet, and each calamity heralded the end. Yet their unfounded fears were forgotten the moment the storm passed, and they remained blind to their folly and began wringing their hands once more when the gales inevitably returned.

"As there have been no deaths or injuries reported, I have no idea why anyone believes themselves in danger," murmured David.

"How can you be so calm? The newspapers are full of reports concerning the destruction the rioters are wreaking," pressed Mr. Standish with a scowl.

David huffed out a halting chuckle. "Do not forget that newspapers are a business like any other. For all that they tout to be the purveyors of truth and knowledge, fear-mongering sells papers more than rational discourse. But as to your question, I assure you I have seen similar issues arise with the mill workers. Whether it be uprisings, shifts in our economy, bad harvests, or any number of unforeseeable downturns, something bad is bound to happen sooner or later. Any business can weather such storms with the proper preparation—set aside savings and diversify your investments."

Benjamin's gaze darted between the gentlemen, his brow furrowing as all the doomsayers continued to spout their poison, and David held back a sigh. Seven years' difference was hardly noticeable in more advanced ages, but in their twenties, it was quite the span of time. More often than naught, David felt more like an elder brother than a friend to the young man.

Every other year some new fear swept through the country, determined to keep people convinced that death and penury were nipping at their heels. And at moments like these, David couldn't help but think that perhaps he ought to be more concerned, as he was the only one in creation who didn't seem bothered. Not that he didn't foster concerns about what was to come, but this crippling belief that destruction was about to rain down was ridiculous and nonsensical.

Hardships would come, to be certain. One could not live without experiencing them regularly. David's chest tightened at the thought of all those laborers displaced by the new threshing machines. Transition was always difficult, and people feared change. But even bad shifts in the world brought with them new possibilities in time.

The workers who had rioted against the mechanization at the mills now had other work, laboring in the factories that produced the parts for said machines. And though it was not a blessing to all, David knew the history of his family's mill well enough to know that he had more journeymen on staff to maintain all those machines than they'd required in the past. Men who were mere weavers in the past now had new skills and higher pay.

No matter how often newspapers and politicians predicted ruination, the country still stood and life continued on as it had before. Altered, certainly, but not destroyed. The world would not end tomorrow, the next day, or anytime soon.

"Oh, I do believe you are underestimating the trouble," said Miss Leigh, trotting out her driest of tones, and a smile tickled the corners of David's lips. "Surely they will be beating down our doors and dragging us from their beds, ushering in a revolution unlike anything we've ever seen before. The streets will run red with the blood of our threshing machines."

David forced himself not to laugh and give her jest away, though it was doubly difficult when the other gentlemen stared at her in varying states of confusion and horror. Her own brother blinked at her, shifting from foot to foot with a furrowed brow. David stared at him until Benjamin finally met his gaze, and with raised brows, he tried to send the fool a silent message. Could he not understand her humor? Certainly, it was odd, but that made it all the more amusing, for so few seemed to grasp it. But Benjamin simply frowned.

Shaking his head, David left the fellow to his confused thoughts and turned back to the lady at his side. The conversation continued on as it had, but Miss Leigh glanced at him, catching his eye. The faintest of smiles tipped up the corners of her lips as the pair shared a silent laugh.

...

Autumn was a trying time. Though Katherine enjoyed the changing foliage and shift from summer to winter, Michaelmas stuffed their social calendar to the brim. With that holiday starting to fall out of fashion, she'd hoped it would mean quieter Septembers and Octobers, in which she could simply enjoy blackberry tarts and the crisp autumn air.

Unfortunately, the popularity had simply shifted, bringing Christmas into more prominence, and with it, a slew of new parties and gatherings. Thankfully, that meant the time between events was greater. However, it also meant that the torture was strung out for months at a time as Michaelmas blended into Christmas. But with Rosanna's masquerade and the Hyatts' picnic concluded, the rest of September might be far more enjoyable. The concert was arriving shortly, but Katherine hardly counted that as a social event, as it involved music rather than conversation.

Mama's voice buzzed in the background, recounting the many ills of the world (most of which were Katherine's doing for being so unlucky as to be born plain, bespectacled, and with the likeability of a trout), but it was easy enough to ignore, for she rarely required responses. Papa tucked away his newspaper before alighting from the carriage and walking into the house; Benjamin and Mama followed suit, though the lady didn't pause in her litany.

Tucking her hands behind her, Katherine drifted behind them, and the family scattered to their separate spaces in the house the moment they crossed the threshold. She took the stairs to her bedchamber, but as she stopped on the landing, she paused as Benjamin called behind her.

"Do you have feelings for Mr. Archer?"

Ice spread through her veins, freezing her in place. Despite her having counted the gentleman as a friend for some time, no one had ever asked that question before. Katherine quickly took stock of her actions and words, searching for any reason that Benjamin might ask such a thing.

Turning in place, she peered at him as Benjamin perched on the bottom step.

"I beg your pardon?" she asked, her heart swelling with gratitude that her tone was even.

Climbing the stairs, he lowered his voice and watched her as he'd never done before. Benjamin's eyes narrowed, and his tone was cautious, though it was certain enough.

"Do you care for Mr. Archer?" he repeated.

Katherine's heart stuttered, and her pulse raced. Such a question. And such an answer to give. In a trice, her mind sorted through all the possibilities, both in what she might say and the subsequent consequences. Unfortunately, few of them ended in anything resembling happiness for her and Mr. Archer.

"I do not know what you mean," she replied.

Benjamin frowned. "I do not think my question is terribly confusing. I've seen you two together, and I wish to know if you view him as more than my friend."

Her lips pinched together. "*Your* friend? Is it so difficult to imagine that he and I are friends as well?"

"I cannot pretend I don't find your friendship unusual, especially as you are far happier alone than with others," said Benjamin, scratching at the back of his head.

Her brother was not a cruel person. Not purposefully, at any rate. Though Katherine couldn't claim a close relationship with him, she knew enough of Benjamin Leigh to know that. Yet his words cut her to the core, not merely due to his confusion about her friendship with Mr. Archer, but because he stated those feelings in such a bald manner—as though it wouldn't hurt her in the slightest.

Did he think she had no heart? That her insides didn't twist at the thought that her own brother couldn't comprehend why his friend might enjoy her company? Or that he thought her some hermit who counted Mr. Archer a friend, despite her dislike of humanity?

"The way you two spoke at the picnic today made me wonder if there was something more. Do you care for him?" Benjamin waved his hands about as though searching for the answer. "Do you feel something more than friendship? Something romantic in nature."

The previous pain faded from thought. Katherine's heart beat against her ribs, and her hands quivered enough that she hid them behind her.

Could she not simply tell him the truth? No doubt, he would tell Mr. Archer. That would land her in the exact predicament she was avoiding by not telling him herself. No more friendship. No more conversations. No more silent jests. The thought was inconceivable.

But then another thought struck, and her heart fluttered.

What if Benjamin was asking because Mr. Archer, himself, wished to know?

It was a silly thought, easily batted aside, for though people were often timid in love, Katherine couldn't imagine Mr. Archer sending another to ascertain the truth when he was quite capable of asking himself.

So, Benjamin was asking for his own curiosity. And if word were to get back to Mr. Archer, then he'd know the truth without Katherine having to declare it herself. Surely it was less embarrassing if Mr. Archer were to discover her feelings from a third party. Wasn't it?

Katherine's heart swiveled back and forth, longing to be done with this charade, yet knowing how likely it was that the ending would not be the one she wished. Could she risk it? Could she trust Benjamin with this delicate truth?

That question silenced all others, leaving Katherine firm in her resolve. Drawing in a deep breath, she forced herself to calm. She could do this. It may not be the right choice, but it was the only one she could make at this juncture.

"He is a friend, Benjamin. That is all."

Chapter 17

Despite earning their bread from the mill, the rest of the Archer family never cared for the sounds of the machinery and had chosen to reside in Stratsfield House rather than any of the townhouses situated nearer to Rawlston Mill. To David's thinking, that thrumming and clanging was the sound of their financial stability. Quiet was far more bothersome.

Vibrations echoed throughout the mill office, soothing David's thoughts as he stared at the letter. Mr. Cox was a sensible fellow and was well worth trusting, but it was never wise to blindly surrender all control of the family's investments to the man of business. That had been one of the first lessons David had learned when he'd begun poking his nose into Father's responsibilities and discovered just how much of a muck their previous one had made of things; no oversight led to complacency, and the world was changing too quickly for such things.

The door to the office opened, and a gust of wind from the courtyard swept through the room, disturbing papers throughout the long space. The mill manager stood from his desk at the far side and greeted the intruder, though David did not look up from Mr. Cox's missive.

"You are making yourself quite at home in your father's seat," said Mr. Culpepper, sweeping past Mr. Fenn to stand before David's desk.

"As he is not currently at home, someone must step in," said David.

Mr. Fenn stood behind the intruder, his hands tucked behind him as he glanced between his employer and Mr. Culpepper. With a nod of his head, David dismissed the mill manager, and Mr. Fenn bowed in reply and moved back to his desk.

"When is he expected to return?" asked Mr. Culpepper.

David hid a sigh and met that question with a smile. "How might I assist you?"

But Mr. Culpepper waved the offer away. "I wish to speak with the master—not some young pup."

From his desk on the far side of the room, Mr. Fenn glanced up before turning back to his ledgers with a shake of the head.

"As my father is often occupied with urgent business outside of Greater Edgerton, I suggest you write a letter," said David. "I will ensure it is reviewed and a reply will be sent posthaste."

Mr. Culpepper stiffened, his brow dipping low. "That is a shabby way to conduct business."

"Nevertheless, it is how we do things here at Rawlston Mill," replied David. "You are free to express your displeasure in the letter."

With a huff and a few muttered oaths under his breath, Mr. Culpepper turned on his heel and stormed out of the office. David puffed out his cheeks and smiled at Mr. Fenn before turning back to the letter from Mr. Cox. Setting it down, he scribbled out a reply and signed Father's name to the bottom.

For all that an entail on the Leighs' property had caused no end of troubles for Benjamin, David understood the sentiment behind the action. An estate grew over generations, becoming so much more than a mere income or house. It was a legacy. David's own grandfather had grown this mill from nothing, creating something of great value with strength enough to withstand many of the twists and turns of fate that upended so many other businesses.

But neither estate nor mill could survive a single negligent owner, and any father of sense would wish to protect that legacy from wastrels. An entail allowed the estate to continue on, protected from men like Mr. Leigh, who would sell off bits of the land that provided the income for their family. So many families were laid low by such actions, and David couldn't help but toast Mr. Leigh's father for seeing what was to come and doing what he could to protect Whitley Court.

Granted, the gentleman was also directly responsible for indulging in his son's indolent behavior and raising his child to be a wastrel. David hadn't met the man, but he'd known his own grandfather well enough to imagine it was true.

Rubbing at his forehead, David set aside those thoughts and turned his attention back to the work at hand. Whitley Court was protected from Mr. Leigh, and Rawlston Mill was blessed to have a master who rarely stirred himself to insert himself into its happenings, leaving David free to guide it along.

A chiming clock near Mr. Fenn's desk pulled David from his work. Glancing at the pocket watch propped up on one side of the desk, he growled at himself and shuffled the papers on his desk into proper stacks before rising from his seat and putting on his jacket.

Leaving was hardly the responsible thing to do, but his appointment with Benjamin wouldn't wait. David knew better than to throw his friend over, for the fellow would simply descend upon Rawlston Mill, and then nothing would get done. If the last few hours of the work day were to be wasted, David might as well do it properly.

Besides, there was other important business that needed seeing to.

With a nod at Mr. Fenn, David strode out of the office, his mind sifting through what he'd done today and what still needed to be addressed. Ticking off the items, he refused to let his shoulders droop as he considered just how little he'd accomplished. Mr. Fenn was quite capable of managing the day-to-day operations, but there were so many broader issues that were beyond the mill manager's purview, and the mountain of missives waiting on his desk attested to David's failure.

Drawing in a deep breath, he forced his feet forward. Workers moved about the courtyard, hauling deliveries of cotton into the store rooms, and he dodged them and stepped into the streets of Olde Towne. The buildings were worn, and the faint pall of coal dust darkened the red brick facades. Yet another reason his family avoided the mill itself, as this portion of town was so much gloomier than that of New Towne, but the streets were filled with commerce and life, and David adored the sight.

Too many businesses had shut their doors in the wake of the economic upheaval and panic that took hold five years ago, and the country was only just healing. And so, David ducked around the people and vehicles clogging the streets and sent out a silent prayer of gratitude for the noise and congestion.

Following the street, he crossed River Dennick, the sounds of Olde Towne's industry and mills fading as he wandered into the new side with its cottages, houses, and shops. It was like two towns fused into one, though both had always been Greater Edgerton.

Turning down the road that followed the river, David made his way past the townhouses and shops that made up the heart of New Towne until he reached the edge, where the close-stacked buildings began to spread. Little gardens and courtyards cropped up around the edges, and further still stood Whitley Court.

Unlike many of the buildings in town, this was made of gray stone, giving it a unique appearance that set it apart from all the other red block-like buildings. Gravel crunched beneath David's feet as he walked the drive to the front door. The maid greeted him and ushered him into the parlor to find Benjamin stretched across a sofa, his eyes fixed on a novel.

"Finally," he said, tossing aside the entertainment and rising to his feet. "I had almost given up on you."

David checked his pocket watch. "I am barely tardy."

With a sigh, Benjamin dropped back into his seat. "Yes, well. I've had nothing to do all day. Your visit is the only thing I have on my schedule this week."

A tart response came to mind, but David held it back. At present, having nothing to do sounded brilliant, but a quick study of his friend's drawn expression silenced that thought. Troubles were troubles for a reason, and comparing them was hardly helpful or fair. Besides, he and Benjamin were merely two sides of the same coin at any rate. If not for Mr. Fenn's silent assistance, David wouldn't be allowed to do anything for the family, and he would be sitting about, twiddling his thumbs.

"Well, I am here," said David, taking a seat opposite. "And I was hoping I might enlist your aid."

Benjamin's brows rose, and he straightened. "With what?"

"I understand your family is familiar with Mrs. Ellery," said David. "I had hoped you could get her an invitation to the concert next week."

With a vague huff, Benjamin relaxed back into his seat and waved a dismissive hand. "I have no connection to the lady, nor do I have any sway over the concert. But I can ask my mother if you wish."

"No." David's response held more of a bite than he'd intended, but the memory of her offering up poor Miss Hooper at the Hyatts' picnic forced the word out. Softening his tone, he added with a smile, "My thanks, but I wouldn't wish to bother her."

Benjamin's brows rose as he sank deeper into the seat. "Ah, but you do wish to bother me?"

"I do hate to disrupt your busy schedule," replied David with a wry tone.

With a sigh, his friend smiled and shook his head. "Katherine is the better Leigh to ask, as she is heavily involved with the concert."

David considered that. "True. And likely, she'll know if Miss Hooper and Miss Lyons are planning on attending."

"I thought you had dismissed both of them as your Mystery Lady," said Benjamin with a cocked brow.

Drawing in a deep breath, David let it out in a heavy sigh. "Something your sister said has me reconsidering my position. People are far freer with their behavior when hidden by a mask, after all. I might've been too quick to dismiss them because they did not immediately remind me of the Lady."

Crossing his arms, David reconsidered that. "I do not believe a second conversation will improve Miss Lyons, but your sister had a fair point. Fancy dress has a way of altering people, and it is unfair to expect my Mystery Lady to behave as she had when in costume. It may take time to discover the truth."

"I must say I am flummoxed."

David turned his gaze to his friend, brows furrowed, but before he could ask, Benjamin clarified, "You clearly didn't care for either lady when you spoke to them at the Hyatts' picnic, yet you are forcing another meeting. Why are you so determined to find this Mystery Lady of yours?"

Straightening, David stared at his friend. "I discovered a lady with whom I shared a significant bond. Despite only spending a few hours together, it was clear we were kindred spirits. Why wouldn't I be determined to discover her identity?"

Benjamin scratched at his cheek. "No, I understand that quite well. I would do the same. But every time you've spoken about her, I cannot help but think you're describing precisely the sort of bond you share with Katherine."

Sinking back into his seat with a laugh, David shook his head. "Ah, since your matchmaking at the picnic failed, you're now trying to foist your sister on me?"

"That is not at all what I am doing," said Benjamin with a scowl. "I am speaking in earnest, David. I watched you two together at the picnic, and for all that we are friends, it's clear you prefer her company. The two of you understand each other in a way that I do not. There is more to you two than mere friendship."

The smile fled from David's face, and a chill swept across his skin. "I am giving her that impression? Have I raised her expectations? Do others believe we are courting?"

Good heavens above, the implications in that question flitted through his mind in rapid succession. A gentleman didn't do that to a lady. To cause her and her reputation such harm demanded only one course of action.

"Not at all," said Benjamin, holding up his hands in placation and pulling David from those panicked thoughts. "I've never given it a thought before, but with your hunt for the Mystery Lady, I do find myself genuinely curious as to why you are searching for another lady when Katherine fits the bill quite nicely."

That answer allowed his pulse to slow, and David shook aside the remnant fear that had taken hold of him. Not that spending a life with Miss Leigh was an unpleasant prospect, for he adored her, but a forced marriage would not be a happy ending for either of them.

When David's thoughts cleared enough for him to answer, he struggled for the words. "Your sister is a wonderful lady, and I am lucky to count her as my friend, but one cannot simply decide to love another."

"As you keep spouting about the 'connection' and friendship you shared with your Mystery Lady, I had expected a better answer than that," replied Benjamin with a frown. "Do you truly believe this lady, whom you knew for only a few short hours, is preferable to someone you've known for years and clearly care for?"

"Marriage hasn't been on my mind," said David with a shrug. "I cannot say that I gave it any thought before."

Benjamin raised his brows in challenge. "But you have now, so why not Katherine?"

"I have never considered her in that light. Neither of us has. She is like an older sister—"

"She is only five years older. A number that no one would even consider if your ages were reversed."

David nodded, though it didn't settle the restless feeling. Standing, he walked the length of the room and stopped, his hands tucked behind him.

"So, why not Katherine?" prodded Benjamin.

Turning his thoughts to the question at hand, David shrugged. "In all the years I have known her, I have never considered her as anything more than a friend, and that isn't going to suddenly change simply because you tell me I ought to. One cannot command love."

"Are you so enamored with your silly Mystery Lady that you cannot see you have something far better within your grasp? What does this fantasy lady have that is so much better than a lady whose company you crave and whose opinion you value?"

With a scoff, David narrowed his eyes. "Quite the question from a man who treats that lady like a pest."

Holding up his hands in surrender, Benjamin shook his head. "I may not understand the appeal, but this is not about my relationship with her. You prize her above all others, so I am at a loss to comprehend why you are searching elsewhere."

David turned away and paced the length of the parlor. "Leave it be, Leigh. There is a lady out there who fits the bill, and I am going to find her."

The edge of the book dug into her skin, piercing her arms as Katherine clutched it to her chest, but she couldn't feel the pain. As she stood just beyond the parlor door, her feet were frozen to the floor, unable to make herself known or flee as she listened to her friend and brother debate her merit as a woman.

There was a vast difference between suspecting a thing and knowing it to be true. Despite all the many times Katherine had told herself Mr. Archer did not view her in a romantic light, hearing his laughter at Benjamin's suggestion made her heart shatter. The icy shards sliced through her, leaving her chest a gaping wound.

His *older sister*?

Even if Katherine had been able to ignore Mama's constant harping about her unappealing features, the dismissive manner in which others treated her was proof enough. Had any man ever viewed her favorably? At best, the men thrust upon her had been aloof. Gentlemen like Mr. Mowbry deigned to glance in her direction only if other prey was unavailable. No man asked her to dance of his own accord. No man sought out her company. Few even looked her directly in the eye, as though giving even that vague acknowledgment might raise expectations.

Except Mr. Archer.

Yet even he did not view her as a woman. He danced around it, never going so far as to call her plain, but it was rife in his meaning. For all that the euphemisms were intended to soften the blow, in many ways, they made it all the more painful. "Ugly" was not a terrible thing, or ought not to be. It was simply a description. A word. But when one said "unappealing," it carried all the same meaning but with the connotation that ugly was something shameful. Elsewise, one needn't be afraid to say it.

And oh, how he avoided those blunter words.

No, Katherine Leigh was not his precious Mystery Lady. It was an impossibility. Thinking of Miss Katherine Leigh as his bride was laughable. Though the response was born more from surprise than the mockery with which others had dismissed her charms, Katherine's heart still broke.

Their voices moved to the parlor door, and she lurched away, sneaking down the hall until she was out of sight. The gentlemen emerged, excitedly planning the rest of their afternoon, and she stilled, remaining fixed in place, just out of sight.

"What about a drive?" asked Benjamin.

"With such fine weather, we ought to make use of it," said Mr. Archer. "But do you think we ought to invite your sister to join us?"

Words that would've warmed her heart mere moments ago

now stabbed that brittle organ, and she kept out of sight as her brother climbed the stairs to seek out her bedchamber. Closing her eyes against the sound of Mr. Archer standing just out of sight, Katherine remained hidden and silent as Benjamin called out to her.

With hopping steps, her brother skipped down the stairs. "She doesn't seem to be about."

"That is too bad," said Mr. Archer as the pair then moved to leave.

Once the front door closed, Katherine lurched from her hiding place and hurried up the stairs and into her bedchamber. With a flick of the key, she locked it tight against everything and everyone and dropped onto the bed. The book fell to the side, but she ignored it as she clutched a pillow to her chest, strangling it in her arms.

Her lungs heaved, and she focused on the movement. In and out. The clean air swept through her, and she blinked rapidly, forcing away the prickling in her eyes, but there was no stopping the blurring. Clenching her teeth, Katherine fought against the pressure building in her, but her control wriggled from her grasp.

A single tear was all it took for the torrent to sweep in, and she buried her face in the pillow, stifling the sobs that wracked her body. Her spectacles dug into her nose, and she ripped the wretched things free, tossing them on the side table before burrowing back into the bed.

Even friendship was not enough. Mr. Archer cared for her, but that powerful connection couldn't outweigh her plain features. Had she truly believed that a man of Mr. Archer's caliber would suddenly embrace her as though she were the most desirable creature in the world? That her sparkling wit was so great that it would overcome such an impediment? That a gentleman who could win the heart of any lady in town would ever lower himself to choosing a plain nobody like Katherine Leigh?

When no other man had ever looked at her as more than an annoyance, how had she believed Mr. Archer would ever love her as a woman and not as an *older sister*?

Only fools ignored reality in favor of fantasy, and Katherine was a fool of the highest order. Else why had she ignored that Mr. Archer had never treated her as anything but a chum—until her face had been covered? Oh, no. Katherine had clung to false hopes, hoping and praying for the day when her friendship would outweigh her hideousness.

Vulnerable hearts were always crushed, and for all that she'd believed hers well protected, it now lay crumpled and cracked beneath Mr. Archer's boot.

Chapter 18

When empty, the Garrisons' drawing room was cavernous, the rectangular space seeming to stretch out *ad infinitum*, but with dozens of chairs lined up like a battalion of soldiers and the hoard of people waiting to employ them, the room was filled, making it feel quite tight. Their hosts employed a veritable fortune in candles, but even that and the light blue walls didn't alleviate the heavy feeling so many people instilled.

Shifting in place, David tried to ease the tension from his shoulders, but they were as rigid as stone. Managing Mother's nerves had taught him much about the subject, and he'd honed those skills with his sisters. Thankfully, David hadn't been cursed with an anxious demeanor, so he rarely felt overcome by the sentiment. Yet standing in the Garrisons' drawing room, he was inexplicably on edge.

Clinging to the glass of punch, David focused on the task at hand, ignoring the prickle of anxiety that ran down his spine as he considered the coming evening. Weaving through the crowd towards his quarry, he cast a glance over the other guests, his gaze flicking across their faces. But Miss Leigh wasn't there.

David forced a smile on his face and turned his attention to his destination, offering up the glass to the lady. "Here you are, Mrs. Ellery."

"You are a dear, Mr. Archer," she said with a smile before taking a sip. "That is perfection. Are you looking forward to the music?"

"Certainly," he replied, availing himself of his drink. "I do not know why there aren't more concerts. I cannot claim to be an expert at music, but I enjoy it when I hear it."

"Then you are not musical yourself?" asked Mrs. Ellery, matching his bright expression.

"Not in the slightest," he said, his gaze drifting from his companion to search the crowd. "And you? Are we to be graced with your talents?"

Mrs. Ellery laughed, shaking her head. "If entertainment is the goal for tonight, I am better left out of the program. That would be a disaster for all involved."

David's grin broadened, though his gaze continued to scour the faces around him. "I would say you are doing yourself a disservice, but you do not seem the type to feign insecurities."

"I never have understood that behavior," she said, taking another drink. "It is one thing to boast, but why do so many ladies insist on denigrating their talents? One can be humble and acknowledge one's skill in the same instance."

David nodded, his attention drifting to the gathering around them. His eyes darted to the edge of the room, though he knew he was unlikely to see Miss Leigh there—not when there were last-minute details to address before the concert began. Most of the musicians were occupied elsewhere, so it was little surprise that Miss Leigh was missing. Flora had gone straight to the staging area for the performers when they'd arrived, as well. David shifted in place, looking for any sign of either lady.

"Do forgive me for being forward, Mr. Archer, but is something amiss?" asked Mrs. Ellery, and when David met her gaze once more, she added, "You seem a bit anxious."

He straightened and forced himself to focus on the task at

hand. "I apologize, madam. My sister rarely performs in public but was prevailed upon to do so tonight. I fear she was a bundle of nerves when we arrived, and I cannot help but feel it by proxy."

"The poor dear," said Mrs. Ellery with wide eyes. "That is one of the many reasons I never bothered to hone my musical skills. Once you have them, you are forever pestered to play or sing in public, and I have no desire to do so."

Nodding, David felt a small pang of guilt for that half-truth. It didn't seem proper to admit that his attention was divided; looking for one lady whilst speaking with another was hardly conducive to a friendly exchange. But David couldn't help that his gaze kept drifting towards the crowd.

Shifting his coat, he tried to force his thoughts back to Mrs. Ellery, but his eyes kept searching for Miss Leigh. No doubt she'd been very occupied with concert preparations, and between her absence and Flora's fretting, he was quite ready to see the evening concluded.

"Do any of your other sisters play or sing?" asked Mrs. Ellery.

"Unfortunately, the majority of my family take after our mother, who, despite her best efforts, hasn't a jot of musical talent," said David, swinging his gaze back to his companion as he took another drink. "But as I said, I do enjoy music and am looking forward to seeing what the evening shall bring. I have a friend who is playing several pieces, and I am eager to hear her perform. As well as my dear sister, of course."

"Ah, and who is the lady?"

"Miss Katherine Leigh."

Silence met that, and David realized his attention had been diverted away from Mrs. Ellery once more. Turning his gaze back to her, he found her watching him with raised brows.

"Oh, Miss Leigh," she said with a strained smile. "Yes, I have heard her play many times before. She is an enthusiastic pianist."

David's hold on his glass tightened at the lady's stilted tone.

"Enthusiastic is the precise word. Miss Leigh adores music. As I am good friends with the family, I am often at Whitley Court and am blessed to hear her practice quite often."

"That must be nice," said Mrs. Ellery, taking another drink from her glass as her gaze drifted away. When her eyes snapped back to him, she quickly asked, "I understand your family owns a mill. That is exciting. Do you assist your father in his work or are you still enjoying your free and easy bachelor years?"

"Oh, that is far too tedious a subject," he said with a laugh. "I understand you were raised in London. Surely that is far more interesting."

And needing no further prompt, the lady launched into a description of her childhood, and David nodded at appropriate times, all while his gaze kept scouring the crowd.

...

Organization was not a difficult thing. One simply needed to consider the relative importance of each item, and place it in order from least to greatest. Surely anyone with sense could do so. But as Katherine followed Mrs. Garrison through the sitting room whilst the musicians flew about, gathering music and readying themselves, she couldn't believe their hostess had not a shred of understanding.

But then, Mrs. Garrison wasn't a musician—not truly. Most ladies played or sang a little, but their dear hostess was like so many of their ranks, who preferred to sit in silent judgment amongst the audience rather than risk their pride by performing.

"Mrs. Turley must be last in the program," said Katherine, following on the lady's heels. If Mrs. Garrison thought to outpace her, she was sorely mistaken.

"Yes, I understand that is what you wish to do, but I am of a different opinion, and this is my concert," said Mrs. Garrison, giving her a narrowed look over her shoulder. "And that is my final word on the subject."

Katherine paused at the unyielding tone with which the lady spoke. Even her stubborn pride recognized the battle was likely lost. Anyone with sense knew better than to poke the beast, and it wasn't her concern, after all. Being all too familiar with social mockery, Katherine wasn't intimidated by the prospect of having the clearly superior Mrs. Turley perform early on in the program.

But the other young ladies would wilt beneath the pressure, and they didn't have the fortitude to fight their ferocious hostess. Mrs. Garrison was thoroughly in the wrong—something that was soon to be proven, but not at her expense. For all that she might believe the quality of the program reflected on her as the hostess of the concert, it was the performers that were lauded or criticized.

Katherine couldn't remain silent if no one else was brave enough to force the issue. Gathering her courage close, she straightened and jutted out her chin before marching to Mrs. Garrison's side once more.

"It is difficult to perform at the best of times, and Mrs. Turley was a professional singer and is by far the most talented of any musician here tonight. Following her piece would be difficult, to say the least, and invites unfair comparison. There is a reason that concerts place the most talented performers at the end. To do otherwise is to ensure that the evening will be unpleasant both for your performers and the audience."

Mrs. Garrison pulled to a stop in front of the doors that connected the staging area to the drawing room and turned to face Katherine. "Miss Leigh, you may believe yourself to be the font of all wisdom, but I assure you I am quite done listening to your unsolicited advice. I only included you out of pity, as you are so determined to put yourself forward at every event. Now, let me be."

The words were like the snap of a whip, and Katherine stood there, blinking after the lady.

Why did no one ever listen to her? If not for Mrs. Garrison's sharp reprimand, she might believe herself to be invisible, for it seemed as though everyone was quite happy to pretend she did not exist. And why, when they deigned to listen, did they turn it about on her as though she were the source of trouble?

Every word that sprouted from Prudence's lips was treated as though they were gifted from Athena, Goddess of Wisdom. And no one would dare overlook Rosanna, for the mighty Aphrodite would never countenance a slight against the Goddess of Love and Beauty.

Katherine, on the other hand, had more in common with the goddesses' cousin Hephaestus. The powerful God of Fire and Volcanoes he may be, but at one look from his mother, the imperfect creature was cast out and despised. Even when he showed more sense than the rest of his Olympic family.

She certainly felt as though a volcano were erupting in her chest, and no one cared.

Mr. Archer would.

That traitorous thought sent fire burning through her, though the entirety of its heat was directed inward. How long would she continue to think of the man who had thoroughly rejected her? Was she so pathetic? Katherine scowled at herself.

For all her experience, she was a dunce of the highest order. She was done with Mr. David Archer. If he did not want her, that was his prerogative. However, she needn't prostrate herself before him, begging him to see her as something more than a chum. No, thank you.

Katherine Leigh may be unwanted and disliked by the vast majority of people, but she had learned long ago that one's value was not determined by worldly acceptance, and she wouldn't allow anyone—even Mr. Archer—to diminish her. And she was done feeling anything towards the man.

"There you are, my dear sister."

The endearment once again set Katherine's teeth on edge, and she drew in a deep breath and adjusted her spectacles before turning to face her brother.

"I've been looking for you," said Benjamin with a vapid

smile.

"Shocking though it may be, I am busy assisting with the concert that is about to begin," said Katherine, moving to step around him. Mrs. Garrison may not welcome that aid, but there were others who might.

"That is good of you, but surely you have a moment," he replied in a dismissive tone that so utterly reminded her of Rosanna that Katherine couldn't help the way her jaw tensed.

But was it any wonder that he waltzed about life expecting everyone to attend to him immediately when Rosanna and their dear baby brother were the favored children? The beautiful daughter and the son who could break the entail. The rest of their siblings had no value; their lives were like dandelion fluff, dancing about on the breeze with no purpose or meaning. After all, the very world itself ground to a halt when Benjamin and Rosanna were not about to witness it.

Drawing in a sharp breath, Katherine forced her thoughts to calm. It was not an easy thing to do, but she allowed air to fill her lungs, calming the heat that seared her veins. Her foul mood wasn't Benjamin's doing, and it was not fair of her to treat him as her whipping boy.

But that was when she spied a gentleman at Benjamin's back, and her eyes narrowed.

"The concert is about to begin," she said, "and I still need to place my music on the pianoforte, as I am accompanying the first singer."

"Ah, well, we shan't keep you then, but I do wish to introduce Mr. Edward Tryck," said Benjamin, motioning for the gentleman.

For all that Katherine wished to simply ignore the interruption, she paused at that name. Having never met him, she couldn't know for certain that it was the same Mr. Tryck of whom she'd heard, but the name wasn't commonplace.

"I was speaking to your brother concerning the wretched state of the decorations," said Mr. Tryck, glancing at the door leading into the drawing room. Though it was closed at present, he wrinkled his nose as though he could see the offending objects. "Such drab things wouldn't have been tolerated in London, I tell you. Even the poorest of families would've managed something grander than a few scraggly arrangements of flowers."

Benjamin tucked his hands behind him and glanced between the pair with bright eyes and a smile that held more than a touch of eagerness.

"But then, what can one expect from such a backwater town? When one associates with frogs, one is bound to get wet. I jest." Mr. Tryck laughed and held up his hands in placation as though it was only a lark, but the ruthless quality of his observations rang truer than his claim that they were witty.

Brow wrinkling, Katherine swung her gaze to her brother whilst nudging her glasses up her nose. But Benjamin merely blinked back at her and gave a subtle nod at Mr. Tryck as though she ought to encourage a conversation with such a snide gentleman.

"Please excuse me, gentlemen, but I must see to my music. And you ought not to be here. This room is for performers only," said Katherine, turning away and moving towards the side table, upon which she had left her portfolio of sheet music.

"Katherine, a moment," said Benjamin, following after.

"I haven't the time, Benjamin."

Chapter 19

S natching up her music portfolio, Katherine slipped into the drawing room and edged around the gathering to where the pianoforte sat on the far side. Bunting draped the wall around it, framing the area in which the performers would stand.

"Ladies and gentlemen, please take your seats," called Mr. Garrison.

Katherine stiffened, turning her wide eyes to their host. Gripping her sheet music, she hurried to the piano, but there was no time to adjust the seat. Why had she allowed herself to be distracted? And why did the Garrisons insist on beginning without consulting the performers first? There was a flurry of activity from the staging room, and the pulse of frenetic energy spiked through the air as others were caught unawares as well.

Flipping open the portfolio, Katherine snatched her music out and placed it upon the pianoforte, but her hurried movements caused one sheet to fall to the ground. The resulting snickers from the audience made it clear she was not going unnoticed, even as their host began to wax poetic about the joys of the evening.

"My dear Miss Leigh, would you please surrender the

stage?" asked Mr. Garrison with a deceptively light tone.

For all that she preferred to simply leave, Katherine refused to allow herself to be cowed. Only when she had assured herself that the sheets were placed in the proper order did she move to take her seat amongst the other performers along the edge of the stage.

Curse Mrs. Garrison for being such a stubborn mule, curse Benjamin for stalling her, and curse Mr. Garrison for beginning without warning. She fought to keep her expression passive, but an anxious glance from the lady to her right made Katherine soften the frown pulling at her lips.

Why did people always laugh at her? What was it that they found so irritating? Though not silly enough to believe herself without flaw, Katherine didn't think herself so wholly offensive that people should throw aside all sense of decorum or kindness and openly mock or deride. Though when her own family—those who ought to know her best—believed her irritating, was it any wonder that those who never deigned to speak to her directly would think so as well?

The answer clung to the back of her thoughts, whispering dark taunts. When one possessed siblings with such charm, it was easy enough to see the truth. Humanity existed on spectrums, and if there existed people with natural talents for drawing people near, then the opposite must exist as well.

People attributed Rosanna's popularity solely to her looks, but Katherine had witnessed other beauties who had not a fraction of her sister's popularity. And conversely, there were ladies who would never be considered objectively attractive who drew beaus like flies to honey. Outward attractions aided to a degree, but there was a *je ne sais quoi* to some that transcended physical appearances. Rosanna had a presence that Katherine could never mimic, even if she boasted her sister's golden curls, voluptuous figure, or perfect eyes.

And wasn't that a happy thought?

Letting out a sharp sigh that drew the attention of those around her, Katherine forced aside such thoughts. Dwelling in such darkness wasn't helpful, and it did no good to lament that which she couldn't change. Nor to blame the whole of her situation on unchangeable things.

Mr. Garrison stood before the crowd, and though he spoke of the revelries to come in glowing terms, he mostly thanked himself for the evening, despite having nothing to do with it (beyond funding and housing the thing) before turning it over to the performers.

Katherine rose and followed Miss Collette to the front, taking her seat at the pianoforte whilst the singer stood center-stage. Her seat was far too close to the instrument, and she had to rise and adjust it several times before it was in the proper place; Katherine ignored the impatient murmurs as she did her due diligence.

Focusing her thoughts on the here and now, she stared at the notes and focused on the piece. Only then did she raise her hands to the keys.

A movement from the audience drew Katherine's attention, and she spied Mr. Archer on the edge of a row, his hand slightly lifted in greeting. Forcing her gaze from him, she looked at Miss Collette, and with a nod from the young lady, Katherine began the introduction.

For all that her family cringed at her "excessive" practicing, a performer never did better in public than she did in the privacy of her parlor. Mistakes were inevitable, so one needed to know the piece so well that having the sheet music in front of her was merely a formality.

At that moment, Katherine rather wished she were less diligent. As she knew the piece by heart, her fingers moved without prompting, following the singer's dynamics with little thought. Which left her free to ponder the interlude with Benjamin and Mr. Tryck—the gentleman her brother wished to "foist" upon her, as Mr. Archer had put it.

Why Benjamin wished to do so was a mystery Katherine no longer wished to consider; she had pondered it enough times over the past sennight, and the answer wasn't important. As

Mama and Rosanna were keen to be rid of her, it mattered little that Benjamin had decided to join in their efforts. Besides, it wasn't that surprising: he was Mama's darling boy, after all.

No, it was the man he'd chosen for her that startled Katherine.

Mr. Tryck was not a nice man. True, he wasn't violent or loose with his morals and money, but he was an arrogant fool who delighted in belittling others. He cloaked his cruelty in wit, but it couldn't hide his sour soul. And that was the gentleman her brother wished her to consider marrying.

Katherine knew her features were unlikely to win many over, but did they truly think so ill of her that the only personalities she might entice were those no one wished to marry because they were so sinfully boring or beastly? But then, could she really cast stones when it was clear that few people thought her interesting or engaging?

Her fingers stumbled, but she did not flinch; the first lesson of performing was to school one's expression. Most never noticed as long as the musician didn't give herself away with a wince. And thankfully, that rule held true, for Miss Collette was the entire focus, and Katherine's playing was merely the background support for the girl's voice.

Forcing her thoughts back to the music, Katherine stared at the pages. But her eyes grew unfocused. She didn't need its guidance to know what notes to play, and her hands ran up and down the keyboard, easily hitting each note without conscious thought.

With so many set against her, why did she believe herself worthy of someone better than Mr. Tryck? How could she say she had value when no one else saw it? Pride was simply an overinflated sense of self, and if everyone believed her to be a sour-faced hag with all the personality of a viper, who was she to say it wasn't true?

And how pompous was it of her to say that Mr. Tryck wasn't good enough for her?

Katherine's throat tightened, and she blinked at the music.

Drawing in a deep breath, she held it for several long seconds before letting it out. Forcing herself back to the music, she refused to let her mind wander into those dark corners again.

Thankfully, the song came to an end, and Miss Collette took her applause whilst Katherine gave a small bob from behind the piano. A room full of people all watching her, and not a single one of them knew or cared how much her heart ached.

But when she lifted her gaze from the ground, her eyes fell straight to Mr. Archer, who was applauding with all the rest, though his attention was fixed on her alone. His broad smile lit up his face, and he called, "Brava," with far more gusto than an accompanist garnered. Katherine's brows pulled low, and she jerked her gaze away. Another voice echoed his, and her eyes flew to where Pamela and her husband sat, both of them clapping for her as well.

A few people who saw something of value. But was their affection enough to balance out the vast ocean of apathy?

The applause ended, and she took her seat once more amongst the performers, her gaze turned to those who claimed her and Miss Collette's previous positions. However, Katherine's attention was well and truly occupied.

At various intervals, her internal thoughts were interrupted when she was called to accompany again, but she couldn't free herself of the melancholy that had taken hold of her heart. Or the unease she felt every time Mr. Archer called out with far more exuberance than was warranted for her part in the performance.

Then the moment Katherine had feared. With many years of experience amongst the musical set of Greater Edgerton, she knew full well how aggravating some of them were. Creativity and talent did not make one inherently better than another, and there were far too many musicians who believed themselves to be a gift from heaven to bless lives with their music. And more often than not, those with the least amount of talent were the most pompous.

Mrs. Turley was one whose talent deserved acclaim, for

having earned her living with her voice before her fortuitous marriage to Mr. Turley, she was by far the greatest amongst the ragtag set of amateurs gathered tonight. And how her voice soared.

Katherine lost herself in the music, reveling in the clear sound; though she far preferred the lower registers of altos, Mrs. Turley's bright soprano lacked the shrillness so often found in those higher ranges. Having never traveled outside of Greater Edgerton, Katherine had never graced the theater, and the professionals she'd heard were few and far between. The tears she refused herself surfaced as Mrs. Turley's voice hummed in the air, warming Katherine's heart as the lady sang of love and loss.

When the final notes sounded, applause erupted, and Katherine shot to her feet. Her gloves muted the sound, and she longed to rip them from her hands; though the others joined in, it was still not enough, for the lady deserved far more. Despite the dwindling sound from the crowd, Katherine remained on her feet, and she wanted to scowl at the others, for a few seconds of appreciation was hardly worthy of that performance.

Finally, Katherine took her seat and wished Mrs. Turley was the entirety of the program. Lost as she was in that thought, she entirely forgot about what was to come next until she spied Miss Flora Archer standing center stage, staring out at the crowd with large eyes.

Katherine's muscles clenched as she watched the poor young lady. To follow Mrs. Turley would be difficult for any performer, but it would be impossible to avoid comparison when attempting a soprano solo directly after. And when Miss Flora's first note faltered, Katherine's heartbeat stilled as the pianist and singer fumbled to align with one another.

In any other instance, it would've been a small misstep. Embarrassing, to be certain, but not devastating. But it was easy to see the panic in Miss Flora's eyes as her gaze darted to Mrs. Turley. It was a simple country tune, and it suited the performer, but Katherine could well imagine the thoughts flying through Miss Flora's mind at that moment. The song wasn't as grand as Mrs. Turley's aria; it never could be.

Miss Flora struggled through it, and the difference between the two performances was clear in the faltering applause that followed. The young lady took her bows and hurried to her seat with cheeks burning scarlet, and though Katherine was not one for embracing strangers, she longed to give the poor young lady one.

"I do not know why some people insist on performing when they haven't the talent," murmured a voice from behind Katherine.

Spinning in her seat, she glared at the pair of ladies, but they gawked at Katherine as though the rudeness was all hers. Though she longed to say something to them, there was little point in it. Especially when the person to her left nudged Katherine in the ribs, drawing her attention to the empty stage.

Her time of reckoning had arrived, and as she stood and moved to the piano, a smile tugged at her lips. She couldn't alter what had happened, but that didn't mean she was powerless to help.

Chapter 20

W ho in the blazes had organized the program? David cursed the person—likely their ridiculous hostess, Mrs. Garrison—to Hades as he watched his sister take her seat. Anger flared in his chest as she refused to lift her gaze from the ground, though it was probably for the best that Flora was seated on the other side of the room, for he longed to put his arm around her, which would embarrass her further. But that would be better than doing nothing. Or pummeling Mrs. Garrison, which was unlikely to make Flora feel better.

What had she been thinking, placing Mrs. Turley so early in the program?

"The poor dear," murmured Mrs. Ellery, her brow furrowing as she shifted her gaze from Flora to David. "That is one of the many reasons I do not like performing in public."

David ground his teeth together and forced himself to smile as though nothing were amiss. The evening would conclude quickly enough, and then he could sneak his sister home. No doubt there were biscuits or cake or some sweet sitting around the pantry. Heaven knew David could use a treat as well.

His discomfort doubled when Miss Leigh came to the front

of the room, her chin held high as she took her place at the piano. Her gaze met his for the briefest moment, but when he nodded, she gave no sign of recognition. Logic said that she was simply focusing on her music, but David couldn't help but feel she was dismissing him.

Which made his heart pang.

Despite his visits to Whitley Court, Miss Leigh was never about. Always occupied. And though it had only been a sennight since he'd seen her last, it felt far longer. David didn't know why he'd begun spending so much time with her, but she'd become a constant in his life. And now, rather than look pleased as their reunion, Miss Leigh seemed unaffected.

No, that was a bit of foolishness. He'd been busy with work, and she had been occupied with the concert. Entirely understandable.

David shifted in his seat and forced himself to still as the lady raised her hands to the keys.

The song began simply, halting and sputtering like a rusty music box, moving through the softer introduction and growing into the transition. When her fingers tripped, Miss Leigh stopped, pulling her hands from the keyboard. The audience straightened and raised their hands as though to clap, but Miss Leigh started from the very beginning with the same gusto as before.

Though David was no connoisseur of music, even his uncultured ears thought the piece was dreadful. At one point, it sounded as though she was stuck in a loop, forever playing the same measures again and again, as though she couldn't remember how the piece transitioned into the next section.

Mrs. Ellery fidgeted at his side, and David glanced at her. The lady didn't go so far as to wince, but her smile was pained as their gazes met. Tittering laughter echoed behind him, and he cast a look over his shoulder to see Miss Lyons pressing a hand to her mouth, her eyes alight with mockery as others around her fought hard to keep their laughter to themselves.

And that clarified one question, for he had no interest in

anyone who would treat his friend in such a manner. Mystery Lady or not.

David's brow furrowed as he watched her falter to a stop once more. Lifting her hands from the keys, she paused, and just as someone hazarded a clap, she launched back into the piece, beginning over again. Though he didn't have his pocket watch on him at present, David would wager she'd stretched out this three-minute piece into a full ten, and she was still not finished.

What was happening? Miss Leigh had practiced far too many times to play this poorly. Her actions all seemed genuine as she faltered through the piece, but David couldn't believe it.

But as quickly as he posed the question, the answer sprang to his thoughts, filling him with such clarity that his heart burned. This was no accident or byproduct of nerves. With one ungainly and loud performance, Miss Leigh guaranteed that the focus of everyone's laughter and pity would be herself—not Flora.

Gooseflesh rose along his neck, traveling down his spine as he watched Miss Leigh serve herself up as a sacrifice to the vengeful gods of society. The lady was truly magnificent.

Mistakes were simple things. Usually. Unpreparedness and anxiety were a potent combination, making it easy for musicians (however skilled) to fail.

With Katherine's dedication to practice, the former was never the issue. The latter was another matter altogether, for her nerves manifested itself by leaving Katherine's hands weak and shaking (a most inconvenient habit to have when playing the piano). However, unease only arose from a desire to do one's best, which was the opposite of her intent at this moment.

For once, Katherine was quite calm and composed as she made her way through the piece. Enough so that it was quite difficult to mangle the music.

One of the main objectives of practice was to train one's

hands to play without thinking; it was as though the very muscles memorized the piece, moving on their own and hitting each note to perfection. Once instilled, it was difficult to break the habit. Even intentionally. Which was the precise reason why musicians dedicated so much time to playing a song again and again: the less one had to think about the notes themselves, the more they could dedicate themselves to the musicality of the piece.

Unfortunately, Katherine had chosen this particular Mozart piece as it required little in the way of dynamics. The sound did range from the softest pianissimo to the booming forte, but the skill of the piece involved dexterity and speed, rather than artistry.

In short, it was a piece perfectly suited for Katherine's skill, and she'd taught her hands too well.

Finally, a sour note was struck, and she seized upon the opportunity. Pausing, she returned to the beginning of the piece, starting from the very first measure. But that wasn't enough to leave an impression. Which was how she found herself repeating the same line of music several times over. As songs often repeated previous melodies and themes, it was simple enough to repeat the measures, playing in an endless loop.

For all that Katherine Leigh believed herself to be kindhearted, she stifled a smile and wondered how long she could torment her audience before someone forced the issue and ended her performance. And for all her low opinion of human decency, she was quite impressed with how patient people were when she came crashing to a halt once more and began again.

Were they truly not going to do a thing to stop her?

But on her third attempt to restart, the applause came quickly and forcefully enough that Katherine had no choice but to consider the piece finished.

Rising to her feet, she curtsied to the crowd, ignoring the varying snickers and sighs of relief that wafted through the room. Katherine glanced at Miss Flora, whose teary eyes had cleared and cheeks had returned to their usual paleness; the young lady was counted among the more vigorous applauders, her smile conciliatory as their gazes met. Katherine's heart lightened, and she knew that no matter what else happened tonight, this was a fine evening.

"Brava!" called Mr. Archer, and Katherine's cheeks immediately heated at seeing him standing, clapping with far more enthusiasm than any performance had warranted. The sound drew attention from the rest of the crowd, who stared at him with puzzled frowns, so Katherine quickly relinquished her place on the stage.

Seated amongst the others, she felt the gazes on her and heard the titters, but ignored them; warmth suffused her chest as Misses Maybury, Fortescue, and Hanbury took their places in the front without the slightest sign of nerves. But then, why would there be? No one could do worse than Katherine.

The piano and violin struck up with the singer quickly following, and the music was quite good, though Katherine couldn't focus on that whilst her heart was expanding, pressing against her ribs. Her lips turned up of their own accord, though she forced them back into place.

Let others laugh. They did so whether she failed or excelled, so what did their mockery matter? To them, she would always be the eyesore and the irritant. But Katherine had spared others that same fate, and in her own quiet and strange way, she had made the world a better place. That was no small thing.

It was a miracle she remained in her seat, for she felt as light as a breeze. Despite being surrounded by others, peace filled her to bursting, and she held fast to it as the concert ended and she was forced to face the sneering crowd. Jeering glances surrounded her like a fog, and the contentment in her heart burned through it, leaving the day sunny and beautiful.

Moving away from the others, she paused as Mrs. Hamstall stepped in her way with a snicker.

"That was quite the memorable performance, Miss Leigh."

"As that was my intent, I am pleased it succeeded."

Mrs. Hamstall flicked open her fan and batted it a few times. "I find it so inspiring that you are so determined to put yourself forward again and again."

Drawing nearer, the lady dropped her voice to a low whisper and spoke gently, as though attempting to share a secret with a friend. "Though I would be remiss if I didn't point out that you needn't play at every event. One ought not to put oneself on display always. Especially when one's talent is so...unrefined."

"So that is why you've stopped performing." Katherine didn't bother softening her retort, though she did lower her voice much as Mrs. Hamstall had and added, "Though if we are exchanging advice, I would say one cannot refine a talent if one doesn't risk public failure. But then, it is easier to sit in the audience and judge another's skill rather than develop it oneself."

Rosanna may have a natural charm, and Katherine may be her opposite in that respect, but she couldn't blame the entirety of her unpopularity on some uncontrollable otherness, gifted to them at birth. To ingratiate oneself among people, one must play society's games, and Katherine detested them. Even if she learned the rules as well as her elder sister, she didn't wish to follow them.

Mrs. Hamstall's insult had been no less pointed than Katherine's, regardless of how the lady attempted to dress her hateful words, and Katherine couldn't muster the interest or desire to follow her example. But from the shocked expressions of the onlookers, it was clear that she was once more the villain of this piece.

"That was rude," said Mrs. Hamstall with her nose in the air. "I was merely offering you some kindly meant advice, and you snipe at me?"

As the lady's singing voice sounded like a cat being gutted by a dull sword, Katherine thought her own reply had been quite kind, but she was forestalled when Pamela swept in and took her by the arm, giving Mrs. Hamstall one of those sharp smiles that the ladies employed when facing down an opponent.

"Ah, my dear Mrs. Hamstall. Wasn't tonight divine? It is a shame you chose to abstain. Your singing voice is unparalleled." Pamela gave a bright and beaming smile, speaking with that vaguely snide tone ladies used, and Mrs. Hamstall stiffened, her chin tipping upwards before she turned away.

Chapter 21

"Making friends, are we?" whispered Pamela.

"I haven't the patience to deal with the subtle jabs. When someone is rude to me, why is it acceptable as long as it isn't overt? I matched her meaning."

Pamela sighed and nudged her friend. "You are never going to learn diplomacy, are you? But then, I suppose that is one of the things I enjoy about you. Honesty is sadly lacking in society."

"Bluntness makes them squirm, which is far more entertaining than playing their games," replied Katherine. "I've had my fill of calling people 'dear' and behaving as though we are all good friends when we treat each other so horribly. We pretend as though everyone is content and our community is close-knit, but everyone is quick to laugh at another's downfall and revel in the gossip to come. It is disgusting."

"Do not measure your words, Katherine. Tell me what you truly think," replied Pamela with a stilted (but amused) tone.

Katherine chuckled, though it died on her lips as she glanced over her shoulder at the rest of the room and caught sight of a particular gentleman weaving his way through the crowd. Snapping her head back around, she glanced at the drawing room exit and dragged Pamela in that direction.

"Where are we going?" she asked, tugging against Katherine's hold.

"I need some air."

"In the hallway?"

Katherine gave Pamela a vapid smile. "Isn't 'needing air' one of society's euphemisms for wishing to get as far from a place as possible without saying, 'I have no desire to be amongst those vipers any longer?'"

Pamela cast a glance over her shoulder just as they slipped out the door. It shut behind them, leaving them in the staging room, in which a few performers wandered about as they gathered their sheet music. Katherine cursed herself. She'd abandoned her portfolio beside her seat, and she'd need to return to the drawing room to retrieve it. But not this very moment.

With her friend following closely, she drifted into a quiet corner of the room.

"How are you?" asked Pamela with a weighty tone.

Katherine waved the question away. "I do not care about the performance tonight. I know how well I can play that piece, and I do not need to prove it to anyone else."

Pamela's brow arched. "Of course. Not all performances can go as we planned, though I suspect yours went exactly as you intended. However, I was speaking about Mr. Archer."

"Pardon?" Katherine dropped her friend's arm and stiffened, casting a glance about the room. As it was mostly empty, it was easy enough for anyone to overhear, though the three lingering performers were more focused on discussing their pieces and collecting their things.

Drawing closer, Pamela lowered her voice. "What has happened between you two?"

Katherine remained fixed in place, her eyes wide despite her best efforts to shutter her expression. And then they began to prickle without warning—traitorous things that they were—and she forced herself to blink the tears away. Not here. Not now.

A loud clatter had Katherine moving, turning away from the others in the room as they righted whatever it was that they had dropped. Pamela shifted with her, taking her friend by the arm, before taking refuge in the far corner of the room. They weren't out of sight, but it was as close to privacy as they could manage at present.

"Oh, Katherine," murmured Pamela. "Tell me what is the matter. And why haven't you come and spoken to me about it?"

Pressing a hand to her forehead, Katherine tried to knead the agony away, though it burrowed deep into her skull. "You are so busy with the children. You do not have time to listen to your friend complain."

"I always have time for you," said Pamela, her brows pulling low.

As much as Katherine wished to believe that, the truth was that her friend's life was very full at present, and the utmost priority was her family. As it should be. Katherine might steal away an afternoon every fortnight or so, but no more than that. However, the truth would only cause Pamela pain, and Katherine would never wish to place extra burdens on her friend.

So, she gave a different, yet still honest, answer.

"What would I do?" she whispered. "Arrive on your doorstep to tell you I've been a fool for thinking Mr. Archer might actually care for me? Admit that I allowed myself to actually hope and dream that for once a gentleman might see me as a romantic possibility? And even though he saw past the surface and came to know me as a person, he still finds the idea of courting me unthinkable. Laughable. A merely a much older sister in his eyes."

Katherine's throat tightened, and she drew in a sharp breath. When her voice was steady, she added, "It is terrible enough to know that I've harbored such foolish fantasies, but to admit it aloud—"

"You are not a fool," snapped Pamela.

A pang shot through Katherine's heart as she met her friend's eyes and saw the tears shining there. "Yes, I am—"

"Sister, dear, there you are," called Benjamin as he burst through the doorway.

Katherine jumped, and Pamela swiped at her own eyes. Only once all signs of their conversation were wiped from view did her friend take her arm, and the pair turned to see him striding up.

"I wanted to continue our conversation," he said.

"Conversation?" asked Katherine with a frown.

"I was speaking to Mr. Tryck about taking a drive out tomorrow."

Not now. Not this moment. The usual protections around Katherine's heart were peeled back, exposing the bleeding flesh beneath. The concert would have been emotionally strenuous enough, but with the added strain of Mr. Archer, and Pamela's skill at seeing through pretense, Katherine had no strength left to manage her emotions.

Her gaze narrowed. "As you are so keen on him, I am sure you and he will have a lovely time, though I cannot imagine anyone enjoying his company."

With a laugh that was far too sharp to be believed, Benjamin shook his head. "I meant you would accompany us—"

"No," she said, not bothering to regulate her tone or soften it in the slightest. It was firm and decisive. Unyielding as stone.

Yet Benjamin merely scoffed. "We'll have a grand time. I can invite a young lady, and we will make an afternoon of it—"

"No."

Pamela squeezed her arm, and Katherine hazarded a glance at her friend. The lady's brows pulled together, a clear question in her gaze, though she knew Pamela well enough to know it wasn't her actions she was questioning. No doubt, she knew Mr. Tryck's reputation as well. He made quite the impression.

Turning an exasperated look at her friend, she begged for some assistance, and Pamela's polite smile tightened as she turned narrowed eyes to the Leighs' favorite child.

"Katherine has made herself clear, Benjamin," said Pamela. "Best cry defeat, and let it be."

"Nonsense," he said with a scoff. "Mr. Tryck is a tad diffi-cult, true, but I think they are well matched. He has a decent income and would make a fine husband for Katherine."

Something inside her shattered. She might've thought it was her heart, but the past weeks had ensured there was little left of it. The concert had mended a few of the fractured pieces, and the knowledge that she'd done some good—whether or not it was known or ever acknowledged—helped to strengthen it, but that could not undo all the damage done.

Drawing in a deep breath, Katherine narrowed her eyes on Benjamin. "Oh, Mr. Tryck is a good match for me, is he?"

Pamela's brows rose at the coldness in her tone, but her own brother seemed not to notice.

With a shrug, he pulled his brows together as though her question was ridiculous and the answer entirely obvious. "Cer-tainly."

So often, fury was described as a hot, burning emotion, and whilst Katherine certainly had fire enough in her heart at times, at that moment, her anger was ice cold. Like an arctic wind swept through her, she stared at her brother as ice swept through her veins.

"Why does it matter to you if I marry, Benjamin?" she asked in a tone as hard as steel. "I have spent years fending off Mama and Rosanna's 'well-meaning' matchmaking efforts as they trotted out gentlemen who are empirically awful and wretched men. But you never threw in with them. You left me alone. Now, you are determined to make yourself just as irritating. Why is that?"

Benjamin's eyes widened, and he shifted from foot to foot. "You speak as though I do not care about you, but that isn't true. I wish to see you happy."

"With a man like Mr. Tryck?" Katherine's voice rose of its own accord, and she didn't care that the others in the room fell silent. "Someone who is cold and cruel in his humor, and deter-mined to pull apart everyone and everything to amuse himself— that is what you believe will make me happy?"

Scratching at the back of his head, Benjamin stared at her. "I am trying to aid you. Why are you being so brusque?"

Katherine scoffed. "If this is your idea of aid, I beg you to stop. You have made it clear since your arrival home from school that I am a bother; you only tolerate me when Mr. Archer forces you to include me. And for all that you, Rosanna, and Mama insist you are acting on my behalf because you care about my happiness and well-being, not a single one of you has ever bothered to know me well enough to know what that entails. So, do not pretend that you are acting in my best interest, Benjamin. We are not friends."

Dragging Pamela forward, Katherine ignored her brother's gaping (and the expressions of the others around them) and marched from the room. She didn't wish to go to the drawing room once more, so she veered towards the door that led into the corridor.

"Brava, Katherine. It was about time you spoke up," said Pamela, squeezing her arm. "Do you wish to leave? I can have Ralph send for the carriage. Now that the concert is over, we needn't linger."

Uncertain whether or not she could form the words, Katherine nodded. Pamela echoed the gesture and stepped away.

"You are staying with my family tonight, and we are going to talk all about this," said Pamela before she wandered off in search of her husband.

Katherine nodded again, though with her anger fading, her strength leached out of her, leaving her limbs quivering. Scowling at herself, she shook it away and straightened. Blast that wretched Benjamin and Mr. Archer. Blast all those people in that room who found delight in laughing at her. And blast her family and all the horrid Mr. Trycks they'd foisted on her.

Tonight was a triumph. Not in the manner she had intended, but it was a triumph nonetheless. And Katherine wouldn't allow anyone to diminish that victory.

Chapter 22

Whitley Court was much like any other house of little distinction and mighty pretension. Little more than a rectangular block dropped at the roadside with a middling garden at the rear, it looked like any number of houses in the area. Though earlier architectural styles employed natural woods, giving the interior a warm—if small—feel, modern sensibilities had painted over all those rich browns, leaving the rooms more open and airy. And cold.

But that might simply be David's current mood.

Being a frequent visitor to Whitley Court meant he was allowed more liberty than other guests, especially as he was the favored friend of the favored son. Except for the private quarters, he'd explored most of the house, but still, he felt a bit like a sneak thief as he slipped through the corridors and up the stairs.

He was here to visit Benjamin, after all, who was in the parlor, but Miss Leigh was unlikely to be at his side. Of course, he didn't hear any piano music coming from the drawing room, so it was unlikely she was there, either, but he had to try.

Pushing open the door, he poked his head inside and found precisely what he had expected. No Miss Leigh. But David paused on the threshold as he realized something was odd about the room. Frowning at the instinct, he tried to identify the source, and it took him a moment to realize that the space between the two grand windows, which utilized the light to its best advantage, was empty. Her pianoforte was gone.

Odd that.

With little other furniture in the room, there was no reason for Miss Leigh to linger. Parlor it was, then. David took the stairs back down and prayed his good fortune would hold out. Sweeping through the door, he ignored his friend as Benjamin rose to his feet in greeting and cast his gaze about the space. No Miss Leigh.

"Thank heavens you arrived," said Benjamin as he moved forward, ushering David back out. "I was about to expire from boredom. With the weather so fine, we shouldn't waste a moment of it. Winter is coming on fast, and before too long, we won't be able to ride at all."

With a nod, David allowed himself to be led back towards the door. "How is your sister faring? I haven't seen her in an age."

"She is otherwise occupied," said Benjamin in a tone that warned him not to make any further inquiries, though it had the opposite effect on David.

"Where is she? I didn't call yesterday as I assumed she would be resting after the strain of the concert, but I had hoped she would be up to riding out with us today."

"I assure you, she doesn't wish to ride out with me," mumbled Benjamin whilst nudging his friend out of the parlor. Glancing over his shoulder at his friend, David frowned, but when his gaze swept over the parlor once more, something else stole his attention.

"Where is your sister's piano? I didn't see it in the drawing room, and I thought it must've been relocated back to the parlor, but I do not see it."

"How can you ask that after her debacle of a performance? Once we arrived home, Mama locked herself in her bedchamber and hasn't stirred all yesterday or today," said Benjamin, shepherding him into the corridor and towards the front door, but David planted his feet.

"What does that have to do with her piano being moved?"

When David refused to follow his prodding, Benjamin stepped around him and strode out the front door.

"What does it matter? Katherine is determined to make a mockery of herself and the family. And whenever I attempt to be the slightest bit helpful, she shouts at me." Pausing on the drive, Benjamin turned and glowered at David as though the rift between siblings was his doing. "I do not know why you bother with her. Katherine is sharp-tongued and rude, forever finding offense when none is meant! The lady is spiteful and ill-tempered!"

David stared at his friend, still uncertain what this had to do with the subject at hand, but Benjamin seemed not to notice as he railed against his sister.

"I was being kind, and she threw it back in my face. I am done attempting to win her over, and I do not blame Mother for reaching the limit of her patience, as well," said Benjamin, his jaw tightening as he shifted in place. Tugging at his jacket, he straightened it and scowled, but for all that his words were forceful, David didn't miss that his friend wasn't looking him in the eye.

"What has happened?" asked David, narrowing his gaze on his friend. "Out with it, Leigh."

Drawing his hands behind him, Benjamin straightened (though without lifting his eyes from the gravel at their feet). "Katherine is the only one who plays, and my parents won't allow her to make us a laughingstock any longer."

David stared at his friend, his brows lowering and pinching together as Benjamin's meaning clarified in his thoughts. Ice swept through his veins as he turned away and closed his eyes. Pinching his nose, he could well imagine the scene that had played out, and his pulse quickened, sending little sparks of pain through him at what Miss Leigh must have suffered. And still was.

"Your parents got rid of her piano," he murmured.

"It wasn't hers. It was the family's, and it was well within my parents' rights to sell it," said Benjamin with a decisive nod.

David's jaw tightened, and he whirled around to scowl at his obtuse friend.

"You believe it is within their rights to strip your long-suffering sister of the one source of solace she has in that blasted house?" he asked, pointing back at Whitley Court, which stood behind them, looking far too serene. "She loves music more than anything, and you have taken that from her. Can you truly stand there and say she deserves that all because she bruised your family's pride?"

Straightening, Benjamin lifted his chin in a defiant manner that was so like his sister, though his friend's gaze darted across the lawn and yard—avoiding David.

"Again and again, she forces herself into the public eye, parading her abysmal talent about and subjecting herself to mockery. Ought we to encourage such destructive behavior?"

"Musicians cannot improve if they remain hidden in their parlors. She chooses pieces that are challenging, and yes, at times she fails mightily, and no, she will never match your eldest sister's skill. However, your sister is not as poor a pianist as you all believe her to be. Rather than joining in with her detractors, her family ought to applaud her attempts to improve."

Crossing his arms, he stared at Benjamin. "Did it never occur to you that perhaps others judge her playing so poorly because of your family's obvious disgust? And perhaps if you all applauded, rather than sneered, others might think kindly of her?"

Raising his brows, David spoke slowly as though explaining it to a child, which his friend was certainly acting like at present. "Better yet, did you never consider that she sacrificed her pride at the concert to save others that pain? And perhaps this was not the first time she has done so?" Not bothering to wait for an answer, he continued, "Ah, no. Instead, you simply dismiss her as the family pariah and punish her, rather than treat her with dignity and understanding. Good gracious, man!"

David threw his arms wide, his voice rising. "You stand there, cloaking yourself in virtue as though you are the injured party, but this has nothing to do with the concert or your family's overblown pride. I heard all about your matchmaking with Mr. Tryck, and you deserved the tongue-lashing she gave you. Frankly, she showed great forbearance. You toss horrid men at her, expecting her to graciously accept them since she cannot hope for better, and then you act affronted when she is wounded by your low opinion of her."

Heat suffused the ice, burning it away as the enormity of all that had occurred crashed down upon him. All Miss Leigh had suffered. And all alone. Nary a friend or companion to help her through the past few days. Even the one person in her family who had treated her with a modicum of kindness now sneered at the thought of her.

Miss Leigh was truly alone at Whitley Court. So few in the world spared a passing thought for the poor lady, and she deserved so much more.

Benjamin shifted in place, drawing David's attention back to the blackguard. The furrows of his brow deepened, and when the young man spoke, his voice was far less certain than before. "Katherine brought this upon herself."

"If you can say that whilst looking me in the eyes, then I might believe your indifference. But you know you and your parents are wrong on all accounts."

"I will admit our actions might seem a bit harsh, but you do not understand how frustrating Katherine can be," said Benjamin, finally deigning to meet David's gaze.

"You are correct, sir. I do not. I cannot. She is engaging, intelligent, witty, and loyal, and I am honored to count her as one of my closest friends—and you would feel so, too, if you bothered to know her!" David stared at Benjamin for a long moment. "What has she ever done to deserve such poor treatment?"

Letting out a sharp sigh, his friend turned on his heels and marched down the drive. "She makes it impossible! Believe it or not, I care deeply for her. She wasn't merely a sister to me—until she turned into this harpy."

David hurried to catch his friend and pulled him to a stop. "Explain yourself."

"What does it matter?" asked Benjamin with a scowl before turning to head towards the stables.

"Move again, and I shall brain you. Clearly, this is troubling you both, and as you two are my dearest friends, we're not leaving this spot until you elaborate."

Tossing his hat down, Benjamin sighed and followed it to the ground. He leaned against a tree whilst his gaze drifted towards the gardens and lawn stretching around Whitley Court. David lowered himself to the grass and waited as they sat in silence for several long moments.

"When I was a child, Katherine was my favorite sister," said Benjamin. "I adored Prudence as well, but she was more of a mother than a friend. Rosanna and Francis were always too occupied with their own lives to pay close attention to their much younger brother. But Katherine was always so tender with me. She used to sneak into the nursery and read books with me. Then I left for school—"

"And did everything you could not to return home during the breaks," murmured David with a knowing raise of his brow.

Benjamin raised his brows in return with another sigh. "Wouldn't you? At school, I was given a view into a wider world and my place within it. If left to my parents' devices, I would've become a spoiled terror, but my dear teachers and headmaster taught me a better way to be. Yet when I returned home, it was too easy to revert to old habits and embrace the role of the pampered princeling. So, I avoided returning until school was over, when I was forced home for good. The one blessing to be found in that dismal prospect was reuniting with my sister..."

Reaching over, Benjamin plucked at the grass and frowned.

"And?" prodded David.

"And rather than the sweet Katherine I remember, she was cold and distant," said Benjamin, snatching up a handful of blades and tossing them to the wind. "She never speaks, unless it is to spout a biting remark or harp at others—even me."

Then, straightening, Benjamin met David's gaze. "I understand why she struggles with Mother and Father. They treat her horribly. But Prudence and Rosanna have both tried to extend a hand of friendship, and she rebuffs them constantly. I've seen it countless times. And felt it myself."

For all that David believed the Archers to be plagued with troubles, the more he came to know the Leighs, the more grateful he was for his family's foibles. Keeping Father from bankrupting them was trying, to be sure, but David had the skill and acumen to do just that. Exhausting, certainly. But manageable.

And that effort was handsomely rewarded by his mother's and sisters' affection. There was nothing he wouldn't do for them, and David's heart hummed happily at the knowledge that they felt the same. That he was tasked with so much of the family's trials and tribulations was merely a byproduct of his ability to manage such things.

Was it any wonder that the Archer ladies suffered from nerves when their futures were inextricably linked to such a careless patriarch? David had control of the business now, but if Father stirred himself, he could easily unseat his son and destroy their finances with little trouble.

The Leighs suffered from many of the same maladies but without the affection. Mr. and Mrs. Leigh pitted their children against each other in such a manner that it was a miracle any of them were on friendly terms. The more David came to know the Leighs in all their wretched glory, the more remarkable Miss Leigh became in his eyes.

And it was time that her brother understood why.

Chapter 23

Rising to his feet, Benjamin brushed off his trousers and turned towards the stables, as though that was the final word in their conversation; David narrowed his eyes but followed nonetheless. Coming up beside his friend, David tucked his hands behind him as they wandered around the house towards the stables.

"Have you ever considered what it was like for your sister to be raised in your family?" asked David.

"It wasn't easy on any of us," replied Benjamin with a shrug. "She may not believe our parents' doting to be a burden, but both Rosanna and I have suffered because of it."

David opened his mouth, but his friend held up a silencing finger and added, "Believe me, our previous conversation on the subject did not fall on deaf ears, and I have considered how the family treats Katherine. I see your point, and it chills me to see how our parents mistreat her. Even Francis often followed in Mother's footsteps. However, the rest of us have only ever tried to be her friend, and she is forever sniping at us. I am doing what I can to help her, and she is resentful of it."

With a neutral grunt that was neither affirmation nor condemnation, David considered just how to explain it. Though he didn't disagree with Benjamin's statement—all of the Leigh children had been broken by their parents in various ways—the wounds inflicted had left them with different scars.

"Irene once took in a stray dog that she found wandering a field at the edge of town," said David. "She didn't even hesitate to bring the starving beast home and was lucky the animal wasn't rabid or diseased in some manner. My sister simply saw a struggling creature and insisted on helping it."

Pausing to consider just how to word it, he felt Benjamin's attention on him, though the fellow remained silent as David gathered his thoughts. It had taken him a long time to understand this about Miss Leigh, and how did one distill two years of hard-won experience into a few minutes?

"It had clearly been a pet or hunting dog, but we could never discover where the animal had come from—not that Irene would've returned the creature to a home where it had clearly been beaten and neglected. She stuffed it full of food, bathed it, and coddled it as best she could."

David arched a brow as he glanced at his friend. "Or she attempted to. No matter how kind she was, the dog snapped and growled at her. Forever biting the literal hand that fed it."

Benjamin huffed and added in the tone of one who believed himself wise beyond his years, "And with time and patience, the creature eventually learned to trust Irene—"

"No." Turning to face his friend, David met his gaze and said, "Despite all her best efforts, the dog ran off some weeks later and disappeared. Irene searched all over for it, but we never discovered where it went. When a creature is so mistreated for so long, it can be impossible for them to trust kindness in any form."

"Katherine does have a difficult time of it, but it is a bit of a reach to say she is..." But Benjamin stopped as though he couldn't finish the sentence. His brow scrunched.

"And though you think your other sisters are kind to her, their assistance is always in the way they wish to help—not what Miss Leigh requires." David pointed himself towards the stables once more as Benjamin shuffled beside him. "I've seen Mrs. Tate reach out in friendship, but only to include Miss Leigh in her social circle—something that is extremely uncomfortable for her—rather than attempting to meet Miss Leigh on common ground."

David sighed. "And Mrs. Humphreys is hardly any better. Miss Leigh doesn't ask for assistance often because she is so often ignored or treated like a burden. So, when she does ask for something, it is not merely a passing fancy—it is a true cry for help. Yet I've seen Mrs. Humphreys and the rest of you dismiss her petitions because you judge them as less important than whatever is happening at that exact moment."

Stopping in place once more, David studied Benjamin. "Do you have any idea what it says to her that you think Mr. Tryck, Mr. Moody, or Mr. Pine is a good match for her? Because though she has said not a word of it to me, it's clear as day that your opinion is low."

"I didn't mean it like that," replied Benjamin with a heavy sigh.

"That is the point. You and your sisters are not purposefully cruel to Miss Leigh, but all those little signs make it clear how you view her. She is not dour or cruel. She is reserved and slow to trust, but once you win that trust, she is loyal and giving. If she is willing to embarrass herself publicly simply to help people she hardly knows, what do you think she would do for someone she adores?"

Benjamin huffed, throwing his arms wide. "It's not that I don't adore her. My actions of late have proved that."

Though it took significant effort, David didn't scoff or laugh at that statement. Ludicrous though it was, his friend meant it. Such honest conversations were always delicate and needed to be handled carefully. So, instead, David studied his friend as he thought through the last few weeks. Though there was little (or rather nothing) to support that assertion from an outsider's perspective, he grasped onto the only thing that might be considered brotherly concern.

"Are you talking about your sudden interest in her matrimonial state? Why are you so keen on it? You've never given it a second thought before."

More fidgeting as Benjamin shrugged. "I want to see her settled."

David narrowed his gaze. "Out with it."

Drawing in a deep breath, Benjamin sighed. He nodded towards the stables. For all that they'd been out of doors for some time, they'd made little progress toward their destination.

"I am nearly one and twenty," he finally said.

As that was something they both knew, it required no response, so David waited as his friend gathered his thoughts.

"My entire life, my parents have spoken of the time when I would finally reach my majority and break the entail on Whitley Court, for they cannot without my assistance," said Benjamin, tucking his hands behind him.

With a frown, he shook his head. "I know what is expected of me, yet I know it would be a mistake. Our family is not in dire straits. We do not need to sell off bits of the property to live comfortably, yet Father is already planning to dispose of several small transactions to fund an expansion of his library. Mother wishes to improve the drawing room to host larger parties. Each time they speak of the changes, they couch them as though it will have little impact on the estate's health as a whole, but I cannot trust that they won't continue to do so until there is nothing left of our family's legacy."

As they had spoken of that subject many times, David merely nodded and waited for Benjamin to arrive at the point, all while hoping this trail of thought was heading in the direction he anticipated. This was Benjamin's life and decision, to be sure, but David knew what he hoped his friend would choose.

"I do not wish to break the entail," said Benjamin with yet another heavy sigh, his shoulders dropping. "Grandfather placed it on the property knowing he needed to protect it from Father, and I do not think it is right to go against that decision for no better reason than that my parents aren't content with what they have. Father keeps insisting that isn't the case, but Grandmother Cora spoke to me about it on more than one occasion. Sometimes she joined Katherine in the nursery, and she'd speak of the future, begging me to be strong enough to stand against my parents."

David sucked in a sharp breath. If his memory served him correctly, the old Leigh matriarch had passed some ten years ago, which would make Benjamin only ten years old at the time. Good gracious, who would place such a burden on a child?

Yes, the Leighs certainly had caused damage to all their children.

Lifting a hand to his forehead, Benjamin rubbed at it. "If I tell them no, I am afraid of what they might do to persuade me otherwise. I fully expect to be cut off, so I am considering my options at present, and with the assistance of my brothers-in-law, I am certain I shall be able to find a position. But if my parents set their sights on Katherine, I will give them what they want. Whatever our relationship at present, she shouldn't be made to suffer, and Father has all but stated he will cast her out if I refuse to break the entail."

And what did a fellow say to that? For all that he felt he knew Benjamin, and for all that the fellow often spoke of his troubles, David was surprised to hear such a thing. Despite his low opinion of Mr. Leigh, he hadn't anticipated such coldness—but in the same vein, it was entirely fitting. Though not familiar with all the details, David had heard enough whispers to know that Mr. Leigh had schemed to ensure his loveliest daughter married well, even at the cost of his elder daughter's feelings.

Despite Benjamin's poor execution, his intentions had been well-meaning. But it was said that they paved the road to hell, so it was little surprise that his plan had crumbled so spectacularly.

"I am her brother, and it is my responsibility to ensure she is protected, but I will be in dire straits myself and unable to care for her," he said, his brows pulling tight together. "Francis treats Katherine as poorly as our mother. Prudence hasn't the space in her house for Katherine. Rosanna has the means, but the two of them are always at odds, and it isn't Malcolm's responsibility to take on his sister-in-law. The best solution would be for Katherine to settle in her own home. She ought to have that. I think it would make her happy."

Raising a challenging brow, David said in a sharp tone, "Her music makes her happy, yet you are relieved that your parents ripped it away from her."

Benjamin's mouth opened as though to refute the remark, but no sound came forth. His brows furrowed slightly as though considering it, but they pulled tighter together with each passing second.

"I hadn't thought of it in such a light."

Clearly, he hadn't, but now that the seed was planted, there was no use in pressing the issue. So, David turned back to the conversation proper.

"Have you spoken to her about your concerns and this plan?" he asked, refraining from calling said plan either "foolhardy" or "ludicrous."

"And burden Katherine with it?"

Miss Leigh's words concerning her escape plan rang in his ears, but that was a confidence he couldn't share. Not that he knew enough for the information to be of any value. Yet it was clear that Benjamin was making a mighty mistake planning for his sister's future without consulting her.

And so he told him.

"Speak to her, Benjamin. I assure you that she is curt at times and may be slow to trust you entirely, but I believe she is eager to do so." Something was keeping her at Whitley Court, and as David considered it, he couldn't help but wonder if the motivations of both brother and sister were aligned. "I believe she has an idea for her future that doesn't include marrying the likes of Mr. Tryck."

"I have tried speaking with her in the past—"

"No. Not truly."

Chapter 24

They paused once more, but at least they'd reached the stables proper. The grooms moved about, readying the horses as he considered what to say.

Drawing in a deep breath, David said, "You say you've given her no reason to distrust you, but I would ask you if you've ever given her reason to trust you. How many times have you sought out her company? Searched for some common ground between you and her? Been eager to see her, rather than allowing her to join us simply because I asked it? I promise you are not as subtle as you think yourself to be, and she is far more perceptive than any of you give her credit for."

For all that his words were entirely true, David couldn't help a pang in his heart as he considered his feelings when they'd first met. Though he had never disliked Miss Leigh as so many others did, it had been more compassion than desire that had pushed him to reach out to her with the hand of friendship. And thank the heavens his conscience had prodded him to do so.

Benjamin kicked at the ground, digging into the grass with the heel of his boot as he stared at his feet. "You are my friend. That means you ought to take my side over hers, you know."

"She is my friend as well," said David, cutting his words short before he admitted the full truth, for if he was forced to rank the two, Miss Leigh would certainly take the premier position.

Benjamin's friendship was a blessing, to be sure, but it was vastly different from what he shared with Miss Leigh. The young man was still only twenty years of age, and David felt far older than his own seven and twenty. A man didn't become the head of the household at sixteen without maturing quickly, and Benjamin had much more growing to do.

The world was forever about to collapse around them. Benjamin's troubles were always insurmountable and cataclysmic. Though his friend was level-headed enough to accept good advice when given, David's role was far more that of a mentor than a peer. The truest of friendships required a give and take, and he couldn't say that Benjamin offered as much of the former as he did the latter.

But that wasn't a confession to be shared. Thankfully, the fellow accepted David's statement with no further argument.

With a nod, the pair strode towards the stables and their waiting mounts, but if David had thought to enjoy an easy ride, he was sorely mistaken; Benjamin pushed them and the horses hard as the young man tried to work out his troubles. Unfortunately for David, it did little to quell his unease. Despite the physical toll it took, both on his muscles and concentration, he couldn't stop his mind from drifting to Whitley Court and Miss Leigh.

A sennight's separation was hardly evidence that the lady was avoiding him, but that niggling concern he stuffed into the back recesses of his thoughts lunged forward as he considered her behavior at the concert. Something wasn't right between them. Despite his best efforts to speak to her, Miss Leigh had snuck away without ever deigning to acknowledge him.

David supposed that was understandable if Benjamin had spent the evening hounding her about Mr. Tryck, but Miss Leigh hadn't even smiled at him or waved back when he'd drawn her attention. She was by no means a demonstrative lady, but he knew the signs and hadn't seen a single flicker of pleasure in her gaze when she'd looked at him.

Despite scouring his memories, David couldn't think of anything he'd done or said to deserve such cold treatment. The story of Irene's dog sprang back into his thoughts, but he quickly quashed the fear nipping close on its heels. His friendship with Miss Leigh hadn't been the easiest to cultivate, but they were well past the time when she'd snapped at his metaphorical fingers.

Not wishing to damage their mounts, the pair forced themselves into a slow walk, and both horses and riders were breathing heavily. Benjamin made no move to break the silence, and David was quite content with that.

Only a sennight, and he missed Miss Leigh. It was a strange thought, but a true one nonetheless, and he couldn't say that he felt that way about any other friend.

"What does this fantasy lady have that is so much better than a lady whose company you crave and whose opinion you value?" Benjamin's question surfaced from the hidden depths of his thoughts. Though David had been dismissive of it at first, the blasted thing had continued to resurface.

David shifted in his seat and adjusted the reins in his hands, ruining the proper grip he had and forcing him to settle the straps of leather back where they'd been. Reaching over, he rubbed Brutus's neck, and the beast shook his head.

There was no denying that Miss Leigh was his dearest friend. Though other gentlemen might scoff at giving a lady that designation, David preferred her company over any number of his peers. Though his actions hadn't been deliberate, he couldn't deny that it was no surprise that he'd ended up at her side at the Hyatts' picnic. She was his calm in the storm.

Thinking of Miss Leigh in such a manner brought a smile to David's lips, for she was not a peaceful and serene creature. Her exterior hid so much fire in her soul, and for all that her own family believed her heartless, David knew she possessed one of the strongest and truest hearts he'd ever known.

So, why was he seeking out another lady?

Benjamin's question had surprised him at the time. Between the possibility of his having raised expectations and the damage it might've done to Miss Leigh's reputation, David hadn't been of the proper mind to truly consider the whole of that question when first posed.

The world labeled Miss Leigh plain. His heart twisted at that cruel descriptor, for it was entirely inaccurate, and he had never thought of her in such terms. Yes, she was far too thin for fashion's liking, but Miss Leigh had a regal bearing that suited the lithe frame. And her chin was prominent, but it made it all the more amusing when her feathers were ruffled and she jutted the thing out like a weapon. Her spectacles may be a bane to her mother, but they suited Miss Leigh, adding an extra sparkle to her gaze whilst she was delivering a dry retort or jest.

No, she wasn't plain by any means. But did she inspire a burning desire?

Attraction wasn't the premier consideration for a wife. Friendship was a far stronger foundation for a marriage, and David wanted a wife who was first and foremost his confidant and companion. However, that did not mean that passion was unimportant.

That was the missing piece that his Mystery Lady possessed. An attraction of body and mind. A desire for companionship and kisses. Not adoration or affection, but a perfect blending of the two. Their tokens shared in the garden weren't mere trifles, and a man would be a fool if he gave up on finding such a lady. David cared deeply for Miss Leigh, but he wanted a spouse who stirred his blood—they both deserved that.

For all that Benjamin spoke cavalierly as though it was a simple matter of David deciding to take Miss Leigh for his bride, he'd never considered her in such a light before. And having spent a fair amount of time considering the past, David felt confident that Miss Leigh had no romantic intentions, for she certainly had given no sign that she desired anything beyond their platonic relationship.

They were friends, nothing more—though even that was suspect at present, for Miss Leigh was most determinedly ignoring him at present.

David's ribs constricted, squeezing his heart anew as he considered all that she had suffered of late all on her own. That was a friend's role, after all. Protector and supporter. David hadn't been able to protect her from her parents' machinations, and now she wouldn't allow him to comfort her through those trials, either.

Drawing in a sharp breath, David clenched his jaw and leaned forward, urging his mount back into a gallop. Benjamin followed, though he strained to keep up as the two tore across the hills surrounding Greater Edgerton. Only when the pair were both well and truly exhausted did they return to Whitley Court.

Despite the speckles of dirt and mud coating his riding jacket and breeches and the ripe smell of horse enveloping him, David approached the house and asked after Miss Leigh—who was still not at home. Nor was she anywhere to be found the next morning. And the following afternoon, she was resting and not to be disturbed. A visit to Mrs. Kitts was the next excuse given, though when David lingered along the path Miss Leigh would've taken home, she never appeared. Then a megrim made it impossible for her to meet him in the parlor.

Had it been her mother or his, David wouldn't have questioned the excuses; those ladies were forever flitting about town or laid low by dramatics and frail constitutions. However, it was a miracle Miss Leigh hadn't expired with all the various maladies afflicting her of late.

And when the maid stood before him with yet another excuse, David stared at the girl.

"Smallpox *and* scarlet fever?" he asked in a monotone.

"Yes, sir. She said she is suffering from a bout of both," she said with a bob, her voice quivering. "And a touch of consumption."

David huffed and nodded at the maid, turning on his heel. As he strode out the front door and glanced back at the house, he saw the curtains flutter at her bedchamber window. Even a fool would understand Miss Leigh's dismissal, but she was the greater fool if she believed he would surrender.

If she was truly set against him, he would respect that. Miss Leigh was not one to mince words and would tell him to leave her be if she truly wished it, but he recognized this behavior easily enough. However, he didn't know what he'd done to damage her trust; he would simply have to think of a way to lure her out.

The corner of her curtains pulled back, just enough for a set of brown eyes to peek out at him from her bedchamber window. David met her gaze and lifted his hat to dip into a deep bow. When he straightened, she was gone.

Turning on his heel, he marched down the drive, the gravel crunching beneath his heels as a vague outline of a plan formed in his mind.

Chapter 25

Whilst walking the streets of Greater Edgerton, there were plenty of subjects that could occupy Katherine's thoughts. The streets were clogged with people and commerce, all vying for attention as they wove down the lane. Movement and sound surrounded her, offering plenty of distractions, but as her feet trudged along the pavement, Katherine couldn't turn her thoughts from spiders.

In her younger years, she had nursed an interest in nature and read many books on the subject. Though she'd abandoned it soon after, her efforts had stuffed her mind with an assortment of tidbits concerning the world around her, including those eight-legged pests.

Katherine couldn't stand the creatures when they crossed her path in the real world, but from the confines of a book, they were fascinating. Despite having seen plenty of examples, she still found it impossible to believe they were able to weave such delicate webs, stretching out to trap their prey.

And at present, she felt a close kinship to the flies and insects trapped in their sticky embrace. Of course, those poor things didn't see the web until they were held tight, and Katherine was well aware of the one she was walking into.

Pausing on the street corner, she watched as crowds passed her by. Carts filled with goods of every sort lumbered by, whilst riders and coachmen attempted to navigate around the hulking beasts. There were no vendors in this area, and Katherine rather thought the air seemed empty without their cries drawing in potential customers—though there was a bakery a street over, pouring the heavenly scent of baked breads and sweet things into the air. Perhaps she ought to stop and enjoy a treat.

Shaking herself free of that thought, Katherine continued on her way, weaving between the people and vehicles. To dawdle would only increase the possibility of being caught in Mr. Archer's well-laid trap, though she was fairly certain she wouldn't escape. Not indefinitely, at any rate. The enticement was too great, and they both knew it.

Katherine clutched her reticule and felt the crinkle of paper. Bringing the note was entirely unnecessary, but she hadn't been able to leave it behind. Just to be certain.

As it was unseemly to call on a bachelor and she hardly knew the rest of his family, Katherine had never visited Stratsfield House before—though she knew its precise location. Weaving down the streets, she moved deeper into town. She hesitated only a moment before she knocked on the front door.

"Yes, miss?" asked the maidservant as she opened the door.

Katherine's throat tightened. Ought she to present the maid with the letter? Or simply state her business there? Despite having settled on doing the latter, she found it difficult to form the words. But she forced herself to speak.

"I am Miss Katherine Leigh."

The girl's eyes brightened, and she bobbed. "Yes, of course, miss."

Ushering her in, the maid divested Katherine of her bonnet, gloves, and cloak before leading her down a corridor and up a set of stairs. Pushing open a door, the maid led her into a drawing room with a few high-back chairs scattered around the edge of the empty space.

In one corner sat a piano, and Katherine stepped closer, her hands resting atop the polished lid. It was not as fine as her family's had been (for though Mama couldn't play well herself, it wouldn't do to have an inferior instrument residing in her home), but as her hand drifted across the silky wood and touched the keys, she knew the Archers' piano was clearly well maintained. Plinking a single note, she listened as it rang through the silent house.

"Mr. Archer said you were to have free use whenever you wish and are not to be disturbed, miss. He had it tuned and polished for you," said the maid. Then, motioning to the far wall, she added, "And should you wish for any refreshment, simply give the bell a pull."

Katherine nodded, for she was certainly unable to speak. The door closed behind the servant, leaving her alone. Having spent a fortnight avoiding Mr. Archer, it was strange to be standing in his family's home. It was thoroughly selfish to ignore the gentleman and then immediately accept his invitation, but Katherine hadn't the strength to deny the pull of the instrument. Sitting herself before it, she let one hand drift across the smooth surface of the keys.

For all that she'd seized control over her feelings, Katherine couldn't help the prickle in her eyes as she dropped her reticule to the floor and raised both hands. Despite trusting Mr. Archer's note, her hope had been too fragile for Katherine to bring music with her and tempt fate. Thankfully, she had enough of a repertoire in her head that she didn't require the sheets.

Beginning with a few easier compositions, Katherine allowed her fingers to acclimate to the new instrument. For all that every piano boasted the same eighty-eight keys across roughly the same keyboard, each instrument had its own touch, and it was not always easy to adapt to the different feel.

But soon, she settled into music, drawing deeper into her repertoire.

Beethoven's style required too delicate a touch for Katherine to master it for public consumption, but that did not mean she did not indulge in it whilst in private. The slow melody poured out of her fingers, moving up and down the keys as the notes swept her away. The faster movements of the sonata were better suited for her talents, but the lilting quality of the piece gentled her teeming heart, allowing her to breathe for the first time since her parents' edict had ripped her piano away.

Closing her eyes, she allowed her fingers to move of their own accord, focusing entirely on the emotion of the piece—poor though her delivery may be. There was such inherent sadness to the music that it was little wonder the piece was titled "Pathétique," for her pathetic soul felt that melancholy in every note. Yet as she drew to the end of the movement, there was a moment of brightness: trilling little notes that gave the piece new life. Even in the darkness it painted, there was a small light of hope.

The final chord was meant to be held for only one count and a half, but Katherine kept her fingers in place, ignoring the rests that would cut it short and allowing the sound to linger for several heartbeats. When she lifted her hands from the keys, applause broke the silence, and before she turned, she knew what she would find.

Mr. Archer stood in the doorway, his hands outstretched as he clapped, a far too satisfied smile resting on his lips. But Katherine couldn't help but notice that despite his casual pose, his chest was heaving as though he'd run a great distance.

She refused to smile at that.

"Brava, Miss Leigh," he said, doing a passable job at hiding the winded quality of his words.

"Did you run all the way from the mill?" she asked, turning her gaze back to the keyboard.

"As I knew you would only come if you thought I wouldn't be there, I asked that the servants send word the moment you arrived," he said, looking entirely unrepentant. "Good thing, too, for I was ready to storm your bedchamber and drag you out if you turned me away one more time."

For all that the sentiment made her heart leap in her chest,

Katherine couldn't smile as he intended. She closed her eyes and drew in a deep breath. She had known this moment was coming. One couldn't visit a gentleman's home and not expect to see him at some point.

"My invitation was in earnest," he quickly added as his voice drew closer. "As Mother and my sisters are often around, there is nothing untoward about you visiting, and you may use the piano whenever you wish."

Mr. Archer drew into her peripheral vision, though Katherine forced her eyes to remain on the keys.

"Though I hope you will speak to me on occasion," he added with a slight chuckle that felt as forced as this "chance" encounter.

And this was the precise reason she had avoided him for so long. Mr. Archer was too kind for her good. Or for her heart's good, at any rate. How did a lady answer such a petition? And with such an offering laid before her?

"I know you've been avoiding me, though I do not know what I have done to offend you," he said, resting a hand on the edge of the instrument. Katherine couldn't bring herself to look at him directly, but her gaze couldn't move from those fingers.

"I've spent countless hours considering what may have happened, and I haven't the foggiest notion. I am sure there is a good reason behind it—please tell me what it is, so I can remedy it," he said with another forced bit of lightness. There was a long pause before he murmured, "I have missed you greatly."

Drawing in a sharp breath, Katherine forced her gaze to the window. If he had said anything else, it would've been easy to maintain her distance. But hearing Mr. Archer assume all the responsibility made her chest tighten.

What had he done wrong, precisely? What sins had he committed that were worthy of her cutting him from her life? He did not want her as a sweetheart, and that was no capital offense. It deserved no censure. He was quite free to throw his heart into loving as he wished, and it was unfair of Katherine to punish him simply because her silly heart desired more.

"I apologize, Mr. Archer," she whispered, shaking her head before turning to face him, though she couldn't raise her gaze to meet his. "I have been out of sorts lately, and I bear the blame for it—not you."

And never were truer words spoken. Katherine's heartbreak was of her own making. What did Mr. Archer have to apologize for? Though his reaction had stung, it hadn't been maliciously meant. For goodness' sake! Her eavesdropping had caused the fracture. Mr. Archer had never intended to tell her directly that he found her unappealing.

With each passing day, her anger ebbed, and reality settled back into place—right where it ought to have been. Katherine couldn't lay an ounce of fault on his shoulders. Mr. Archer had treated her with respect and decency, and that did not make him obligated to fall madly in love with her.

No, her ridiculous dreams and hopes had been of her own making. Mr. Archer had never asked for more than friendship, and yes, he was a blind fool for not recognizing her as the Mystery Lady, but what did that signify? She was the fool who refused to speak up and tell him the truth, so their sins balanced each other out.

Friends. That was all.

And that was no small thing. So few people wished to fill that role in her life, and each was all the more precious for it. Was she truly willing to cast him aside simply because of her bruised pride? Especially after she'd treated him so shabbily of late, and his response was to offer a new piano to replace the one her parents had stolen from her.

"What has you so out of sorts?" asked Mr. Archer.

For all that Katherine had known he would ask that, she had no ready answer. Reaching for the keys, she struck up a new song, and though she ought to have chosen a livelier tune, it was a somber piece that matched her mood far too well.

Chapter 26

Head bent low, Miss Leigh closed her eyes and sank into the music. For all that she claimed she did not play well, it was entrancing to watch her. Perhaps he ought to drag Benjamin over to hear one of these private sessions; anyone seeing her thusly couldn't walk away thinking she was aloof or unfeeling.

But then, perhaps that was the trouble. Miss Leigh was not a demonstrative lady. Life had taught her to guard her heart well, and one could not play such music without giving others a window into those hidden parts of one's soul. David's heart thumped in time with the rhythm, slow and languid as he considered just how lucky he was that she allowed him to see her in such a vulnerable state.

A gentle smile stretched his lips as her expression softened, her brows drawing together as though searching for something within the notes. It was lovely and heartbreaking all at once to see her find such contentment in a thing when life offered her so few joys. The longing and sadness blended together into a bittersweet melody. Her features softened, shining with the sentiment she so often kept locked away.

The song was stirring, filling his heart with a warmth that

he'd been without for far too long. When it wound to a close, she opened her eyes and stared at the keys.

"You may think to avoid the question, but I shan't be put off. As I was made to bear the brunt of your fury, surely you should divulge the cause," he said.

Miss Leigh huffed and turned an arch brow to him, and David couldn't help but grin at the sight of her tartness sparking there. "Ah, I owe you, do I?"

Holding a hand to his heart, David nodded. "You have wounded me grievously, my lady. Surely that has earned me a bit of honesty."

Her expression fell, and he cursed his wayward tongue.

"Ignore me if I am making matters worse, Miss Leigh."

Shaking her head, she met his gaze, her eyes so full of sadness that David's ribs squeezed his heart. "No, Mr. Archer. I apologize for how I have behaved of late. It has been quite unfair of me. And though I appreciate your offer of assistance, I fear I cannot accept."

David's brows pulled low. "Surely there is something I might do to help."

"You have your family's mill to oversee in secret, your mother and sisters all demanding your attention, your father constantly causing megrims, and do not think for one moment that I do not recognize just how much my own brother relies on your wisdom. And that is all without even considering your own personal troubles. That is quite enough for one person, Mr. Archer," she said, straightening. "I assure you I can manage on my own."

"I know you can, which is precisely why I enjoy assisting you, Miss Leigh," he said with a wan smile. "You are quite capable of managing alone, so it isn't an obligation. I am simply allowed the pleasure of doing so because I can. Am I making sense?" David wasn't sure, for in many ways it was insensible. However, it was true. Helping Miss Leigh was never a burden.

"That is kind of you," she said, turning back to the keys and striking a few chords. "And I assure you, the offer of your piano has done more to help than anything else."

Straightening, David watched her. "Truly?"

Miss Leigh's gaze rose to his as her hands moved across the keys, her eyes bright, though he knew all too well that she would not allow those tears to fall.

"Truly," she whispered. "I feel as though I can breathe again."

"Good," he said with a nod. Far from the imagined burden Miss Leigh believed she was, it felt as though one had lifted, leaving him all the lighter. "You are free to come as often as you want. My mother and sisters enjoy music, and I suspect Flora will enlist you to accompany her often, if you will allow it."

"As often as she wishes," she replied.

They lapsed into silence, though Miss Leigh's music filled the void. David didn't recognize the song, but then, with his limited understanding of music, it wasn't surprising. Resting his right arm against the instrument, he watched Miss Leigh as she slipped back into serenity, and a flicker of anger flared to life within him at the thought that Mr. and Mrs. Leigh had stolen this away from their daughter.

But it was quickly followed by another squeeze of his heart at the thought that he had been able to return it to her. Whatever other burdens she may bear, David swore she would never be made to bear the loss of her instrument again.

"I haven't had the opportunity to offer up my thanks," he said.

Miss Leigh's eyes popped open, though her fingers didn't pause as they ran along the keys. "For refusing to see you?"

David smiled at that, though it had less to do with the jest itself as it did the fact that she was making any lighthearted remark. In truth, the past few days had not been pleasant ones, and it would be some time before he could laugh at them. If ever.

"For your assistance with Flora at the concert. She did a fine job, but I know she would've only remembered her mistakes. However, you guaranteed that no one, including herself, could."

Miss Leigh's gaze dropped to her keys, and though her complexion showed no signs of it, David was certain that if she were wont to blush, she would be quite red at present.

"How do you know it wasn't a mistake?" she asked.

"I am surprised anyone else believed it was an earnest performance," he replied with a chuckle. "I've heard you play many times, and even at your worst, you could never do that by accident. Besides, it is just like you to sacrifice your own dignity to help someone else. You are a good friend to me, Miss Leigh."

Miss Leigh's hands stilled on the keys, her brows furrowing. "That is kind of you to say, but I didn't do it for you, Mr. Archer."

David straightened, but before he could say a word, she waved it away and returned to her playing.

"Not that I did not wish to help your sister, but every performer following Mrs. Turley felt the strain of following that impossibly high standard and was bound to flounder because of it," she said with a shake of her head.

"And so, you set an impossibly low standard to counteract it," he said with a chuckle.

"I wanted to make certain no one could do worse than me; thus, there would be no need for them to fret," she said with a lift of a single shoulder. "A concert is entertainment, both for the performers and listeners, and it was thoughtless of Mrs. Garrison to do what she did."

Whatever mirth he'd been feeling fled as David considered just what she was saying. Miss Leigh's actions hadn't been motivated by friendship. It wasn't Flora she'd been saving.

No, Miss Leigh had opened herself up to public mockery, knowing she would pay a high price, to help all the other musicians—including many who had not treated her with kindness. Those people were going about their days, unaware of the price Miss Leigh had knowingly paid. And she didn't expect them to ever acknowledge it.

In all honesty, David didn't know if he had the fortitude or

kindness of spirit to do such a thing. The lady was truly remarkable.

Miss Leigh's lips pinched together, and she lifted her gaze
to his with a hint of her usual laughter brightening her eyes.
"And I will admit it was exceptionally entertaining to annoy all
those people in the audience who sat there, criticizing the performers when they, themselves, have not a shred of talent or
ability."

That brought about the first genuine laugh David had given
in some days. Though a smile flitted across Miss Leigh's face for
the briefest of moments, her hands paused once more, her gaze
falling down to the keys.

"Miss Leigh?" he prodded.

She shook her head and continued with her song, the notes
flowing from her memory to her fingers. Did she truly believe
that she could avoid yet another question from him? For all that
Miss Leigh was an intelligent creature, she did not learn
quickly.

"What is it, Miss Leigh?"

Hands stilling, she gathered them in her lap, lowering her
head as she stared at her fingers, entwined together. David
watched her, not willing to allow the moment to slip, but not
hurrying it along, either.

"Thank you," she whispered, her eyes bright with tears that
would not fall. Miss Leigh's eyes shone with her heart, as lovely
as any lady could ever hope to possess.

Again, David's soul lightened at the tenderness in her gaze.
He couldn't claim himself to be brilliant and possessing the
quickest of minds, but he knew all too well how well the world
had taught Miss Leigh to shy away from such vulnerability. That
she allowed him that glimpse into her heart filled his own with
such pleasure.

Yet still pain pulsed beneath that happy haze at the anguish
hidden in those brown depths; David could well imagine how
difficult the past few days had been for her.

"It is nothing. Hardly anyone uses it, and Mother and the

girls will enjoy the music."

Miss Leigh shook her head and dropped her gaze once more, gathering her nerves before raising her eyes and trying to speak, her voice wobbling the slightest bit.

"I wasn't referring to the piano—though I do appreciate that more than I can ever say. Thank you for not assuming the worst of me. For recognizing my performance for what it was. Mama won't stop speaking of it—" Miss Leigh's voice halted, and she drew in a deep breath.

"I shall never understand why your family is so determined to see you in such a poor light," he said, for there was no point in disagreeing with her. The Leighs had set their minds against her, and it seemed that no amount of evidence to the contrary would turn them from their path. "You are magnificent."

David stood at her side, watching as she withdrew into herself. With furrowed brows, he tried to understand it. What was troubling her so much that she had cut him from her life? And what was the escape she had planned? For the first time, David began to wonder if they were connected somehow.

Was she leaving soon? Wishing to cut ties with him as well as her family?

His stomach burned, and he found it difficult to draw in a deep breath. Inching closer, he wished he could hear the thoughts churning in her head. It was clear that her mind was never quiet, yet she rarely gave voice to it. Would she ever share it all with him?

David didn't know when he'd drawn so close, but he couldn't help it. But neither did he know when Miss Leigh had become such an integral part of his life. She was always nearby with a teasing comment and a wry smile, and the past fortnight had proven to him just how intertwined their lives had become. Despite having survived without her for years, now that Miss Leigh was a part of his life, his heart throbbed at the thought of her disappearing. And David knew she would not return to Greater Edgerton.

Hang convention, he would insist on writing to her—let

others make of it what they would, but he wasn't going to deny himself that little contact. Even if it wasn't enough.

Reaching out, he brushed a hand against her shoulder, drawing her gaze to his once more. Truly, he didn't understand why so many believed her to be a heartless creature, for anyone could see it shining there in her eyes. Her expression showed no other indicators, but he felt her heartbeat pulsing in those brown depths.

Her wide neckline allowed his fingers to brush against the skin of her shoulder, and David jerked his hand back, his face heating as he cleared his throat. There was friendship and there was being overly familiar, and he'd crossed that line. Even if it was to offer comfort.

"Would you play me your concert piece?" he asked with a crooked smile.

Her brows rose at that. "So you may hear it properly?"

"Heavens, no. They cut short your performance that night, and I wish to hear it in all its wretched glory."

Miss Leigh laughed, though it was closer to a snort, and she covered her mouth with a wince. "Dear me. I do not know if I shall ever be able to recreate that magnificence. Such magic cannot be recaptured."

"Oh, but I insist," he said, striding over to the far side of the room where a straight-back chair rested and dragging it to the piano's side. "Come now. Don't be coy."

Screwing up her face, she moved as though to slam down her hands on the keys, but softened it at the last moment, playing the piece as the composer intended, rather than her unique interpretation.

"I shan't abuse your instrument in such a manner," she said, glancing at him as he leaned in. "I didn't care two jots about Mrs. Garrison's instrument, but I refuse to treat yours so shabbily."

"No, it is only its owner you enjoy abusing."

Miss Leigh arched her brow. "At every opportunity."

Shifting his seat so that it was next to hers, David leaned

over to nudge her shoulder with his, causing her hands to slip. Which earned him a narrowed look as she continued, but it didn't stop him from doing so again.

"You are ridiculous, sir."

"At every opportunity, Miss Leigh."

Chapter 27

Every estate and property boasted soothsayers in the form of an ancient tenant or retainer with miraculous aches and pains guaranteed to predict the coming weather. Yet despite Greater Edgerton's best fortune tellers predicting a long and warm autumn, winter swept with a flourish.

Snow was nowhere to be seen, but the temperature was low enough that driving out was hardly an enjoyable occasion, even with hefty lap blankets and bricks warming their feet. But there were few avenues by which a gentleman could secure a lady's company without raising eyebrows, and an open carriage ride gave them a semblance of privacy.

And thank the heavens that was the case, for there was no one to witness this debacle with Mrs. Ellery.

With the reins wrapped around his hands, David guided the pair of horses down the narrow country lanes surrounding the town. Pulling to one side, he allowed a cart to pass before nudging the horses forward, and he cursed himself for having chosen a more sedate course.

If they were in the town, he could blame his silence on needing to concentrate as he drove. But beyond the occasional passing cart or carriage, there was no excuse when the conversation lapsed once more. David didn't recall such awkwardness at the concert, but that had been over a fortnight ago, so perhaps his recollection was hazy, or all the hubbub had hidden the fact that they had little to say to one another.

Taking both reins in one hand, David rubbed his face and forced his eyes open. Mrs. Ellery's gaze drifted to him as a yawn hit him hard enough that he couldn't stifle it.

"I apologize," he said with a grimace. "It is not you. The past few weeks have been exceptionally busy, with many long hours spent poring over my family's business."

For all that it was the truth, he couldn't help but think that it was far less difficult to keep his thoughts engaged when Miss Leigh or Benjamin was about.

"Think nothing of it," she said with a smile. "With your father absent, I do not doubt that many of his responsibilities have fallen on your shoulders, which must be difficult to manage without him to guide you. Besides, my husband was much the same. Forever burning the candle at both ends."

Ducking her face away from him, she added in a rush, "And now, it is my turn to apologize. I suppose it is uncouth to speak of him when driving out with another."

David ignored her statement concerning his father and shrugged away the rest. "I would find it more disconcerting if you never wished to mention him. Many are trapped in unhappy marriages, and I am glad to know that was not true of yours—however short it might've been."

Mrs. Ellery nodded, though she said nothing more. Her hands clenched the blanket draped across her lap, and she turned her attention to the passing trees as David stared down the road. With their branches and the fields bare, the world was stuck in what was the ugliest time of year. Neither autumn nor winter. Simply a brown, barren mess waiting for the snow to cover it in white.

Investing in the railroad in Manchester was a fine idea. Risky, to be certain, but as Mr. Cox thought it sound, David couldn't help but agree. All speculation was uncertain, but their man of business never put anything forward that was too precarious, and they had plenty of other investments to keep the loss (if there was one) to a minimum. That was good.

Another yawn struck, but he was able to suppress it.

Forcing himself back to the conversation, David scrounged his thoughts for something to say. "Do you read, Mrs. Ellery?"

"I am capable," she replied in a dry tone.

David glanced in her direction and found her smiling.

"I am glad to know your education was not neglected," he answered in kind. "But do you enjoy it?"

"I am fond of ladies' magazines, and I read any pamphlet I can get my hands on, but I fear novels are too expensive a pastime for me to indulge often." Pausing, Mrs. Ellery straightened with a wince. "Forgive me for being gauche. One of the basic tenets of polite conversation is not to mention money, but I fear it is too often on my mind for the topic not to slip out occasionally."

David nodded. "Quite understandable. Don't fret. I would much rather have an honest conversation than sit about discussing the weather. I cannot stand the pretense."

And it wasn't as though Mrs. Ellery's financial troubles weren't known. Her husband's income had never been great, and his untimely death hadn't improved matters. However, one didn't acknowledge such things—no matter how well-known they were. And as David considered it, he realized just how much he disliked the falseness of it all. It was little wonder that Miss Leigh was such a dear friend, for she avoided pretense as much as he.

Unless she was pretending to be a poor piano player. That was quite amusing.

Jerking his thoughts back to the present, David turned his attention to his companion again, but the young widow was staring off into the distance, her thoughts clearly wandering far from this moment as much as his. Surely that was not a good sign.

Four candidates for his Mystery Lady. Miss Hooper seemed a sweet enough girl when she managed to string three words together, and she was infinitely more suitable than Miss Lyons. And Mrs. Ellery was pleasant company, he supposed. But even when employing a generous dose of allowance for the difference in behavior, as Miss Leigh had suggested, none of them enticed David. Even if his Mystery Lady was more reserved without the mask, there was no way that any of these three could be her.

There was still Miss Sheridan, and with more consideration, David did think her the likeliest of the four. He supposed he would discover the truth tomorrow night, as he had it on good authority that the family had returned home and were to attend the Breadmores' party. That knowledge warmed his heart a touch, though it couldn't chase away the chill seeping into him with each passing mile.

David frowned at the road ahead, guiding the horses in their circuit around the town. A niggling thought warned he was being rude, and he ought to say something to Mrs. Ellery, but each subject he attempted fared as well as lighting a fire in the wind: conversation sparked for a bright moment before dying.

Shifting his reins again, David rubbed at his face. He'd been foolhardy to make this appointment today, for he was in no fit state to converse with the lady. To his thinking, friendship was an easy thing or it did not exist. Not that it didn't require effort at times, but such sputtering was hardly promising.

And foremost, David wanted a wife who was a friend and a sweetheart. Not one or the other.

Father was likely home by now. The thought made David's chest ache. Having him in residence was a double-edged sword; it was easier to curtail his antics whilst he was in Greater Edgerton, but maintaining the pretense that Mr. Thaddeous Archer was the master of Rawlston Mill took so much more effort. Father cared little either way, but too many of the gentlemen trusted the elder Mr. Archer's years over the younger's experience and sound judgment.

And it was beyond vexing to have everything humming

along at the mill, only to discover that Father had struck up a terrible deal with someone line Mr. Kellen.

A pox on Grandfather. Father's decisions in life were certainly his own, but had the old man insisted on Father taking more responsibility in his youth, perhaps things would not be so complicated for David. But the self-made man had wanted a gentleman for an heir and treated him as such, leaving Mr. Thaddeous Archer with the business sense of a horse. Perhaps less, for at least a horse was trainable. Father refused bridle or saddle.

Scrubbing at his face once more, David struggled to keep his eyes open. They felt as though they were made of lead, sinking lower despite his best efforts. But Mrs. Ellery remained silent at his side, providing no distraction from his exhaustion.

Thankfully, the town came back into view, and they quickly arrived at Mrs. Ellery's cottage. It was a small and simple building, though tastefully situated, with vines crawling up the sides and large bushes circling it, and in high summer when everything was blooming, it was a picture of tranquility. David needed a bit of peace, but instead, he was left struggling to know what to say to Mrs. Ellery as he helped her down.

"That was quite enjoyable," she said, though there was a tightness to her smile that belied her polite words.

"Thank you for joining me," he said with a nod.

Pausing on her doorstep, Mrs. Ellery held his gaze. "Perhaps we might go again?"

Only the mightiest exercise of self-control kept David from frowning. Though her question might be deemed a polite inquiry, the hope in her eyes testified that she was in earnest. Despite the fact that he would lay a large wager that she hadn't, in fact, enjoyed herself at all.

But then, a struggling widow had few options for securing her financial position, and with Mr. Ellery's debts, David doubted she could be discerning about her second husband—which sent a skitter of unease running down his spine, both for the terrible situation and that he might've given her reason to believe he would welcome such a transactional marriage.

Mrs. Ellery was pleasant enough, but David desired so much more.

"I fear the weather won't allow it," he said with a bow. "Though I have no doubt our paths will cross from time to time."

Mrs. Ellery managed not to frown, though his tone made his intention clear. Drawing in a deep breath, she nodded. "Certainly, Mr. Archer. I wish you well."

"And you, Mrs. Ellery." David turned and all but ran back to the carriage. Not every outing led to courtship, yet he still felt as though he'd pained her.

Blast this wretched business! How was a man to know a lady without an outing or two? Yet to do so gave rise to beliefs that too often left one of the pair hurting. But there was nothing to be done about it. That was the nature of courtship. Like its name, one could liken it to a boat that sank every time but once; as such, the mariners ought to be hesitant to take it out on open water.

David's thoughts swirled about, touching on Father, business, Mrs. Ellery, and his Mystery Lady, before settling once more on Miss Leigh and the many questions that surrounded her. So many aspects of his life were unsettled.

For all that he hadn't thought much about matrimony before the Mystery Lady swept into his life, he'd spent plenty of time considering the subject since then. That night at the masquerade, he'd been given a glimpse of something magnificent.

He knew no one comprehended why that evening had mattered so much to him, but only a few hours in her company had shown the Lady to be engaging and empathetic, understanding him better than any stranger ought. It was as though the bits of himself he'd shared had been lifted from his shoulders, borne up by more than him alone, allowing him to breathe as he hadn't done since taking the reins of his family's finances at the tender age of sixteen.

With so many depending on him, David had no desire to

add a wife to his burden, but in those few hours, he'd glimpsed the possibility of what being a marriage could be. A wife was a partner, not an obligation. And now that the hope had taken root in his heart, he couldn't turn it aside.

Was his Mystery Lady only a mirage? A mere trick of his addled wits? Or the desperate longing of his heart manifesting?

Shoulders falling, David forced himself to focus on the horses and guided them through the town, narrowly avoiding a few collisions as he struggled to keep himself awake. Thankfully, the grooms were on hand in a trice once he arrived home, and with heavy footsteps, he trudged through the front door.

Despite crossing Mrs. Ellery from the list of candidates, David felt no closer to an answer.

Chapter 28

"**D**avid?" called Mother's voice as he crossed the threshold, and heaven help him, he cringed and eyed the nearby stairs. But she called several more times, the sound coming closer as she hurried through the corridor. Emerging in the doorway to the parlor, she stared at him with wide eyes. "Have you read the newspaper?"

Drawing in a low breath, David held it for a count of three. He'd taken the newspaper with him to the mill this morning specifically to avoid this conversation. How had she gotten her hands on a copy?

"Do not worry yourself, Mother—"

"But the riots are growing worse!" she said, thrusting the paper at him and shaking it.

"They concern the farm laborers," he said with a shake of his head, tugging the paper from her grasp. "It has no effect on mills."

Not directly, at any rate. Such things were bound to send a ripple of changes and troubles outward, but that was why varied investments and large savings were so important. However, it was better to nip Mother's hysterics in the bud, rather than attempt to explain all he'd done to prepare the family.

"But your father is in the South. He decided not to return, despite his promise," she said, thrusting another scrap of paper at him. David didn't need to read it to know what it would say. He recognized the handwriting of his Father's valet; his father was fond of saying, "There is no need to waste one's time when a servant can do it."

Mother clutched it to her chest. "What shall we do if something happens to him?"

In truth, the absence of his expenditures would be a boon—though as quickly as David thought that, he cast it aside. Whatever his father's flaws, it wasn't fitting to think such dark thoughts.

"Can you not give your son a moment to breathe, Mrs. Archer?"

A small and simple statement, yet the tension in David's shoulders eased as Miss Leigh strode down the corridor, a tea tray hefted before her. With a gentle but unyielding nudge, she herded Mother back into the parlor.

"Does Mr. Archer spend his time in the fields?" said Miss Leigh as she set the tray on the table. Flora sat at the far side of the room, clutching her book, whilst Clarissa looked as teary as Mother. Thankfully, Irene was not present to add to the hysterics.

Mother took a seat and the cup of tea Miss Leigh offered. "Of course not."

"Then there is nothing to fear, Mrs. Archer. And you have a devoted son who will ensure all is well, so there is no need to work yourself into a dither and accost him when he has only just returned after a tiring day. The poor man looks ready to collapse."

David fought to keep his wince hidden whilst gathering his thoughts on how to smooth Mother's ruffled feathers after Miss Leigh's blunt comment.

But then something astonishing happened. For all that David considered himself a faithful man, he knew little of miracles. There were certainly tender little mercies he couldn't attribute to logic or reason, but a grand manifestation? Never. Until now.

Mother held her teacup close and straightened, her gaze fixing on David. With wide eyes, she set it aside and rose to her feet.

"Oh, you are absolutely correct, Miss Leigh. My dear boy. I do apologize," she said, coming to his side and nudging him towards a seat. "Do sit down. You look ready to expire."

But David couldn't do as bidden, for his attention was fixed on Miss Leigh, who was bustling about the parlor, handing out tea and biscuits with a little word here and there that was kind but firm. Only once the ladies were occupied with their refreshments and chatting of the Breadmores' upcoming party did Miss Leigh sweep over to him.

"Now is your chance to escape," she whispered. "Take it while you can."

Never one to turn aside sound advice, David spun on his heel and slipped away whilst Miss Leigh distracted the ladies. As quickly as he could, he moved through the corridors and up the stairs to his sanctuary. With the afternoon sun dipping in the heavens, the library's windows were full of golden light, making the room quite cozy, which was just what his chilled bones needed.

Grabbing a blanket left folded on the armchair, he dropped into the seat and leaned his head against the back whilst draping it across his lap. Just a few moments of quiet, and he would go down to relieve poor Miss Leigh, who had somehow been pressed into the role of caretaker to his fretful mother. As Miss Leigh had quite enough of that at home, it was hardly fair of him to add to her burden, but he needed a few moments to warm himself and rest.

David wasn't sure when or how, but despite his best efforts, he fell asleep—only realizing it when he was jolted awake when the library door opened. Bleary-eyed, he watched Miss Leigh manhandle a tray through the opening, belatedly realizing he ought to assist her only after she managed it on her own.

Leaving the door open, she bustled in and set the tray on

the small table beside him. With quick work, she had a plate of treats arrayed for him and a cup poured, which he gratefully took and sipped, allowing the hot liquid to work its magic.

"How is it that you've been conscripted into being an Archer family servant?" he asked with an arched brow.

"Your mother and sisters make an impressive press gang." There was no smile on her lips, but Miss Leigh's eyes shone with mirth as she took the seat opposite him.

David chuckled, nearly spilling his tea, and set the cup aside. "Is that so?"

"In truth, whenever I come to play, I often spend much of the afternoon with them. I had planned on leaving some time ago, but your mother was in such a state, I couldn't leave her."

Straightening, David frowned. "That is kind of you, Miss Leigh, but you are not their keepers, and it is not your responsibility—"

"I have enjoyed it, Mr. Archer," she said with a faint smile. Her gaze fell to her hands, and she fiddled with her skirts. "You have everyone demanding something from you, but I fear no one wishes anything from me. My own mother would be happy to see the back of me. For some reason I cannot fathom, your family has taken to me. As much as keeping your mother and sisters company was my excuse for staying, the truth is that I enjoy them."

Her gaze drifted from his to stare out the window, and her smile grew. "That I am able to relieve some of the pressure you are under is merely an added reward. All in all, being at Stratsfield House makes me feel as though I matter. That I am doing some good."

"You do matter," he said with a furrowed brow. "Greatly."

But Miss Leigh waved that away. "And what have you been up to today?"

David's lips thinned into a sharp line as he studied his friend, though he knew well enough that pushing the issue would do little good; Miss Leigh was blunt, but there were some subjects in which a gentle hand was required.

"Much of the same," he said, taking up his tea and cakes once more. Between bites, he shrugged. "The usual mess, though now I will have to spend some time hunting down my father and begging him to return, or Mother won't rest easy. And I just passed a miserable hour with someone who is most certainly not my Mystery Lady."

Miss Leigh's fingers clenched together. "Yes, I can imagine that would be frustrating."

"It is so vexing to have been given a glimpse of something wonderful, only to have it ripped away," he said with a sigh, discarding his dishes to the side.

"I can well imagine," she murmured.

But before David could say another word, Mother's voice rang through the corridors. "Katherine? Could you please play for us?"

Miss Leigh's gaze turned in that direction, her eyes brightening as she rose to her feet, but David caught her by the hand and stopped her before she left.

"You needn't go if you do not wish to. It is kind of you to take care of her, but it isn't your duty, and you shouldn't feel obligated..."But his words trailed off as her brows rose in challenge, a slight smirk curling her lips.

"For once, someone is requesting me to play, and you think I accept out of obligation?" she asked, and David grimaced at the ridiculousness of his assertion. Of course Miss Leigh would wish to do so. "And you needn't fear, Mr. Archer. I am quite comfortable with saying 'no' when I wish to, but hearing her words is as close to heaven as I can find in this world."

David smiled, nodded, and released her. Reaching over, Miss Leigh straightened the edge of the blanket and tucked it up to cover him better. With one final smile and a nudge of her glasses, she turned and hurried out the door, leaving him frowning at the empty library. A bit of solitude was precisely what he had wanted—but not this much.

But then, Miss Leigh wasn't company. And being with her was no burden. Quite the opposite.

What a wretched day. Three candidates eliminated, and only Miss Sheridan remained. Thankfully, their meeting tomorrow would provide the answers he sought. Hopefully.

But what if she proved as poor a choice as the rest? What would he do then? Was it time to simply surrender? Benjamin certainly thought so, but he'd made his indifference concerning David's search clear many times. As though it was a simple thing to ignore such an incredible connection and throw his heart into loving another.

As he contemplated that, the first notes of the piano sang through the house, and David rested his head against the back of the chair and listened to the melody. His breathing grew even and steady, and his eyelids lowered as her music lulled him into the sort of peaceful state he never seemed to find on his own.

For all that Miss Leigh was not an inherently tranquil person (she possessed far too passionate a heart for such a description, regardless the outward calm she projected), she had a way of bringing peace into his life. Her friendship was such a blessing.

"What does this fantasy lady have that is so much better than a lady whose company you crave and whose opinion you value?" Benjamin's question surfaced to plague him once more.

No doubt, it was merely coming to trouble him during a weak moment. Another failed attempt to find his Mystery Lady, only to arrive home and find his dear Miss Leigh slipping into his life with such ease. Naturally, he would question his present course in favor of the easier path. However, it didn't resolve the one lingering issue that stood between them.

Miss Leigh was a passionate creature, but she didn't inspire passion within him, nor he in her. They were merely friends. That was all.

Yet as the days had passed, David's thoughts returned again and again to her first visit to Stratsfield House. The image of her seated at the piano came quickly to his mind's eye, her gaze fixed upon him with such tenderness and feeling. Even the memory of it made his heart burn, filling him with a warmth he'd never attributed to the lady before.

And then, there was that touch.

David flexed his fingers, though that couldn't erase the feel of her skin. He'd only meant to comfort, but his cheeks reddened at the memory of his hand grazing that delicate shoulder.

Straightening, he allowed the blanket to fall away. Could he develop a tendre for Miss Leigh? Having never considered her in such a light, it felt like such a strange question to ask, but his pulse quickened at the thought of it.

Miss Katherine Leigh. His sweetheart?

Of course, it still didn't resolve the issue of her own feelings towards him—and he wasn't settled on any course of action in the first place—but it was a strange yet intriguing prospect. From the very first, his only true answer to Benjamin's question had been the issue of attraction, but if one were to remove that obstacle, what was left?

His Mystery Lady and Miss Leigh were indistinguishable.

David's brow furrowed, and he turned his gaze to the fireplace. The maid hadn't bothered lighting it as the family rarely graced the room in the afternoon, but his eyes weren't seeing it at any rate.

Benjamin had jokingly tossed his sister into the list of contenders, and the whole idea had seemed too far-fetched to consider. Yet as David compared the lady behind the mask and the friend he knew so well, there was little to differentiate the two. The Mystery Lady shared so many similarities with Miss Leigh that he couldn't help but linger for a long moment on that thought.

Yet it was impossible.

One month since the masquerade. The subject of the Mystery Lady had arisen many times during those four weeks, and not once had Miss Leigh given any indication that she knew the masked lady. David scoured his memory and couldn't think of any concrete sign. Surely that was evidence enough that they were two separate ladies.

Yet he knew his friend as well as anyone could boast, and

Miss Leigh was a cautious person, quick to hide her heart if she feared it might be hurt. Having him burst into their home the day after the masquerade speaking of some other woman whilst her family all laughed at her was certainly reason enough to guard that delicate part of her.

Was Miss Leigh his Mystery Lady?

It was a pleasant thought, for it would resolve David's troubles quite easily. The question of his attraction would be settled, and his Mystery Lady's response to that evening would remove any doubt as to whether or not Miss Leigh would welcome his advances. In truth, it wrapped up this quest in a nice and tidy package. Simple.

He let out a heavy sigh and sank into his seat once more; resting his hand against the arm of the chair, he drummed a rapid beat against blue fabric. The prospect was enticing but ignored reality and all the evidence set against it.

Miss Leigh hadn't been wearing fancy dress.

That was an indisputable fact.

He'd seen so with his own eyes.

And Miss Leigh's feelings were clear on the subject. For years, her family had attempted to force her into the frivolity, and never once had she bent to those attempts. Not only did she not approve the expense of the costumes, but Miss Leigh would never surrender her spectacles and embrace blindness for the evening; David couldn't imagine a scenario in which the lady would willingly make herself so vulnerable.

For all that it would be nice to resolve the question so easily, life was rarely so straightforward, and David couldn't deny the truth.

Miss Leigh couldn't be the Mystery Lady.

Chapter 29

"Forfeit!"

The single word echoed across throughout the Breadmores' drawing room, bringing with it a gale of laughter as Mrs. Leggatt stripped off her blindfold to discover that the gentleman whom she couldn't identify was her very own husband. Mr. Leggatt waggled his brows at her as she gaped at the man, shaking her finger at him whilst warning of the dire consequences that awaited him at home.

"Peace, my lady," he said, rising to his feet and giving her knuckles a buss as he offered her his seat and took her place in the center of the gathering.

"She isn't free yet," called Mr. Ewings.

But Mr. Leggatt silenced that with an arched brow, adding, "A husband knows when to throw himself on his blade. We'll be here all night paying back her forfeits if I do not."

His wife gaped and swiped a teasing smack at him, which he dodged before tying the blindfold around his eyes.

"You'd best check that it's firm," said Mrs. Leggatt, crossing her arms, though her eyes sparked with laughter. "He likes to cheat."

Mr. Leggatt gasped with all the drama of a stage actress, lifting up the blindfold to stare at his wife with mock-innocence. "I never cheat at Buffy Guffy. It is a very serious game, and I am offended that you would impugn my honor in such a way. It is unforgivable!"

Slipping the blindfold back in place, he stood in the center of the group, but Miss Breadmore swept up behind him, shifting her forfeit ledger under one arm as she tightened the bit of cloth and adjusted it to properly cover his eyes.

"Thank you for securing it," he said. "I would hate to be tempted to peek."

"Steady on," said Mr. Leggatt.

Miss Breadmore nodded at the circle of people all seated around him, and they quickly rose and shifted places, firmly scrambling their ranks. Stretching out his legs, David watched as Mr. Leggatt inched towards Mrs. Fitzgibbon, who struggled not to laugh. Holding her hands to her mouth, she stared up at Mr. Leggatt as he fumbled his way around the circle to stop before one of the players.

At his side, Miss Sheridan turned towards him. With a hand clasped over her mouth, her eyes were ablaze with a laugh, and David couldn't help but respond in kind. Despite having only spoken with her briefly before the games, it was clear she was a lively soul with a kind heart, and it was easy enough to enjoy her company.

Miss Sheridan reminded him of Mrs. Rosanna Tate. Not in looks, for though the young lady was quite pretty, she boasted dark ringlets and rich brown eyes as opposed to Mrs. Tate's fair coloring. However, she shared that lady's presence and magnetism—an ease around others that drew them to her like bees to honey. And for all that Mrs. Leigh had objected to the young lady's age, even a short conversation proved her to be intelligent, witty, and self-possessed, with the bearing of a lady beyond her years.

Mrs. Tate had been correct, and all the hours he'd spent with the other candidates only served to further the point. If any of the four were his Mystery Lady, it was Miss Sheridan. Even without that possibility, David would have found her appealing. Her easy manners, quick wit, and beauty all recommended her.

Miss Sheridan's eyes were aglow as she met his gaze, but when the group erupted in laughter, her attention was torn away from him.

David drew in a deep breath, his attention waning from the game as Mr. Leggatt began his attempts to ascertain the identity of the person seated before him. With exaggerated movements, and adopting a voice that sounded like that of a young miss rather than a married man, he began to ask questions, hoping to elicit some extraneous sound that might give the person's identity away. But Mrs. Fitzgibbon was a terrible player and struggled to contain her answer to the solitary grunt that was required.

The Breadmores were excellent hosts, providing ample entertainment and food to delight their guests, yet David couldn't throw himself into the thick of things—which was clear enough when he considered how many forfeits he'd earned himself already this evening. His thoughts were far too occupied to invest in the game before him.

David joined in with the laughter as Mrs. Fitzgibbon's identity was quickly and easily guessed (despite the lady always seeming so genuinely surprised at having been caught), but his gaze drifted through the room. Leaden Court was a fine townhome. Though by no means as large as the estates circling town, it was perfect for functions such as these. Large rooms with space aplenty for the various entertainments that were scattered throughout the house.

But it wasn't the autumnal floral arrangements dispersed around the drawing room or the myriad of candles burning bright that caught his attention. It was his sister. As this was the largest room, this was where the Breadmores had chosen to hold the active parlor games, and the long shape of the room allowed for plenty of space in which onlookers could gather to watch. Flora stood in a far corner, her wide eyes staring at the gentleman standing before her as her shoulders rounded.

David couldn't see the man's face but knew who inspired such trepidation. As he rose to his feet, the others cried out for his forfeit, but he waved them away without glancing backward. With quick steps, he moved to her corner, but he was not quick enough.

"There you are, my dear!" said Mrs. Rosanna Tate, sweeping in and taking Flora by the arm. "There is someone I wish you to meet."

"Do excuse my frankness, Mrs. Tate, but I was speaking with Miss Flora," said Mr. Kellen with a smirk.

Mrs. Tate turned her gaze to him with such utter surprise that David could almost believe she was truly shocked to see him, despite the fact that the gentleman had been standing there when she had approached.

"Oh, Mr. Kellen," she said with a laugh before patting him on the arm. "I do apologize, but you must excuse me. And I am certain you won't be alone for very long. I heard Mr. Jemmet was in attendance tonight and quite keen to speak with you."

Tugging at his cuffs, Mr. Kellen glanced about, his eyes darting as though the gentleman might appear that very moment. "Is that so? I heard he was still in Bath."

"I assure you he is not," said Mrs. Tate. "My husband spoke with Mr. Breadmore to ensure he was invited to tonight's festivities, and I believe he arrived home early for that very purpose—as he's had trouble locating you in the past. He is quite eager to speak with you."

Despite her smile never faltering, there was a thread of steel in that last statement, and David couldn't help but grin as Mr. Kellen blanched. Without another word, he turned on his heel, and though David wouldn't say the gentleman scurried away, he certainly moved with purpose towards the exit.

"Do not fret, my dear Miss Flora," said Mrs. Tate, patting the girl's arm and then leading her in the opposite direction. "Now, I would be grateful if you could assist me with a young man. He's a cousin of my husband's and has come to stay with us for a few weeks, but I fear he is overwhelmed by all the strangers, and I know you are the perfect companion to help him feel at ease."

Flora blinked at the lady, though a small smile crept across her lips as her cheeks pinked. David stood there staring at the pair as they moved away, quite at a loss to understand just what had happened. Oh, it was clear that Mrs. Tate had managed to thwart Mr. Kellen's advances and find Flora a pleasant distraction, but David didn't know when or how his sister had come under Mrs. Tate's protection.

Despite his friendship with the Leighs, his sisters were not acquainted with them—especially the Tates, who were well beyond the Archers' station. That social disparity was the very reason why David hadn't used his connection to Benjamin to foster the introduction; he didn't want to be numbered among the obsequious toadies, desperate to use the Leighs to gain access to the Tates and further their standing in town.

But then, the answer to that mystery was easy enough, for there was now a second connection between his sisters and the Leighs.

David turned his gaze out and spied Miss Leigh standing on the far side of the room. Despite being alone, she did not look like the other wallflowers, who held themselves with the fragility of a wilting blossom about to lose its petals. Miss Leigh stood with a straightened spine, looking out at the room like a queen gazing upon her subjects, appearing to all the world as if the solitude was self-imposed and to her liking. A blooming rose amongst wildflowers.

There was no need to ask, for it was clear she had fostered the connection between her elder sister and his younger one, for that was just the sort of thing Miss Leigh was wont to do. David would wager a hefty sum that she'd felt Flora's discomfort as though it were her very own and did what she could to ease it; Miss Katherine Leigh was no social butterfly who could aid his sister's entrance into society, but she had a close connection to one.

David's heart burned at the thought. The heat spread through him as he watched Miss Leigh. Why could others not see the treasure she was simply because she had a few thorns? Everyone did.

"Are you going to do something about your young lady?"

David jerked, though he kept himself from doing something entirely embarrassing like squawking, and he turned his gaze to his mother, who had somehow snuck up to his side. He stared at the lady, but she simply took his arm.

"You are rather preoccupied tonight, aren't you?" she asked, giving him a pat.

"I have much on my mind at present."

"No doubt." The lady nodded and gazed out at the gathering, though her brows drew together. "I am proud of you, David. You know that, don't you?"

"Of course," he replied, though his throat clamped shut on the last syllable. He couldn't say his response was entirely truthful, but then, neither was it a lie. Never would he have claimed his mother was embarrassed by or disgruntled with him, but that was a far cry from being proud.

Mother glanced at him from the corner of her eye, and that furrowed brow deepened. "I know I do not say it enough, David, but I am. You do so much for us. I wish I could do more to aid you, but I fear I am such a useless creature."

"Nonsense," said David, turning to face her once more—but her head lowered, her eyes falling to the ground.

"Ignore me," she said, waving it away and taking his arm once more to turn him towards the crowd. "I didn't come here to speak of myself. I want to know what you are doing with your young lady."

"I do not have a young lady—"

But David's protests died when his mother gave him a raise of her brows.

"I am quite optimistic." Though he spoke the words and believed them, they rang a touch hollow even to his ears. "I like Miss Sheridan, and I think she may very well be that lady from the masquerade."

With a furrowed brow, she shook her head. "Not that nonsense. I was speaking of your Miss Leigh."

Chapter 30

David stiffened, his gaze darting across the room to where she stood. "She is not *my* Miss Leigh."

Mother wrinkled her nose. "She is a bit too brusque at times, but she has a good heart—forever playing for us and keeping me company, and she is endlessly kind to the girls. It's been such a short time since Miss Leigh first graced our home, yet it feels as though she's a long-standing fixture in our family."

Of their own accord, his eyes drifted to his sisters' positions in the room. Though Irene was nowhere to be seen, David was certain Mr. Gould was keeping a close eye on her. However, Flora was quite happily situated with the gentleman Mrs. Tate had introduced her to, whilst Clarissa was ensconced in Mrs. Tate's circle.

Yes, Miss Leigh was kind to his sisters. And to his mother.

"What are you going to do about your Miss Leigh?" prodded Mother.

"She is not mine. We are friends."

Mother gave a low hum that sounded more like a scoff, and David glanced at her to find her watching him with narrowed eyes.

"Are you? Or are you simply overlooking a good match because you're not swept away in some flight of fancy?" she asked. "Love is not only racing hearts and wild attraction, David."

"That doesn't mean it ought to be ignored—"

"Oh, my dear son," she said with a sigh. Despite the exasperation in her tone, David couldn't help but feel warm at the endearment. The Leighs employed it all too often in meaningless manners, but there was nothing feigned about his mother's affection in that word. And it helped to ease the sting of what she said next.

"Memories are funny things, twisting and distorting the past, and I fear yours is leading you down the wrong path. Is that lady everything you imagine her to be, or have you inflated that sweet moment into something grander than it was?"

With brows pulled together, his mother moved to step in front of him, raising her hand to pat his cheek. "Do not allow a fantasy to distract you from the beautiful possibility before you, and ask yourself if you had to choose, which lady would you pick?"

Reaching over, Mother kissed him on his other cheek before leaving him to his thoughts—though David didn't know what he ought to think at such a moment. They said by the mouth of two or three witnesses the truth was established (or something to that effect), and David couldn't easily brush aside his mother's words when they aligned with what Benjamin had said not long ago.

He glanced over at the other guests all gathered together. The game was in full swing, with laughter and merriment aplenty, and his seat by Miss Sheridan remained unoccupied. It would be easy enough to return to his place and take up the hunt again.

But David's gaze drifted towards Miss Leigh, standing by herself.

...

Jealousy was an ugly sentiment. Rather than celebrating the blessings in another's life, it festered in selfishness and resentment. A miserable feeling for a miserable person who desired one's own happiness above anyone else's. There was nothing wrong with regrets or longing, but one should be able to wish for something whilst celebrating when another achieved it.

Life was full of disappointments, and no good came from focusing on the things one lacked and others possessed—a philosophy Katherine tried to hold firm to, though it was difficult at times.

Katherine Leigh was not jealous of Pamela. On her friend's wedding day, she had celebrated wholeheartedly beside the new Mrs. Kitts, and though spinsterhood loomed before her, Katherine had refused to allow it to taint a beautiful day.

Of course, she hadn't truly realized just how much their friendship would alter.

Pamela may not have been a darling of society, but she'd had gentlemen admirers aplenty, and thus, Katherine had thought she knew what it was like to share her friend's attention. However, there was a vast difference between a courting lady and a married one—especially with each additional child requiring more of their mother's attention. And Pamela was an attentive mother. As she should be.

Mrs. Kitts' life was with her family, and Katherine did not resent that felicity, but neither could she stop herself from feeling all the more alone at functions like this.

Spinsterhood was not such a terrible thing. It was not her desired state, but many people did not have the lives they wished for, and Katherine had always thought it far better to be a spinster (even an unhappy one) than an unhappily married woman.

Granted, that would be far less true if she didn't have her escape plan at the ready. Katherine Leigh was not at the mercy of her parents or siblings; spinsterhood was not something to be feared. But for all that she understood and embraced it, dissatisfaction struck at the oddest of times, reminding her just how lonely such a life could be.

Laughter burst from the revelers, and she watched as the circle of people in the center of the room erupted into chaos, doing who knew what. Humor was such a variable thing, and Katherine rarely understood the amusement gained from parlor games like Buffy Guffy. But then, most of the guests imbibed freely their hosts' wine and spirits, making even the most ludicrous things uproarious.

A hand appeared before her gaze, holding up a glass of fresh cider. Her eyes traveled the length of the arm to find Mr. Archer standing beside her.

"I thought you might be parched," he said, nudging the glass towards her.

Katherine's brows rose. "I am, thank you."

Taking a deep drink, she enjoyed the sweetness of the apples mixed with the bite of cinnamon, nutmeg, and allspice. And the faintest kiss of orange peel. Although it was room temperature, the cider sent a wave of heat through her—though that had more to do with the gentleman who had given it to her.

Katherine straightened and drew in a breath, forcing that ridiculous sentiment aside. Mr. Archer had been attentive. He was a gentleman, so that was of little surprise. Even if he was the only one who ever seemed to pay her any heed.

"I ought to say thank you," said Mr. Archer.

"For what?" she asked as the pair watched the frenzied antics of the gathering. For all that poise and gentility were prized behavior, such decorum was immediately forgotten when it came to parlor games. An oddity, that.

"For everything you have done for my family. Introducing my sisters to yours, keeping my mother company, being a friend to them all."

She gave a little shrug. "I have little to offer them, but your sisters are just the sort of young ladies Rosanna enjoys assisting. An introduction and a few minutes of my time are not such mighty things."

"They are to them," he said, nodding at his sister and mother, who stood at Rosanna's elbow, gazing up at her with such adoration. It was the sort of expression that Rosanna had earned every day of her life. A simple smile and everyone was entranced.

"I am glad to be of assistance," murmured Katherine whilst sending a scowl inward. Jealousy truly was a wicked thing. It wasn't Rosanna's fault that she'd garnered all attention from the moment of her birth. But Katherine couldn't help but wish that she had just a touch of that radiance; being raised next to such perfection had only made her flaws stand out in stark contrast.

Good gracious, she was maudlin tonight.

Mr. Archer stood at her side, silently sipping his cider as they watched the antics, though Katherine's mind was far from the goings-on of the Breadmores' party. And she suspected from his heavy silence that Mr. Archer's thoughts were just as distant.

"Are you going to return to the games?" It was a silly question to ask, for Katherine wasn't interested in chasing him away, but she required a distraction, and a conversation was just the ticket.

"I am not in the mood for it tonight," said Mr. Archer, slanting her a glance. "You?"

Katherine scoffed, drawing forth a knowing smile from his lips.

"I didn't think so," he replied before nodding at the door. "Would you join me for a round of whist? I heard Mr. Davis bragging about his prowess, and I would love to see you trounce him."

The corners of her lips tipped upwards. "That does sound amusing."

Taking her empty glass from her hand, Mr. Archer placed their two glasses on the side table and motioned towards the door with a solicitous grin. "After you, my lady."

"Certainly, my good sir," she said, lifting her chin with a smile.

They fell into step, and Katherine longed to take his arm. Sadly, the floor was devoid of holes and uneven bits, and she required no assistance. As they weren't courting, there was no need to take hold of Mr. Archer, but she couldn't help but wish it all the same.

Shaking free of that thought, she sent another scowl inward. There was no good to be had in such musings. Mr. Archer was her friend, and that was a fine blessing to have. Hoping for anything more was a fool's errand—especially when he'd made his feelings clear on the matter. Katherine had enough dignity not to chase after a man who didn't desire her.

And so, she straightened and glided out of the room at his side, content to spend a few hours trouncing him at cards. Mr. Archer did not love her, but he desired her company, which was far more than many of the ladies in this room could say of their husbands.

"Come now, Mr. Archer," called Miss Breadmore. "Do not think you can slip away without paying your forfeits!"

"Rum business, man," called Mr. Leggatt. "A gentleman always pays his debts."

Mr. Archer paused and turned back to the room with hands held up in surrender. "And I fully intend to. However, I wasn't certain we would have time to see to mine when your list of forfeits is so very long, sir."

Holding a hand to his chest, Mr. Leggatt glanced at his wife. "Do you hear how the fellow maligns me?"

"It isn't maligning if it is true, my darling," she replied with a pretty bat of her lashes.

"Such treachery, woman!" he said, clutching his heart once more. "My list is only long because you always have me pay yours."

"Hush, you blowhard," said Mrs. Leggatt before nodding for Miss Breadmore to continue.

"Now, what shall his punishment be?" she asked, glancing

down at her tally sheet. "It seems you owe four forfeits—"

"Might I pay them all at once?" asked Mr. Archer, glancing at Mr. Leggatt. "I can only stand so much of his antics, and I find I have reached my limits for the evening—"

"For shame!" cried the maligned man, though he looked undisturbed by the accusation.

"—And I promised Miss Leigh I would play a few rounds of cards with her," finished Mr. Archer.

But before he finished speaking, Katherine spied Benjamin sneaking up next to Miss Breadmore. Leaning in close, he whispered into the lady's ear, and Katherine's eyes narrowed as her heart sank. She couldn't say what worried her so, but instinct sent a flush of gooseflesh across her arms as she watched Miss Breadmore beam.

"Brilliant, Mr. Leigh!" she said, turning a bright grin at her intended victim. That dread grew as the young lady's gaze flicked between Mr. Archer and Katherine. "Mr. Archer, to repay your forfeits, you must kiss Miss Leigh!"

The room erupted with more laughter, the ladies and gentlemen braying like donkeys. Gentlemen nudged each other, ladies sent mocking glances one to the other, and Katherine raised her chin as the sound enveloped her. It rang off the walls, filling her ears before settling into her heart.

They all thought it such fun. So amusing. Just the height of ridiculousness. Forcing Mr. Archer to kiss the Leigh spinster.

Katherine swallowed, but her throat clamped tight, and she forced herself to keep her gaze upon the crowd. She would not be cowed. Not by them.

She gripped the sides of her skirts, her fingers digging into the cloth as she stared them down, her eyes narrowing. And Benjamin had the gall to stand at Miss Breadmore's side with a little smirk on his lips. But then, this was naught but a bit of fun for him. A laugh at his sister's expense.

Her brother.

Turning on her heel, Katherine escaped.

Chapter 31

Teeth grinding together, David forced himself not to shout at the hyenas as they guffawed, but his gaze bored into Benjamin's. With narrowed eyes, he promised retribution before turning to follow Miss Leigh. Leaden Court was bursting at the seams, and though she was only a few steps ahead of him, the lady was quickly swallowed by the crowd.

Thankfully, she was no petite miss, and David spied her simple bun popping up here and there as she wove through the revelers. Following those little signs, he quickly found himself dumped out of a side door and into the night air.

"Miss Leigh," he called, but she delved deeper into the gardens. David might've believed that she hadn't heard him, but her shoulders stiffened at the sound of his voice, making it clear she had.

Being situated in town, the gardens behind the building were meager, so Miss Leigh did not have far to go, but she did not slow as she moved further away from the candlelight shining through the windows. And David did not surrender, continuing to follow her until she reached the far wall that divided the Breadmores' property from the adjacent one.

Upon reaching the impediment, Miss Leigh didn't pause as

she turned to follow the line of masonry.

"Miss Leigh, please," he said.

"What do you want, Mr. Archer?" she snapped, not slowing one bit as she marched beside the wall. "To assure me they meant no harm? That it was all in good fun?"

David forced his feet to match her pace, coming up beside her as he wove between the shrubs. "I—"

"I am not a fool, Mr. Archer. A kiss is a common enough forfeit, and they would never have laughed quite so hard had it been some pretty young miss they wished for you to kiss," she said, clutching the sides of her skirts until they were hopelessly wrinkled.

Miss Leigh continued to storm about, and when she stopped to draw breath, David hurried to speak.

"You are correct."

Stopping in place, Miss Leigh turned to face him, her chest heaving from the force of her breaths. Through the fire in her gaze, David spied the spark of sorrow that drove her, and his heart burned at the sight of it.

"They were mocking you, and it was wrong of them." His hand itched to draw her into his arms, though the impulse left him blinking. Comfort was freely given between them, but not in that fashion. However, David couldn't deny that the feeling had struck him—and lingered.

Miss Leigh dropped onto a bench nestled into the corner of the garden. "It feels as though the only time anyone pays me any mind is when there is a chance for mischief, and I do not understand why."

David opened his mouth, though he didn't have any words to offer up in explanation.

Though the shadows leeched the color from the world, the moon hung high above them, illuminating her face as Miss Leigh turned her gaze upward to meet his. "I know I am blunt and lack my sisters' way with people, and my humor is far too dry for many—"

"You are delightful," said David, though the lady seemed

not to hear him.

"—and that I am not pretty or attractive in any fashion, but what is it about me that invites people to deride me? My own family..." Her voice quivered, and she dropped her head, rubbing at her forehead.

"I do not understand it at all, Miss Leigh." David dropped onto the bench beside her, and following the impulse, he took her free hand in his.

"Why did Benjamin do it?" she whispered. "What have I ever done to earn his displeasure? I do not understand it at all. I suppose it is little wonder when the entire family treats me as though I have the plague, but never did I think he would embarrass me in such a fashion—"

"I do not believe he was trying to do so," said David, scratching at the back of his head with his free hand.

"Then why?"

But David had no answer for that. Or rather, he had one, but it was not to be shared with her. For all that Benjamin likely had thought his actions subtle, clearly, the fool was trying his hand at playing matchmaker. And though anger flared through him at Benjamin's heavy-handedness, another thought niggled its way into his mind.

The masquerade had been a difficult night for Miss Leigh because of her family's matrimonial machinations, and his Mystery Lady had jested that she was fleeing a blackguard determined to woo her. Had Mr. Mowbry's overtures been so repugnant that Miss Leigh embraced a costume and chosen blindness to obscure her identity entirely?

The thought sent a jolt straight through him, and despite his efforts to wrangle logic and reasoning back into his mind, David struggled to piece together anything coherent. The idea was too ridiculous. Too strange. It couldn't be true, yet it wouldn't leave him be.

But such ponderings mattered little when Miss Leigh sat there, pleading for an answer. Her furrowed brows rested above the rim of her spectacles, pinching together with such longing, begging him to provide her with some assurance.

"Your brother wanted to humble me," he blurted. Miss Leigh's brows rose at that, but before she could say a word, he continued. "Friends ought to do so at every opportunity, and what other lady in attendance would flee in horror at the thought of kissing me?"

With a huff, Miss Leigh shook her head. "I did not flee in horror."

"Oh, no. You had more self-respect than to give them that satisfaction," he said with a knowing nod. "You stared daggers at them all, fairly cursing them all to Hades, and then strode out the door with the regality of a queen."

"I didn't do that, either."

David chuckled. "Believe me, I described it precisely as it happened. But regardless, it is clear you are greatly offended at the thought of kissing me, even when such things are common-place in parlor games."

The words sprang forth before he could think better of them; David couldn't help it. Now that the question had taken hold in his thoughts, he needed to nudge the situation forward. There was one definitive way in which he could discover the truth, and for all his blundering about, Benjamin had handed it to him. An easy test to see if they could view each other in a romantic light. If not, they could laugh it away with no damage done to their friendship.

Miss Leigh stiffened and turned her head to stare at him.

"I know I am as repulsive as Mr. Mowbry and as annoying as Mr. Tryck, but is it truly so awful to give me a little kiss?" he said with an impish grin, pointing to his cheek.

"The forfeit was for you to kiss me, sirrah."

"Sirrah, is it?" he asked with an arched brow. In a quick movement, David rose to his feet, sweeping Miss Leigh along with him. Standing flush with his arms around her, he fought against the laugh that threatened to emerge when Miss Leigh's eyes bulged until they were liable to pop from her head.

"Might I steal a kiss, Miss Leigh?" But for all that David had intended the question to be lighthearted, there was a roughness to his voice that he couldn't hide. One of her hands rested against his chest, whilst the other gripped his arm, and David's heart stuttered when her fingers brushed across his shirtfront.

What was happening? Katherine didn't think herself a dunce, but that question ricocheted about her thoughts, demanding an answer. Yet she had none to give. If she were anyone else, she might say Mr. Archer was looking at her in a romantic fashion. His dark eyes held hers, and the humorous quirk of his lips vanished as his hands rubbed at her back.

"Please allow me to pay my forfeit, Miss Leigh."

Mr. Archer didn't sound like himself at all. His voice was low and rough, and her heartbeat quickened as her skin flushed with the memory of those fevered kisses they'd shared at the masquerade. Standing in the darkness, it was easy enough to believe she'd donned her mask once more, and it was the Mystery Lady and the rascal Dick Turpin stealing a feverish moment in the gardens. But the moonlight allowed them to see clearly enough that it was Mr. David Archer and Miss Katherine Leigh.

Surely he didn't mean anything by it.

Yet Katherine couldn't ignore the softness in his gaze. She might've called it tenderness if it had been directed at anyone else, but it wasn't. Mr. Archer was looking upon her. And he knew it. There were no masks to hide behind.

His arms remained circled about her, his fingers brushing gently against her back, and for all that Katherine clung to good sense and the memory of his dismissal so many weeks ago, she couldn't help but wonder if something had changed. Mr. Archer's voice echoed in her mind, fairly laughing at the thought that she was his Mystery Lady. And only that lady would do.

Yet now, Mr. Archer held her close enough that the scent of his cologne surrounded her, filling her nose with the faint aroma of cinnamon, which blended with the remnants of the cider they'd been drinking. The last lingering rational thought in her mind pestered Katherine, reminding her of her resolve to ignore her feelings for him, but the strength of that conviction faded beneath the feel of his arms around her.

Was this a jest? Was he in earnest? She couldn't tell.

Leaning forward, he drew his lips near to her flushed skin, and his gaze echoed the question that he'd asked. Would she allow him a kiss? For all that the scandalous forfeits drew forth laughter, the truth was that those little tokens were intended for the cheek or hand—not the mouth.

The way he held her, Katherine couldn't say where he'd planned to place the kiss, but before she allowed herself to think better of it, she turned into him, her lips meeting his.

Brows shooting upward, David felt his pulse leap at the sudden feel of Miss Leigh's lips touching his. Despite that being his intended target, he'd anticipated some careful maneuvering to achieve it. And there she was.

He was kissing Miss Leigh.

Despite fully knowing what to do in such a situation, David found himself wondering how he ought to proceed. His arms remained circled about her, and while they normally felt free to rest against the lady's back, it felt like too much of a liberty in this situation—which was ridiculous, as they were kissing, which was far more shocking than a hand at the small of her back.

But this was Miss Leigh. One did not tease and flirt with one's friend. Or steal kisses from her in a darkened garden.

Her hand rose, brushing a featherlight touch against his cheek, and David's pulse jumped. His brows rose for a heartbeat before his thoughts grew foggy, and the surprise of what they were doing fading away. What started as a little touch of the lips deepened, his eyes closing as he surrendered to the feel of her. It wasn't some swell of emotion that took over and stole away all reason and stoked the passion, but it felt so very natural.

Miss Leigh's hand slid up around his neck; David felt the trembling of her fingertips as they brushed against the edge of his collar, and he felt like smiling, though that would've disrupted their kiss. His pulse slowed, growing in strength like the beat of a drum, pushing him further into the embrace.

For all that the situation had seemed strange, the feel of her in his arms felt right. Proper. Which was laughable, as they were doing something very improper at that very moment. Had David ever thought kissing Miss Leigh would be enjoyable, he would've indulged far sooner, but despite knowing that she was the lady in his arms, he still couldn't believe Miss Leigh inspired such pleasure.

This was his friend.

Yet as David reveled in the feel of her, he couldn't quite deny the frisson of awareness that ran down his spine. As pleasant as the kiss was—and it certainly was—it answered the question he'd been considering before the embrace. Miss Leigh was not his Mystery Lady.

Chapter 32

For all that Katherine had tried to forget the masquerade, one's first kiss was impossible to erase from one's memory. It invaded the quiet moments in her life (of which there were far too many) and haunted her dreams. And she'd given up hope that another would ever follow. Yet here they were, David and Katherine, wrapped in moonlight and each other's arms.

His embrace felt like home, as though they were two parts of a puzzle fitting snugly together. So perfectly. Katherine's pulse quickened, and she gathered that pounding passion and poured it into her touch whilst her heart hummed with a silent prayer that he would see, he would feel, and he would know the truth. This was where she was meant to be. He had to know that. How could he not?

The kiss slowed, and David's arms fell away, leaving her shuddering against the chill night air. Slowly, she opened her eyes to see a flash of disappointment in his. There and gone in a flash. Katherine wanted to ignore it. But she couldn't.

Mr. Archer cleared his throat and fidgeted. "That most certainly paid my forfeits."

Her jaw slackened, and she stared at him as everything

within her stilled. The stone at her feet seeped into her, spreading through her body until everything was as hard as granite. If only her heart would stop beating, but the aching pain in her chest couldn't be stopped.

The gentleman winced and scuffed the ground with the heel of his boot whilst rubbing at the back of his head. "I didn't mean that to sound cavalier."

Blinking, Katherine stared at him, her thoughts swirling about, trying to make sense of this moment. Surely there was some explanation. Mr. Archer stood there, awkwardly mumbling, and Katherine's pathetic little heart tried to twist his stuttering words into something good. But she knew better.

Turning on her heel, she sped back to the house. Mr. Archer called after her, but that only made her move faster. The gentleman was quick enough to keep pace, but when he tried to step in front of her, she dodged around him. He babbled some nonsense, but it was a blur of sounds that made no impression on her.

Katherine swept through the side door, and though Mr. Archer was at her elbow, she wove through the crowd, forcing him to slow enough to avoid collisions with the other guests. And a little distance was all she required.

In one aspect of life, a wallflower and a rake shared a similar education, coming to know every private nook and cranny of the houses in the neighborhood—though they used that knowledge for very different purposes.

Dodging around a group of ladies, Katherine closed her ears to Mr. Archer's call and slipped through a circle of gentlemen before darting behind a curtain. The Breadmores always kept them drawn during parties (to better display the expensive fabric, of course), and most assumed they hid only a straight pane of glass. To Katherine's utter relief, the alcove was unoccupied.

Placing a hand to still the fabric as she slipped into the darkened place, she held her breath. She found it exceptionally difficult to do so, as her lungs were heaving. Her chin trembled, and she forced air in and held it. Clamping a hand over her mouth, she scowled at herself as the breath spasmed.

Katherine Leigh would not cry.

She would not.

Crying was something silly girls did when their hearts were broken because they were too foolish to accept reality. Katherine had learned long ago not to hope for a man to gaze upon her with longing, to whisper sweet nothings and declare his undying devotion. A lady like Katherine Leigh was too sensible for such flights of fancy. So, she was not crying.

Katherine huffed and swiped at her cheeks.

Leaning to the edge of the curtain, she peered out at the gathering and watched as Mr. Archer strode past, his gaze searching the crowd before he disappeared into it.

What had she expected? Mr. Archer to kiss her and suddenly look at her as a woman, rather than some chum who happened to wear dresses? That he would recognize his delectable Mystery Lady hidden behind his friend's guise? That he would be seized with instant adoration for a plain spinster who was five years his senior? The *older sister* in his life.

For all that Katherine thought herself a sensible creature, she was proving herself just as silly as Mama and all the other girls who allowed sentiment to dictate their behavior. She knew better than to hope for such a thing, so why was she upset when Mr. Archer proved the point?

Her breath shuddered, and she swiped at her cheeks once more as the image of his expression played out in her mind again and again. Disappointment? Was there anything worse a lady could see after an embrace?

Ripping her glasses from her nose, she tossed them onto the sill and covered her face with her hands before dropping onto the window seat. What had she been thinking? No doubt, he'd only been jesting and had intended to kiss her cheek or forehead or something equally innocuous, but she simply had to offer up her lips.

Had her good sense flown out the door?

Katherine lowered her hands and leaned against the glass, the cold seeping through the thin layer of cotton at her back. The chill in the alcove felt good against her flushed skin, though it did little to extinguish the fire burning through her.

What had she been thinking? But the answer was simple enough.

For all that Katherine had determined to let go of the fantasy, the hope hadn't died. Not entirely. Some part of her had longed to see love in his gaze. To hear him whisper her name and tell her just how much she mattered to him. That he desired her.

Love grew from friendship. Katherine knew such a thing to be true. It was easy enough to see that their marriages were strong and flourished because they genuinely respected and enjoyed their husbands; Parker had only come to love Prudence after they'd become friends, after all. It had been so easy to convince herself that if a man became a friend, one day he might view her with adoration.

But she had been wrong. Mr. Archer was as close a friend as she could boast, and there had been no passion in his eyes when he'd looked at her mere moments ago. His heart was so full of that wretched Mystery Lady that he couldn't believe it had been the plain Katherine Leigh beneath the mask.

She covered her face once more, bending over with a low groan.

What had she been thinking? She hadn't. Or at least, not in any discernible fashion.

Silly, foolish girl! Making a mockery of herself at every opportunity—

Dropping her hands, Katherine straightened, jutting her chin out as though to challenge her own thoughts. Whether or not she'd made the proper choice, she did not deserve such castigation. Those poisonous words were her mother's, and whatever mistakes she'd made, Katherine wouldn't allow herself to wallow in such filth.

Fool! Dimwit! Imbecile! For all that the English language had many colorful turns of phrase, there were not curses enough for the lackwit David Archer.

He was a man of business who had successfully managed his family's finances for over a decade. He had the social grace to earn himself a decent place in society. He clearly possessed skill and brains enough to navigate most situations with aplomb, even from a young age. Yet when it had mattered most, he'd uttered that ridiculous statement.

"That most certainly paid my forfeits."

What had he been thinking? Clearly, he hadn't. A jest was a good way to ease tension at appropriate times, but not when one had just soundly kissed a lady. His friend.

Rubbing at his forehead, David cursed himself again and again as he tried to comprehend what had happened. The fact that he'd kissed her was disorienting enough. That he enjoyed it so much was doubly so.

And then he'd said that idiotic statement and sent her fleeing.

Turning this way and that, he searched the sea of faces, but he caught not a single sight of Miss Leigh. He paced the drawing room, then surrendered, marching through the corridors to the parlor, but she wasn't there either.

Heavens above! What would he even say to her once he found her? What could he say?

David didn't know what he was thinking then or now, and his nerves weren't helped by the memory of her eyes fixed on him as he'd spoken. Despite being a closed book to many people, Miss Leigh's eyes spoke volumes if one bothered to look, and with her wrapped in his arms, David hadn't missed the pain and anguish his thoughtless statement had caused.

What had he done?

Lifting back the edge of the curtain, Katherine scoured the

corridor and found no sign of Mr. Archer. Sitting here was doing no good, and she was done with the evening. Time to return
to Whitley Court. Thankfully, the Breadmores' home was not
far from hers. No—the Leighs'. For all that Katherine had spent
the whole of her life within those walls, the place did not feel
like her home. It was merely the stack of bricks in which she
resided.

And perhaps it was time to change that.

Striding down the hall, she kept her head ducked low to
keep from drawing attention, and in a trice, she had fetched her
shawl from the footman and stepped out into the night.

"Katherine!" called her brother.

Crunching footsteps hurried down the gravel drive, following after her. She didn't slow. Benjamin was the last person she
wished to see at this moment. No, Mr. Archer held that distinction. And Mama would be equally vexing, for the lady could
make any irritation all the more irritating. In point of fact, there
was only one person Katherine wished to see at that moment,
and Pamela was bundled up in her home with her darling husband and sweet children.

She gripped the edges of her skirts as she marched along,
refusing to stop when Benjamin placed himself in front of her.
His brows rose as she barreled into him, shouldering past without slowing a step.

"Do not tell me you are piqued—" he began.

"Do not speak to me! You said enough tonight."

Proving himself a fool of the highest order, Benjamin fell
into step beside her. "I apologize. I was attempting to be subtle—"

Katherine scoffed. "Oh, yes, Benjamin. Standing up in front
of everyone and whispering in Miss Breadmore's ear was quite
subtle. Everyone in that room was quite aware of your subtlety.
Bravo!"

"I—"

Throwing her arms wide, she rounded on him. "What have
I done to earn your scorn, Benjamin? What reason do you have

for opening me up to such ridicule? I've had to bear it from Mama and Papa, and even our sisters to varying degrees, but you? I..."

Katherine closed her eyes, turning away with a shake of her head as her chest squeezed tight. What good would it do to dredge up such things? Benjamin had made his choice. It ought not to hurt so very much that yet another person thought her worthy of derision, but her heart panged and her footsteps grew heavy as she continued down the gravel drive.

"I didn't intend for you to be laughed at, Katherine. I give you my word—"

She refused to look at him, though he sounded earnest enough. Shaking her head, she murmured, "What does it matter, Benjamin? You are like all the rest. At your best, you only tolerate me, so I don't know why I have hoped for anything different. I've been a fool to linger..."

But her throat clamped tight, and she straightened her shoulders, forcing her feet onto the road.

"I—" he began.

"Let me be," she said.

"But—" Benjamin grabbed her elbow, and Katherine yanked it free.

"Leave me alone!" She didn't know if he fled or simply remained standing where he was, but it didn't matter, for she walked along the road and didn't hear his footsteps following her. Only the breezes in the trees broke the silence, scattering their foliage along the pavers.

Staring at her feet, Katherine trudged along. And in the stillness of the night, she felt certainty settle upon her. She'd been a fool to linger in Greater Edgerton. With the means to forge her own path, why was she so determined to remain at Whitley Court?

To help a brother who despised her? What good would it do when he cared not two jots for her opinion? Benjamin would choose as he saw fit; it was his future to decide.

To support a gentleman who had enough responsibilities to

manage without fending off the advances of a lovestruck spinster? Mr. Archer was quite capable of making other friends.

To retain a friendship with a lady whose life was far too full
for an awkward wallflower? Pamela's letters would be more
plentiful than their visits had been of late.

Hope had trapped her here with false promises of a better
resolution with the former two, and Katherine was finished allowing that silly emotion to hold sway over her any more. There
was no good to be had remaining in Greater Edgerton, and that
knowledge wove through her until she felt it in her very bones.

The time to leave had come. Katherine was done sitting
about, waiting for the life she longed to have.

Chapter 33

"**M**iss Leigh is not at home, sir," said the maid. The girl gave a good show of remaining firm in the face of David's consternation, but she couldn't help the slight tremor in her voice at what was clearly a bald falsehood.

Euphemisms were such useless things. For all that they were purported to be a kinder way to communicate, what did it matter how the message was presented when the meaning was clear? Miss Leigh wouldn't see him.

"When will she return?" he asked.

"I do not know." And with that, the maid shut the door, leaving David standing on Whitley Court's doorstep. Drawing in a deep breath, he dropped his head back and stared at the clear sky above.

Had he ruined everything? He liked to think he knew the answer to that question, but the truth wriggled in his conscience, not allowing him to confidently respond. But then, he knew the lady in question quite well.

Drawing in a deep breath, he forced himself to step back from the door. As much as he longed to beat on the blasted thing until Miss Leigh saw him, he possessed at least a modicum of sense that told him such a move would do little to earn her favor. As he turned on his heel, his boots crunched against the gravel as he marched down the drive and made his way home.

For all that Miss Leigh was a tempestuous lady, they rarely quarreled. There were disagreements aplenty, to be sure, but how did a man make amends when the lady refused to see him? Again. David hadn't another pianoforte to lure her out. He supposed he merely had to be patient and wait for her to pay call at Stratsfield House, but that decision sat uneasy in his stomach, demanding he settle on another solution.

What ought he to do?

That question haunted his steps as he moved about the streets of Greater Edgerton, his feet drawing him home as he stared at the pavers and his thoughts drifted far and wide.

Many believed England incapable of sunshine, but nothing could be further from the truth. If anything, one was bound to experience the entire gamut of weather possibilities in a single day. The morning may be blustery, only to clear into blue skies by afternoon, and end with drizzle in the evening. And today was no exception. Though the winter chill had settled quickly into Lancashire, another mercurial shift found the cold fleeing once more as the sun climbed the horizon, warming everything it touched with its golden rays.

It truly was a magnificent day despite the bare trees and muddy streetscape. If David bothered to notice. He trudged along the roads of Greater Edgerton, but despite the press of the crowd surrounding him, his thoughts refused to drift from Miss Leigh. Stifling a yawn, he forced his feet forward.

That kiss.

For all that he knew Miss Leigh as well as anyone could claim to know her, David had never expected such a stirring embrace. Not from his dear friend.

Their embrace was as different from his Mystery Lady's as night and day. The kiss at the masquerade had been all fire and passion—the sort of heady delirium that poets wrote about as the pinnacle of love and adoration. But Miss Leigh's had been something altogether different from anything David had experienced. Despite spending the rest of the evening and morning trying to quantify it, he couldn't put it into words.

Comfortable? That made it sound too staid and boring. Yet he couldn't help but feel as though that encapsulated the thrumming in his heart. Despite the initial awkwardness, there was something so comforting about her embrace. Something right and proper.

What he felt for Miss Leigh was no inferno, bound to consume him. No, it was the light and warmth that sustained a man through the darkest and coldest of nights.

When so many ladies looked like explosions of muslin, flowers, and curls, Miss Leigh's simplicity was quite refreshing. A gentleman needn't worry about being jabbed in the eye by feathers or about his hands getting caught in braids and dangling loops. The feel of a woman in his arms, rather than puffs of fabric.

There was something truly appealing about Miss Leigh. Even if that thought made the world tilt around him.

"...if you had to choose, which lady would you pick?"

Mother's question added to the cacophony in his heart, and the more he considered it, the larger its meaning became. There was no scenario in which he could maintain ties with both women. A man didn't have female friends. Though some believed such relationships innocent, David knew of too many similar situations that ended in heartbreak; he wouldn't risk his and his future wife's happiness.

No, to choose the Mystery Lady would be to say farewell to Miss Leigh. Not merely a few days or a sennight apart, but to never see her again. To lose her forever.

David's chest constricted, his footsteps moving quicker as he imagined this fracture between him and Miss Leigh growing until they were little more than strangers. If he continued his hunt for the Mystery Lady, it only made sense that he ought to simply let things lie. To pester Miss Leigh any more would do no good.

"What does this fantasy lady have that is so much better than a lady whose company you crave and whose opinion you value?"

A man must choose, and when considering the whole of the question before him, the answer seemed so clear that David struggled to understand how he'd overlooked it for so long.

As he frowned to himself, his feet carried him through the streets of Greater Edgerton, his mind churning over his past, present, and future.

...

Blast this wretched trunk! Katherine was not one to blacken her tongue with profanity, so she did not speak the words aloud, but after having spent the past half hour battling the gargantuan thing, the epitaph was perfectly suitable in her thoughts. Tugging at the handle, she heaved, and it slid a few inches along the floorboards of the attic—and stopped.

Wiping at her forehead with her forearm, Katherine was certain she looked a fright, with a pink and shining face whilst her spectacles kept slipping down her nose. Thankfully, she didn't care in the slightest. Though she did not like the way her underthings clung to her dampened back.

She moved behind the trunk and bent over, pushing it along, but had no greater success with that effort than the first. Drawing in a deep breath, she gathered her strength and shoved, though even if she had the strength of Hercules, her slippered feet found no traction on the floorboards, leaving her unable to shift it.

"Move!" she groaned before dropping down beside it with a sigh. Leaning heavily against it, Katherine propped up her chin on her hand and stared at the tiny window that provided the only light in the small room.

"What are you doing?"

Katherine stiffened at her brother's question and glanced over to find him standing in the doorway, his hands on his hips for a brief moment before he held them up in surrender.

"Peace, dear sister," he murmured.

Teeth clenching together, Katherine narrowed her gaze. "Do not call me that."

Benjamin straightened, his brows rising. "Sister?"

"*Dear* sister," she replied with a frown. "I am done with hearing our family spouting that hypocrisy."

"Did it ever occur to you that we mean it?" There was a slight hint of humor to his tone, and Katherine forced herself not to do something childish, like slam the attic door in his face.

"Oh, I assure you I feel Mama's meaning every time she tacks it on after some derogatory statement concerning my looks, talents, or intelligence. They say actions speak louder than words, and I would add that her insults speak louder than the shallow affection in 'dear.'"

"I am not our mother," he replied, crossing his arms.

Drawing in a deep breath, Katherine sighed. "Did you come here to argue with me?"

Benjamin loosened his stance and winced. "I didn't. I was curious. What are you doing?"

"What does it matter?" she asked, her chin lifting a touch.

Holding up his hands in surrender again, Benjamin scowled. "It sounded as though you required assistance, and I wish to offer it."

She waved a dismissive hand. "I can manage—"

"No doubt you can, but that doesn't mean I cannot help." Lowering his brows, Benjamin looked at the trunk.

"Do not worry about me," she said, rising to her feet and coming around to the front.

"Simply telling me not to do so won't change a thing," muttered Benjamin.

She straightened and turned to look at him. "Pardon?"

His cheeks flushed pink, and drawing in a deep breath, he let it out in a long sigh. "I have been meaning to speak with you, but as you've been avoiding me completely for the past two days, I've been unable to tell you something important that I ought to have said before."

Her brother straightened and tucked his hands behind him. Looking in her direction, but not directly at her, he shifted and said, "I apologize for what I did at the Breadmores'. I truly did not mean to embarrass you."

With a scoff, Katherine stared down at the trunk. How was she to get this thing downstairs?

"I freely admit my actions were poorly planned, but I had good intentions," he added.

"Which were...?" she mumbled, crossing her arms to glower at the heavy item. The only solution would be to take everything out of the box and carry each item down individually. It would take time, but probably less than this monumental effort required.

Examining her options, Katherine fairly forgot that Benjamin was still there, and his voice ripped her from her thoughts.

"I think you and David are a good match, and I wanted to encourage it."

Her mouth dried, her heart thundered in her chest, and Katherine tried to stop the frantic beating with a deep breath, though it did little. Those words were no less startling than if Benjamin had announced that he intended to become an acrobat in a circus.

Benjamin sighed. "But you know him better than most. The fellow requires time and some none-too-subtle prodding before he can make up his mind on something, and this situation is doubly difficult because he's blinded himself with this silly search for the lady from the masquerade."

"You believe we're a good match?" she asked, her brows rising at how even her words sounded. "Have I given you the impression that I wish for that?"

Thank the heavens that Benjamin was standing behind her, or he would've known just how deeply her feelings ran on the subject. Memories flashed through her thoughts, churning up every interaction, looking for the subtle signs others might interpret. The humiliation of rejected affection was painful enough when only she knew just how much it pained her. If others suspected...

Katherine shuddered. Then, shaking her head, she turned around to face him. "Do not answer that. I do not need to know."

Benjamin opened his mouth, but she gathered her dignity close and wrapped it around her heart.

"What does it matter, Benjamin?" she asked, crossing her arms. "Even if it were true, *and* you felt you had no other recourse than to publicly mock me, why should you bestir yourself? You do not care for me in the slightest."

"That is not true," he said with a huff, throwing his hands wide. "Why do you keep saying that? I want to see you happily situated like all my sisters—"

"And you think a gentleman like Mr. Moody, Mr. Tryck, and the rest is what will make me happy?" she asked with raised brows and more than a bit of bite to her tone.

Benjamin held his hands up in surrender. "I fully admit those were missteps on my part, and we do not need to rehash the past. David has already raked me across the coals for it. But I was at my wit's end."

With a grimace, he scratched at the back of his head and glanced about the attic. Only when he stilled did Benjamin meet her gaze once more.

"Father has made it clear that if I don't agree to break the entail, it will be you who suffers for it," he said in a resigned tone. "I thought marriage was a better option for you."

With a few quick words, he told her all, and Katherine's legs grew weak beneath her. Sliding down, she dropped atop the trunk, her unfocused gaze fixing on the floorboards. It was one thing to recognize her parents cared little for her, but to be handed clear evidence of their selfish desires and apathy towards their own progeny was chilling.

Despite having thought herself immune to her parents' barbs, it felt as though they'd scooped her heart from her chest, leaving a gaping hole behind.

Chapter 34

Coming to stand before Katherine, Benjamin shook his head. "I am sorry. Perhaps I shouldn't have told you the truth. And I know I've gone about this all wrong, but I couldn't bear to see you made to suffer for my choice. I won't break the entail and allow the family's legacy to be pulled apart because of their negligence, but neither will I allow you to suffer because of it—I don't know if I could remain strong if that were to happen."

"Pardon?" Katherine's gaze jerked up, meeting her brother's eyes with a furrowed brow.

But he responded with his own puzzled frown. "Is it truly so surprising that I would care what happens to you?"

As much as she wished to give him the answer he clearly wanted, she couldn't help but say, "Yes."

Benjamin's head jerked back, and he stood there, staring at her for a long, silent moment before nudging her over and taking a seat beside her.

"I know there are twelve years difference in our ages, but before you left for school, I had thought we shared a bond," she said with a sigh. "I wrote, but you never replied—"

He opened his mouth, and Katherine rushed to add, "I realize you were a child, and I didn't truly expect much correspondence, but it isn't easy to maintain a correspondence with someone who never responds. My life is not interesting enough to fill pages. When you returned home, I hoped we might rekindle a friendship of some sort, yet you only tolerate my presence. And even then, only when Mr. Archer is present."

"You do not make it easy to be close with you, Katherine," murmured Benjamin. "Every time I have attempted it, you bristle and snap at me."

"Is it any wonder with our family?" she replied, slanting a look in his direction. "Whether or not we wish to admit it, our parents made us fight for our place in this family, and I learned from a young age that I am on my own. Prudence treated me like one of her responsibilities—one she didn't have time for. Rosanna only deigned to notice me after Prudence married, when her favorite sister was no longer around. Francis, like our mother, only ever saw my flaws. And I embarrass you."

"That isn't—" he began, but Katherine gave him a narrowed look.

"Do not deny it, Benjamin. I've seen you cringe when I approach a piano, but I am not as poor a pianist as the Leighs believe me to be."

Benjamin frowned, his eyes turning to the ground.

Shaking her head, Katherine ran a hand down her knees, straightening her skirts. "You say I'm prickly and combative, but is it any wonder when those closest to me treat me like an imposition? When those who ought to be my greatest supporters are constantly critical and cold, do you not think it is natural to assume everyone views me in that manner? That I might wish to protect my heart against further damage by keeping you at arm's length until you prove you aren't going to crush it beneath your boot?"

Her ribs tightened, and her eyes prickled, but she forced air into her lungs and blinked any sign of weakness away, straightening as she clenched her hands in her lap and stared at the wall opposite.

"I wish I could contradict you, but I suppose I hadn't given it much thought," murmured Benjamin. With a grimace, he amended, "Or not until David gave me a tongue-lashing. Several, in fact."

Again with Mr. Archer. Katherine longed to ask him more about it, but there was little point to it. Her future was now decided, and it did not include David Archer.

"I apologize. As much as I have tried to be a good brother to you, it seems I have failed," he said with a sigh. "But I assure you I had good intentions. However misplaced they were."

The corner of her mouth quirked upwards. "And that is the only reason I am speaking about any of this to you. I cannot recall the last time I spoke to Mama concerning anything more important than hair ribbons."

"You refuse to talk to her about hair ribbons."

"Precisely," she added in a wry tone, which drew a half-smile from Benjamin.

Shaking his head, he reached over and gave her clasped hands a squeeze. "I apologize for the Breadmores' party. I wish I could say that I was simply mistaken, but I was a bungling fool."

Katherine forced herself not to draw her hands away, though the reminder of the other night was hardly conducive to a tender sibling moment.

"In truth, I ought to thank you," she said, "for it clarified things quite nicely for me."

Benjamin's brows shot upwards, and his gaze filled with such hope that she couldn't help but free her hands from his. Rising to her feet, Katherine straightened her skirts and stepped away from her brother's seat, wandering between the trunks and crates cluttering the attic.

"Do not mistake my words, Benjamin Leigh," she said with a shake of her head. "It clarified that Mr. Archer and I are not suited for one another. We are friends, that is all."

"Fustian," he replied. "You two are happiest when together.

And it's clear you have feelings—"

Katherine whirled about to scowl at him. "Who said such a thing? Cannot a lady and a gentleman be friends without people speculating about them? It is ridiculous. I have already told you I do not have feelings for him, so why do you persist in pressing the issue?"

Heat filled her cheeks as she realized just how much her response said about her feelings. A lady needn't be defensive if she felt nothing for the gentleman, but Katherine couldn't unspeak the words.

Holding up his hands as though calming a rearing horse, Benjamin winced. "I didn't mean to offend you, Katherine, but I have seen you both together enough times to see the truth."

More words came to her lips, sharp and stinging, but Katherine forced herself to hold them back. With a hand over her mouth and the other curled around herself, she fought to keep a hold of her tongue, though her defenses were all primed and ready to repel Benjamin's words. But there had been no attack. It was clear from his earnest gaze and the gentleness in his tone that her brother meant no harm.

"Is it so obvious?" she whispered as her pulse raced.

Benjamin rose from his seat with a shake of his head. "Not at all. Do not forget that I see you two together more often than anyone else."

However, Katherine couldn't help but wonder if he was simply being generous and giving her the words she longed to hear. But then, whilst he was playing matchmaker, the rest of the Breadmores' gathering had thought the coupling excruciatingly hilarious.

Forcing another deep breath, she dropped her hands and faced her brother. "I believe you meant well, Benjamin, but please promise me you will stop. Please do not tell Mr. Archer anything and let things lie as they are. I assure you he does not view me as a sweetheart or even a woman."

He huffed and scratched at the back of his head in a manner that reminded Katherine so very much of the gentleman in question, and her heart panged at the sight.

"Whatever disappointments or fears you are fostering, Katherine, he cares for you—"

"As a friend, but nothing more."

Benjamin shook his head. "It is more than that. David has been out of sorts. You know he can be blind at times, but I've never seen him so distraught and discomposed—"

"Give me your word you will say nothing—to him or anyone." And heaven help her, Katherine's voice trembled. Drawing air deep into her lungs, she forced her breath in and out and refused to allow her chin even a single tremble. "Please, Benjamin."

"Would you at least accept a visit from him? He's called several times—"

Coming to his side, she grabbed his hands in hers. "Please promise me! I have been patient with him, and short of declaring my feelings, which is unthinkable for a lady to do, I have done everything I can to convince that man. If he cannot see what we share, then I do not want him. I refuse to beg him to love me."

Benjamin held her gaze for a long moment, and Katherine echoed her pleading words in her eyes, begging him to see and understand. With a heavy sigh, he nodded.

Then his arms were around her, holding her tight against him. Katherine stood, fixed in place, as she blinked at the sudden shift. It took several quickened heartbeats for her to realize just what was happening. And several more passed as she remained stiff in her brother's arms before she relaxed enough to bring up her arms and hold him in return.

How long had it been since anyone in her family had held her in such a fashion? Grandmama Cora had died ten years ago, so she supposed that was the likely answer.

That wretched chin of hers betrayed her with another tremble, but Katherine refused to allow herself to fall to pieces. Even if it felt so very wonderful to have her brother holding her. Drawing in a quick sniff, she cleared her eyes of any hints of tears as he pulled away, and Benjamin's own gaze was a touch brighter than before as he stood before her.

"I give you my word, I will not tell him anything of your feelings." Then, with a grimace, he added, "It's not as though my efforts to bring you two together have done any good."

"You are dreadful at matchmaking," she quipped with a tart sniff.

Benjamin gave a sharp chuff of laughter and shook his head. "Though I thought him insane at first, I do believe David is correct. You are quite humorous."

Katherine's heart panged at the mention of that man, but rather than allowing her mind to drift down those darkened roads, she narrowed her eyes at her brother and said with her driest of tones, "Yes, it is a shock to discover that your sister is witty."

Letting out another snort, Benjamin placed his hands on his hips and turned his gaze to the trunk. "Now, are you going to tell me why you are up in the attic, banging about?"

Motioning at the trunk, she said, "Our *dear* mother doesn't care for me rooting about in the attic, so she ordered the servants not to assist me, hoping I would give up this foolish endeavor."

Benjamin gave a wry smile and a hint of a chuckle. "Does she know you at all? Saying such a thing only guarantees you will stay up here all day until you manage it."

"If she were a conspiring sort, I would think she did so on purpose to keep me out of her hair for the rest of the day."

"And what is so very important about this trunk?" he asked, nudging it with his boot.

Katherine paused, considering that question and what answer she might give. For all that she felt the warmth of familial affection for the man asking it, the sentiment was far too new to simply embrace without question.

"I require something inside it."

"Clearly," he replied in a dry tone that matched the one she so often employed. But without further question, Benjamin reached down and lifted it up. Katherine gaped at the sight of it moving in any fashion after having spent so much time attempting to shift the wretched thing. Her pride was salved only by the fact that he strained beneath the load.

Nodding at the door, he said, "Lead the way."

Hurrying forward, Katherine moved ahead of her brother, opening doors as they made their way down to her bedchamber—all while she attempted to think of some reason for what they were to find there. She stepped through the door and around the trunks spread across her floor, their lids open and the contents spilling out.

Benjamin placed the new one where she indicated and straightened, staring at the mess. "I didn't think you kept your room in such a state."

Clutching her hands in front of her, Katherine smiled (or what she hoped was one), but when he stood there, staring at her, she didn't know what to say.

"I may not know you as well as I thought I did, but that doesn't mean I'm an utter fool, Katherine," he added in a dry tone. "What are you up to?"

Katherine's hands twisted together, and she shifted in place while Benjamin watched her with a narrowed gaze. They stood there for several long moments before he spoke again.

"If you do not wish to tell me, that is your right, but is there anything I can do to assist you? More than shift trunks?" he asked.

"You wish to help me?" she asked with a frown.

"Of course."

Her brows drew closer together. "Without question or explanation?"

Drawing in a deep breath, Benjamin tucked his hands behind him. "Someone, who shall remain nameless, has been chastising me of late about my treatment of you, and after what has happened and our conversation, I believe I am finally realizing the extent of my sins. If you require anything, you need only command, and I will do it—without question or explanation."

Katherine's fingers twisted together. "That is generous of you, but I assure you I am quite capable—"

"Your capability is not in question, dear sister," he said, though the endearment he tagged on was spoken with far more affection than the words usually held. With a wry smile, he added, "You are able to do anything you set your mind to, but that doesn't mean you need to do so alone. How can I be of assistance?"

Chapter 35

Shrugging out of his jacket, Benjamin dropped it on the chair at the far side of the room and then crouched down next to a trunk.

Nodding at the mess, he asked, "Are you removing everything or looking for specific items?"

Katherine stared at him, and he simply stared back, his hand on the edge of the opening, waiting for her orders. "You truly wish to help me?"

Benjamin's head lowered a touch, and he drew in a deep breath, but when he met her gaze once more, there was none of the irritation or impatience she expected to see.

"I have already said so, Katherine, and I mean it. Now, unless you wish me to simply start unpacking everything, you'd best give me my marching orders. What do you require?"

Drifting backward, she dropped onto her bed whilst staring at him. "You truly mean it."

Benjamin huffed, leaning heavily against the trunk, and with more than a hint of amusement, he said, "Good gracious, woman. Need I say it again? You are my sister, and though I have not shown it properly before, I do care about you and wish to do what I can to make you happy. Is it truly so difficult to believe?"

But before she could answer, he held up a staying hand. "No, don't answer that, as you've already done so. Can we move beyond all the disbelief and allow me to prove myself to you?"

Wasn't this precisely what she'd desired for so long? The moment Benjamin had arrived from school, Katherine had wished for blunt conversation and genuine interest, yet now that it had arrived, unease settled in her stomach. Again and again, a question sprang to her thoughts, and she couldn't ignore it.

Could he be trusted? He surely hadn't shown himself worthy of it.

Yet a thought wormed its way past that, planting itself deep in her heart. If she wished to resurrect her relationship with her brother, trust was required. And though her pulse quickened at the thought of laying it all bare to him, telling him of her plans was no less scary than admitting her feelings for Mr. Archer.

Most of all, Katherine felt deep in her bones that Benjamin was being earnest with her. This was no halfhearted olive branch like those Prudence and Rosanna had offered from time to time. He wished to help her. And despite her best efforts and insistence that she was capable, she wasn't certain how to proceed with her plans.

Besides, what did it matter if Benjamin disapproved? It wouldn't stop what was to come, after all. But if he was being honest with her, he could be of assistance. Katherine Leigh would take control of her future one way or another, but if he wished to help her, why not accept it?

"You must give me your word that you won't tell our parents about this," she said. "It will not alter my plans one jot, but they will make my life a misery."

Benjamin's brows rose. "That sounds ominous."

"I want your word."

"Then you have it," he said without further quibble. "I will not tell our parents anything you say to me. However, I will add that you seem to be under the misconception that I speak to our parents about anything. I avoid them as much as I can."

With a sharp nod, Katherine held his gaze and said, "I am leaving Greater Edgerton."

Her brother's gaze widened for a moment, but before he could say a word, she continued, "Grandmama Cora left me an inheritance—enough to let a small cottage and live on my own. It would be a humble life, but I've done the calculations, and the interest is enough to cover food, heating, rent, my personal expenditures, and even a maid-of-all-work. I will be quite comfortable. More than that, I will be quite happy to live my own life without my parents dictating my social calendar, harping about my clothes, and bemoaning my despicable spinsterhood."

Benjamin dropped from his crouch to the ground, his mouth agape as he stared at her. "You are leaving?"

She lifted her chin and watched him closely. "I am."

"And Grandmother Cora left you that much money?" he said in a monotone.

"With instructions to the solicitor to tell no one but me, lest our parents get wind and attempt to wrestle it away from me," she added with a wry smile.

Benjamin let out a low whistle, shaking his head as he leaned against the trunk. "That crafty old biddy."

"She knew our parents well."

"That she did," he said with a chuckle. "And clearly, she knew you, as well."

"She was the only one at Whitley Court who enjoyed my company."

Katherine's gaze dropped to the ground, her heart growing heavy in her chest. Before Benjamin could say anything to that, she shook the melancholy away and met his gaze once more. He watched her carefully, his brows pinched together.

"She passed a decade ago," he said.

"Yes."

"And you are just now deciding to leave?"

She ran her hands down her skirts and straightened the folds of fabric. "I have been waiting for the proper time."

"And now that things with David—"

"This has nothing to do with him."

Benjamin gave her a challenging raise of the brows, and Katherine met his gaze without wavering. The debacle with Mr. Archer might have a small part to play in her timing, but it was not he who had inspired it. As they stared at each other, Benjamin straightened.

"You only met him two or three years ago, so it couldn't be about him," he murmured, and as he studied her, Katherine shifted in place, forcing herself not to flinch.

"Can I simply say my time here is at an end, and it is best that I leave? What reasons I had for remaining are nonsensical and no longer matter."

Benjamin's lips tightened, but he nodded. "I will allow it, though I feel I ought to say I am concerned about this plan of yours. Living alone can be precarious."

"Yet there are spinsters and widows who manage," she replied with a wry tone. "I will take precautions, and there is no reason I cannot be as safe as anyone can reasonably expect to be."

"And it is lonely," he added.

She lifted a single shoulder in a shrug. "I am well used to that. Even when the house was filled to bursting, it always felt lonely. Besides, solitude is preferable to keeping company with Mama and her friends."

Turning her gaze to him, she arched her brow. "You needn't object further, for I have already put my plan into motion. I wrote to my solicitor and enlisted his aid in finding me a home."

Benjamin's brows rose, and he straightened. "What news does he have?"

"I am awaiting his response," she replied whilst picking off a bit of lint from her skirts. Her words were true enough, but as she considered them, Katherine's heart sank.

Writing to him was the only course of action she'd had, but despite having met the man only once, she was fairly certain he would not approve of her plan or assist her in it. He'd been quite concerned about Katherine's plans for the money, and he was unlikely to celebrate a lady striking out on her own.

She lowered her gaze to the rug at her feet, and her eyes traced the swirling scrollwork woven into the pattern.

Prudence's brother-in-law was a solicitor; Katherine didn't know the man, but he might be of assistance. But then, he'd likely reveal her plans to Prudence. She could only imagine what strong words that lady would have to say about this venture. And then there was a greater chance of Mama or Papa discovering it before she was ready to leave. It wouldn't alter her course, but they could make her situation very uncomfortable in the interim.

There were a few other solicitors in town that might be willing to meet with her, but perhaps she could simply choose a town from a map and travel there, staying in inns until she located a home to let. That was a risky endeavor, but it was better than languishing at Whitley Court—

"I will act as your man of business," said Benjamin.

Katherine jerked her attention from her thoughts and the rug's pattern to look at her brother. "Pardon?"

"I will find you a home to let."

Perched on the edge of the mattress, she stared at the fellow—and he stared back. Despite the closeness of the past half hour, Katherine couldn't say she knew her brother well. Their lives intersected quite often, but she couldn't recall the last time they'd truly had a frank discussion like this, so she couldn't quite trust her interpretation of his expression.

But to her eyes, Benjamin looked eager.

"I wish to help you," he added. "And if hauling about trunks is the only assistance I can offer, then so be it, but for once, I can see something you require and cannot do yourself."

Katherine opened her mouth, but he continued, "I can travel there and see for myself if it will suit your needs. It is easy enough for me to do so without raising suspicions. And I would feel better if I saw for myself that you are properly settled, rather than entrusting it to some solicitor you hardly know."

Brows crinkled together, she watched as he spouted off reason after reason as to why she ought to accept his assistance, and she couldn't seem to find the words to answer him. Benjamin truly wished to assist her. Though some dark part of her heart whispered that it was solely so he could ruin her plans, that fear couldn't be sustained with every impassioned argument he gave.

Benjamin's gaze pleaded with her, matching his tone as he expounded at length on just why he was the better choice. And still, she couldn't seem to answer him.

Her brother cared for her. Had she thought such a thing yesterday, Katherine would've laughed at herself. That foolish hope had laid in wait for so many years, desperate for some sign that it was true. And here it was. Benjamin Leigh cared about his sister.

Clearing her throat, Katherine drew in a deep breath and interrupted. "I accept."

Benjamin paused mid-sentence and blinked at her. "You do?"

"Yes."

"Oh," he replied, straightening and drumming his fingers against the floor. "I thought it would take more for you to agree. I still haven't exhausted all my arguments."

She huffed. "I can be reasonable. Isn't that shocking?"

He matched her huff and shook his head. "How did I overlook your humor?"

"A double shock, to be sure," she replied in a dry tone.

Drawing his legs in, Benjamin stared at her with a clear question on his lips, though he didn't speak. Katherine watched him for a long moment before he finally ventured to voice it.

"I hope not to pique your anger, but I fear I must ask if I can divulge your plans to Prudence and Rosanna."

She shook her head. "They will tell Mama—"

"Not if you ask them not to," he replied. "And please notice I did not mention Francis, for not only will she be of no use, she will immediately write to Mother and tell all. However, the others can be trusted."

"Rosanna is Mama's favorite, and she will do what she will to maintain that place—even betray my trust if need be." Katherine crossed her arms and sighed. "She is just as aggressive as Mama when it comes to foisting me off on undesirable gentlemen, and all for the sake of garnering favor with the Leigh matriarch."

Benjamin canted his head to the side, his brows furrowing. "That is not true. Rosanna is convinced you do not like her, but she wishes to see you settled. Unfortunately, she is as blind as I have been. I cannot tell you how often I have heard Prudence and Rosanna bemoan the fact that they wish to know you better—"

"That is ridiculous," she said with a frown. "Rosanna is forever attempting to alter me—just like Mama does—and Prudence continually brushes me aside whenever I ask her for anything or attempt to speak with her. She is forever occupied with something far more important."

With a wince, Benjamin shrugged. "I feel as though we have already established that our family is quite good at misinterpreting each other's motivations. Perhaps we could try again."

Drawing her arms tight around herself, Katherine considered the dueling sentiments warring in her chest. Her heart gave a happy flutter at the mere thought that such a thing was possible. Yet experience had taught her time and time again not to give in to such vain hopes, and her ribs squeezed tight at the thought of opening herself up once more to that possible pain.

She breathed deeply, forcing both emotions into the background as she focused on her brother. "I will, if you promise me one thing."

Benjamin paused, his head canting to the side as he considered that. "Which is?"

"Do not break the entail. Do not sacrifice your future for our parents' selfish desires. They have made their poor choices, and you needn't be made to bear the consequences of them."

"I do not plan on doing so," he said. "And with you comfortably situated there is nothing they can do to persuade me otherwise."

Katherine shook her head, her brows drawing close together. "You have never been the focus of their ire before, Benjamin. In their eyes, you can do no wrong, for you are their salvation. When it becomes clear you are not, they will unleash the very fires of hell. You have no idea how horrid they can be."

Rising to his feet, Benjamin took her in his arms once more and held her tight. "Do not worry, my dearest sister. I will remain strong."

Yet as she reveled in the comfort his embrace held, Katherine's heart chilled at the thought of what was to come for him.

Chapter 36

Focus was not a difficult thing. Having stepped into his father's shoes at sixteen, David Archer knew how to work. For all that people believed the youth lacked determination, to his thinking, much of that was due to a lack of responsibilities laid on their shoulders.

Young men were simply expected to attend whatever schooling their father decided and fill the time between exams and books with drinking, gambling, and sowing those wickedly wild oats. As long as they toed the line when their majority arrived and settled down with a gently bred lady, the heirs of the gentry had few demands to fulfill.

Seeing his family's struggling mill and the inevitable bankruptcy that was bound to come, David had stepped into the role of mill owner without a second thought. Father hadn't been bothered by the shift, for it allowed him to make himself merry, and it had taught David many valuable lessons—including that work was an excellent distraction.

Yet with the ledgers and correspondence stacked around him, demanding his attention, David stared at the window. Faint shafts of light streamed through the glass, though the sky was heavy with clouds. There was just enough sun to keep frost from forming on the pane, but there was a definite nip in the air as winter returned in force again. However, it wasn't the gardens outside the study window that held his attention.

With the door open, it was easy enough to hear noises from the rest of the house. Certainly a piano, if it were being played. But no bright melodies rang through the air.

Scowling at the ledgers, David shoved them away and leaned back into his armchair. He ought to have gone into the mill this morning, as there were issues he needed to discuss with Mr. Fenn, but he couldn't force himself to leave his study. He rested his hands on his stomach and entwined his fingers whilst sinking lower into the armchair.

Since his initial invitation to use their piano, Miss Leigh had visited Stratsfield House daily, yet he'd seen neither hide nor hair of the lady since *the incident*. And David knew her well enough to know that nothing short of the direst of circumstances would keep her from playing the piano for three weeks.

He'd driven her from that passion of hers.

Passion. Such a strange word. Despite having a clear definition, there were so many facets to its meaning. Only a few weeks ago, David wouldn't have put passion and Miss Leigh in the same sentence, but for all that the lady's exterior spoke of one far too sensible for such a heady emotion, he'd always known she had a fire burning in her heart. Just not that sort of heat. Certainly not the sort to steal kisses in the moonlight.

Footsteps echoed in the corridor, and David straightened, his ears pricking up at the noise. Rising to his feet, he moved to the doorway and spied a maid hurrying along to her duties. With a sigh, he moved back to the desk and dropped into his chair.

He was quite willing to admit he'd handled their kiss poorly, but how would he make amends if she refused to speak to him? Groaning, David leaned forward and rubbed at his face. Was it possible for a man to make more of a muck of things than he had? If Miss Leigh was willing to give up her precious piano to avoid him, was there any hope for him?

Shaking free of that thought, David rose to his feet and paced a familiar route around the study. Melancholia was hardly helpful at present. He certainly deserved the sourness in his stomach and the heaviness in his heart, but if he had any hope of winning Miss Leigh's forgiveness, he needed a plan.

Unfortunately, his mind supplied no viable solutions. Calling on the Leighs hadn't worked, and letters were returned, unopened. Perhaps he could bribe the servants to sneak him in. Grimacing at that thought, David paused and rubbed at the back of his head. Flowers were a clear choice, but that was so pedestrian, and Miss Leigh was not the sort to be won over by a simple nosegay.

In truth, he knew patience was required, but no matter how much he tried to embrace that rational course of action, David couldn't help but return to one sickening thought again and again—Miss Leigh despised him so much that even the lure of his piano wouldn't bring her into the open.

Shaking his head, he resumed pacing. That was ridiculous. Music was a part of her very soul, and she could not deny herself indefinitely. A little time, and she would give in to that longing. He simply needed to decide what to say when the opportunity to speak to her arose.

But his thoughts were moving in circles, just like his feet. Dropping into his armchair again, David let out a heavy sigh.

"That most certainly paid my forfeits."

Groaning anew, he scrubbed at his face. What sort of fool said such a thing at such a time?

Footsteps sounded in the corridor, and when they paused just out of sight in the doorway, David straightened, his ears straining to hear who it was. Which was ridiculous: it was likely the maid again. But he couldn't seem to help himself.

"Hello?" he called, and Benjamin stepped through.

David held back a sigh but relaxed back into his chair. It wasn't the distraction he'd hoped for, but it was something. Even if it wasn't a pleasant one. Heat filled his cheeks, and he fiddled with the stacks of paper on his desk, straightening them.

"Come in, Benjamin."

His friend did so, striding over to take a seat across from David and matching his relaxed pose, though Benjamin's was far less comfortable with his jacket restricting his ability to properly slouch. But the two simply sat there in silence.

"Are you going to stride into my study after three weeks without a word and act as though nothing is wrong?" asked David.

"What is wrong?" asked Benjamin with a frown.

David narrowed his eyes, though there was little heat in the expression. "You dare ask that after that debacle at the Breadmores'?"

Holding up his hands, Benjamin shook his head. "It isn't my fault you bungled the kiss with my sister."

Gaping, David scoffed. "That isn't what I was referring to. You forced our hand—"

"I mean no offense, David, but the only person I owed an apology to is my sister. She was the one who suffered the ridicule. You were given an opportunity, and you squandered it. If anything, you should apologize to me. And to my sister."

David let out another sigh, puffing out his cheeks. "I have attempted to do so, but your sister refuses to see me. And I would point out that if you didn't feel that you owed me an apology as well, you wouldn't have avoided me for the past few weeks."

Benjamin scoffed and shook his head. "How wrong you are, David Archer. I've hardly been in town for more than a few hours at a time. I haven't had a moment to spare."

"You've been traveling?" asked David with a raise of his brows. "What for?"

"I've been on an important errand for my family."

"Concerning?"

"None of your business."

David stared at him, not only because of the curt reply but due to the hard tone with which Benjamin spoke. There was no mistaking the fact that his friend would not welcome further inquiries, but David couldn't help his rising curiosity at the evasive answers. Having spent much time advising his friend on matters of business, David knew the Leighs had no income or investments beyond their estate; there was nothing financial dragging him from Greater Edgerton.

"Does this have anything to do with your sister?" asked David.

"I do not want to talk about her with you," replied Benjamin with narrowed eyes as he crossed his arms.

And the pair fell silent. For several long moments, they simply stared at each other as David's thoughts raced. Instinct niggled in his stomach, saying there was far more to this conversation than met the eye, yet he couldn't logic his way to an answer.

Yet still, Benjamin sat there, silent.

With a sharp sigh, David threw his arms wide. "You won't speak to me of what you've been up to, your sister, or anything else, it seems. Why are you here, Benjamin?"

"I have my reasons," he replied.

"Which you are not going to share with me?"

One sharp nod was all the reply he gave.

Drawing in a deep breath, David let it out and forced his fists to unclench. "What can I do to repair things with your sister? I have done what I can, but she will not see me. I cannot make things right if she refuses to allow me any opportunity."

"I told you I do not wish to discuss Katherine. You've done enough harm."

David's pulse quickened at that, and his heart chilled at the description. And once again, the memory of their parting played through his mind, sending a spike of pain through his chest. But quick on its heels, heat swept across his skin at Benjamin's tone and the hard judgment in his gaze.

"This is a laugh," said David. "Only a few weeks ago, I was chastising you for how you treated her, yet now you're rushing in like some shining knight, protecting her from harm. Do not cast stones at me, Benjamin Leigh. I have hurt her, I know it, but it is nothing compared to what you and the rest of your family have done in the past."

Benjamin leaned his head back, his brows rising. "What does it matter to you what happens to her? You have plenty of friends. What does it matter if one of them cuts ties?"

The very breath in his lungs seized, and David wasn't certain they would ever function properly again. His reunion with Miss Leigh had been a given; even if it took weeks or months, he would win his way back into her good graces again. But Benjamin's final question cut him to the quick.

Cutting ties. That was not a small thing. That was definitive. Unyielding.

"What do you mean, 'cut ties'?" he asked.

"That is a fairly simple turn of phrase, David."

Despite its being a 'fairly simple' action, David couldn't breathe. His chest expanded and contracted, yet he couldn't get any air into his lungs. The finality of his friend's tone pressed down on him as Benjamin's words rang through his thoughts. Miss Leigh was cutting ties with him, and with that, he was losing any opportunity to win her back.

Rising to his feet, he snatched his jacket from the side table and shrugged it on, his feet carrying him across the room before he knew what he was about.

Chapter 37

"What are you up to?" asked Benjamin, stepping between David and the door.

"If I have to camp out on your doorstep or break into her bedchamber, then I shall do so," replied David, straightening his jacket as he tried to step around him. "One way or another, I am going to get your sister to speak to me. If she cannot forgive me, then so be it, but I cannot let things stand, Benjamin. And I am not going to let her cut ties without a word."

The two shifted and pivoted around the doorway as David attempted to leave the study whilst the other did what he could to stop him.

"Stop this!" said David. "I need to speak to her."

But Benjamin simply stepped in his way once more.

Shoving against him, David gritted his teeth. "What are you doing? I know I have been a fool—and I certainly deserve to be raked over the coals—but this has gone on long enough. I thought giving her some time might help, but clearly, matters are only growing worse. Things will never mend if she won't speak to me—"

"And I ask you again, what does it matter?" asked Benjamin, shoving back with equal force. "One way or another, you're going to find your Mystery Lady, and you won't have any need for Katherine to hang about—"

"I don't want that wretched Mystery Lady!" shouted David, putting his shoulder into it as he butted against his friend, but Benjamin grabbed him in a bear hug, and the two were as close to wrestling as gentlemen in restrictive jackets could.

"After the way you've been pining for her?" asked Benjamin with a grunt.

"You're the one who has been pushing me to open my eyes and realize the truth, and I have. Katherine is everything I could hope for in a sweetheart. We make each other happy. In fact, the only time I am miserable when it comes to her is when she refuses to speak to me, so let me go. I need to find her. Why are you being so ridiculous?!"

His arms squeezed tight around David, strangling the last words, and though Benjamin stilled, he didn't loosen his stranglehold.

"You truly mean that, don't you?" asked Benjamin.

"Again," he managed to squeak out whilst tugging at the arm holding him in place, "you are the one who has been lecturing me on this subject. Why are you so surprised that I came to my senses?"

With a low hum somewhat akin to a growl, Benjamin released him, and David straightened, tugging at his jacket and smoothing his cravat.

"You care for her?" asked Benjamin.

Brushing off his sleeve, David frowned. "I do not wish to discuss that with you."

Benjamin's gaze darkened, and he stepped forward, reaching for him again. David jumped backward, holding up his hands to ward his friend off.

"I only meant that she deserves to hear what I have to say first."

But his friend did not back away. Benjamin narrowed his

gaze. "I did a wretched job of it in the past, but it is my duty and honor to protect her from blackguards."

David kept his hands up between them, and he nodded. "I understand, and I will say that I have intentions and they are honorable. I was a fool to cling to some fantasy for so long, but I realize my folly now, and I will do everything in my power to win her heart."

Letting out a heavy sigh, Benjamin dropped his arms to his side. His brows drew together as he studied David, who did his utmost to look as genuine as he could. Thankfully, every word he'd uttered was the truth, so it was simple enough to do so.

"I am a distraction," said Benjamin.

"Pardon?"

"You asked why I was visiting, and that is the reason," he clarified. "Katherine is gathering the last of her things she left here, and she asked me to keep you occupied."

David Let out a groan that ended in a sigh and scrubbed at his face. "Promise me that if this interview goes poorly, you will convince her to continue using our piano. If she wishes to avoid me, she need only tell me when she is coming by, and I will leave the premises. Even if she cannot forgive me, she shouldn't be kept from her music."

Benjamin's jaw clenched, and he was silent for a moment before he answered. "I cannot promise you that, but I give you my word Katherine will never be forbidden music again."

Again, the tone with which he spoke was far too significant to be ignored, and David frowned.

"Your parents have replaced her piano?" Though that seemed the clearest meaning, he couldn't imagine it was the case, as Mrs. Leigh was quite clear and unshakeable concerning her daughter's playing.

"Of course not," replied Benjamin, holding David's gaze as though hoping to lead him to the answer.

David rubbed at the back of his head. "If you have something to say, man, then say it. Clearly, something is going on, but I cannot fathom what it is. Out with it."

"I gave my word that I wouldn't," replied Benjamin with an equally heavy tone and expression. "I have already said far more than I probably ought to, but do you recall when you asked me about the escape plan Katherine mentioned?"

Benjamin raised his brows suggestively, and David frowned, his thoughts quickly pasting together the various hints scattered in their conversation. It took no great leap in logic to suspect that his friend's recent absences from town had something to do with it, and David didn't need Benjamin to confirm what his heart already suspected.

When Miss Leigh had spoken of her escape, it hadn't seemed like some small attempt at freedom. David had never thought it would be so grand a thing, but in his bones, he knew it was true.

Cold ran down his spine, settling into his stomach as he stood there, staring off at nothing. She was leaving Greater Edgerton. Leaving him. Knowing he had time to plead his case had been the only modicum of peace to be found in the past three weeks, and now, that was snatched away from him.

David was out of time.

...

In only a few short weeks, Stratsfield House's drawing room had undergone a brilliant transformation. Most families kept that room relatively empty, allowing it to transform into any sort of space they required without much effort. Without sofas and armchairs, it was simple enough for it to become a ballroom. Bring in a few chairs and tables, and it was a card room. Or a music room. As the parlor was the place for comfort when entertaining, it made sense to leave the drawing room for the formal evenings.

However, Mrs. Archer was a lover of music. Katherine wouldn't call the lady a connoisseur, but Mrs. Archer adored hearing the family's piano brought to life under Katherine's fingertips. And so, the drawing room had slowly transformed into something between drawing room and parlor. A sofa and armchair were placed to one side of the room, far enough from the instrument that Katherine couldn't see if anyone listened to her, but allowing Mrs. Archer and her daughters to sit in comfort during their informal concerts.

Katherine's hand rested on the polished wood of the pianoforte. The light from the windows glinted off the mirrored surface, highlighting the beautiful grain that wove through the multi-hued browns. But as much as she would miss the feel of the keys and the clear quality of the notes, it was their company and acceptance she would regret losing the most.

Only a few weeks, and yet her time here had become such a significant part of her day. She doubted Mr. Archer knew just how much time she spent in Stratsfield House. Or *had* spent.

Gently, she set the lid down, closing the pianoforte up tight. No one was likely to use it in the near future, and Katherine couldn't help but feel saddened by that thought, but there was nothing to be done about it. Even if she could fit it in her cottage, the instrument belonged with the Archers.

She brushed one final touch across the top and turned to the stacks of sheet music in the box beside it. A more intelligent person would've kept theirs separate, but in all her visions of the future, she hadn't anticipated needing a quick departure. And so, she was left to comb through each book and sheet to separate hers from the Archers'.

For all that she knew she ought to move quickly, her traitorous heart kept stopping to recall some memory tied to the compositions, and her gaze kept drifting to the empty seats, seeing the family gathered round.

Foolish girl. Drawing in a deep breath, she forced her thoughts to what needed to be done. Benjamin would do his best, but he was no miracle worker, and Mr. Archer was bound to discover her here if she wasn't careful. It would've been wiser to wait until he wasn't here, but ss one cursed with poor luck, she knew having the rest of the Archers absent was the best she could hope for.

Gathering the sheets close, Katherine turned to find Mr. Archer standing in the doorway. She felt the void gaping between them, deeper and darker than before. For all that he looked like the man she'd known for so long, she couldn't see her friend there any longer.

"I pay my staff handsomely, and despite asking them to inform me the moment you arrive at Stratsfield House, I find they ignored my wishes," he said with a wry smile. "Clearly, they prefer you over me."

Katherine clutched the music tight to her chest, her chin lifting a fraction, and Mr. Archer held up his hands in placation.

"I apologize," he said with a wince. "I should know better than to attempt humor in weighty situations, but I fear I cannot help myself—even when they always come out wrong."

And even that was spoken with a hint of amusement. The edges of her music books dug into Katherine's arms, and she moved not an inch as she stared at him through half-lidded eyes. Mr. Archer stood there, blocking the door.

"I—" he began, and the sound spurred her to move. With quick steps, Katherine crossed the room and reached the other exit, but Mr. Archer proved himself quite spry and was there before she could step through.

"Please, Miss Leigh—"

"I do not wish to hear your excuses, Mr. Archer," she said with a shake of her head. "Whatever you wish to explain, it matters not. Please, let me through."

"What about an apology? Surely that is important?" And once more, he attempted a wry tone and awkward grin.

"There is no need to apologize, Mr. Archer. Everyone has the right to feel as they wish, so you needn't apologize for feeling disgusted with our..." Katherine's teeth clicked together as her jaw snapped shut, and she felt like scowling as she stumbled over the word. It was a kiss. Only a kiss! No reason for her cheeks to blaze like a midsummer's day.

"Disgusted?" Mr. Archer gaped, his brows knitting together.

"Do not deny it, sir," she said, tipping up her chin. "I saw the truth in your gaze that night. You were repulsed."

Katherine forced herself not to wince as her voice trembled at that last word. Whatever others might believe of those wilting wallflowers who haunted the edges of society, she refused to allow herself to be cowed by anyone—let alone her own heart.

Yet the memory of his expression surfaced in her thoughts once more. Mr. Archer's gaze filled her, the bare and unmistakable regret shining within his dark eyes. And her heart cracked further.

Chapter 38

Only the strongest display of willpower allowed David to remain where he was. His hands shook as Miss Leigh stood there, the picture of strength and invulnerability. He'd seen her in such a pose so many times before, for it was her favorite when facing down the villains in her life. And like all those other times, he saw the truth in her gaze.

No tears would fall from Katherine Leigh's eyes, but that didn't diminish the pain in those brown depths, and David's own grew misty as his heart twisted in his chest, squeezing in on itself.

He had done this to her. Made her feel unwanted. Rejected. Despised. What had been an awakening for him had left her feeling like that poor discarded little girl who'd spent her life hoping for a morsel of affection from her selfish parents and blind siblings.

"Katherine," he whispered, her name coming easily to his lips, but she stiffened, that defiant chin lifting even further. Holding up placating hands, he amended, "Miss Leigh, I was in no way repulsed or disgusted—"

"Disappointed, then," she said with a huff and turned on her heel toward the other door out of the drawing room, but

David scurried around, stepping in front of her. "But I assure you, the sentiment was clear enough, and even a plain spinster doesn't care to be embraced by a disappointed man—"

"Do not speak of yourself in such a manner!" David couldn't help the sharpness of the words. They came to his lips with such a pulse of strength that radiated through him, and he couldn't moderate them in the slightest. They were fueled by a fire that had been simmering for so long, kindled by every unkind word others spoke of her—even those she spouted about herself.

Miss Leigh merely gave him a placating smile that was as false as paste stonework. "I am well aware of marital status and appearance, Mr. Archer. And you needn't apologize for your natural reaction to my unattractive self. You are free to feel as you wish without needing to beg forgiveness. It is no mortal offense."

David moved before he could think better of it, pulling her flush to him and encircling her in his arms. Miss Leigh's gaze widened, and he dipped his head closer, stopping a hair's breadth from seizing her in a kiss. No matter what he wanted to do, that would not help matters at present.

But with her full attention on him, he spoke in a tone that, though low, held all the conviction he felt. "You are not plain, and I will not stand here and listen to anyone disparage you—even yourself."

Miss Leigh's brows rose in challenge. "No number of hollow compliments will make a lie the truth, Mr. Archer. I heard what you said about me."

The words were spoken as though it was a gauntlet thrown, awaiting a response. She was so certain in it that David's stomach began to sink.

"I do not know what you are referring to," he said.

"You and Benjamin were discussing your possible Mystery Lady—that pinnacle of womanhood—and you couldn't believe for one moment that I could be that goddess among mortals. She was so perfect and lovely—"

"I couldn't believe it because you weren't dressed in a costume. I saw you with my own eyes, so you couldn't be that masked lady, and surely you would've given some sign that it was you," said David with a frown. "It was a shock to consider you in that light simply because it hadn't crossed my mind. I freely admit I was a lackwit for that."

His toes were on the edge of a precipice. One more step would launch him into the unknown. With so much damage done to her poor pride, he knew what needed doing, but his throat clamped shut. Though it was clear that Miss Leigh felt something significant when it came to him, only a fool would trust a declaration would be well received at that moment.

Where did her heart lie? Was it merely pricked because of the supposed rejection? Or did she feel more for him? The odds were too distorted for him to feel comfortable placing any wager on it, but David knew there was no chance this would end well if he didn't try.

Miss Leigh stood like a statue in his arms, but her gaze held his, those lovely eyes of hers saying more than her lips. He could see the stony resolve faltering, and he prayed that he would know the proper words to say.

"I know I have been blind, and that you've watched as I've searched in vain for some phantom of a lady, thinking her the perfect partner for my life, but the expression of disappointment you saw that night wasn't because I didn't enjoy the kiss." He paused, drawing in a fortifying breath before hurrying to say, "It was because I had wanted you to be her."

Her hands rose and pushed against him. "And what does that matter? Am I only worthy of your affection if I am some fantasy, come to life? Otherwise, I am invisible—the plain old Katherine Leigh—"

"No!" he said, the word sharp. "Do not say such things—"

"But they are fitting. I am like an older sister to you." Though her chin did not tremble, her words wobbled just a touch. "After you laughed at the prospect, you said those very words, Mr. Archer."

Closing his eyes, David dropped his head with a sigh. Truly, he was a fool. How many times had he cursed all the thoughtless people who caused her pain? And yet in the end, his careless actions and words had done more damage. His throat tightened around his words, though he didn't know which ones to offer up.

"I do not know what to say. What penance to complete. What reassurances I can offer or explanations to give. I have always respected you greatly, Miss Leigh, but I do know that I have made some terrible mistakes."

With his hands resting on her back, David couldn't help but brush his thumbs against her, gathering the strength he needed.

"I took you for granted, Miss Leigh. You were my friend and companion for so long, slipping into my life with little fanfare, invading every part of it before I knew what was happening. I can't even say when I fell for you, but I know now that I love you. I have for some time, even if I was too blind to see it."

Miss Leigh's muscles loosened, her eyes widening as she gaped at him.

"I admit I was fixated on that silly Mystery Lady because I wasn't thinking of romance or marriage before she swept into my life," he said with a shake of his head. "My thoughts were full of my family and all those responsibilities, and she opened my heart to the possibility of what I could have. And as I searched for her, I came to see that I've had that for so long—with you."

David's mouth dried, his gaze lowering to her collarbone as his fingers grazed her back. "And when I kissed you, I hoped you were the same lady who had inspired those feelings. That there was one lady only who captured my heart. That the answer is and always was you."

That certainly painted her memories in a new light. Katherine struggled to sort out her realities, but her thoughts couldn't seem to make any sense of them. Not with Mr. Archer's hands caressing her back in such a manner whilst he said such tender things.

He loved her?

As much as she'd longed to hear those very words, Katherine couldn't believe he'd actually said them. Had it been her imagination? Was she asleep and her dreams had simply conjured this moment? But she didn't think even her imagination would create such a scenario, with papers and books crumpling in her arms as she struggled to breathe properly.

"Please do not leave me," he whispered, his head lowering closer to hers. "I cannot bear to lose you."

Lightening broke from the heavens and struck Katherine's heart, shattering it whilst the fog in her mind cleared to show her the truth standing in front of her face—Mr. Archer knew of her plans and didn't wish to lose his chum.

Katherine Leigh truly was a fool of the highest order. Despite having known his feelings from the start, her silly little heart couldn't help but pitter-patter with him so close. It was merely the memory of his other embraces that had her pulse racing so, but one's decorum shouldn't be so easily disrupted. Mr. Archer had kissed her a few times now, and it had altered nothing. Not for the better, at any rate, so there was no need to allow it to sway her now.

"Thank you for your kind words, Mr. Archer," she said, freeing one hand to pat him on the chest as though he were a puppy, and that helped her breaths to deepen. "You've always been a stalwart friend."

Mr. Archer's brows drew tight together, and he leaned back to study her, though Katherine knew none of the pain showed at present. It helped that the initial shock of the moment had faded, filling her with a cold numbness and making her feel like a doll held up in his arms rather than a lady of flesh and blood.

"I am not speaking only as a friend, Miss Leigh—though I do count you as my dearest—but the past few weeks have helped me see that you are everything I wish for in a wife." The gentleman fairly babbled as he spoke, his words coming hurriedly as though he was desperate to get out every word before she disappeared.

And that was the trouble, wasn't it? Katherine ought to have known better than to trust Benjamin to guard Mr. Archer without spilling some of her secrets. Mr. Archer's explanations were perfectly sound, and she felt certain he believed them, but if the road to hell was paved with good intentions, the mortar binding the pavers together was desperation.

How long before Mr. Archer realized he'd mistaken the longing to keep his chum as love? Plenty of fools convinced themselves that a fleeting passion was something substantial, especially when fate attempted to pluck the object of their desire away. Nothing rushed love quicker than the thought of losing it.

Patting his chest more forcefully, Katherine freed herself from his hold. "I am honored by your declaration, Mr. Archer. I am. However, I cannot help but feel your epiphany concerning my 'perfection' is rather conveniently timed. You've had months—years, really—to see me as something more than your older sister, and it is only when the clock strikes twelve that you show any romantic interest in me."

"I would say the timing is rather inconvenient," he replied with a frown.

She straightened the music in her arms. "It is flattering, Mr. Archer, and I will miss our friendship as well. But I am not interested in being the lady you settle for simply because you cannot find your Mystery Lady and are afraid of losing my company."

"You are not my second choice," he said, stepping closer, but Katherine moved away and warded him off with a raise of her hand.

"That is kind of you to say, but I will not allow you to bind yourself to me out of some misguided determination to keep me close," she said, turning towards the door.

"I know my own heart, and I won't give up, Miss Leigh," he said, his tone as unshakeable as any she'd ever heard him use.

Mr. Archer stood there, his own chin lifted as though mirroring hers, and his jaw was set as though ready to do battle. But there were no demons to fight.

Katherine paused, swallowing past the tightness in her throat. "Go find yourself a proper love, whoever that is."

Mr. Archer gave no sign that her words shook his resolve, and he watched her with those eyes that so often saw to the very heart of her. "There is no one more proper for me than you."

Forcing her feet to move, Katherine strode towards the door with her head held high. And only once she was safely at home, hidden in her bedchamber with the door locked, did she allow the tears to flow.

Chapter 39

Silence could be such a heavy thing, pressing down with a substance and form all its own. Despite Katherine's sister sitting on the sofa opposite, neither lady spoke, and the sharp tick of the ormolu clock punctured the quiet like the needles in their hands.

Pushing it through the muslin, Katherine stitched the thread along the faint marks of the pencil that outlined the design. Ivy wound along the edge of the white fabric with flowers of pink, blue, and purple sprouting in clumps. She didn't know what images she would put inside the needlepoint frame, though she rather liked the idea of a quote or verse.

With quick movements, Katherine tied off the stitch and clipped the thread. Holding the embroidery hoop, she examined her work. Her eyes fell to an uneven stitch, and she frowned at it. Despite knowing no one else could see the imperfection, it was frustrating to know it was there.

"I have a frame that would look lovely with that," said Rosanna.

Katherine couldn't help but stare at her sister. Clearing her throat, she nodded. "That would be wonderful."

Casting a glance about, as though Mama might suddenly

leap from behind an armchair (despite knowing the lady was paying calls elsewhere), Rosanna added, "I am certain it will look perfect in your parlor. I understand the cottage is near the shore."

"I can hardly wait to see it in person," said Katherine, threading another color into her needle. "Benjamin says it overlooks the cliffs and boasts a lovely view of the ocean. I have long wished to visit the shore."

Rosanna smiled, her own needle making quick work of a torn seam. "Once you are settled, Malcolm and I would love to visit." Rosanna's brows pinched together, and she hurried to add, "If you wish us to, of course."

Good heavens, the conversation was so discomforting. Yet Katherine's heart warmed with each awkward attempt her sister made. The conflicting emotions set her insides churning until she wasn't certain whether or not this was a good development.

"Perhaps you could come during the holiday break and bring the children as well." Katherine paused, searching for something to say to prod the conversation forward, but chatter wasn't her forte. Silence was her preferred form of communication when it came to her family, and it was difficult to undo a lifetime of habit.

She glanced at Rosanna and scoured her thoughts for something to say. "How are Layton and Samuel enjoying school?"

Rosanna's light eyes rose to meet Katherine's, and a smile blossomed on her lips. "Samuel adores it. He is so like his papa and adores being surrounded by all the other boys—"

"And like his mama," added Katherine with a wry smile.

"Yes, and like his mama," amended Rosanna before launching into a description of the boys' letters and the reports the school sent on their behalf. As Katherine adored her nephews, it was an easy enough subject to expand upon, and soon a conversation sprouted from that hastily planted seed.

Katherine kept her gaze fixed on her work, and despite her

mind being engaged with the conversation, her thoughts couldn't help but drift to all the new alterations in her life. Even a few weeks ago, she wouldn't have imagined sitting with her sister and having a proper conversation.

"Oh, and I completely forgot!" Rosanna gaped, dropping her sewing and reaching for her bag. Digging through the contents, she pulled a roll of papers free and handed them to Katherine. "Prudence wanted to join us, but she is feeling poorly—"

"Still?" asked Katherine with a frown. "Is there anything I can do?"

Rosanna's brows rose, and Katherine straightened, her heart clamping shut at the look of surprise. Did she truly think Prudence's discomfort meant nothing to the heartless Katherine?

"I apologize," said Rosanna with a grimace. "I didn't mean to imply you wouldn't wish to help. Of course you would. I just cannot recall—"

Rosanna snapped her mouth shut, and Katherine could well imagine how she would've finished the sentence, for it was true.

"No one ever accepted my assistance, so I gave up offering," said Katherine.

Clearing her throat, Rosanna nodded, her eyes full of another apology. "I fear there is nothing any of us can do. Hopefully, the sickness will fade as she draws nearer to her confinement, but I fear she often struggles to the very end. Thankfully, this new addition to the family should arrive in a few weeks."

Straightening, Rosanna offered the roll of papers again. "And I am determined to forget this all over again. Prudence couldn't come, but she asked me to deliver some music she thought you might enjoy. She is sorry she couldn't bring it herself."

Katherine blinked at the offering, her sewing lying forgotten in her lap. Music. Tentatively, she took the roll and tugged open the twine to unfurl the sheets. John Fields was a bit beyond her ability, and she wasn't good enough at sight-reading to discern the melody simply by looking at the notes, but her heart warmed all the same.

"I—"

But she jerked when the parlor door swung open.

"Good afternoon, ladies," said Benjamin, striding through and coming over to buss his sisters on the cheek, not even pausing as he bestowed the affection on Katherine, as though it was a commonplace thing to do. She couldn't say whether her ribs grew too tight or her heart expanded within her chest, but pressure built there, threatening to burst forth in some ridiculous display. Drawing in a breath, she nudged her spectacles up her nose and turned her attention back to her sewing.

And that was when Benjamin swept into a bow and brought his hand around to the front to show Katherine the nosegay he'd hidden behind his back. As the growing season was long over, there weren't many flowers available even for purchase, but the bundle of chrysanthemums was lovely with their riot of pinks, offset by delicate streaks of white, and wrapped up with a deep purple ribbon.

Her gaze drifted from the flowers, and she met her brother's eyes with an arched brow.

"Another?" she asked.

"David begged me, and I couldn't say no," he said with a wince.

A slip of paper was nestled amongst the blossoms, and despite her best judgment, Katherine unfolded it and stared at Mr. Archer's short note.

I love you. — D.A.

Apparently, he'd forgone subtlety and lyricism in favor of a direct approach. Katherine's pulse quickened at the words, but the twinge in her heart dulled the joyful beat. She'd longed to hear someone—most especially Mr. Archer—say such a thing. But then, she'd imagined it being said by someone who truly believed it.

"He is beside himself," said Benjamin.

Katherine nodded. "It is difficult when friendships end."

He scoffed. "That is not it, and you know it."

Folding the missive up and tucking it back into its hiding place, Katherine laid the bouquet on the side table. "He's had weeks, months, and even years to decide he feels something for me. This hunt for the Mystery Lady ignited his feelings for matrimony, and now I am leaving. He is conflating his friendly affection with true love."

"Katherine—" he began, but Rosanna interrupted.

"Let her be, Benjamin. Besides, it will do Mr. Archer some good to pine for a bit. A little penitence is in order."

Turning her attention back to her sewing, Katherine ignored the pair and their scheming. Despite appreciating her sister's support, it was clear from Rosanna's tone and wording that she believed this rift was temporary. But then, her sister had never known rejection before. No man had ever treated Rosanna as second best, so it was impossible for her to truly understand the heartbreak of having a man settle for her.

Second best. Surely Katherine had enough self-respect to avoid such a future. Forever being compared to another—even if that other was herself in a mask.

Her traitorous heart once more chimed in, begging her to tell Mr. Archer the truth. She and his first choice were one and the same; all that was needed was a bit of honesty, and she would have everything her heart desired.

Katherine paused in moving her needle and stared at the uneven stitches. With a sigh, she pulled the needle free of the threads and unpicked the work she'd done.

Surely, it wasn't wrong for her to want her beau to desire her, and Mr. Archer's disappointment in their embrace was proof enough that he viewed the Mystery Lady as the preferred option. Besides, he'd never seen Katherine in a romantic light until she put on that silly mask. That said enough of his attraction to her. His silly heart was fixated on that wretched Mystery Lady, and Katherine couldn't compete.

Sighing, she rethreaded the needle and began to stitch the

edge of the posy once more.

"That cannot be true." Rosanna's sharp voice cut through Katherine's musings, and she glanced up at her siblings to find her sister staring at her. "Are you leaving on Thursday?"

"The deal has been struck, and the cottage is ready for me. Why would I wait?" asked Katherine as she frowned at the crooked stitches. Another sharp sigh, and she unpicked her work once more.

"But the Angleseys' party is one of the best of the year. You cannot miss it," said Rosanna with such horror, as though Katherine had announced she was joining the navy as a midshipman.

"Parties do not hold the same thrill for me as they do you."

Rosanna's expression crumpled, and she glanced between her brother and sister. "Could you not postpone one day?"

"Our hosts do not care if I am there, and I do not care to attend, so what does it matter?" asked Katherine with a raised brow.

Rosanna's bright eyes fell to her lap, and her fingers worried the fabric she was mending. "I suppose I had wanted one party with you. With everything altering between us, I had hoped..."

Straightening, Rosanna shook her head and adopted a bright smile. "I do not mean to twist your arm, Katherine. Of course, you should do as you see fit. It is a small and silly thing. Of no importance."

Had there been any artifice in those words, Katherine could've easily ignored them and done precisely as she pleased, but Rosanna's disappointment was so genuine, and she tried so hard to hide the pain and simply smile. For once, Rosanna Tate wasn't going to press the issue.

Which was how Katherine Leigh found herself trussed up in her best gown and doing something she'd sworn never to do again.

Chapter 40

"Really, Katherine. Why do you bother going places if you do not wish to make an effort with your appearance?" murmured Mama through gritted teeth as they stepped into the Angleseys' drawing room. Despite the strain in her smile, the lady's bright expression didn't falter, looking for all the world as though she was speaking of the weather or the latest *on dit*.

"You enjoy filling the air with noise, my dear wife. It's a pity it is never anything of value or sense," muttered Papa as he freed his arm from her and strode to the far side, where the door to the card room stood open and ready for him.

Mama lifted her nose in the air. Though her eyes narrowed, she gave no other outward sign of her vexation bubbling beneath the surface. Turning that burning gaze to Katherine, she sighed.

"Must you always embarrass us?" asked Mama.

Katherine turned her own gaze to the people milling about, her thoughts supplying a slew of retorts (with varying degrees of wittiness), but she remained silent. Her time at Whitley Court had come to an end, and despite her desire to flee tonight's "entertainment," Katherine felt as though she could finally breathe. For the first time.

That weight had been an ever-present companion, and it wasn't until her plans had finalized that Katherine recognized the sorrow because of its absence. With peace filling her, it was easy enough to simply ignore her venom. And it helped that Mama was still ignorant of that surprise to come.

"The only thing embarrassing us is your cruelty," said Benjamin, stepping up to offer his arm to Katherine. She stared at it, and him, in turn. The gallantry was still so new that she hardly knew what to do with it. Sliding her arm through his, Katherine held fast to him, though her composure was harder to maintain when Mama shook herself from her surprise and patted her son on the cheek with a laugh.

"You are feisty tonight, my dear boy."

Katherine slanted a look at her brother, giving him a knowing raise of her brows at their mother's epithet, which served as the perfect punctuation for her entire statement. Benjamin drew in a deep breath and turned to lead Katherine away.

But Mama followed. "You really ought to have accepted Rosanna's offer of a new gown. You've worn that old dress so many times."

"I like this dress." Katherine tried to stop it, but her hands couldn't help but run down her skirts.

The pale blue flowers dotting the cream cotton were delicate enough to make even her feel graceful, and though the cut of the gown was rather plain, the fabric's pattern kept it from being wholly boring—even if it wasn't as ethereal or regal as those with flounces and sleeves so large it was a miracle the ladies fit through the doorway. And the gathers around her sleeves showed her shoulders to their best advantage. Katherine Leigh would not turn heads tonight, but she thought herself quite presentable, no matter what Mama said.

"What are you on about?" asked Rosanna, sweeping in to buss her mother's cheek before bestowing another on Benjamin. Then she took Katherine in her arms, greeting her in a similar fashion, though Katherine was too stunned to return the favor before her sister shifted to stand beside her.

"Your sister could've had a lovely new gown," said Mama.

"Nonsense. The dress she has on is fetching," said Rosanna, giving Katherine's outfit an appraising look. "It is simple, but there is beauty in simplicity. And the current fashion suits her figure to perfection. I fear the proportions do nothing for me, but Katherine has such lovely shoulders, and the sloping neckline shows them at their best."

Mama scoffed and waved a hand. "Don't be silly. It is not a poor choice for her, to be certain, but she is too mulish to accept a fine gift or remove her spectacles. I do not know why I bother trying to help her."

"I am an absolute beast," murmured Katherine in a low tone, but when Rosanna slanted a look at her, she realized her comment had carried. However, her sister's gaze sparked with a hint of a smile.

What was happening? In such a short time, the world had turned itself on its head. Mr. Archer sent flowers and tokens of love at every turn, her brother defended her from their mother, and her sister appeared amused by Katherine's mutterings.

"Mrs. Seward was asking after you," said Rosanna, nodding off to the far side of the room.

Before Katherine's eyes could follow the movement or Mama could think to follow, Benjamin took her free arm and led the trio away. Casting a glance over her shoulder, Katherine breathed a sigh when she spied Mama heading after the distraction, and Rosanna patted Katherine's arm as they meandered through the crowd.

Nudging them towards a circle of people, Rosanna lowered her voice and leaned in. "I know you are more like Prudence than myself—preferring the edges of the ballroom to the thick of things—but there are a few people I would love to introduce you to."

Proverbs advised people not to look a gift horse in the

mouth, but they also warned of Greeks bearing gifts, and for all that Katherine had hoped the former more fitting for this sudden shift in her life, her stomach sank as she realized it was the latter. How many times had Rosanna attempted to smooth her way into society? Katherine didn't know why the lady had ever bothered, for it always ended in disaster.

Rosanna tapped a gentleman on the shoulder, and Katherine drew in a deep breath, steeling herself for another Mr. Mowbry or Mr. Tryck. Judging another based on appearances was a terrible thing to do, for one could not help the face one was born with, but surely it was acceptable to base one's judgment on hygiene. She didn't care if her friends were plain or handsome, but smelling of decay or muck was unacceptable. As was having the personality of a rotting fish.

"Mr. Julian," said Rosanna with a broad smile, and Katherine couldn't help but stare at the man. He was quite ordinary-looking. Neither old nor young, tall nor squat, thin nor thick, and with a mop of brown hair and dark eyes, Mr. Julian was entirely unremarkable.

"Might I introduce you to my sister, Miss Katherine Leigh," said Rosanna with a smile, motioning between the pair. "Mr. Julian is a musician and composer."

The gentleman winced at that. "You flatter me, Mrs. Tate, but I fear I haven't the talent to claim either title. It is a passion of mine, that is all."

"Then you do not compose?" asked Katherine.

"I do, but only for my own pleasure," he said with a smile that strained at the edges.

"And you play?"

Mr. Julian nodded but added, "My talent is middling at best."

Katherine raised her brows in challenge. "There are bankers, physicians, vicars, and solicitors that claim those titles without having a modicum of skill, and there are gentry with failing estates and no income to their name, yet not one of them would hesitate to label themselves by those titles. If you play and compose music, you are a musician and composer. What does skill have to do with it?"

Mr. Julian tucked his hands behind him, his cheeks turning slightly pink, though his smile broadened. "I see you will not allow me even an inch."

"Not when you speak nonsense."

Though Rosanna stiffened at the quick retort, Mr. Julian laughed.

Then he dipped into a bow and asked, "Miss Leigh, if you are not otherwise occupied, would you care to dance?"

Katherine stiffened, and she blinked at the gentleman. Had she heard him correctly? A hand at her back nudged her forward, and she followed the prompting, taking his proffered hand. Mr. Julian led her onto the dance floor, where they took their places amongst the dancers as the first strains of music started, and the whirlwind of an evening began in earnest.

Had she been given a glimpse of this evening in the past, Katherine would never have believed it to be true. Mr. Julian was a delightful companion, allowing her to ramble on about composers and compositions, matching her impassioned descriptions with his own as they debated the merits of various styles.

And when their dances were done, Rosanna was there once more, guiding her into another small circle, who delighted in dry humor and discussions on literature and art. With each passing minute, Rosanna led her deeper into parts of Greater Edgerton society that Katherine hadn't known existed. There was the occasional harpy or pompous twit, but the majority were keen to discuss something of substance.

She didn't understand where it had all been hidden. But then, how much of her social circles was determined by her parents' connections? Mama would never deign to spend an evening with people intrigued by such dry subjects.

All in all, Katherine was enjoying herself, which was shocking and strange in and of itself. But then, that was fitting, as everything in her life was topsy-turvy at present. And all the while, Rosanna continued to lead her about, showing her off as though she were a treasured sister.

Katherine's throat tightened, making it difficult to speak, and she reveled in the warmth burning in her heart. It spread through her, heating her far more than the press of bodies and burning candles.

"Stand and deliver," murmured a voice at her shoulder, and it felt as though someone had dumped a basin of water atop her. Those words pulsed through her, and in a flash, Katherine recalled every sweet and wonderful moment of that evening when the man in question had so loved to speak those words.

Why was he saying them now? Did he know? Had he finally realized the truth? Surely calling back to that night was significant, and Katherine's breath quickened as her mind sped through the possibilities. He knew. He must. But for all that the realization had a significant impact on her equilibrium, she couldn't decide if it was for good or ill.

Something that was becoming all too commonplace of late.

Turning in place, Katherine forced herself to meet his eyes. "Good evening, Mr. Archer."

He dipped his head and, with a smile, said in a low tone, "Good evening, Miss Leigh."

Katherine studied every aspect of his face. Was that crinkle of his eye a knowing one, or was he simply delighted to see her? Or did he find it amusing that his Mystery Lady was her? Good gracious! Despite knowing the man as well as anyone could claim to know a friend, she couldn't decipher his expression with any confidence.

"There is no need for that nonsense. You are not dressed as Dick Turpin tonight," she said.

Mr. Archer's gaze drifted across her features, studying them with equal intensity. "True, but I have been giving that evening much thought. It didn't end the way I had intended."

He knew. Katherine's mouth dried, and she tried to think of something to say to him—

"I never did get to dance with you."

She stiffened and stared at him, her heart sinking to her toes. Letting out a quiet breath, she scowled within. How many times would she be so foolish? For all that she believed herself to be a mature and confident lady, Katherine Leigh was a lack-wit of the highest order, quick to throw her heart into believing any fantasy that took her fancy.

A single smile and quiet greeting from Mr. Archer, and she hoped for something else.

Ridiculous.

"What a tragedy," she replied in a monotone.

Mr. Archer's gaze jerked away, his brows twitching for a moment before he cleared his expression once more. "I certainly believe it was. Though I hope to rectify it tonight. Would you do me the honor?"

Two partners in an evening. That was a record for Katherine—even if she didn't wish to dance with the second. Yet she couldn't bring herself to give Mr. Archer the cut direct. Whatever had passed between them, they had been friends. Or still were?

Katherine didn't know how to quantify their current situation, but it mattered little. This was the last time she'd ever see him.

Chapter 41

With a nod, Katherine allowed herself to be led towards the dance floor, though the current set was still in progress. They stood side by side, watching the dancers, and Mr. Archer tucked his hands behind him, rocking on his heels.

"You seem to be having a fine night," he said.

"It has been delightful."

Mr. Archer looked at her from the corner of his eye. "Enough to make you rethink your present course?"

Turning to face him, Katherine met his gaze, her chin lifting. "My siblings have all attempted to persuade me to stay, but why would I choose to live under their roof and off their charity when I can chart my own course in life? Besides, a fortnight of listening to me practice piano would undo all the goodwill we've built."

"Do you truly believe their feelings are so fleeting?"

Katherine drew her strength close, ignoring the tender quality to his voice that hinted at far greater meaning to his words. "I believe it is foolish to expect the world to alter so completely in such a short period. It takes time to bring about true change, and rushing things will only cause more damage."

The current dance ended, and Mr. Archer placed a hand at the small of her back, guiding her forward. Katherine forced her pulse to slow and ignored the heat of that touch. Allowing her heart free rein had done enough damage; it was forever mucking with her life, rushing into things or closing off completely, and it was time for her mind to take control.

And it knew better than to give any meaning to that little movement.

The strains of a waltz began, and Katherine stiffened, her gaze darting to Mr. Archer's. It was easy enough to see that he'd known precisely what dance it was to be when he'd asked. Giving her a bow, he stepped forward, but she refused to clasp his hand. Resting her hands on his shoulders allowed her a little more distance than other dance holds.

Of course, it left his hands at her waist, but Katherine ignored that and moved with the lilting beats as they turned about the room.

"Then you are determined?" he asked as she gazed out at the other dancers.

"Have you ever known me not to be?" She pressed against his shoulders to keep him at a distance—though Mr. Archer made no move to draw closer.

"Have you spoken to your parents?" he asked.

Katherine dropped one hand away from him, allowing it to dangle at her side. "How are your mother and sisters?"

With a quick turn, she found their positions shifted (though she couldn't attest to how Mr. Archer had managed it), and her free hand was now clasped above their heads, drawing them so close that it felt indecent, though others were equally cozy with their partners.

Mr. Archer's face was so near to hers that Katherine couldn't help but recall his kisses, and his gaze held hers with such fire that the ice around her heart began to melt despite her best efforts. Candlelight flickered around them, casting itself across the planes of his face and highlighting the warm hues of his eyes.

"Miss Leigh..." His tone was like melted chocolate, all rich and sweet—and just as delectable.

"Mr. Archer, please." She tried to step back, though her attempt was half-hearted at best. That ridiculous organ of hers had taken control once more, losing itself in his gaze and muddling her thoughts.

"You are so lovely."

Four simple words, yet they struck Katherine with such force, for Mr. Archer said them with such utter sincerity. And she couldn't help but wonder if he truly believed it.

A snort pierced the haze surrounding the pair, and her attention jerked to a couple dancing beside them; the gentleman's gaze swept Katherine and turned away with clear dismissal whilst the lady's lips were clamped tight together as though holding back a laugh. In other settings, she knew how to defend against such barbs, but Mr. Archer had stripped away her defenses, and she felt every prickle of pain as it burrowed into her heart.

Katherine's gaze darted to him, but he was staring at their tormentors.

Her heart's hold slackened, divesting control back to her thoughts, and they raced with the possibilities. Was this just another ploy? A way to convince her to stay? Was that another chuckle? Were they all laughing at her? Entertaining themselves by watching the spinster make cow eyes at the eligible bachelor? Good heavens, she was fairly plastering herself to Mr. Archer, what else were they to think?

Tugging free of his hold, she stepped backward, shaking her head. Mr. Archer moved with her, drawing near, but Katherine held up a staying hand. Turning on her heel, she hurried away from the dancers, weaving through the crowd.

"Mind your business, Stavely!" David couldn't prevent the words from bellowing out, drawing even more attention. The bounder didn't even look the slightest bit chagrined, merely curling his lip as he let out another scoff before he and his partner disappeared into the swirl of dancers.

David forced himself not to shove the others out of the way. It wasn't as though they deserved to suffer for his own stupidity—except Stavely. That fellow deserved a lesson in manners. But Miss Leigh was far more important.

He had to find her.

Holding fast to the sight of her brown coiffure in the sea of ribbons and flowers, David ducked between the people. She wouldn't give him the slip. Not this time. Miss Leigh fled the drawing room, and David fully ignored the others who attempted to stall him with greetings and conversation. Forging ahead, he followed as she stepped through a side door.

A burst of cold air swept through the heat of the house as she disappeared into darkness, and David didn't slow, gaining ground as he reached her exit.

The Angleseys boasted a proper estate, and unlike the Breadmores, they had more expansive grounds than a small garden. However, like most fine houses, the areas closest to the building were carefully manicured, and David found himself once more in a dark garden, chasing after Miss Leigh. At least the curtains inside were wide open, and the candlelight from inside helped him avoid obstacles as he took the twists and turns deeper into the greenery.

"Miss Leigh, please!" Dodging around a shrub, he stepped into an opening surrounded by trees and flowerbeds, though they were all bare at present, ready for the snow to fall.

"Leave me be, Mr. Archer," she said with her back to him.

"No."

Whipping around, Miss Leigh scowled. "Did you come here to mock me some more?"

David gritted his teeth, reminding himself that an instinctual reaction wouldn't help matters, and held up placating hands. "I was not mocking you, and you know it."

"Oh, I do, do I?" she said, placing her hands on her hips and tipping up that challenging chin of hers. "What I know is that a man who hardly knew I was a woman a month ago is suddenly declaring his undying love for me and claiming me to be 'lovely,' with no clear provocation—except my impending departure."

Folding his arms, David sighed. "You are repeating yourself, Miss Leigh, and it hasn't altered my intentions. I am still here, hoping you will believe me."

"When the thought of you and I together is so downright ludicrous that people cannot help but laugh?" Then, holding up a warning finger, Miss Leigh hurried to add, "And do not deny it—this is the second time I've been the butt of the joke. Isn't the thought of you and me in a romantic situation positively hilarious? Prime fodder for a farce!"

It was as though she was driving nails into his heart with each word, but he stood there, waiting as she spouted her troubles once more. Though her expression and posture spoke of defiance and anger, David recognized fear when he saw it.

Miss Leigh finished, and her lungs heaved as though she'd run a race, her eyes blazing with passion—though not the sort David longed to see.

"I know how difficult it is for you to trust. You've been given so many reasons not to," he murmured, creeping close with careful steps. "And your entire life has been upended of late. The upheaval surrounding your siblings would be great enough, and now, I am asking you to be vulnerable as you've never been before—and to trust that my feelings are true."

With wide eyes, she stared at him, and he took the opportunity to slip his fingers around hers. Miss Leigh gave a start but didn't pull away as he lifted her hand to his lips. As they'd begun as friends, he'd been allowed so many freedoms that most sweethearts were not granted, and he knew all too well how soft her skin was there. He longed to feel her elegant fingers beneath his lips, rather than the lifeless silk of her evening gloves.

David held her hand in his as he met her gaze. "I wish I could say your fears are unfounded, but I know all too well the mistreatment you've suffered and how unutterably dense I've been."

His thumb brushed against the back of her hand, and Miss Leigh's gaze widened as she stood there like a startled statue.

"I cannot explain why I did not see the truth sooner—any more than I can explain why I see it now. But I do, and I do not doubt that you are the woman for me. My perfect match."

Despite the careful styling of her hair, a few wisps broke free, brushing across the curve of her cheek. David searched his heart and mind for words to offer her, but as he stared into her eyes, he couldn't understand how he'd spent so long thinking of her in such a platonic light. Even her spectacles appealed to him, as they had the tendency to slide down her nose, perching slightly askew and upending her primness.

"A simple and easy pairing, no doubt," she replied in a tone that held a touch of tartness, though it didn't disguise the tremor beneath it. "Many people marry for convenience's sake."

David nearly ruined it all by laughing at that ludicrous statement. Nothing about this courtship could be considered easy, simple, or convenient.

"True, but if you believe my intentions are motivated by convenience, you are dead wrong, Miss Leigh."

For all that Mr. Archer moved slowly, attempting to do so without her noticing, Katherine was all too aware of how close they stood and his arms drawing around her. And she accepted it solely because for the first time in her life, she felt faint. Despite Katherine being a fine walker and a sturdy lady, her muscles struggled to keep her upright.

Mr. Archer spoke with such conviction, as though he didn't doubt a single syllable, and she fought to hold onto her reasons for rejecting him when everything in his tone and expression spoke of truth. Holding her flush to him, Mr. Archer recited those statements again, echoing what he'd said before, and she couldn't help but lean closer into his embrace.

How she wished them to be true.

Stiffening, Katherine swallowed as her throat clamped shut.

That was the problem, wasn't it? She wanted this declaration to be exactly what it appeared to be. Just as she prayed that the shift among her siblings wasn't fleeting. But how many times must she risk her heart before she learned her lesson?

"It is growing late," she said, stepping away.

Mr. Archer released her, his arms dropping to his sides as he stood there, watching her.

"I hadn't planned on staying the whole evening, as I have much to do tomorrow. My coach leaves early the day after next, and there is still much to be done." Katherine forced herself to swallow and gave him a feeble smile. "As I intend to tell my parents about my plans, tomorrow is bound to be fatiguing, and I ought to get some rest."

Turning away, Katherine began moving back down the path, toward the house.

"That is probably for the best," he said. "Tomorrow shall be quite busy for me as well, and a good night's sleep is required before long days of travel."

Chapter 42

Katherine stopped in place, her spine straightening at those final words. "And where are you going on such short notice?"

"The coast."

Whipping around to face him, she stared at him. "No, you are not."

Mr. Archer had his hands tucked behind him as he replied with a smile, "A little village in Cheshire called Thorngate. I've heard it's quite picturesque."

Tingles ran down her skin, settling in her stomach as she stared at him. Despite the darkness, there was light enough to see the smugness in his smile.

"You are not visiting Thorngate."

Mr. Archer nodded. "You are correct. I am not visiting. I am relocating and plan on being there for some time—"

"No, you are not."

"My things are all in crates and trunks, ready for the 8:43 a.m. coach to Preston. I've got a room at the inn—just until I can locate a house to let. I've heard there is some very beautiful property on the cliffs, overlooking the ocean." With a tilt of his head, he added, "There's a particularly darling cottage that would be perfect, but I fear it is already let. I do hope I might make friends with its mistress, and she might allow me to visit from time to time and enjoy her view."

Katherine gaped, her sluggish thoughts attempting to sort out this revelation, but none of it made any sense. "You are not going to my Thorngate."

"I heard Benjamin was traveling there," he said with a shrug. "You know how much trouble he can get into if left unattended."

"And your solution was to force your way into our traveling party?" she demanded, grasping onto the first thought she could—and leaving her to wonder what it said about her that her first instinct was combative.

Relaxing his shoulders, Mr. Archer let his arms fall to his sides, but he didn't move any closer. "I have told you, Miss Leigh. I am in love with you. I know it. And I am not willing to surrender simply because I have bungled things so terribly. If you require time to trust me once more, then so be it. You are leaving for Thorngate, so I must follow. I won't be parted from you. I cannot bear it."

Katherine's breaths stilled, though her pulse raced.

Jutting her chin, she met his statement with narrowed eyes. "And give up on your Mystery Lady? That gorgeous and perfect specimen? That paragon of women?"

Mr. Archer's head lowered, his brows drawing together as he stared at his toes. "I cannot do anything about the past, Miss Leigh, other than apologize for it, but if you think hiding behind your righteous indignation will deter me, you do not know me at all."

Yes, it was quite impossible to breathe—due to both the accuracy with which he described her present feelings and the sentiment rife in his words.

Then Mr. Archer was standing there with his arms around her once more. It wasn't some sudden thing, but neither could she say when they had come so close again. Katherine was certain she hadn't moved in his direction.

"But to answer your question, Miss Leigh, why would I keep searching for someone else when I have perfection here in my arms?"

Katherine scoffed. She couldn't help it when he spouted such nonsense. She was many things, but perfection was not one of them. But the sound made Mr. Archer frown.

"I am serious, Miss Leigh," he said, giving her a squeeze. "That other lady may have turned my head for a time, but it is you who possesses my heart and soul. It's you who drives me to distraction. I was unhappy when I lost her, but the thought of losing you fills me with anguish. I cannot bear the thought of my life without you in it, and I can say without hesitation or equivocation that I don't want a phantom or some hollow flirtation. I want you."

What did a lady say to such a thing? Katherine's heart knew the answer to that, but she forced her lips closed and studied his expression.

Mr. Archer's gaze softened, and he whispered, "If you think of me only as a friend and cannot accept me as a beau, then simply tell me. However, I will not surrender if your only argument is that you cannot believe my feelings. I know we share something special, and if there's even the smallest chance that I can win your heart, I will move to the farthest reaches of this globe, if need be."

"But your family and the mill—"

"They will find a way to survive without me. But I know I cannot survive without you."

Katherine had hoped that at such a moment, she would have something witty or clever to say (or at the very least, romantic), but all she could manage was to gape at him like a carp. "Are you truly that determined?"

With a hint of a smile and an arched brow to match, he replied, "Have you ever known me not to be?"

Warmth slipped through the ice encasing her heart, melting it away like the first spring breezes sweeping across the frozen hillside, ushering in a new life and changing the world into something new. It filled her until her heart expanded well past its physical boundaries.

Mr. Archer truly meant it.

"I will sort out the rest," he said as one hand drifted to her neck. "I should've realized the truth long ago, but please tell me I have not ruined things beyond repair. Can you forgive me for my blindness and stupidity? Allow us to begin again?"

He paused, his thumb brushing her cheek and sending a wave of gooseflesh across her skin. Mr. Archer's gaze held hers, boring into her as though any answer but acceptance would destroy him.

"You are so beautiful," he whispered in a tone that held far more awe than her plain features deserved.

Mr. Archer's thumb grazed her lips, and his eyes drifted across her face as though committing each feature to memory. Despite having known him so well for so long, Katherine couldn't think of any other time he'd said something with such awe and conviction. This was no mere compliment. Simply stated and stripped of any pomp, he spoke from the deepest part of his soul. And try as she might, Katherine couldn't find any duplicity in his words or actions.

Katherine Leigh was no chum. No convenience. She was his love.

Vision blurring, Katherine's chin trembled, and she drew in a sharp breath, forcing air into her lungs, but it came out in short bursts, breaking past her control and drawing forth her tears. Mr. Archer's eyes widened, his brows pinching together as he quickly wiped at her cheeks.

"I apologize—I don't know what I did—please do not cry—" He stumbled over his words as he held her, and Katherine rested in his arms as her strength leaked out of her along with this ridiculous display. But she couldn't stop it. Five weeks of kindnesses from her siblings, culminating in a truly special evening, was touching enough, but hearing her beloved friend saying such lovely things was more than her fragile heart could handle.

"I—" Katherine tried to explain, but words struggled out of her grasp as she blubbered and gasped.

"Please, do not cry," he murmured.

Katherine shook her head, but still, she couldn't speak. Tugging her arms free of his, she did the only thing she could; when words refused to come to her lips, she had to use them another way.

Brows shooting upwards, David held still as Miss Leigh took hold of his face and kissed him. It was a touch awkward and, with her tears, far damper than one would wish for in an embrace, but his heart leapt, and energy thrummed through him until he was certain he could run all the way to Cheshire.

Miss Leigh was kissing him. His Katherine.

Relaxing into her hold, David poured all that newly found strength into the kiss, reveling in the joy of her touch, freely given. His heart skipped a beat as he considered that this did not guarantee anything was settled between them, but he let his heart lead the embrace, refusing to give his doubts any credence. Katherine was not one to throw about her affection. Especially a crying Katherine.

David deepened the kiss, hoping to give her all the assurance he felt. All the contentment and joy.

How had he ever believed that some flirtation at a masquerade would ever compare to spending his life with his dearest friend? If that heady moment with the Mystery Lady had shown David the possibilities rife in sharing a connection with another, this embrace with his Katherine wove their hearts together as one, binding them irrevocably. This was no mere kiss; her touch flowed through him, filling him as no other triumph had or ever could.

Thank the heavens that foolish and all too blind men did not always get what they deserved. For David could never hope to deserve her.

Katherine's heart creaked open like a door on rusty hinges, forcing aside the locks she'd placed there to protect it. There was no point in hiding now. No point in avoiding the possible pain. Despite all the effort she'd placed into fortifying it, David swept in, erasing all her protections and slipping past her security.

Not that she wished to stop him. This was her David. Her friend and confidant. Her support and protector. Pouring her heart into her kiss, Katherine embraced the moment, and she was swept back into that beautiful memory in Rosanna's courtyard when the fantasy had finally come alive for her and David.

When they parted, his arms were tight at her waist, and her own rested around his neck, their bodies crushed together as they breathed deeply. Katherine forced herself to look him in the eyes, and David stared back at her, his eyes glazed over as though his wits were well and truly addled. The corners of his lips were tipped upward, and his hands massaged her back.

But still, no recognition. If he realized she was his Mystery Lady, there was no sign of it.

Before she could say a word, David closed the distance again, kissing her as though he were a dying man in a desert and she was his oasis. Smiling to herself, Katherine shoved away thoughts of masquerades and dimwitted beaus and reveled in the moment. Their moment.

It was several long moments before they slowed again, and though she wanted to groan at the interruption, the sound of footsteps drew her back to reality—though David refused to relinquish her lips.

Katherine had never giggled before, but she felt distinctly like doing so at that moment when they pulled back and she whispered, "People are coming."

Shrugging, he seized her in another embrace, stealing away her good sense as she ignored all else and nearly giggled once more when his hands rose to brush the nape of her neck.

Definitely footsteps.

She forced her thoughts to clear and pushed David back,

though he refused to let go of her.

"People are coming," she repeated with a narrowed look. "Do you wish to get caught?"

"I have watched you run away from me twice, and I refuse to let it happen a third time," he murmured, his thumbs drawing forth a shiver from her as he caressed her neck. "I do not care if the Archbishop of Canterbury strolls in, I am not releasing you."

Katherine sighed at his unrepentant grin. "But I do not want anyone to force your hand—"

"Then you would be mine and unable to run away anymore," he said with a waggle of his brows.

Her hands slid to his chest, and she stared at him. "Does being a beau mean you've suddenly become a scoundrel, wishing to compromise poor, unsuspecting ladies at parties?"

"Not any lady. Just you." He leaned closer, his lips brushing hers as he whispered, "Of course, you could simply agree to marry me, and we wouldn't need to worry about compromising."

Katherine jerked back, but David's arms remained fixed around her.

"Marry?"

With a halting chuckle, he stared at her. "I have declared my love in no uncertain terms. Did you not think I would want to marry the woman I love?"

"We haven't even courted—"

But David gave her a quick buss on the lips. "We've known each other for far longer than many newly married couples and count each other as our closest friend. To say nothing of the fact that you've compromised me twice now—"

Katherine gaped at that, though as much as she wanted to give him a tart reply, she couldn't entirely disagree, as she had been the instigator twice. Even if he'd been a willing partner in that compromising.

David's hand drifted from the back of her neck to brush his thumb across her cheek, and Katherine couldn't help but close her eyes at the feel of it. Turning her head, she pressed a kiss to his palm and watched as his gaze filled with all the tenderness she'd so longed to see.

"All jesting aside, Katherine, my mind is made up on the matter, but I am willing to wait as long as you need. Whether it's in Greater Edgerton, Thorngate, or on the other side of the world, I will not give up as long as there is a chance for us."

Lifting her arms once more to circle his neck, Katherine pulled him close and pressed her lips to his. Oh, yes, there was more than merely a chance for them.

Chapter 43

A s much as her good sense prodded her, Katherine lost herself in David's embrace once more. Never in her grandest imaginings could she have pictured such a sensation. For too much of her life, she'd been separate from others in every way, and now, her senses swam with sensations.

It was more than the feel of arms, hands, and lips—though the thrill of those touches quickened her pulse, leaving her nearly dizzy from the pace. It was the man himself. Her dear David. It was that heart and soul she loved so dearly that poured from him through each caress.

And then he was pulling back, his lips twisting in a chagrined smile.

"As much as I hate releasing you now, I fear it is for the best. Despite my jest about not allowing you to escape again, I would hate myself if your hand was to be forced, and I've had too many reasons to hate myself of late," he whispered, placing a little space between them. "We ought to return to the party, my love."

The Leighs adored endearments, but even with all the dears and dearests tossed about, they rarely ever spoke of love, and

Katherine's throat tightened at that endearment, making it very difficult for her to speak.

Leaning forward, she mumbled into his shoulder. "Why must you be sensible now?"

"I haven't the foggiest notion," he murmured in return. "But it's for the best. Unfortunately."

Katherine's gaze rose once more, and her breath seized once more at the longing in his eyes. For her. Katherine Leigh. They drifted across her face as though studying each lovely detail, and heat swept through her, settling deep into her heart.

With great reluctance (and one final kiss), she stepped from his embrace and slipped her arm through his, resting her free hand atop his forearm. Then his other hand joined hers, binding them together in such a cozy fashion that Katherine longed to rest her head against his shoulder with a sigh.

It was not as good as stealing kisses in the garden, but it would do.

Weaving through the shrubbery, David led them along, and Katherine couldn't speak. As they passed others enjoying the cool autumn night, her cheeks flushed with heat. No one paid them any heed, and she doubted they suspected a thing, but she couldn't help the silly grin brightening her face.

"Yes, I must marry you as soon as possible," he murmured, slanting an arched brow at her. "I cannot help but want to kiss you thoroughly when you look so radiant."

A thrill coursed through her, filling every inch of her body with such vibrant electricity that Katherine was certain her grin would explode at any moment. And all the while, her dear David smiled with the smug satisfaction of a man who knew he would get his way.

They stepped back into the house and strode down the hall, though Katherine nudged him away from the ballroom as she caught sight of a familiar face striding towards the entryway. She refused to release David's arm, instead dragging him along as her footsteps quickened, speeding towards the only other person she wished to see at this moment.

"Pamela!" she said. "I thought you were not coming."

"I'm afraid we arrived monstrously late and are taking our leave already," replied Pamela, stepping away from her husband just as Katherine released David to sweep her friend into an embrace.

"He loves me," whispered Katherine, though the fact that she managed to moderate her tone was something of a miracle.

"Too right, he does," whispered Pamela in return. "How could he not?"

Despite all the frustrations of his world, David Archer had thought himself a happy man; imperfect his life may be (for every life was tainted by trials and tribulations), he was blessed with many good things. Yet seeing Katherine's broad smile as she embraced her friend added to David's own delight, growing and expanding far more than he thought possible for any person to feel.

"Am I to assume that congratulations are in order?" asked Mr. Kitts in a low voice, glancing at his wife. The ladies stood apart from their men, holding a whispered conversation, utterly unaware of anything else around them.

"That is a question for Miss Leigh to answer," replied David.

Mr. Kitts raised his brows and nodded as the pair stood there waiting for their ladies. Mrs. Kitts shifted, tugging at the shawl draped across her arms, and the movement drew David's attention to the length of cream cashmere, decorated with intricate stitches of deepest blue. His eyes latched onto the article as the world around him stilled. For one long moment, he stood there, transfixed.

He knew that shawl.

Despite his thoughts stuttering at the sight, David's mind leapt through various assumptions and possibilities, and it took no great stretch of logic to make the connection between Mrs.

Kitts and the Mystery Lady. His eyes darted to Katherine, blinking a rapid pace as he struggled to sort out his jumbled thoughts.

Katherine was the Mystery Lady?

Despite that possibility posing itself a few times over the past two and a half months, David hadn't truly believed it—especially considering the tender tokens of affection they'd shared. Yet, staring at the shawl draped across Mrs. Kitts' arms, David had to admit that it must be true.

Pain struck his heart, and he tried to hide it from his expression as the truth of Katherine's deception settled heavily in his chest. For months, she'd kept this from him, watching his struggles without saying a word. And even after having bared his soul to her, Katherine did not trust him with the truth, and that betrayal thrummed through him.

But as quick as the feeling came, it faded.

David knew better than most how fragile her heart was. Hadn't he lectured Benjamin on how difficult it was to earn her trust? And opening oneself to love was among the most vulnerable things a person could do. It was little wonder Katherine had remained silent.

To say nothing of the fact that he was the fool who hadn't recognized his friend beneath the mask. That was his doing— not hers.

And then there were all the ways in which he'd mishandled this courtship from the beginning. Even if Katherine had lied to his face that she wasn't the Mystery Lady (which she hadn't), David had no right to feel anything but bone-deep gratitude that she had forgiven him. It was a miracle she was even speaking to him. Let alone allowing him to kiss her.

Besides, what did that secret signify? Mystery Lady or not, she was his choice—his only choice. Katherine was everything he wanted in a sweetheart and wife, and as long as she was his, it didn't matter if she and the Mystery Lady were one and the same.

Stuffing his hands in his pockets, David watched Katherine, his gaze drifting over the length of her as a smile crept across his face. Katherine Leigh was his sweetheart. Possibly his wife-to-be. As they hadn't officially settled on an engagement, he couldn't say which it was, but as long as she wasn't fleeing from him, he was quite content to take some time to sort the rest of it out.

Casting another glance at Mrs. Kitts' shawl, he frowned. With narrowed eyes, David examined it again and frowned to himself with a shake of the head. Apparently, habits were hard to break, for after two months of searching for the Mystery Lady, he saw signs of her everywhere.

It wasn't the same shawl. Similar, yes, but this was more beige than cream, and the stitching was far darker and less intricate. David was a fool of the highest order.

His attention drifted from that silly shawl back to Katherine. *His* Katherine.

Whoever that Mystery Lady was, her identity meant nothing, and whatever had awakened his heart that night was of no consequence. True love was not some stolen moment or flash-in-the-pan sentiment. For all that he'd had his head turned by the idea of love at first sight, it wasn't real. And soul mates (if such a thing could ever exist) weren't forged in a few hours. Such a connection was built over months, years, and decades. It required forgiveness and sacrifice.

Love was not a shallow flirtation and a few stolen kisses.

But then again, David wouldn't mind stealing a few more moments in the garden with Katherine. Heart ablaze, he allowed his gaze to drift along the line of her shoulders, following up the sweep of her neck and the curve of her cheek. Perhaps he could sneak her out there later.

A chuckle from his side jerked David's attention to Mr. Kitts, who gave him a knowing smile before turning his attention to his wife.

"I hate to interrupt, but I fear we must be on our way," said Mr. Kitts, stepping forward to offer his arm to his wife.

Mrs. Kitts sighed and moved to his side. "I do apologize, Katherine, but I fear we just got word that little Freddy is feeling poorly—"

"Nothing serious, I hope," said Katherine, taking David's arm in a tight grip.

Shaking her head, she sighed. "He won't rest easy while we are gone, and he's bound to get worse if he sleeps poorly tonight. But..."

The mother glanced between her friend and husband, but before Mrs. Kitts could talk herself into feeling more guilty about her choice, Katherine shook her head.

"Don't be silly. I will come by for a visit tomorrow, and we can catch up then. This will keep."

Mrs. Kitts' brow furrowed. "If you are certain—"

"Of course," she said, ushering them towards the door.

"Only if you promise to bring *your* Mr. Archer with you." Mrs. Kitts gave him a wicked grin as her husband led her down the corridor. "Then we can celebrate properly, and you can tell me everything."

"Everything?" asked David, straightening as he glanced between the ladies.

Mr. Kitts laughed and called over his shoulder at them, "You should know there are no secrets between them. Pamela will know every sordid detail."

David raised his brows and glanced at Katherine. "Everything?"

Katherine met his gaze with what was likely meant to be a placating look, but Mr. Kitts laughed once more and said, "Everything."

Then the pair disappeared from sight, leaving David and Katherine alone once more. Drawing closer, she leaned into him, wrapping her arms around him, and he pressed a kiss to her head. Though he desired far more than that, it was all he allowed himself at present. The ball raged just behind the doors to their right, and being caught in such a cozy position would be scandalous enough.

David sighed to himself and gathered the last of his gentlemanly resolve, freeing himself from her hold. Sweeping into a bow, he motioned towards the doors.

Katherine grimaced. "Need we? I do not want to face those people again."

A spark of anger made its way through the contented fog that surrounded him as David recalled just how poorly their first dance had gone this evening. Of course, he was certain Benjamin would be quite pleased to join him on a "visit" to that weasel, Stavely. A little lesson in manners might be just the thing.

Making note of that plan, David turned his attention back to the beauty before him. "But I am very much hoping you will dance with me again."

Straightening, she met his gaze. "You've never danced two sets with me before."

David's stomach clenched, his heart sinking at just how true that statement was. With each passing minute, it was clearer and clearer just how much of a fool he'd been. But that was the past, and he couldn't change it. Thankfully, he could ensure he never repeated the mistake.

"I plan to remedy that immediately," he said, tucking her arm through his as they turned towards the ballroom. "In fact, I plan on dragging you about the dance floor for the rest of the evening."

"And scandalize the entire party?" she asked with a wry laugh.

"What does it matter? A husband and wife aren't allowed to dance together without raising eyebrows, which is absolute rubbish."

Katherine arched a brow at him. "So you mean to get in as much dancing as you can before we are forced to ignore each other in public or be labeled as unconscionably rude?"

Pulling her to a stop, David angled towards her, though he refused to let go of her arm. "I plan to dance with my lovely

Katherine for the rest of my life, so I think it's best to start acclimating them to my scandalous behavior now."

He raised her free hand to his lips, holding her gaze as he pressed a kiss to her knuckles. Katherine's breath hitched, and her cheeks turned a stunning shade of pink.

Her lips turned upwards into a hesitant smile, and in a low voice she said, "Then we'd best get started, hadn't we?"

Chapter 44

One Month Later

Waving off the groom, David reached for the carriage door and opened it, offering his hand to his bride as she climbed inside. *His bride.* Standing on the pavement, he stared into the vehicle and watched as Katherine settled into the cushions.

His bride.

Stepping up, David slid into the seat beside her, and before he could remove his hat or gloves, Katherine leaned into the crook of his arm, resting against him with a sigh. Shifting so he could wrap it around her, David held her close as the carriage rolled forward. Their families and friends cheered from the church entrance, but the sound was quickly swallowed by the noise of the street.

David reached up just long enough to tug his glove free and then rested his hand back on her arm. Despite wishing to make himself more comfortable, he wasn't ready to relinquish this pleasant perch, with his bride tucked into his side.

His bride!

"Are you happy, my love?" he murmured, pressing a kiss to

her head.

Katherine leaned in and looked up at him with a furrowed brow. "Of course I am. I didn't know it was possible to be this happy."

And David had never thought it possible that another's joy could fill him so completely. For all that so many believed one's bliss ought to be the primary consideration, those selfish creatures never understood the true meaning of felicity. David certainly hadn't understood how much being the author of another's joy compounded one's own.

Lying back, Katherine murmured, "Even if you insisted on a proper ceremony."

Gazing out the window as the buildings of Greater Edgerton slowly thinned, David couldn't help but smile to himself. Over the past four weeks, so many of his friends and acquaintances had congratulated him on the fact that, as the groom, he needn't fret over the wedding details, without knowing that he had expended more time and energy on that endeavor than the lady at his side.

Had it been solely up to her, they would've eloped and been done with the whole business. He may not have convinced her to have a wedding breakfast, but any celebration (however small) was better than sneaking away in the dead of night.

Rocking with the carriage, David found it difficult to breathe. It was such a simple action, yet his heart felt so full that it was impossible to fill his lungs. His bride. His wife. Mrs. Katherine Archer.

"I promise never to mention her again, but I feel as though I'm doing her a disservice if I do not express just how grateful I am to the Mystery Lady, wherever she may be," he said.

Katherine's head jerked up, and she stared at him. "Pardon?"

"My life was filled with so many things that I never gave marriage much thought. In many ways, I was a husband and father already to my family, and it just didn't cross my mind to take on more responsibility. I thought a wife was an obligation, not a blessing."

Reaching with his free hand, David brushed her cheek, and heat burned through his veins as her eyes closed, a smile crossing her lips.

"Without her sweeping into my life and upending that belief, I would never have realized that I already had my one true love waiting for me to wake from my stupor," he murmured. "I had all this love and joy waiting for me to claim it. How could I not see it?"

Katherine opened her eyes, and David was struck anew by the woman he'd married. So much heart and soul burned in that gaze turned entirely on him.

How had he not seen? The question came to him again and again, and David had no answer. He doubted he ever would. All he could do was ensure that he spent the rest of his life showing his gratitude for Katherine's patience.

Pulling her into his embrace, he told her of his love in a way no words could convey.

Guilt didn't belong on one's wedding day. Especially when one's groom was Mr. David Archer. Katherine's heart soared as she reveled in his touch. Despite their short engagement and small ceremony, it felt as though he'd been kept from her far too much.

She didn't know how courting couples managed all the interference. As no one had believed David and Katherine's relationship could be anything but platonic, no one had seen fit to cast aspersions on the pair when they'd been friends; the only restrictions they'd faced were those imposed by their schedules. For others, an engagement allowed more freedom to see their sweetheart, but for Katherine and David, it had the opposite effect.

Yet now they were man and wife. Free to pass every hour together. Such a moment ought only to be a joyous thing.

And it was.

Except Katherine couldn't quite ignore the skittering in her stomach that told her she'd done wrong by David. Despite the inauspicious beginning to their courtship, he'd proven himself earnest and loyal, and she didn't doubt his devotion. Yet still, Katherine hadn't told him about the masquerade.

But how did one bring up such a thing? With each kiss, she hoped he would finally recognize the lips he'd kissed that night, but still, the fool didn't seem to realize. The secret tormented her, presenting opportunities to reveal the truth, but Katherine's tongue held fast. The more time passed, the less she doubted his affection—especially now that they were legally and lawfully bound man and wife—but still, she struggled to find the words.

The fears of the past had transformed, whispering new terrors to torment her. What man would be pleased to discover his new bride had lied to him for so long? Surely that was an inauspicious beginning. Would he be angry? Or disappointed? Pained? Surely he would figure out the truth on his own. She needn't tell him outright. Ought she to ruin their wedding day?

Yet the thought of letting the secret remain was like a weight pressing down on her. Love required trust, and Katherine knew she couldn't claim the latter if she was quick to assume the worst of her husband.

"We'll spend the evening in Preston," he said, his hand brushing back and forth against her arm. "It took some doing, but I found a reputable inn to stay in before we set off for Thorngate."

Katherine sighed. "I still feel a little ridiculous about that."

"Paying rent on a small property for a few months is hardly going to beggar us," said David, as he had so many times before. "Besides, this is the perfect wedding trip."

Leaning up once more, Katherine captured his lips in a kiss, channeling the Mystery Lady facade she'd donned during the masquerade. But when they parted, David watched her with that same satisfied grin he always had when they managed to sneak away for a little kissing. Not a single gleam of recognition.

Katherine sighed and patted his cheek. "Oh, my dear, sweet, blind husband. You are never going to figure the truth out on your own."

David's brows rose, and she couldn't help but chuckle and shake her head.

"My love, there is something I need to tell you."

Exclusive Offer

Join the M.A. Nichols VIP Reader Club at

www.ma-nichols.com

to receive up-to-date information about upcoming
books, freebies, and VIP content!

About the Author

Born and raised in Anchorage, M.A. Nichols is a lifelong Alaskan with a love of the outdoors. As a child she despised reading but through the love and persistence of her mother was taught the error of her ways and has had a deep, abiding relationship with it ever since.

She graduated with a bachelor's degree in landscape management from Brigham Young University and a master's in landscape architecture from Utah State University, neither of which has anything to do with why she became a writer, but is a fun little tidbit none-the-less. And no, she doesn't have any idea what type of plant you should put in that shady spot out by your deck. She's not that kind of landscape architect. Stop asking.

Website   Facebook   Instagram   BookBub

Made in United States
Orlando, FL
24 September 2023

37242242R00183